david levithan

ILLUSTRATED BY dion mbd

every day

THE GRAPHIC NOVEL

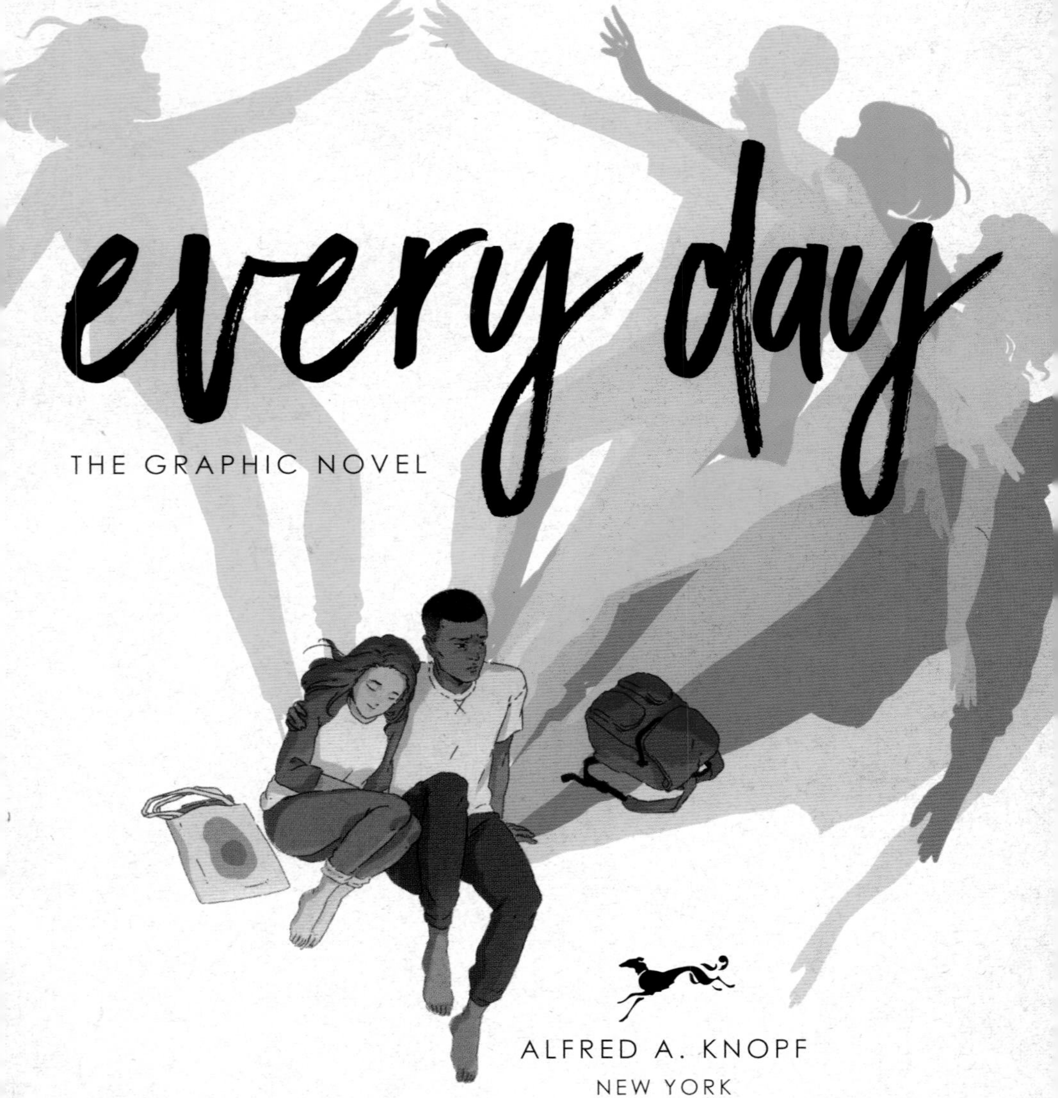

ALFRED A. KNOPF
NEW YORK

THIS IS A BORZOI BOOK PUBLISHED BY ALFRED A. KNOPF

Visit us on the Web! GetUnderlined.com

Educators and librarians, for a variety of teaching tools, visit us at RHTeachersLibrarians.com

Library of Congress Cataloging-in-Publication Data is available upon request.
ISBN 978-0-593-42898-6 (trade) — ISBN 978-0-593-42899-3 (lib. bdg.) — ISBN 978-0-593-42900-6 (ebook) — ISBN 978-0-593-42897-9 (trade pbk.)

The text of this book is set in Brian Bolland.
The illustrations were created digitally.
Interior design by Penguin Random House LLC

MANUFACTURED IN CHINA
10 9 8 7 6 5 4 3 2 1

First Edition

For Paige

(May you find happiness every day)

—DL

To Fanny, who allows me to be all forms

and shapes that make me myself

—DMBD

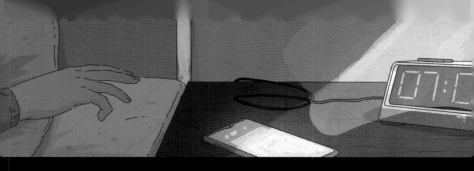

IMMEDIATELY I HAVE TO FIGURE OUT WHO I AM. THE BODY, THE LIFE.

EVERY DAY I AM SOMEONE ELSE. I AM MYSELF—I KNOW I AM MYSELF—

BUT I AM ALSO SOMEONE ELSE. IT HAS ALWAYS BEEN LIKE THIS.

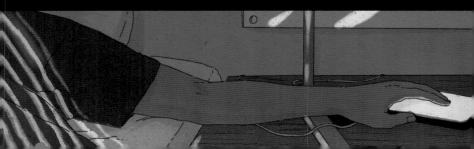

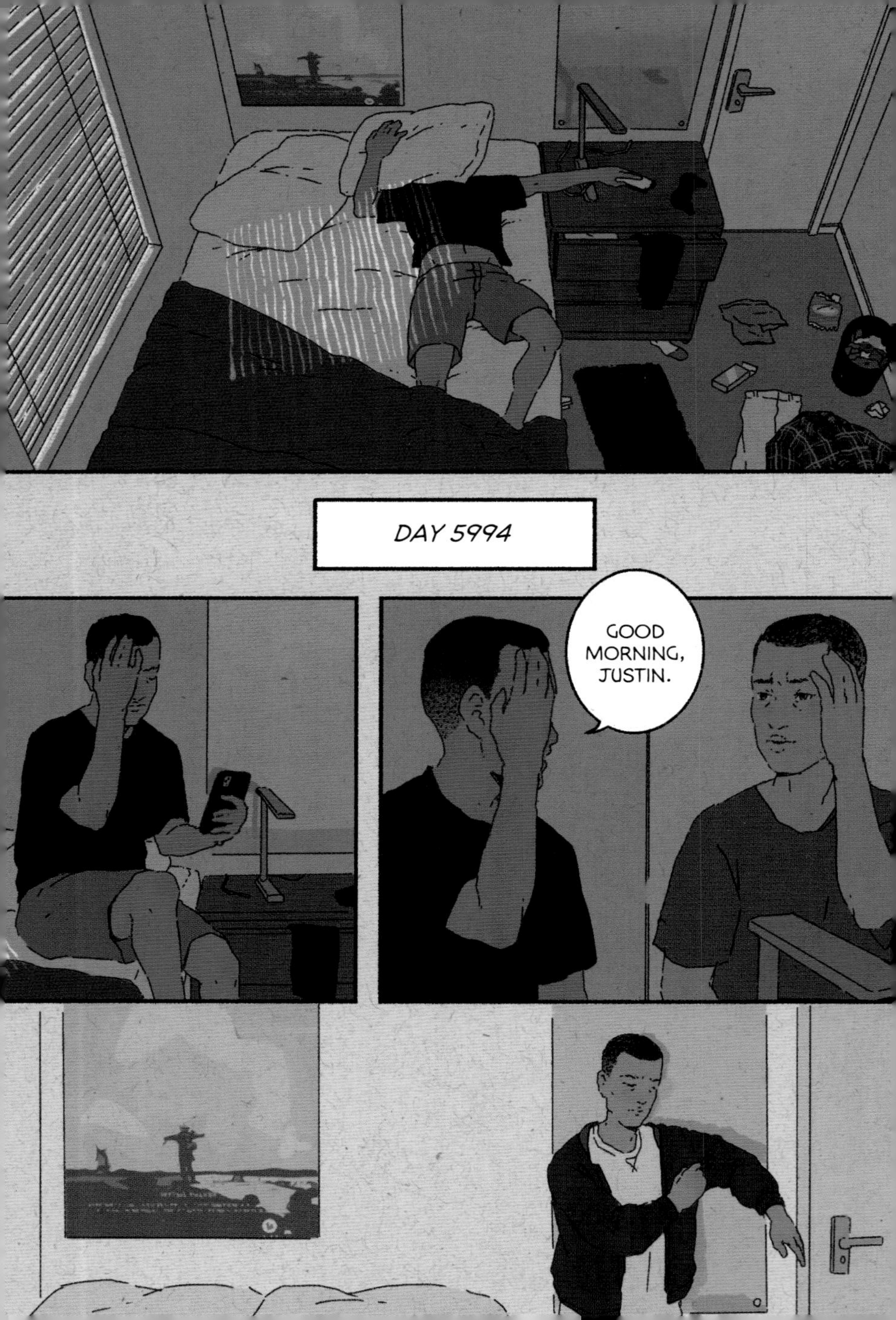
DAY 5994
GOOD MORNING, JUSTIN.

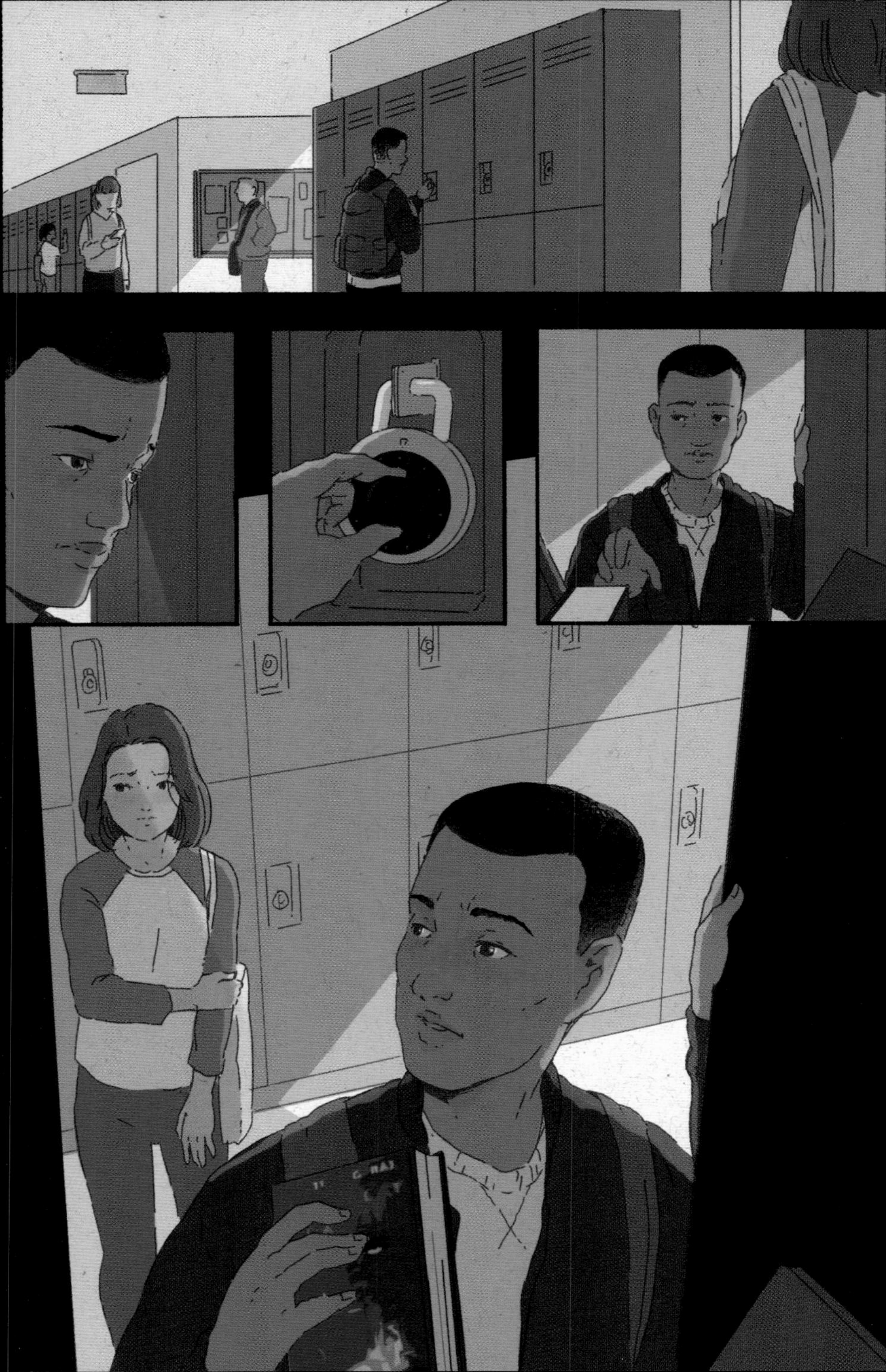

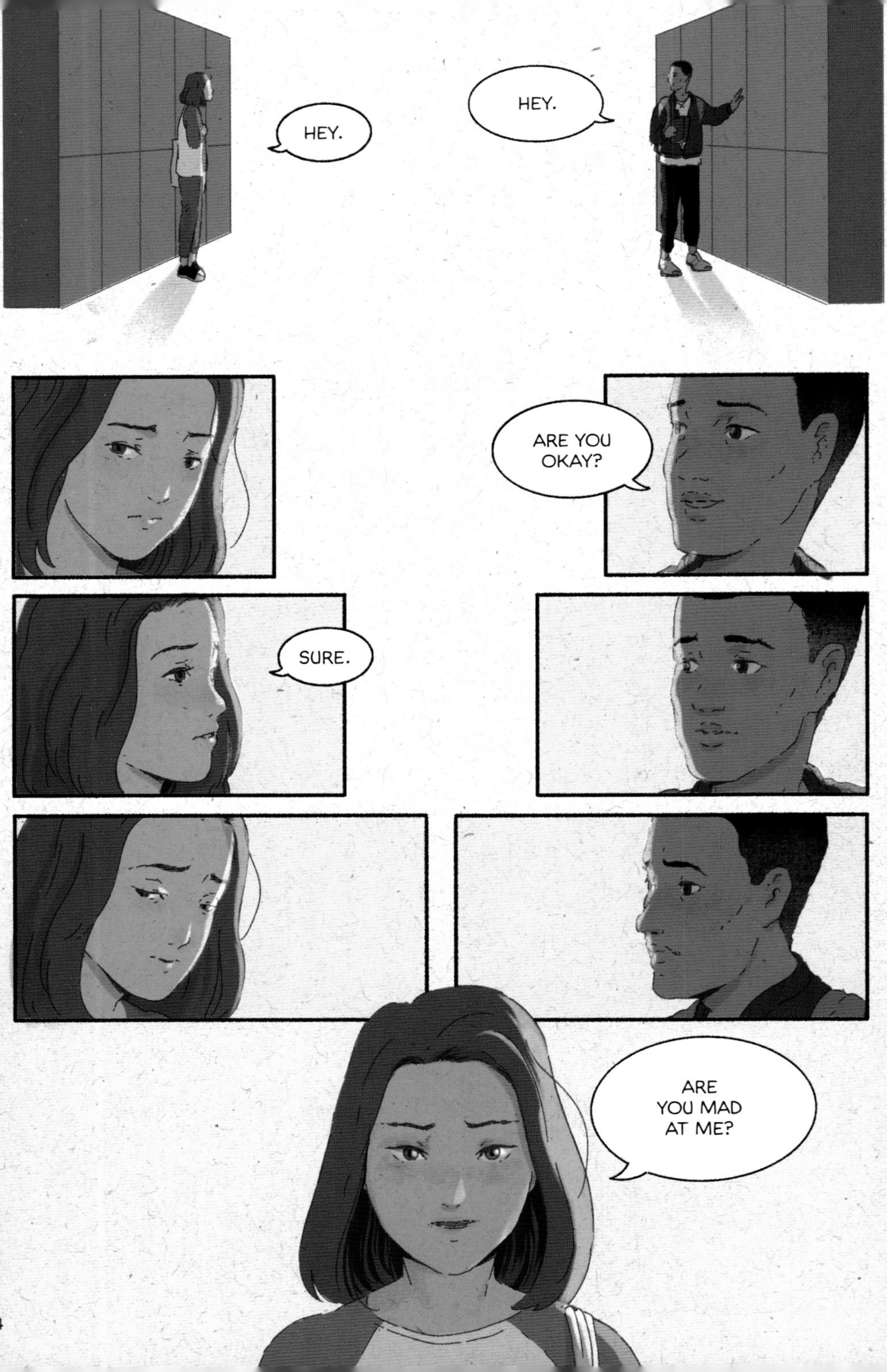
HEY.
HEY.
ARE YOU OKAY?
SURE.
ARE YOU MAD AT ME?

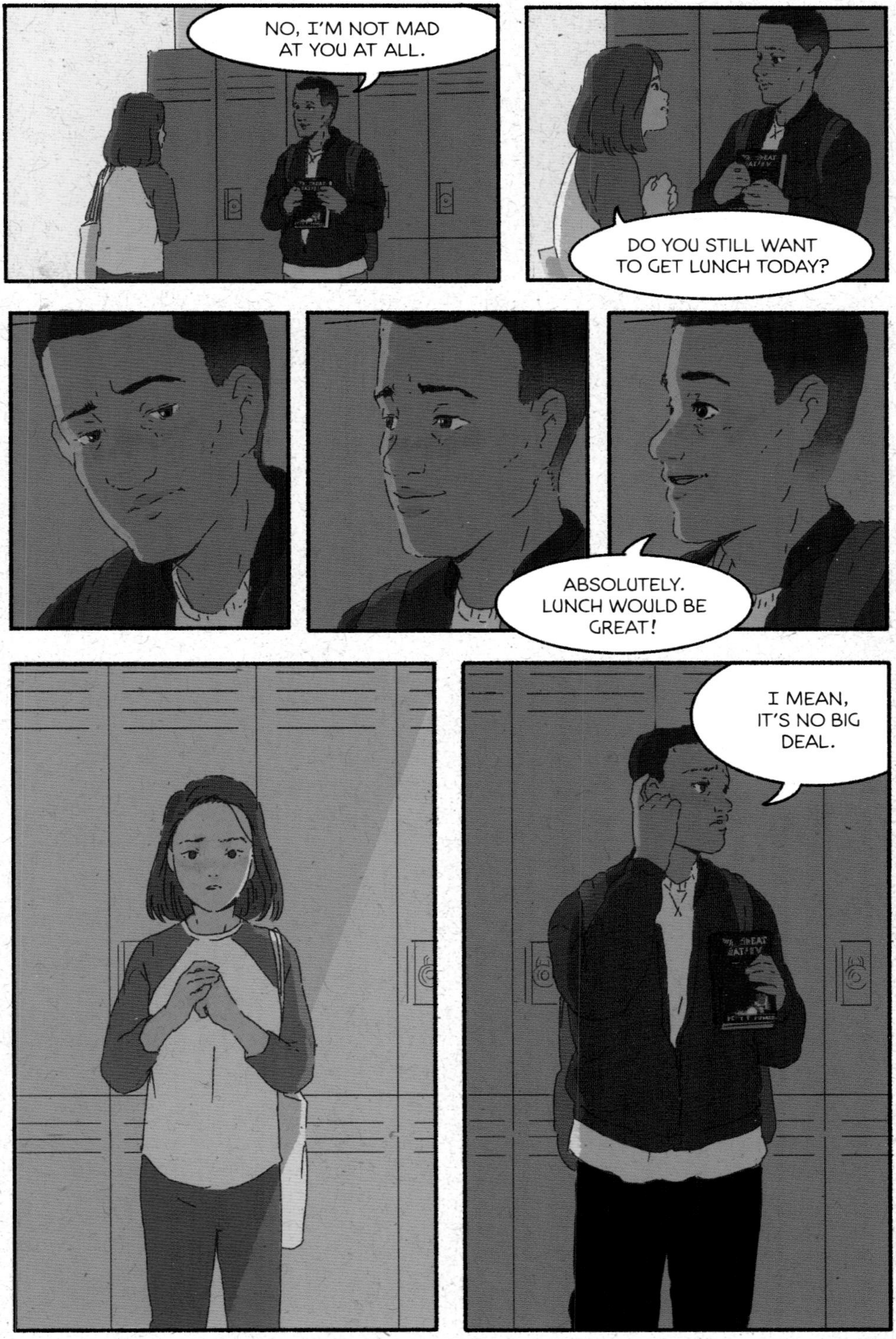
NO, I'M NOT MAD AT YOU AT ALL.
DO YOU STILL WANT TO GET LUNCH TODAY?
ABSOLUTELY. LUNCH WOULD BE GREAT!
I MEAN, IT'S NO BIG DEAL.

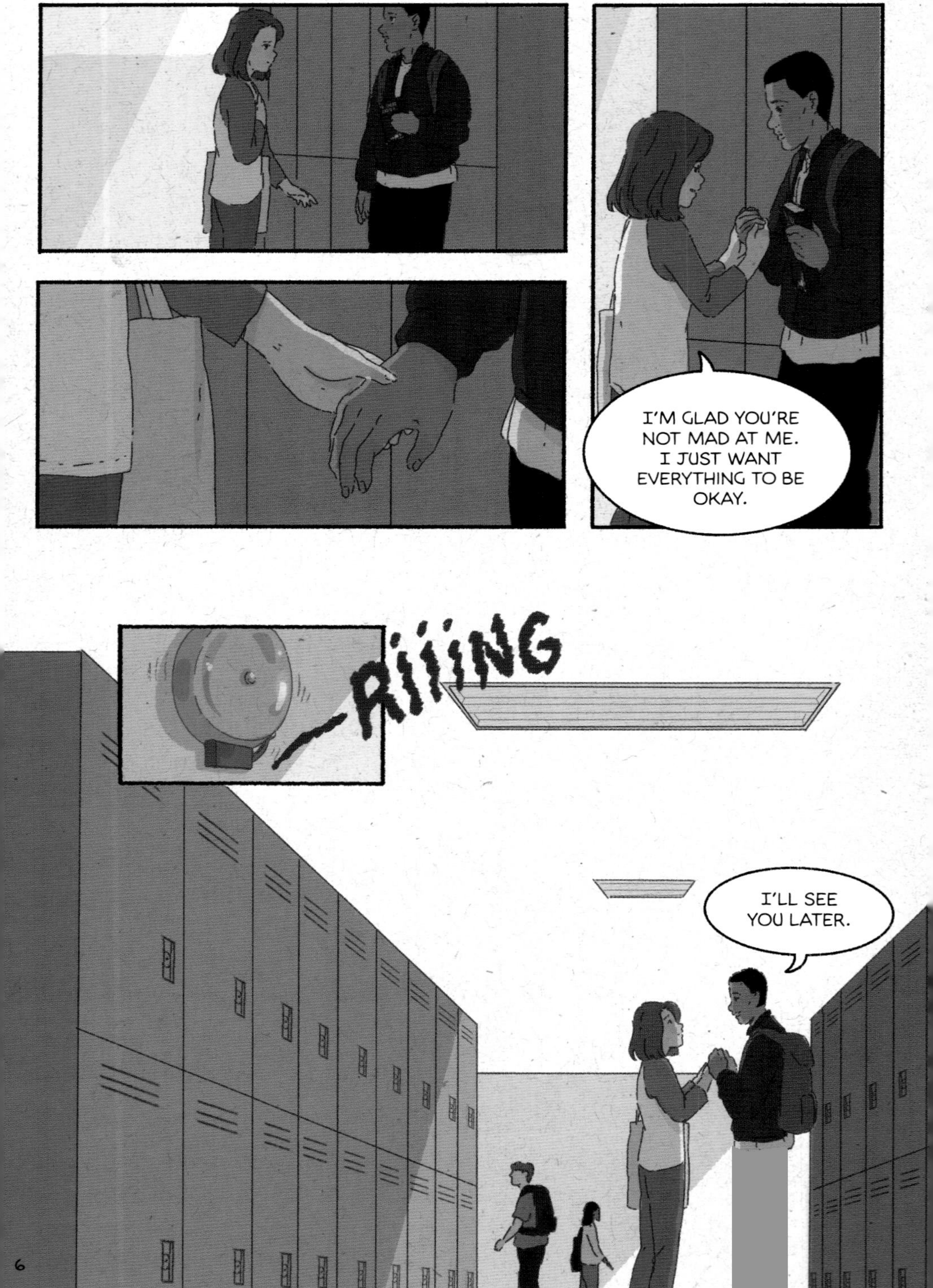
I'M GLAD YOU'RE NOT MAD AT ME. I JUST WANT EVERYTHING TO BE OKAY.
RIIING
I'LL SEE YOU LATER.

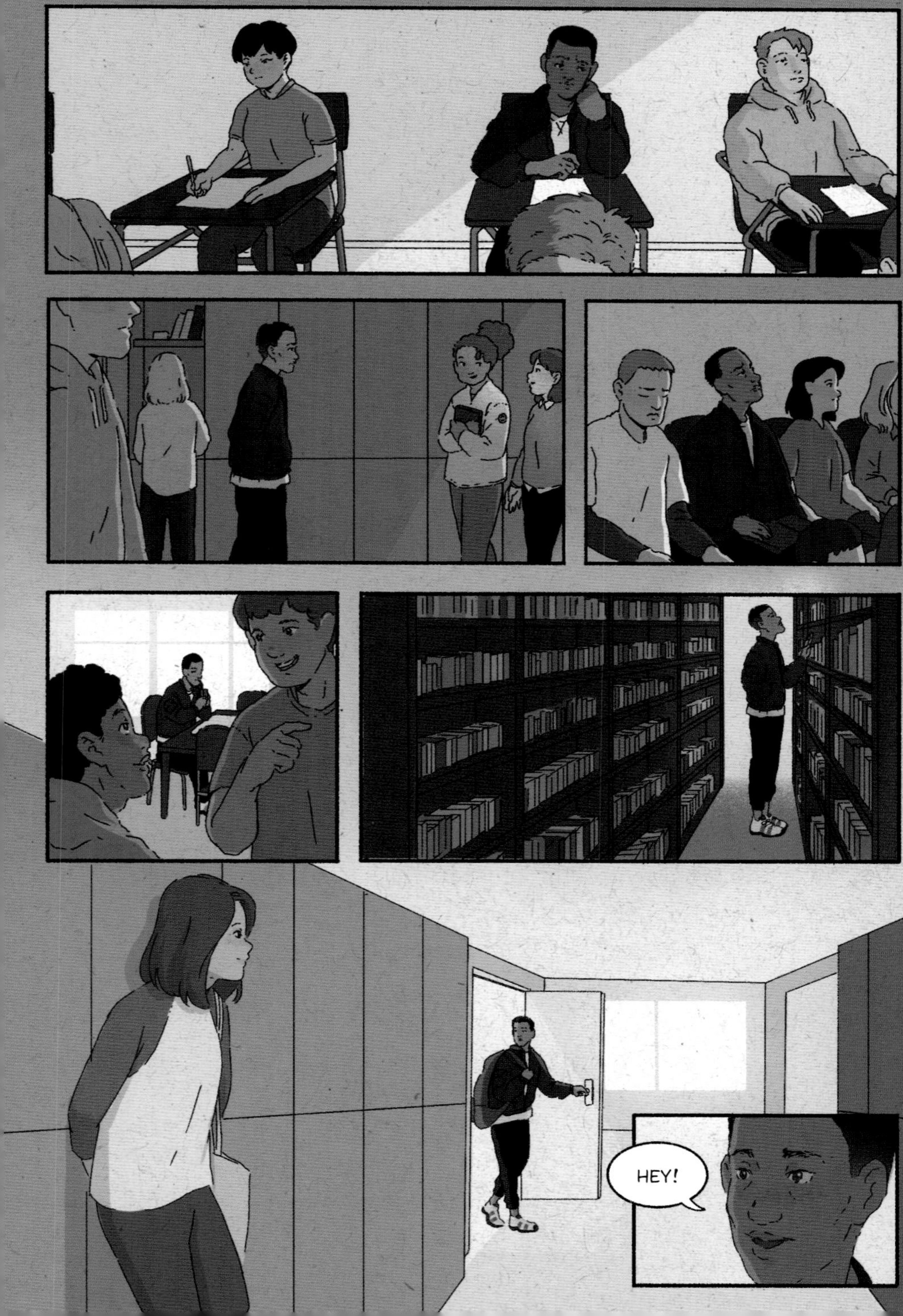
HEY!

HEY.

LET'S GO SOMEWHERE. WHERE DO YOU WANT TO GO?

I DON'T KNOW.

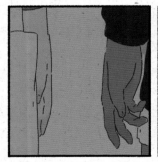

COME ON.

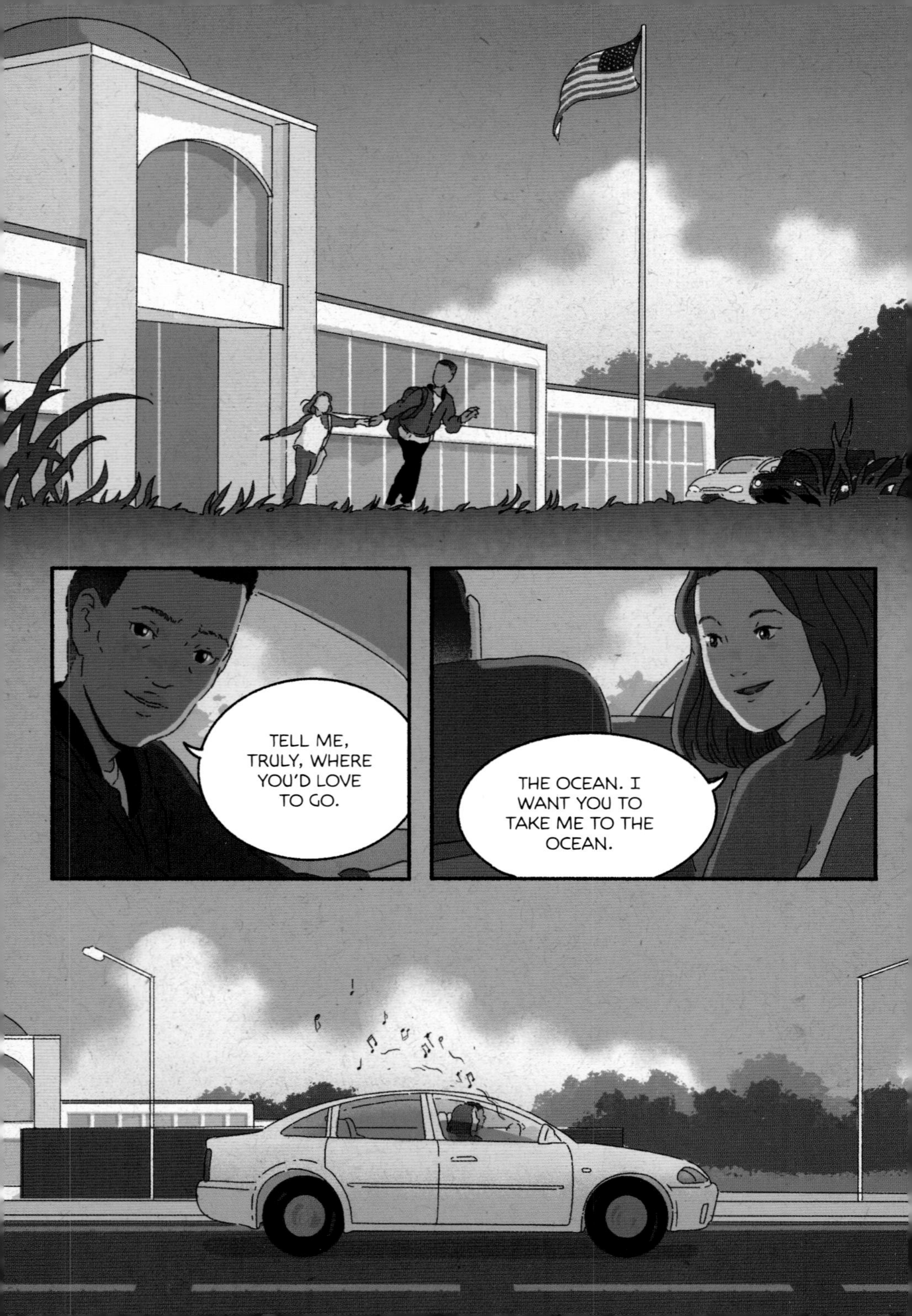
TELL ME, TRULY, WHERE YOU'D LOVE TO GO.
THE OCEAN. I WANT YOU TO TAKE ME TO THE OCEAN.

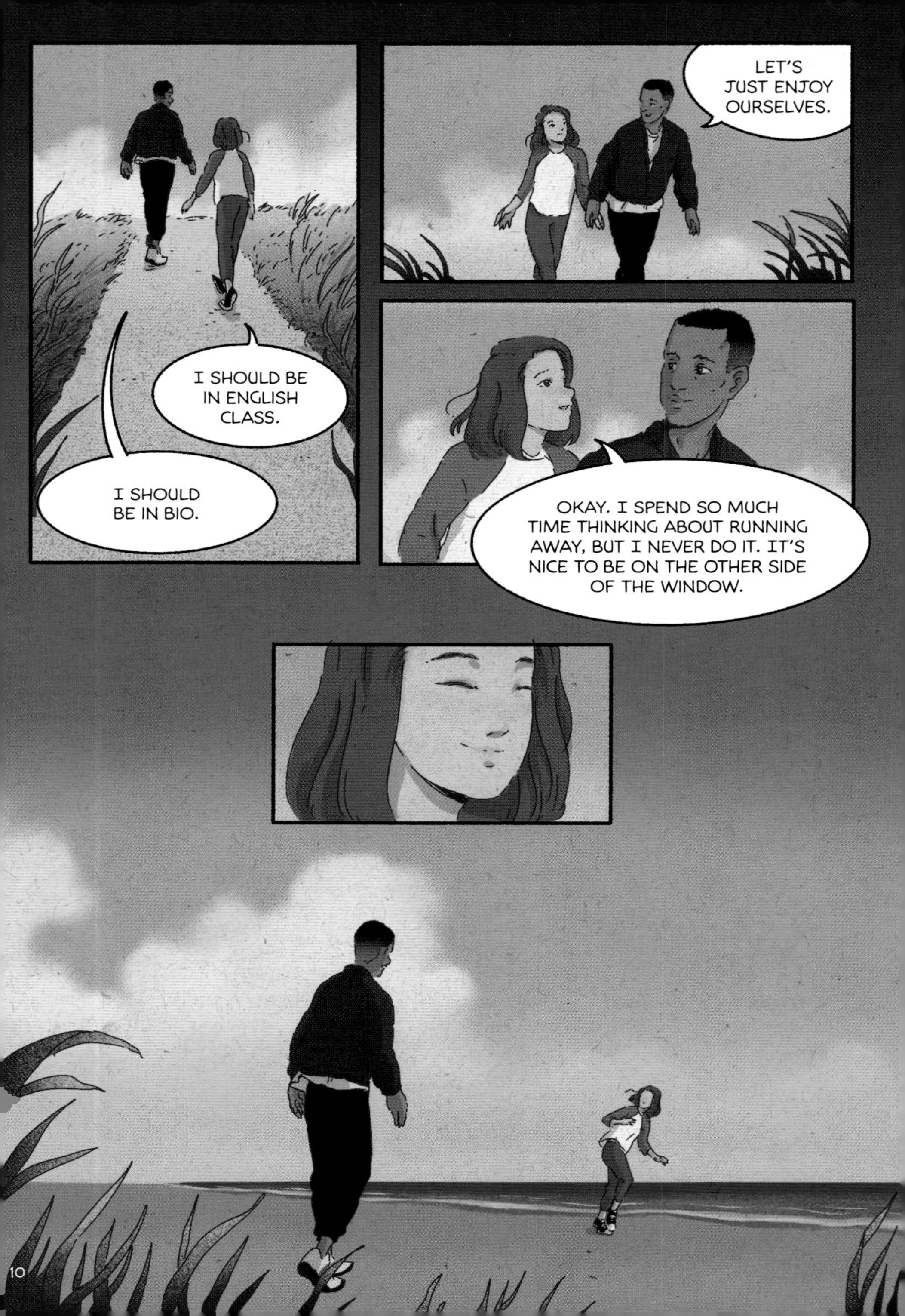
I SHOULD BE IN ENGLISH CLASS.
I SHOULD BE IN BIO.
LET'S JUST ENJOY OURSELVES.
OKAY. I SPEND SO MUCH TIME THINKING ABOUT RUNNING AWAY, BUT I NEVER DO IT. IT'S NICE TO BE ON THE OTHER SIDE OF THE WINDOW.

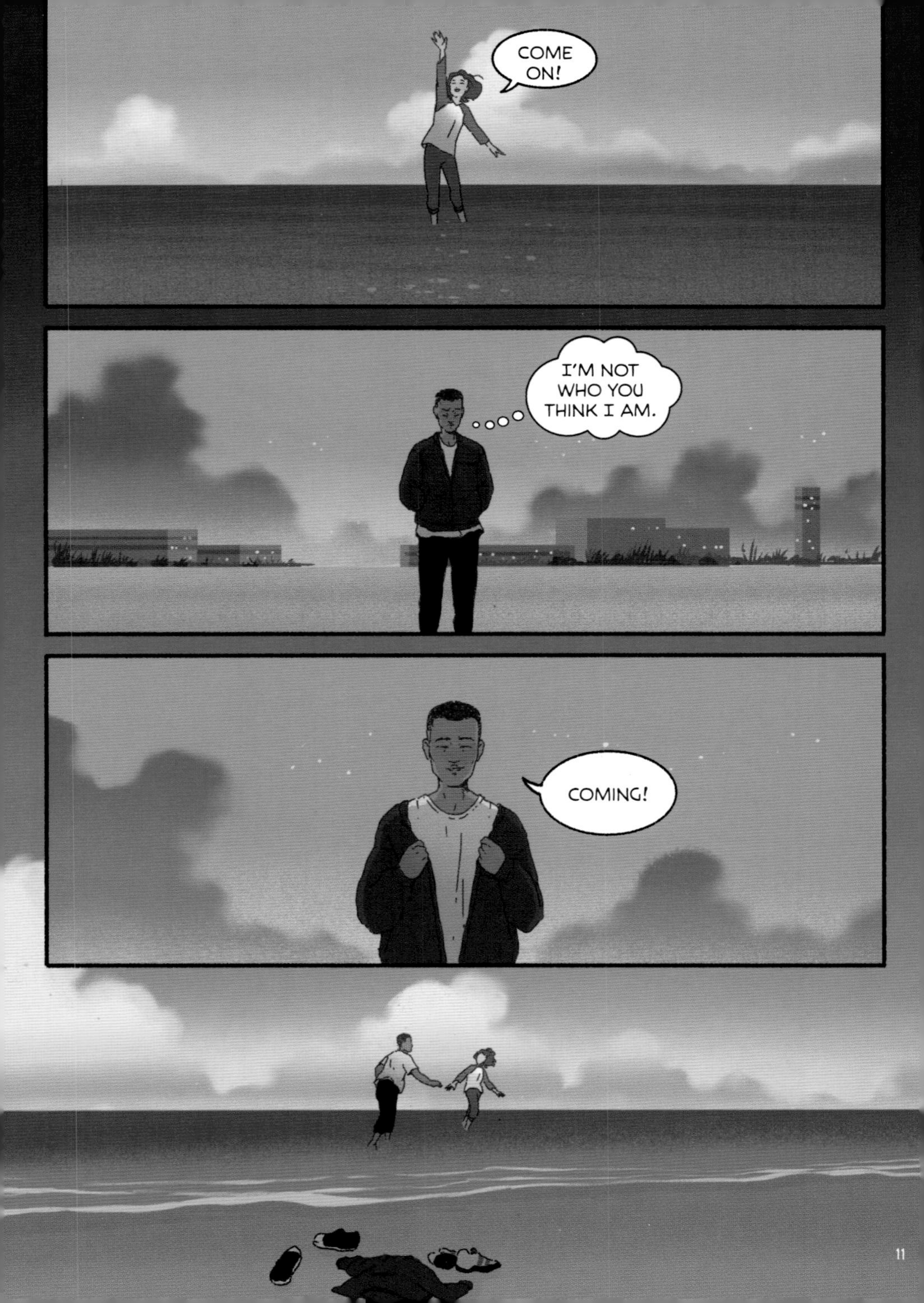
COME ON!
I'M NOT WHO YOU THINK I AM.
COMING!

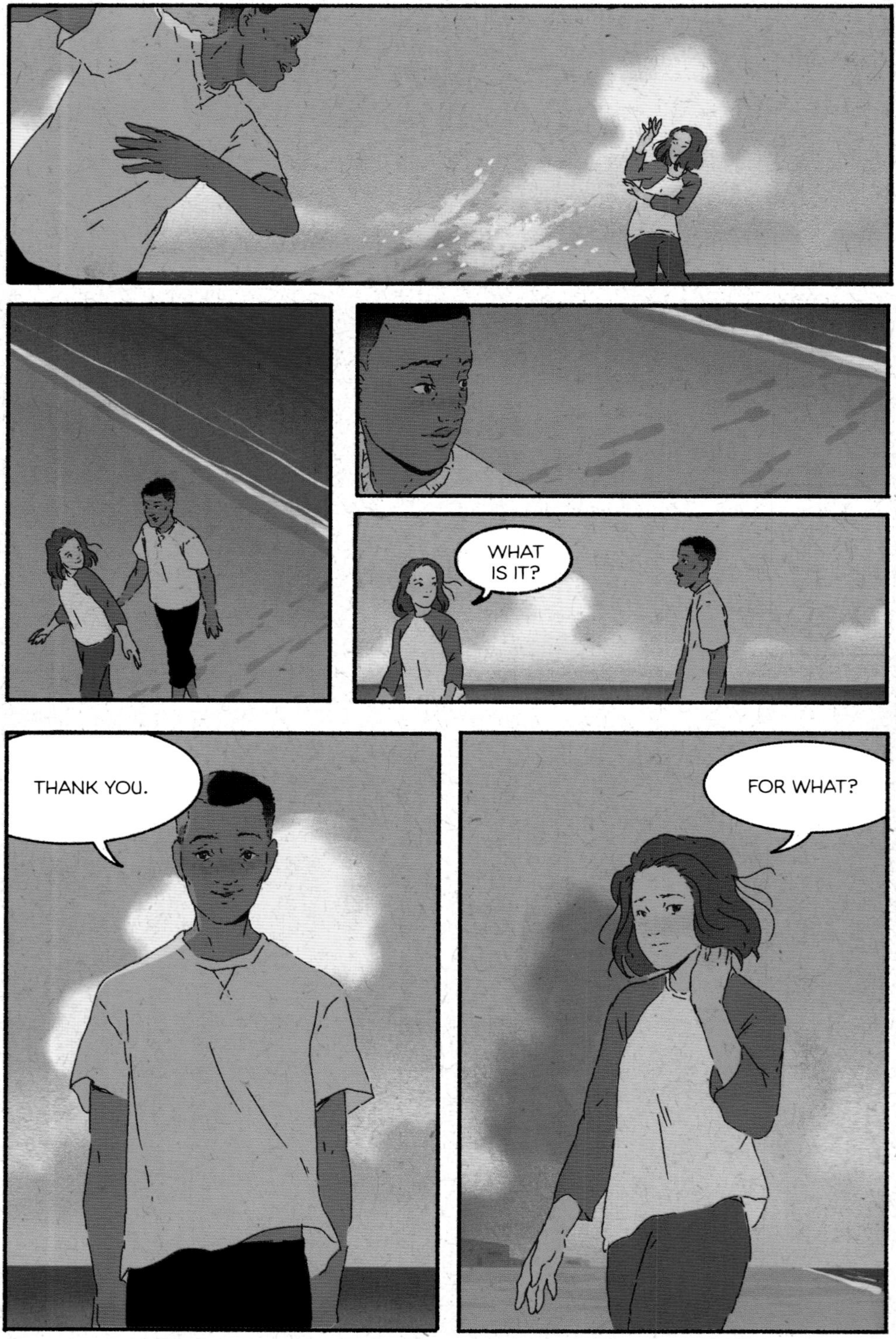
WHAT IS IT?
THANK YOU.
FOR WHAT?

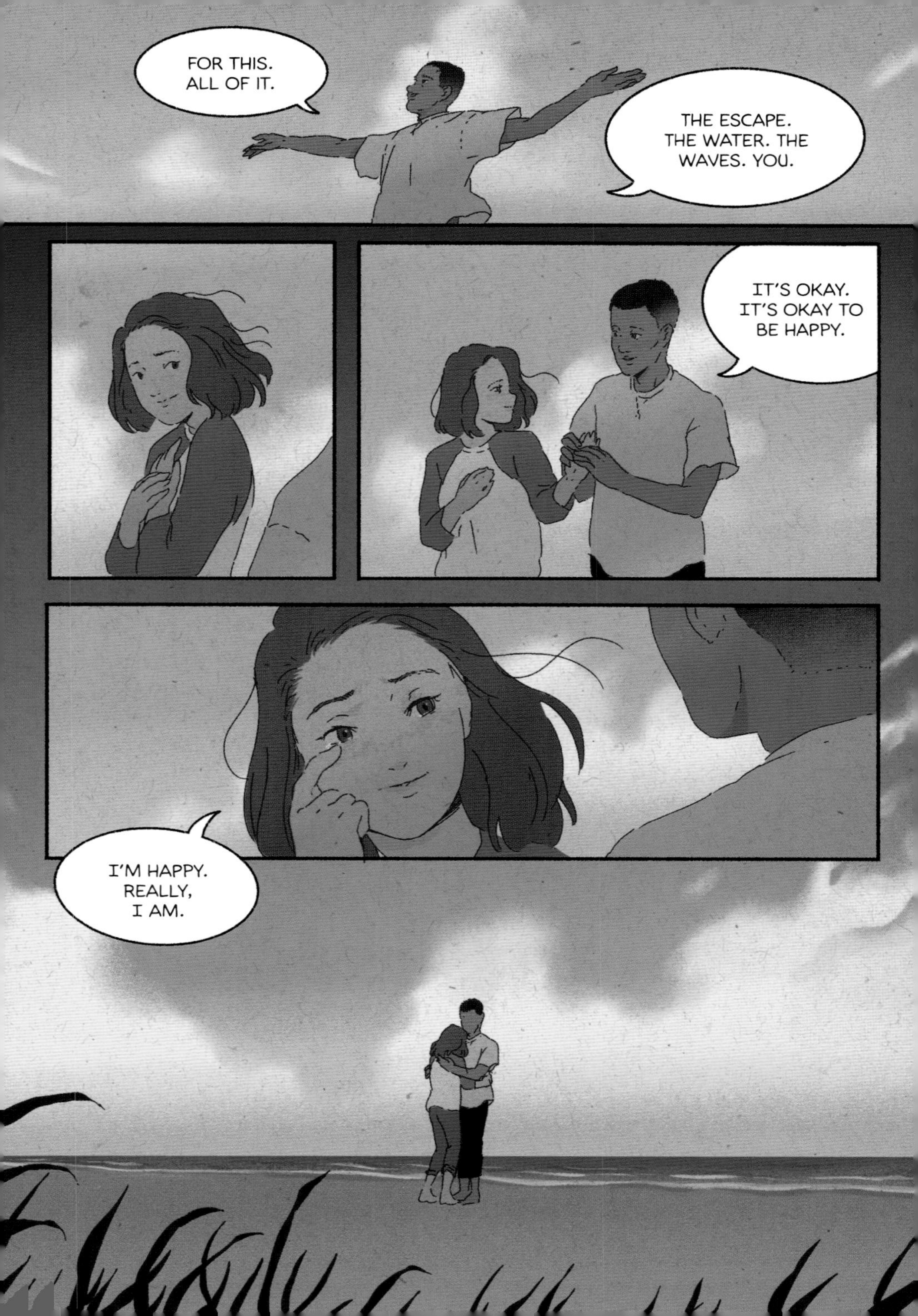
FOR THIS. ALL OF IT.
THE ESCAPE. THE WATER. THE WAVES. YOU.
IT'S OKAY. IT'S OKAY TO BE HAPPY.
I'M HAPPY. REALLY, I AM.

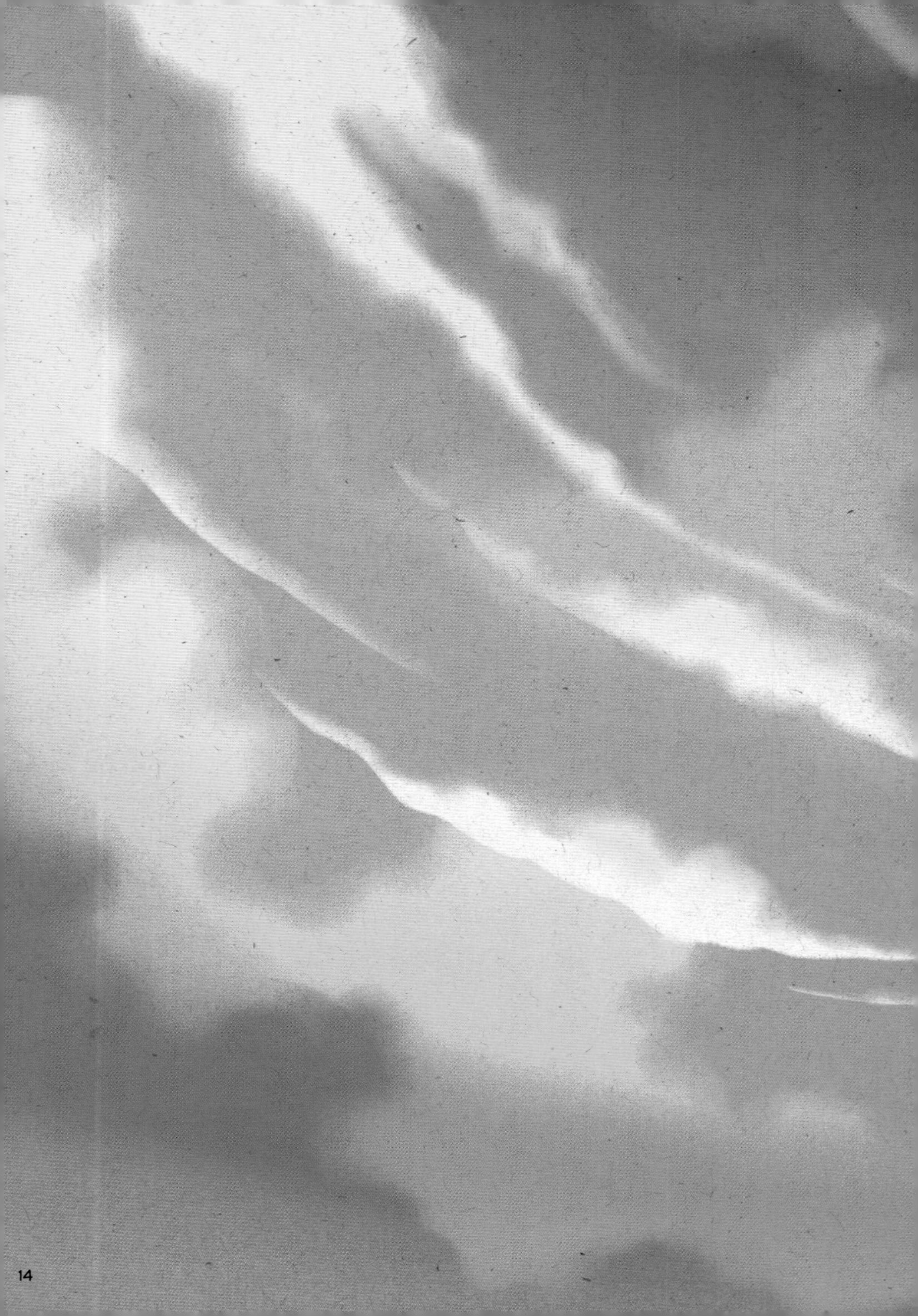

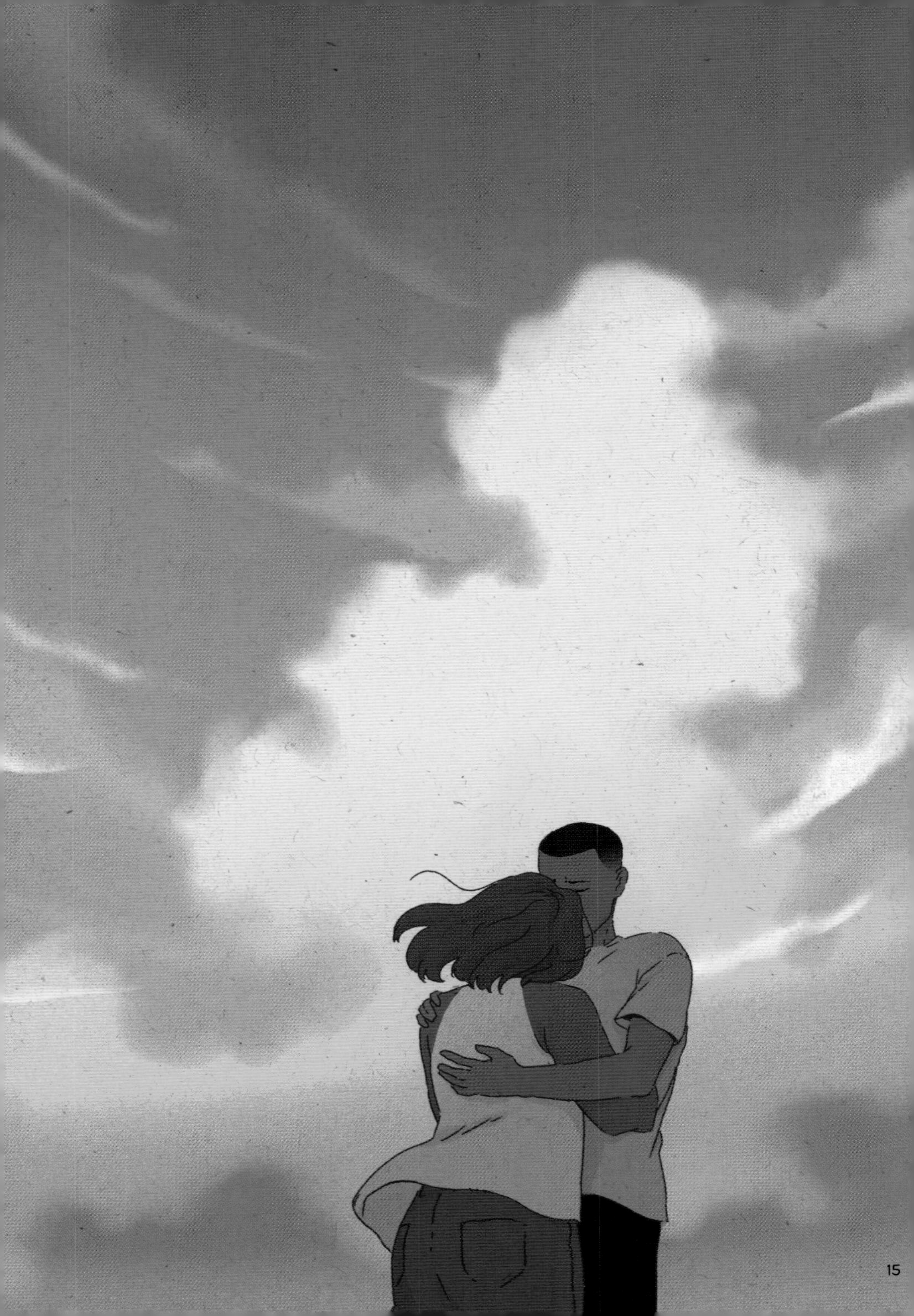

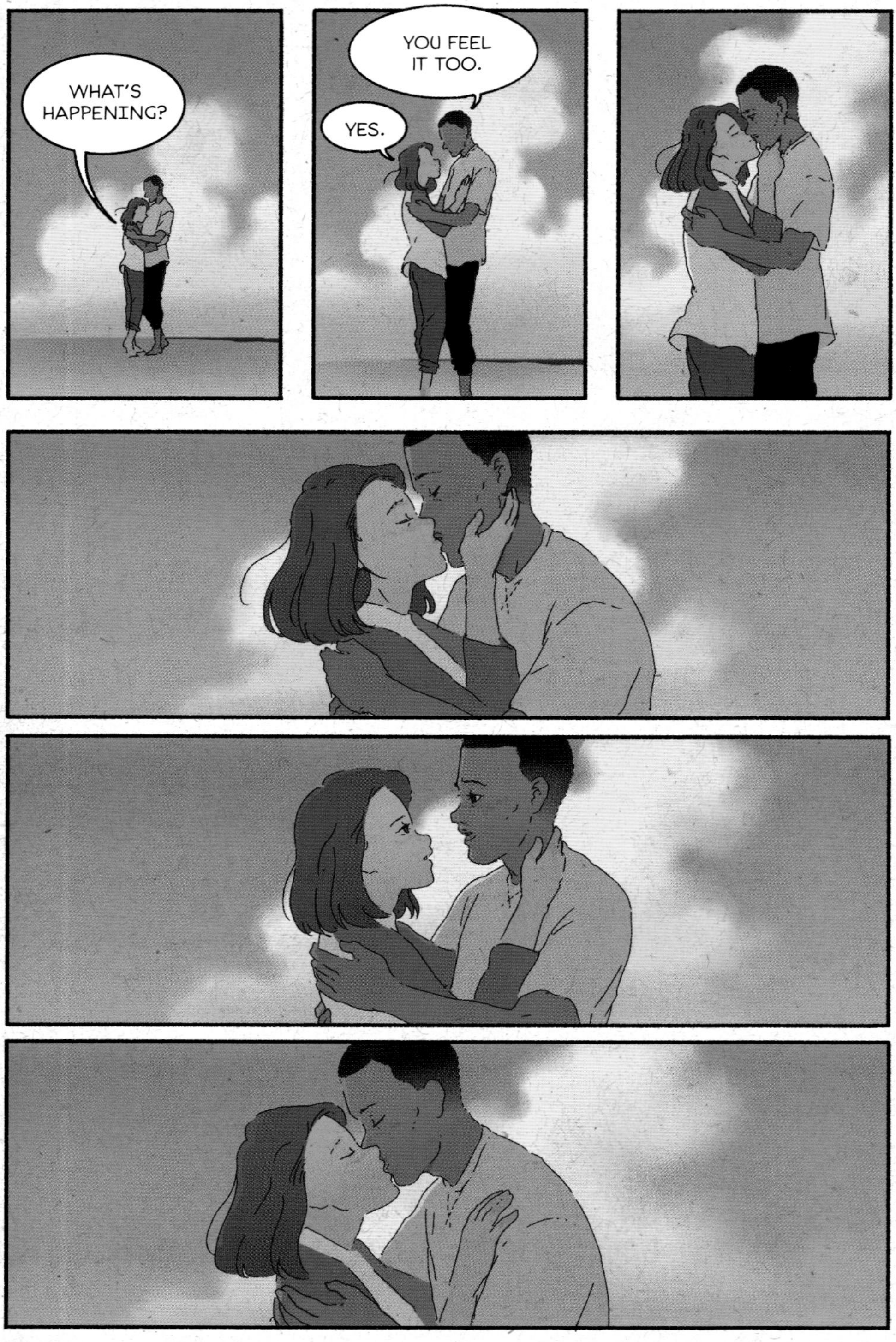
WHAT'S HAPPENING?
YOU FEEL IT TOO.
YES.

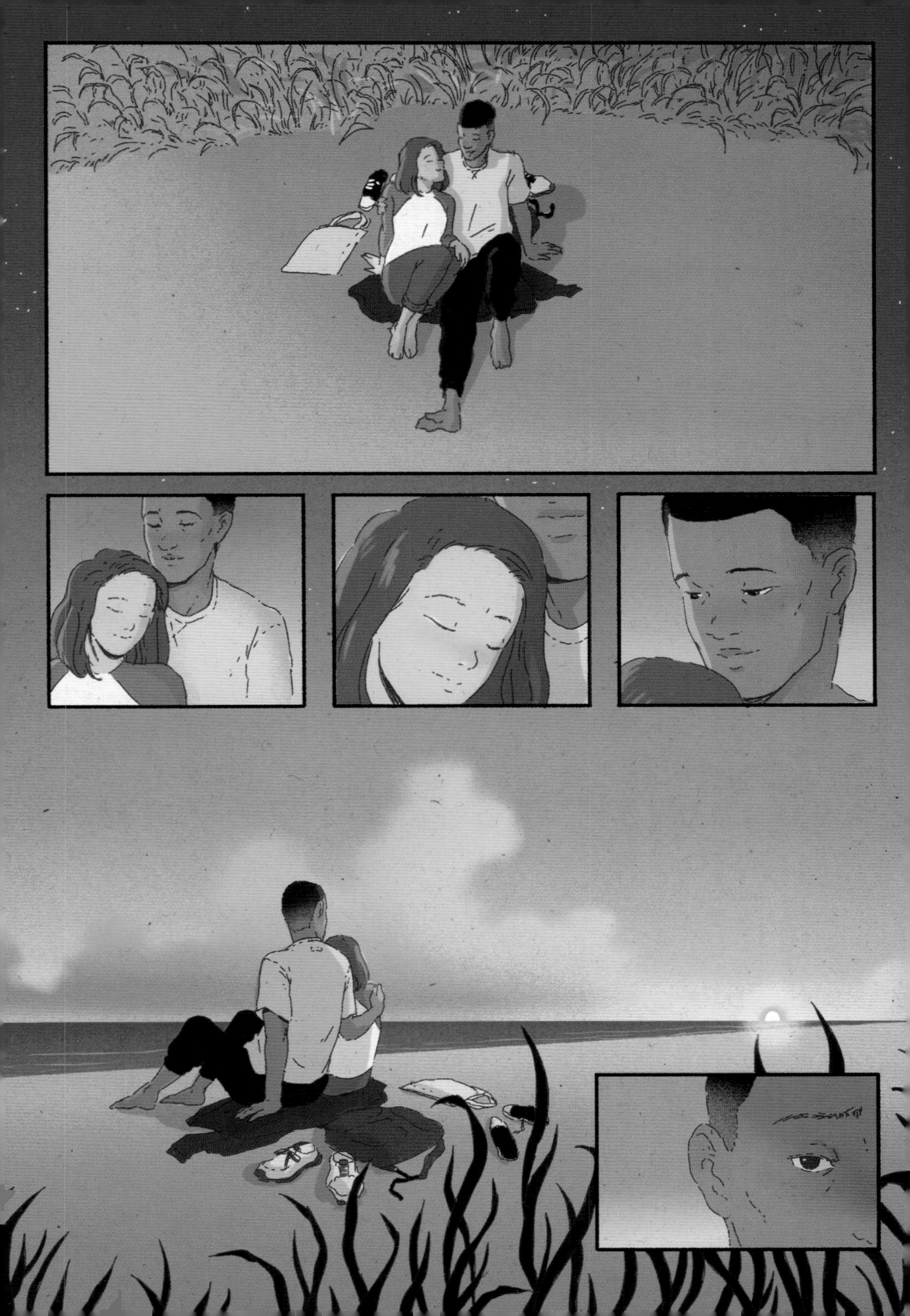

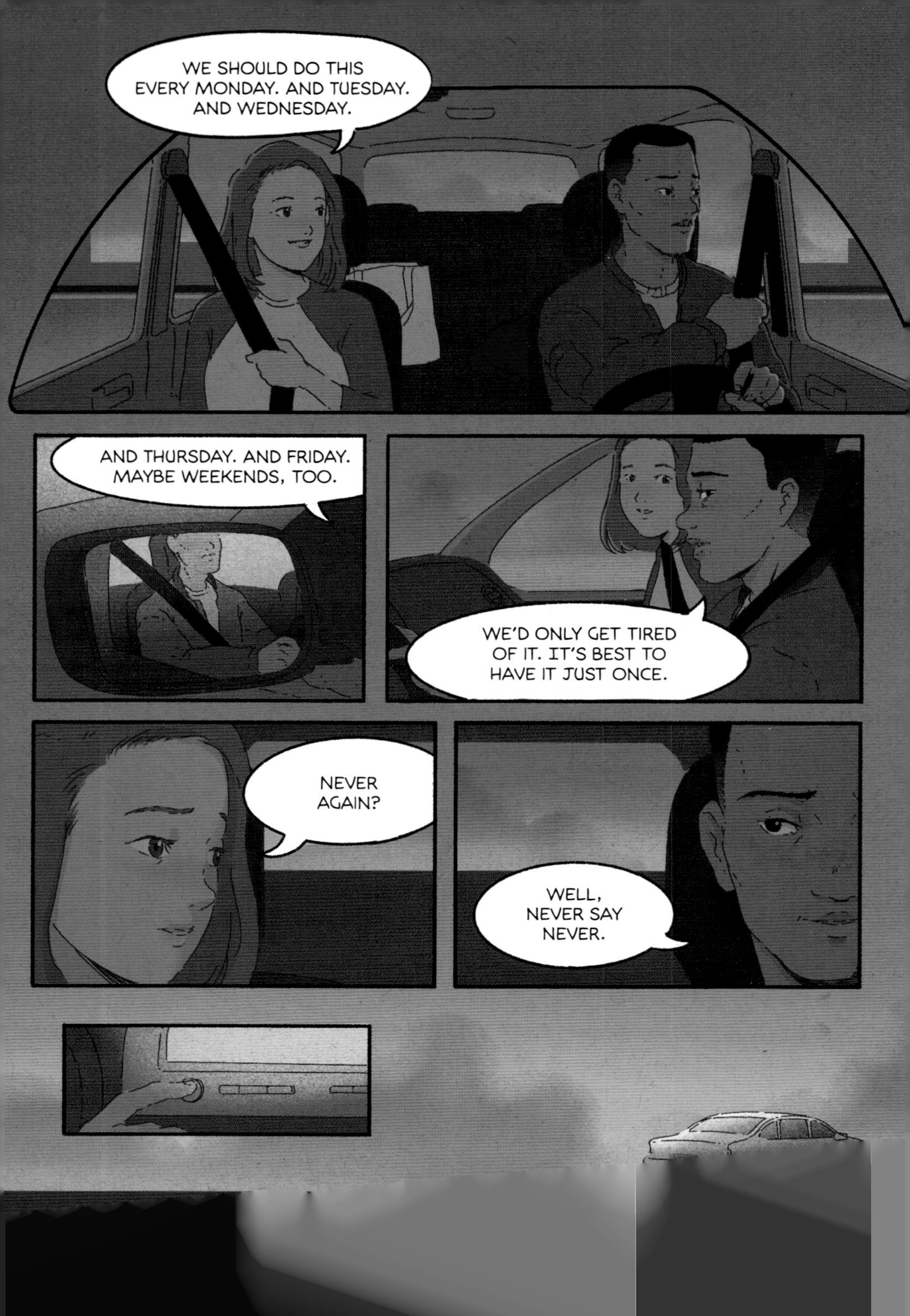
WE SHOULD DO THIS EVERY MONDAY. AND TUESDAY. AND WEDNESDAY.
AND THURSDAY. AND FRIDAY. MAYBE WEEKENDS, TOO.
WE'D ONLY GET TIRED OF IT. IT'S BEST TO HAVE IT JUST ONCE.
NEVER AGAIN?
WELL, NEVER SAY NEVER.

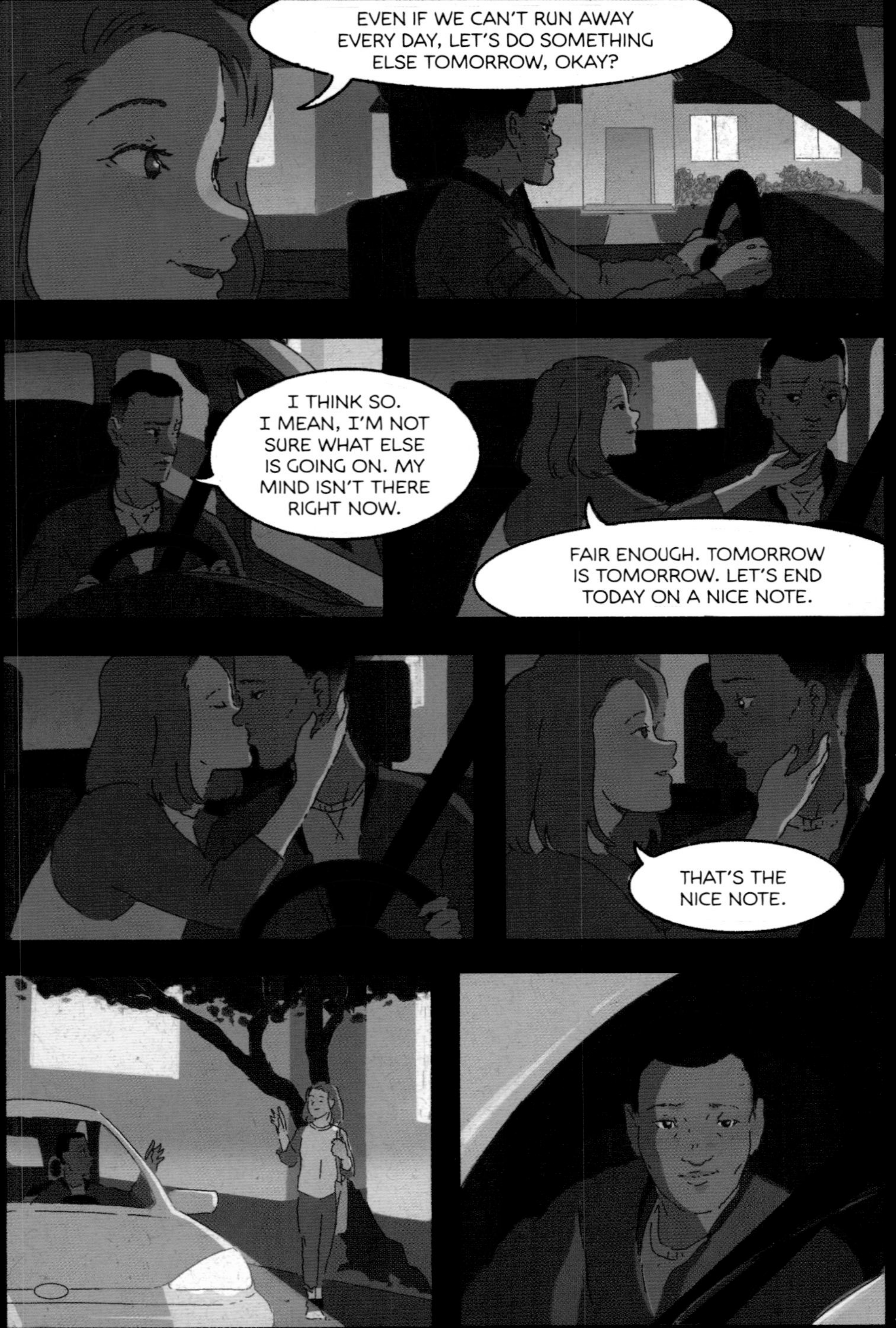
EVEN IF WE CAN'T RUN AWAY EVERY DAY, LET'S DO SOMETHING ELSE TOMORROW, OKAY?
I THINK SO. I MEAN, I'M NOT SURE WHAT ELSE IS GOING ON. MY MIND ISN'T THERE RIGHT NOW.
FAIR ENOUGH. TOMORROW IS TOMORROW. LET'S END TODAY ON A NICE NOTE.
THAT'S THE NICE NOTE.

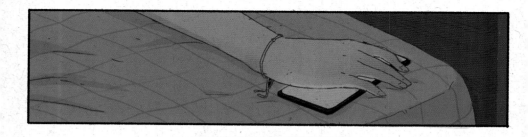

DAY 5995

DON'T SAY A WORD.

LOOK, I DON'T NEED YOUR JUDGMENT, OKAY?

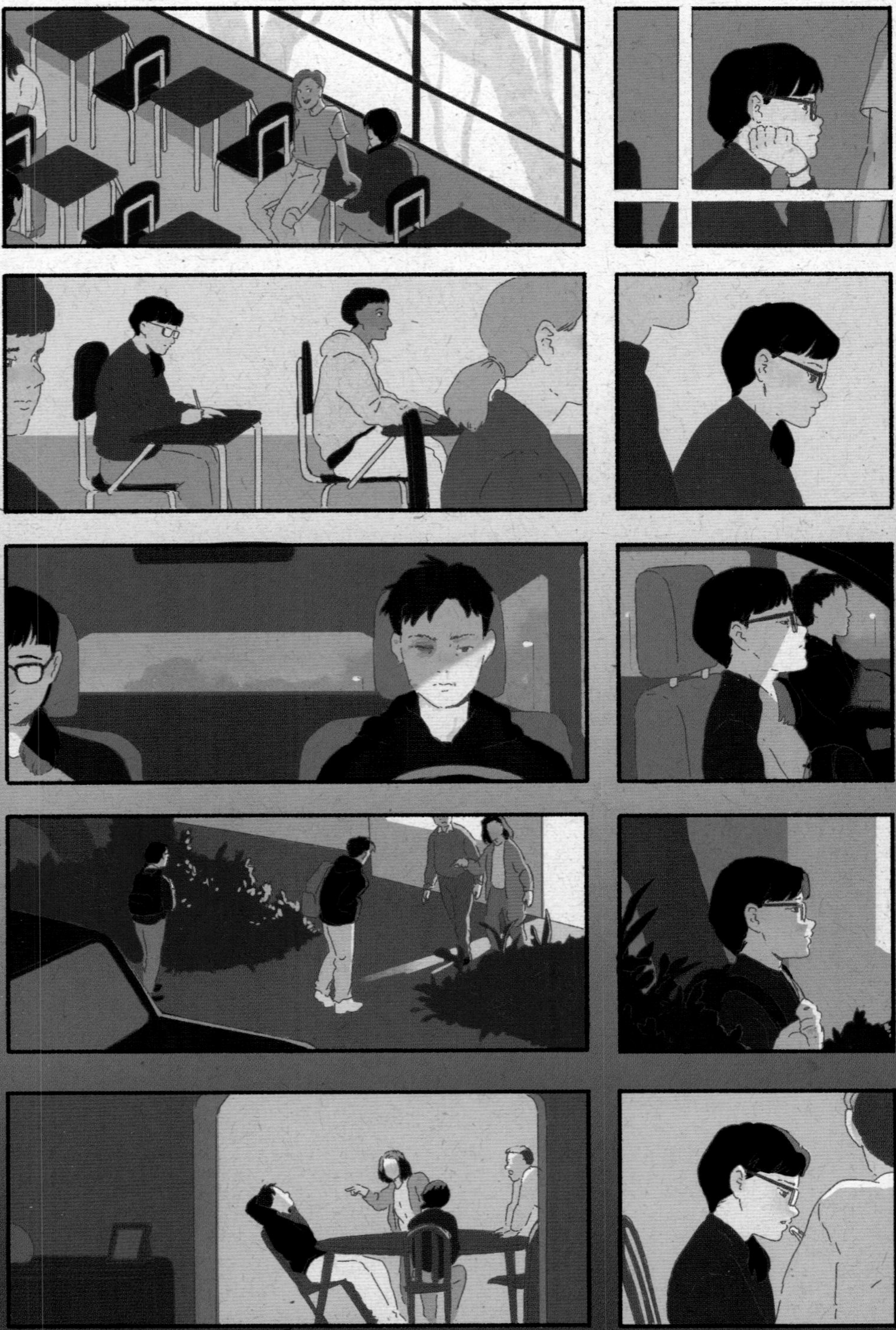

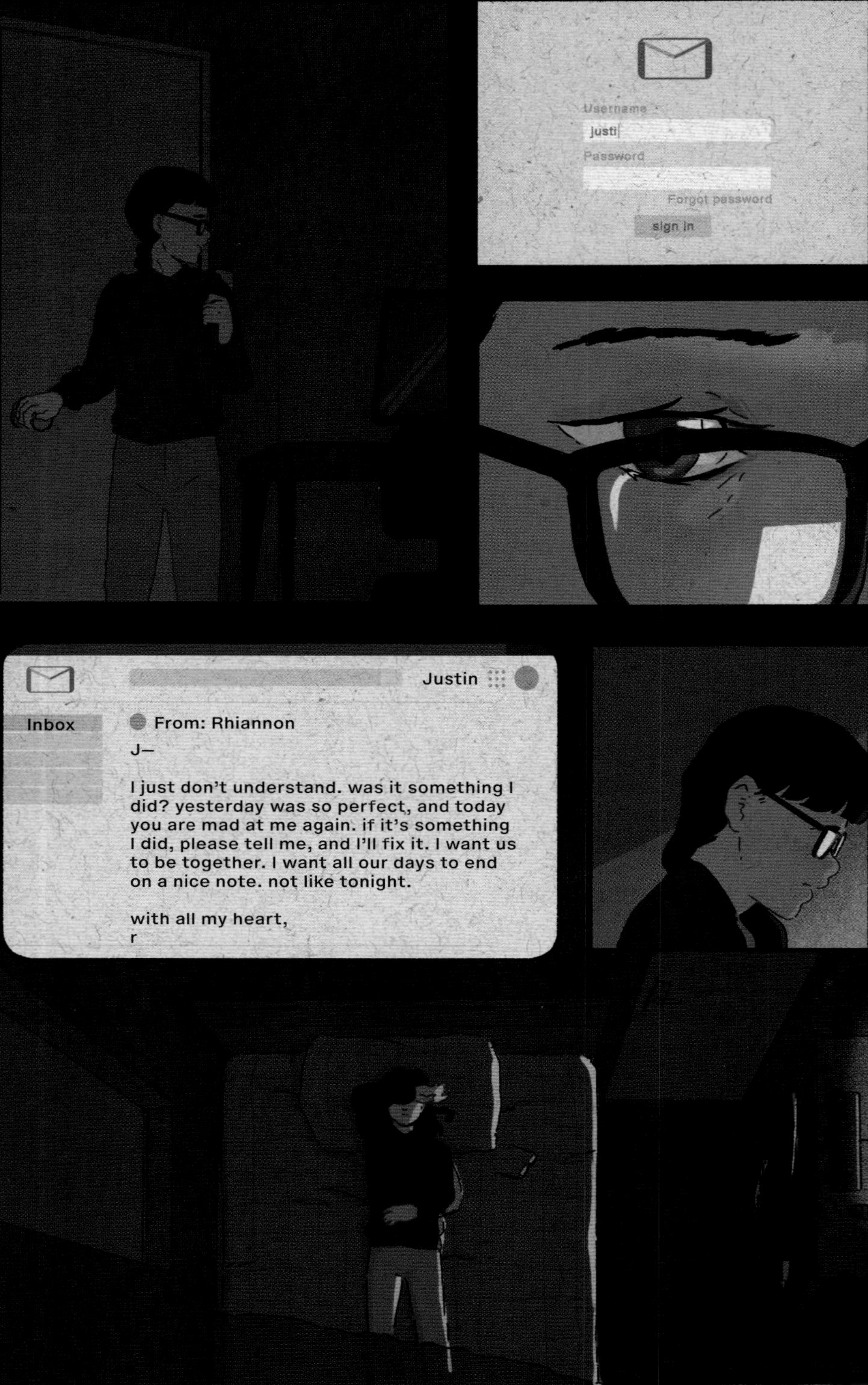
Username
justi
Password
Forgot password
sign in
Justin
Inbox
From: Rhiannon
J—
I just don't understand. was it something I did? yesterday was so perfect, and today you are mad at me again. if it's something I did, please tell me, and I'll fix it. I want us to be together. I want all our days to end on a nice note. not like tonight.
with all my heart,
r

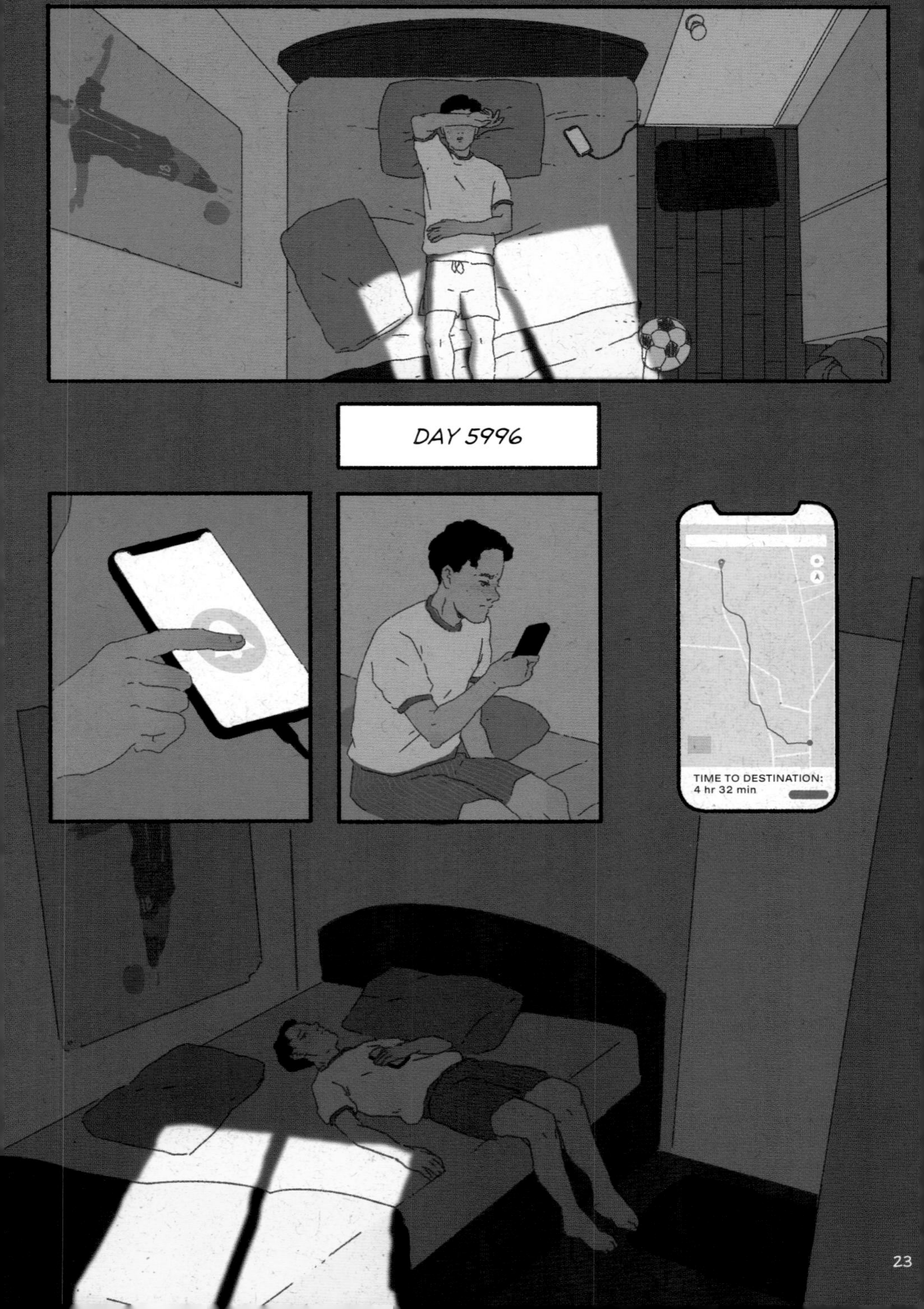
DAY 5996
TIME TO DESTINATION:
4 hr 32 min

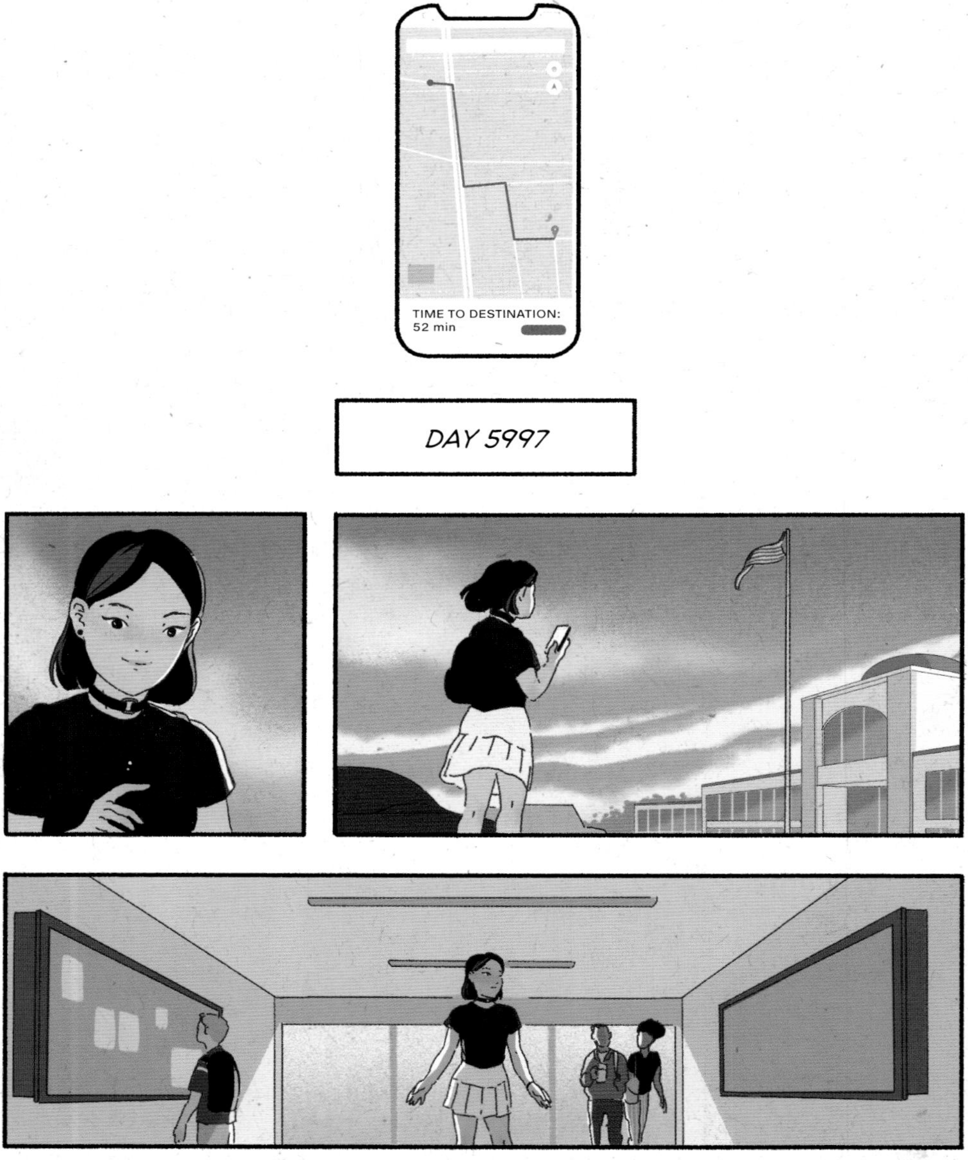
TIME TO DESTINATION:
52 min
DAY 5997

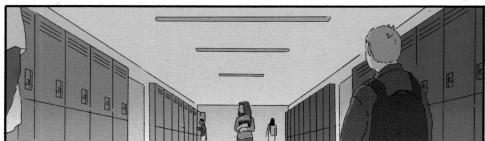

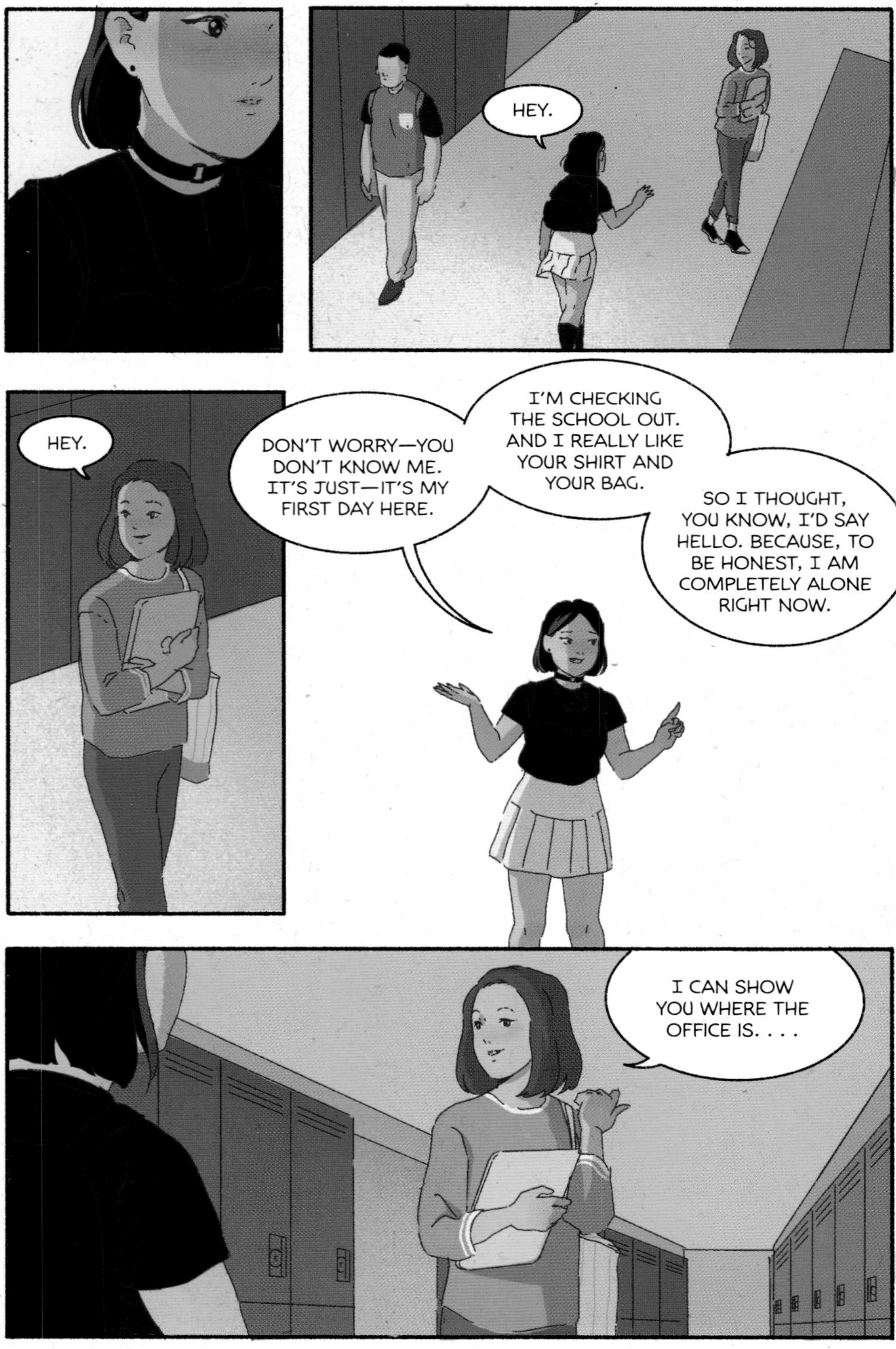
HEY.
HEY.
DON'T WORRY—YOU DON'T KNOW ME. IT'S JUST—IT'S MY FIRST DAY HERE.
I'M CHECKING THE SCHOOL OUT. AND I REALLY LIKE YOUR SHIRT AND YOUR BAG.
SO I THOUGHT, YOU KNOW, I'D SAY HELLO. BECAUSE, TO BE HONEST, I AM COMPLETELY ALONE RIGHT NOW.
I CAN SHOW YOU WHERE THE OFFICE IS. . . .

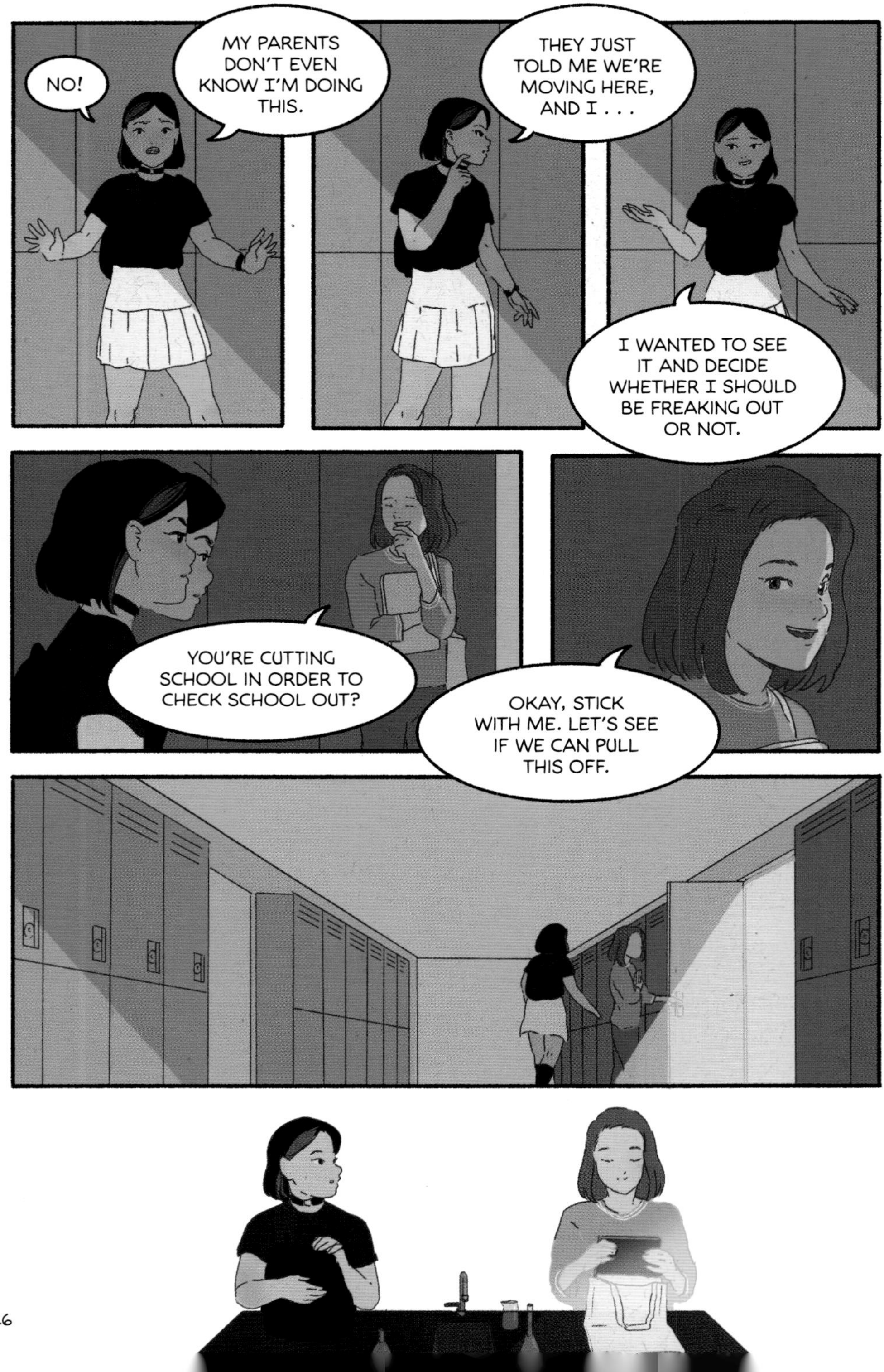
NO!
MY PARENTS DON'T EVEN KNOW I'M DOING THIS.
THEY JUST TOLD ME WE'RE MOVING HERE, AND I . . .
I WANTED TO SEE IT AND DECIDE WHETHER I SHOULD BE FREAKING OUT OR NOT.
YOU'RE CUTTING SCHOOL IN ORDER TO CHECK SCHOOL OUT?
OKAY, STICK WITH ME. LET'S SEE IF WE CAN PULL THIS OFF.

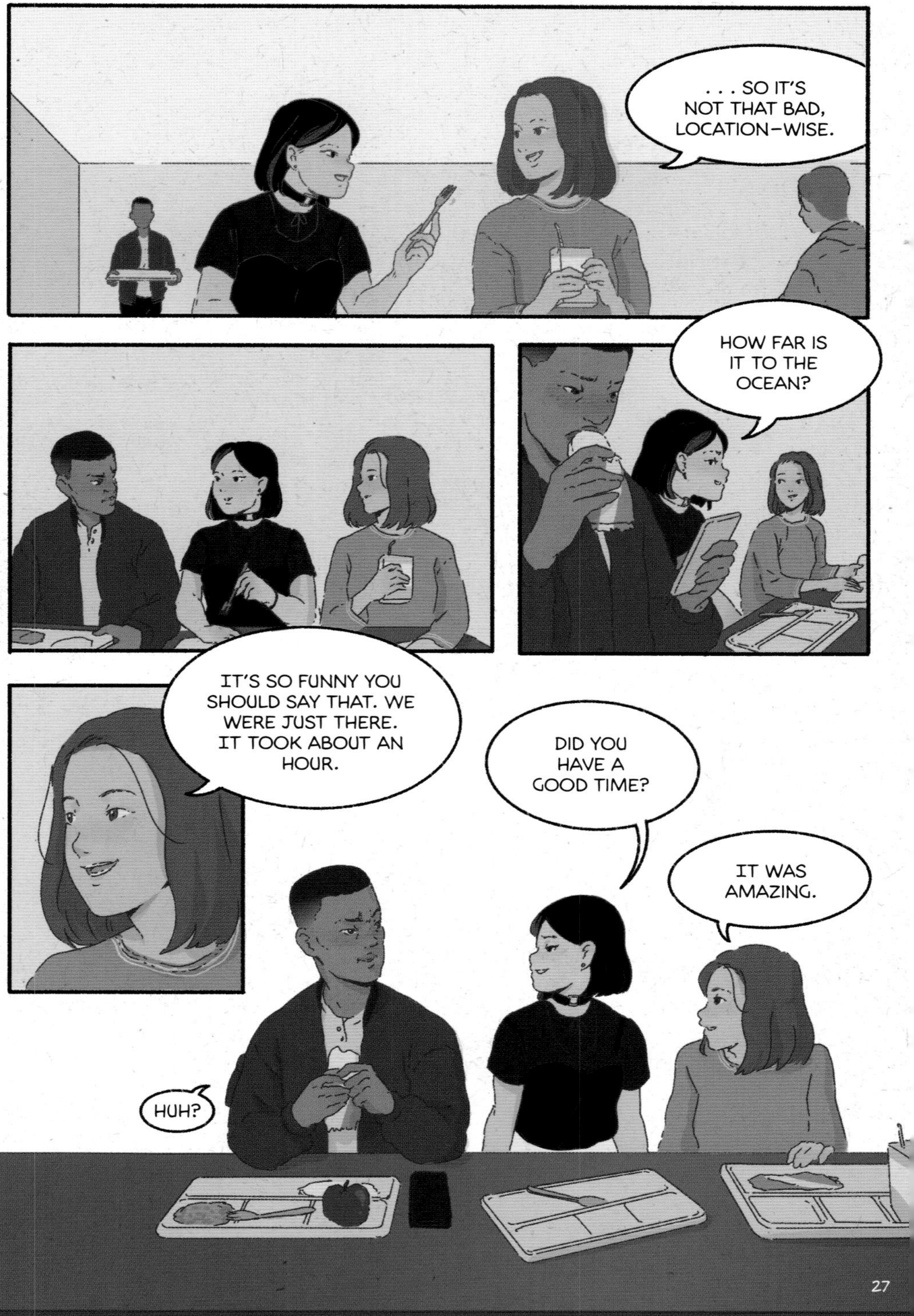

. . . SO IT'S NOT THAT BAD, LOCATION–WISE.
HOW FAR IS IT TO THE OCEAN?
IT'S SO FUNNY YOU SHOULD SAY THAT. WE WERE JUST THERE. IT TOOK ABOUT AN HOUR.
DID YOU HAVE A GOOD TIME?
IT WAS AMAZING.
HUH?

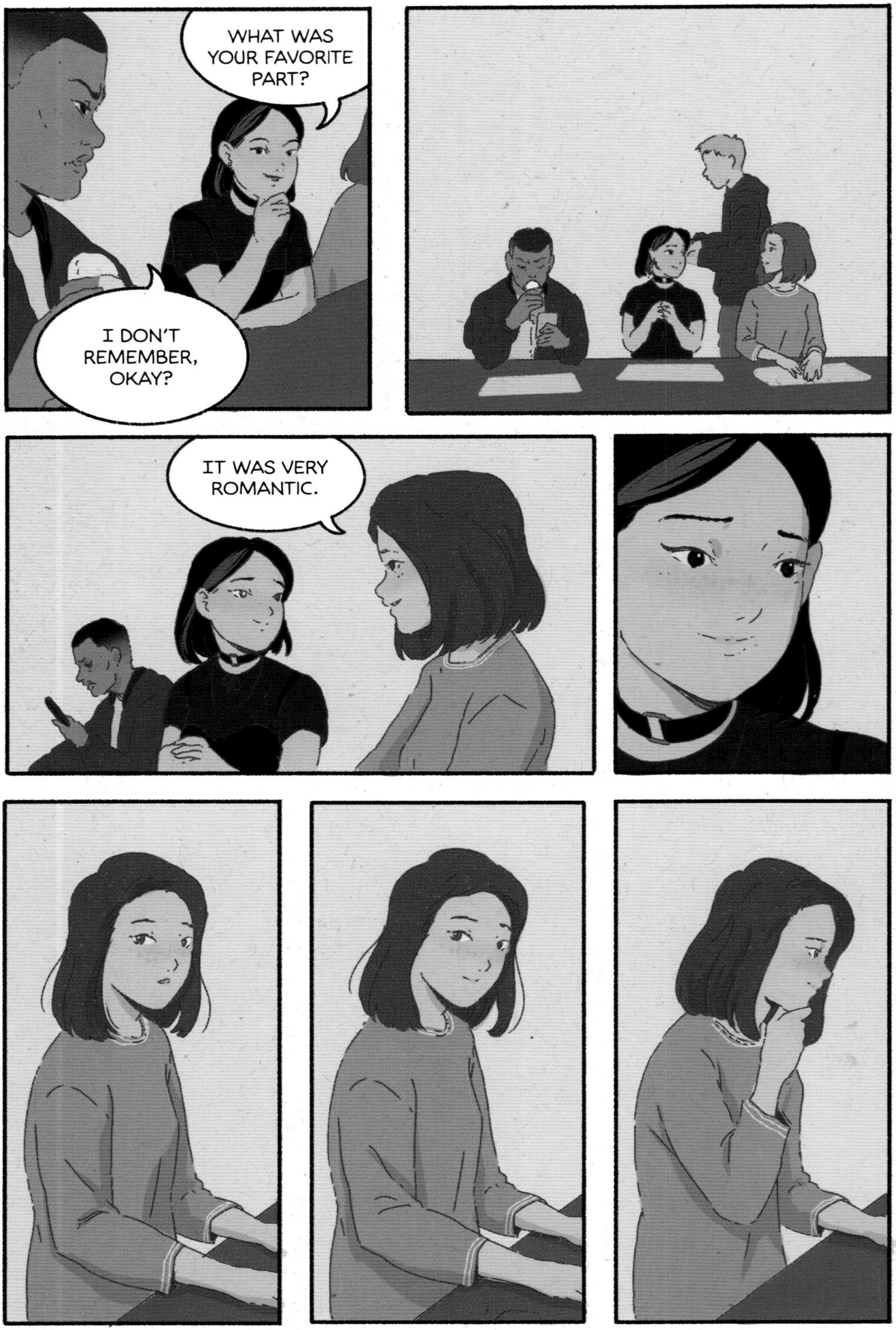
WHAT WAS YOUR FAVORITE PART?
I DON'T REMEMBER, OKAY?
IT WAS VERY ROMANTIC.

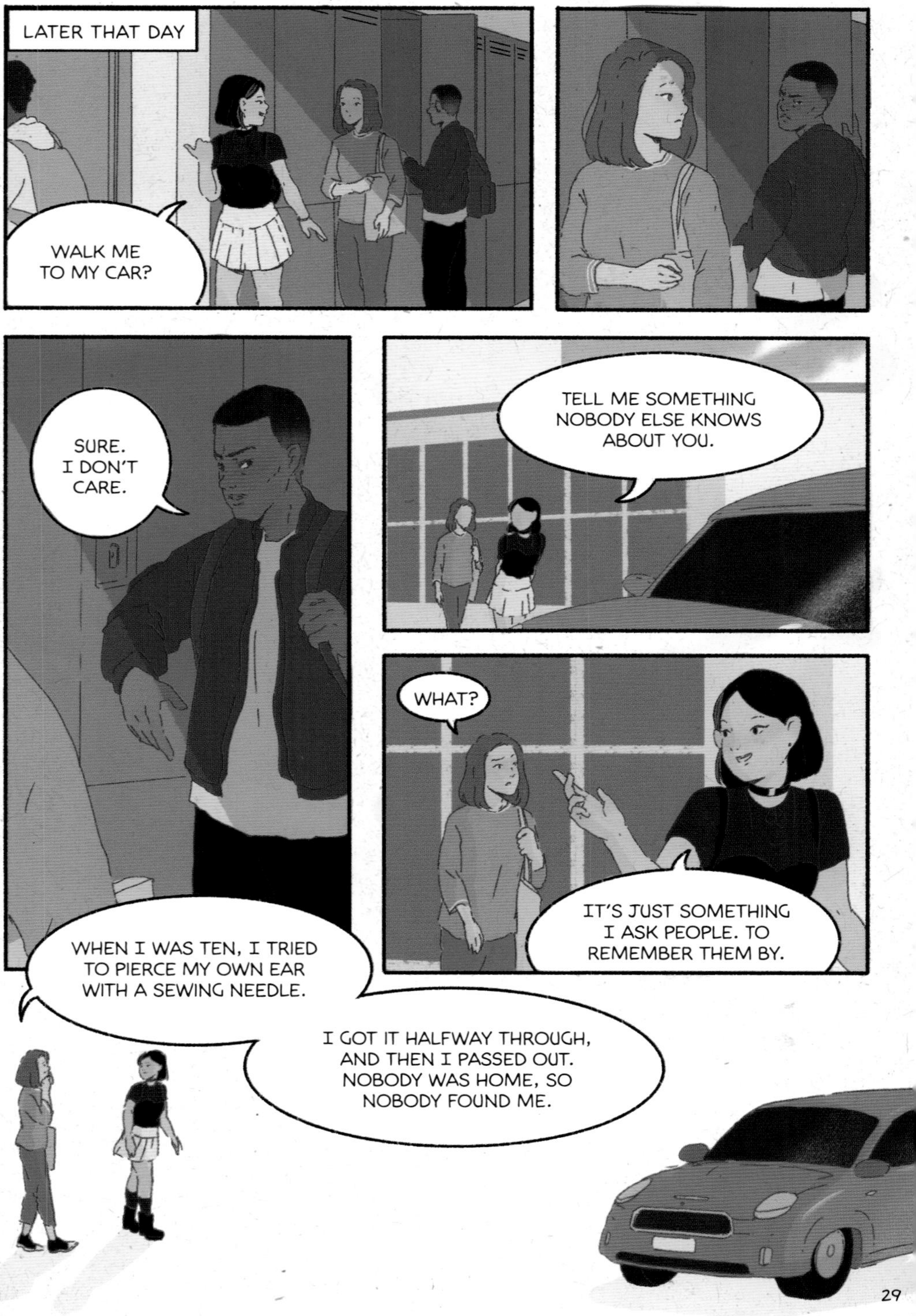
LATER THAT DAY
WALK ME TO MY CAR?
SURE. I DON'T CARE.
TELL ME SOMETHING NOBODY ELSE KNOWS ABOUT YOU.
WHAT?
IT'S JUST SOMETHING I ASK PEOPLE. TO REMEMBER THEM BY.
WHEN I WAS TEN, I TRIED TO PIERCE MY OWN EAR WITH A SEWING NEEDLE.
I GOT IT HALFWAY THROUGH, AND THEN I PASSED OUT. NOBODY WAS HOME, SO NOBODY FOUND ME.

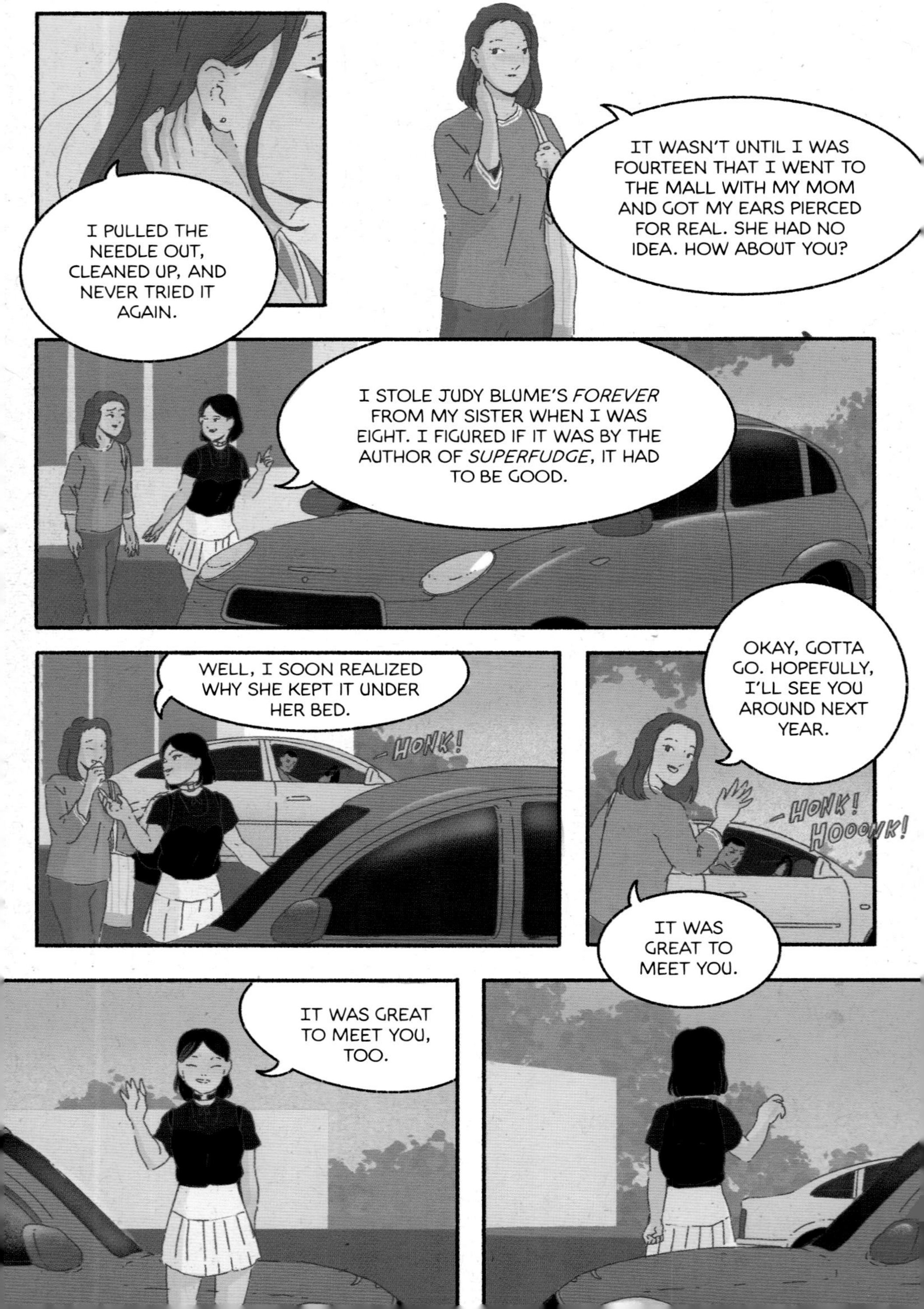
I PULLED THE NEEDLE OUT, CLEANED UP, AND NEVER TRIED IT AGAIN.
IT WASN'T UNTIL I WAS FOURTEEN THAT I WENT TO THE MALL WITH MY MOM AND GOT MY EARS PIERCED FOR REAL. SHE HAD NO IDEA. HOW ABOUT YOU?
I STOLE JUDY BLUME'S *FOREVER* FROM MY SISTER WHEN I WAS EIGHT. I FIGURED IF IT WAS BY THE AUTHOR OF *SUPERFUDGE*, IT HAD TO BE GOOD.
WELL, I SOON REALIZED WHY SHE KEPT IT UNDER HER BED.
-HONK!
OKAY, GOTTA GO. HOPEFULLY, I'LL SEE YOU AROUND NEXT YEAR.
-HONK!
HOOOONK!
IT WAS GREAT TO MEET YOU.
IT WAS GREAT TO MEET YOU, TOO.

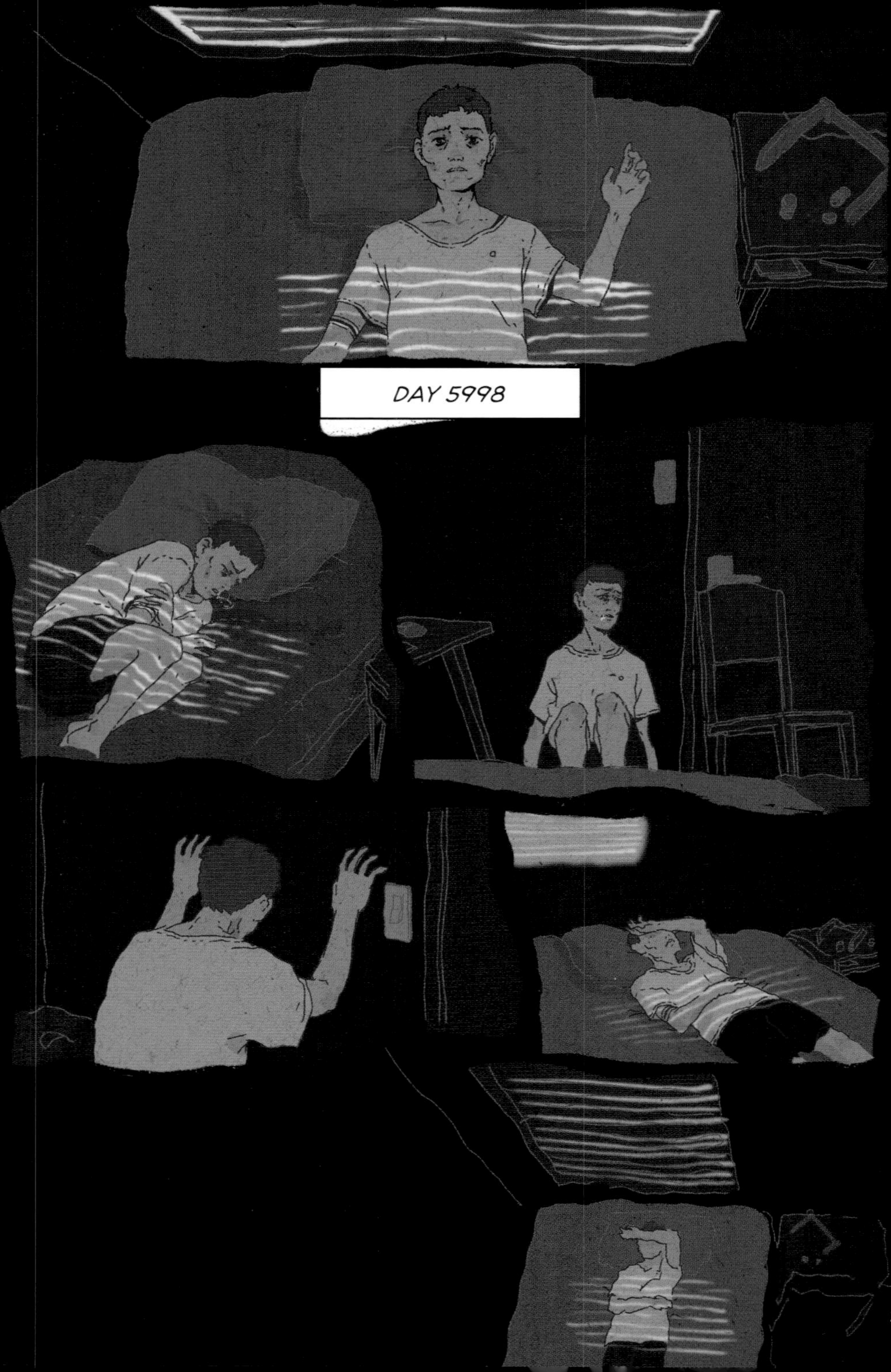
DAY 5998

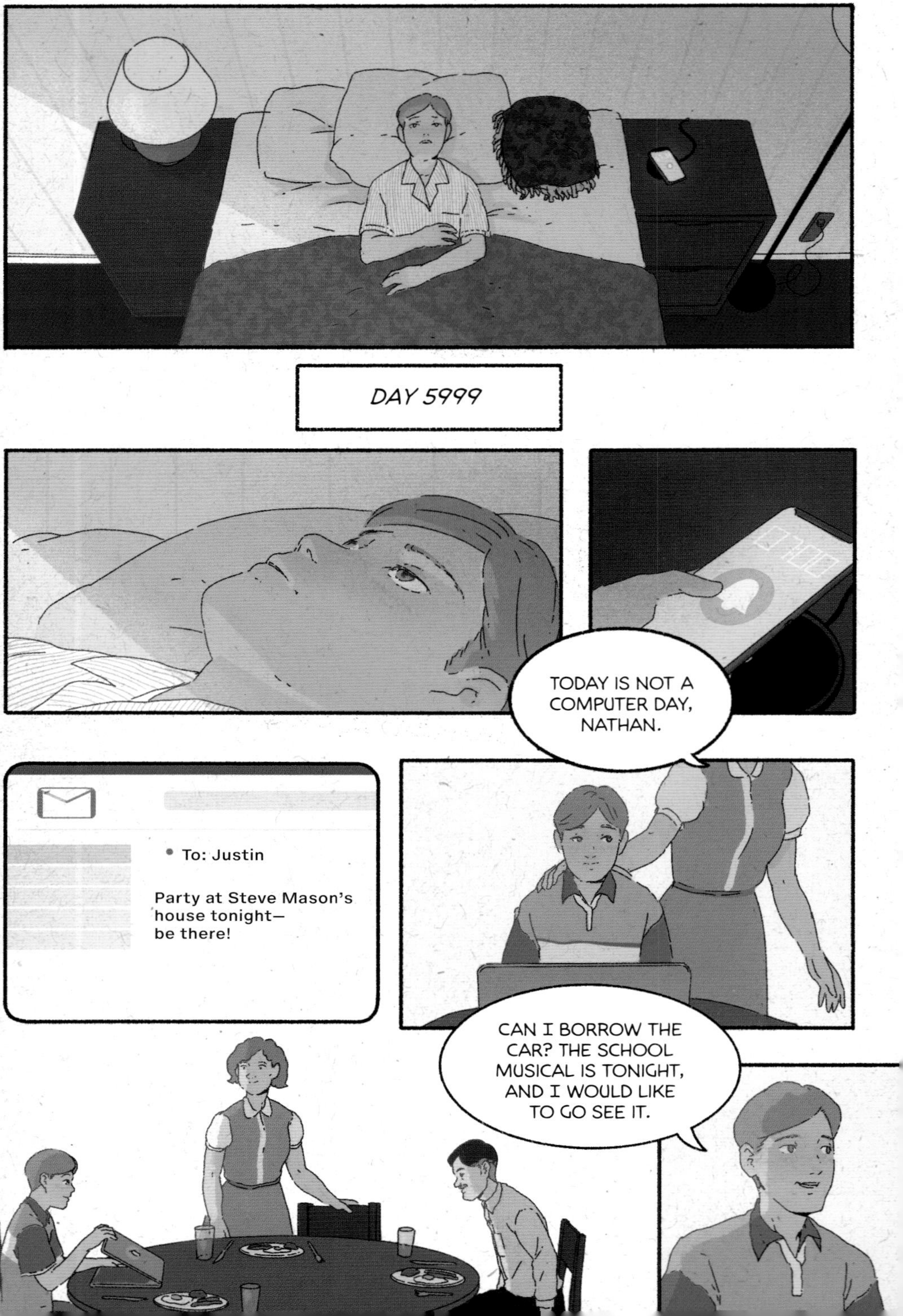
DAY 5999
TODAY IS NOT A COMPUTER DAY, NATHAN.
To: Justin
Party at Steve Mason's house tonight— be there!
CAN I BORROW THE CAR? THE SCHOOL MUSICAL IS TONIGHT, AND I WOULD LIKE TO GO SEE IT.

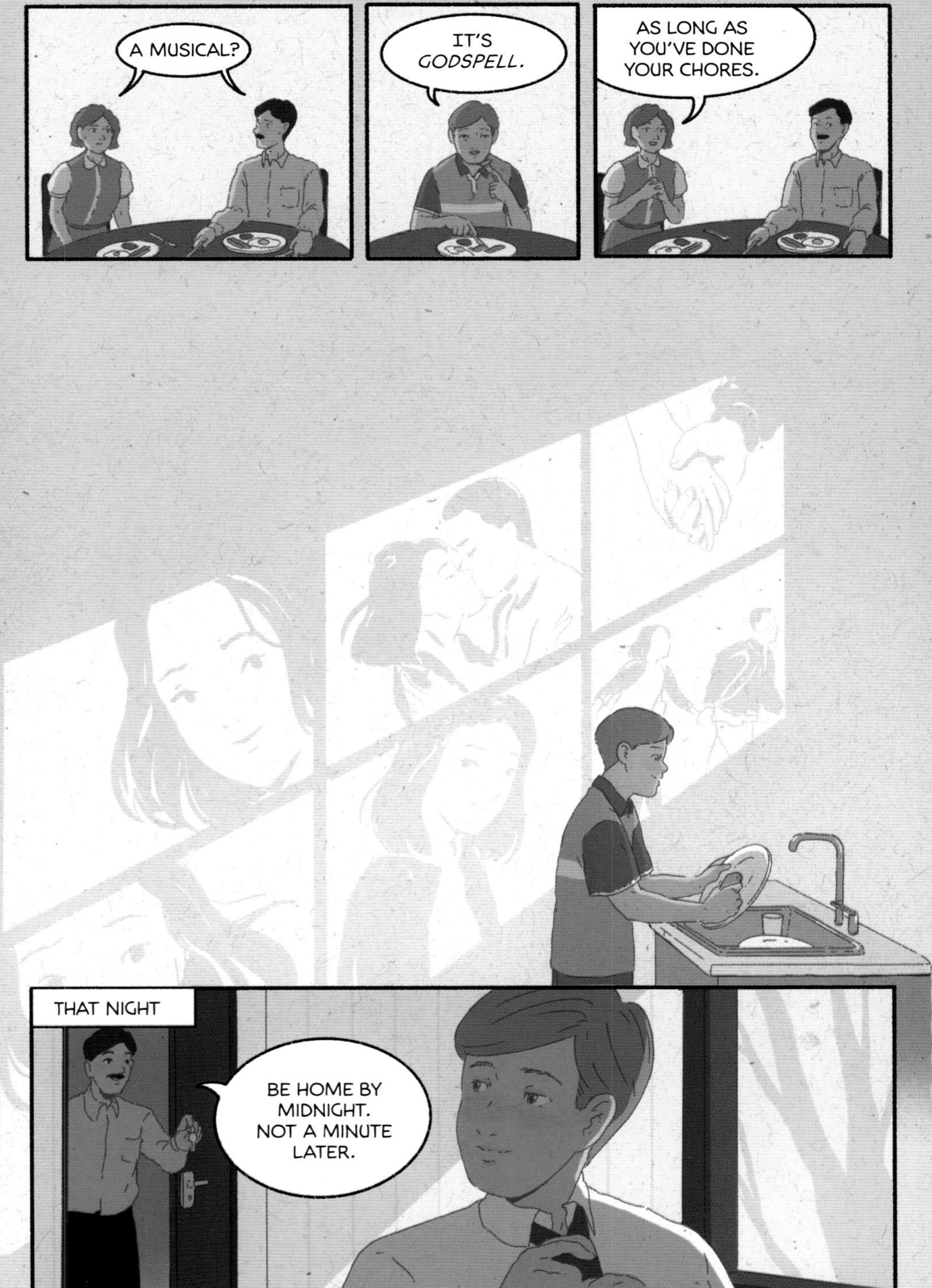
A MUSICAL?
IT'S *GODSPELL.*
AS LONG AS YOU'VE DONE YOUR CHORES.
THAT NIGHT
BE HOME BY MIDNIGHT. NOT A MINUTE LATER.

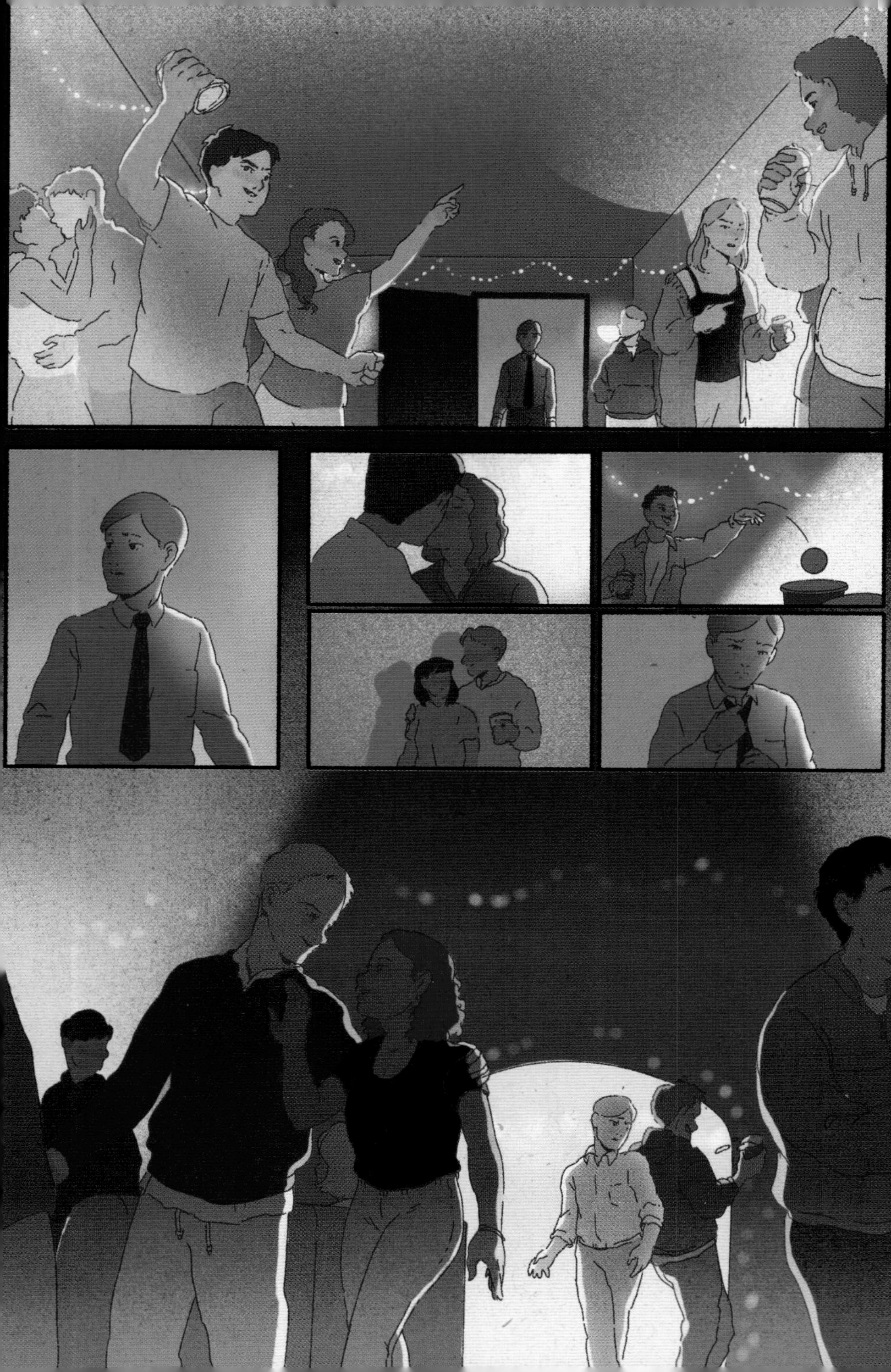

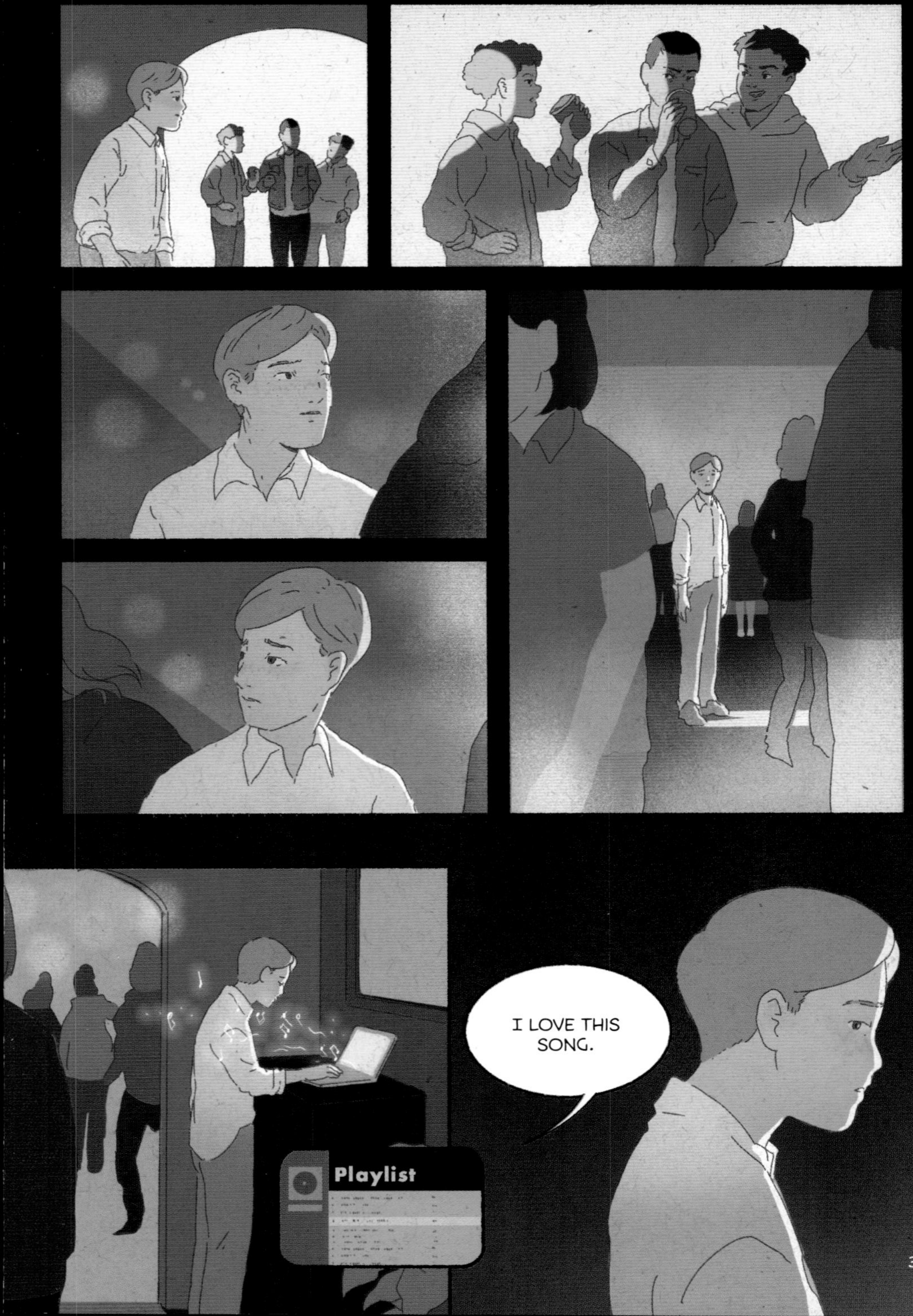
Playlist
I LOVE THIS SONG.

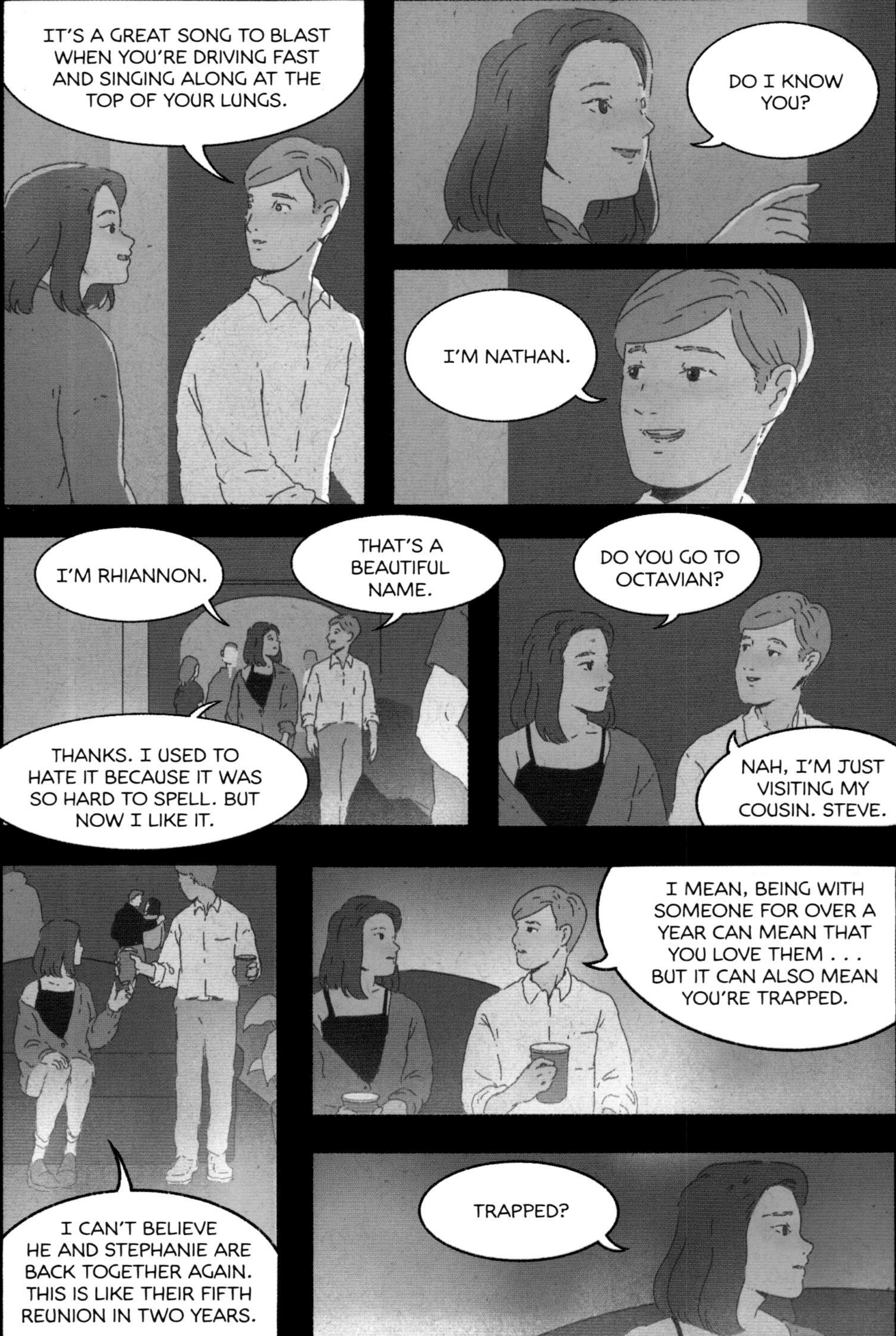
IT'S A GREAT SONG TO BLAST WHEN YOU'RE DRIVING FAST AND SINGING ALONG AT THE TOP OF YOUR LUNGS.
DO I KNOW YOU?
I'M NATHAN.
I'M RHIANNON.
THAT'S A BEAUTIFUL NAME.
THANKS. I USED TO HATE IT BECAUSE IT WAS SO HARD TO SPELL. BUT NOW I LIKE IT.
DO YOU GO TO OCTAVIAN?
NAH, I'M JUST VISITING MY COUSIN. STEVE.
I CAN'T BELIEVE HE AND STEPHANIE ARE BACK TOGETHER AGAIN. THIS IS LIKE THEIR FIFTH REUNION IN TWO YEARS.
I MEAN, BEING WITH SOMEONE FOR OVER A YEAR CAN MEAN THAT YOU LOVE THEM . . . BUT IT CAN ALSO MEAN YOU'RE TRAPPED.
TRAPPED?

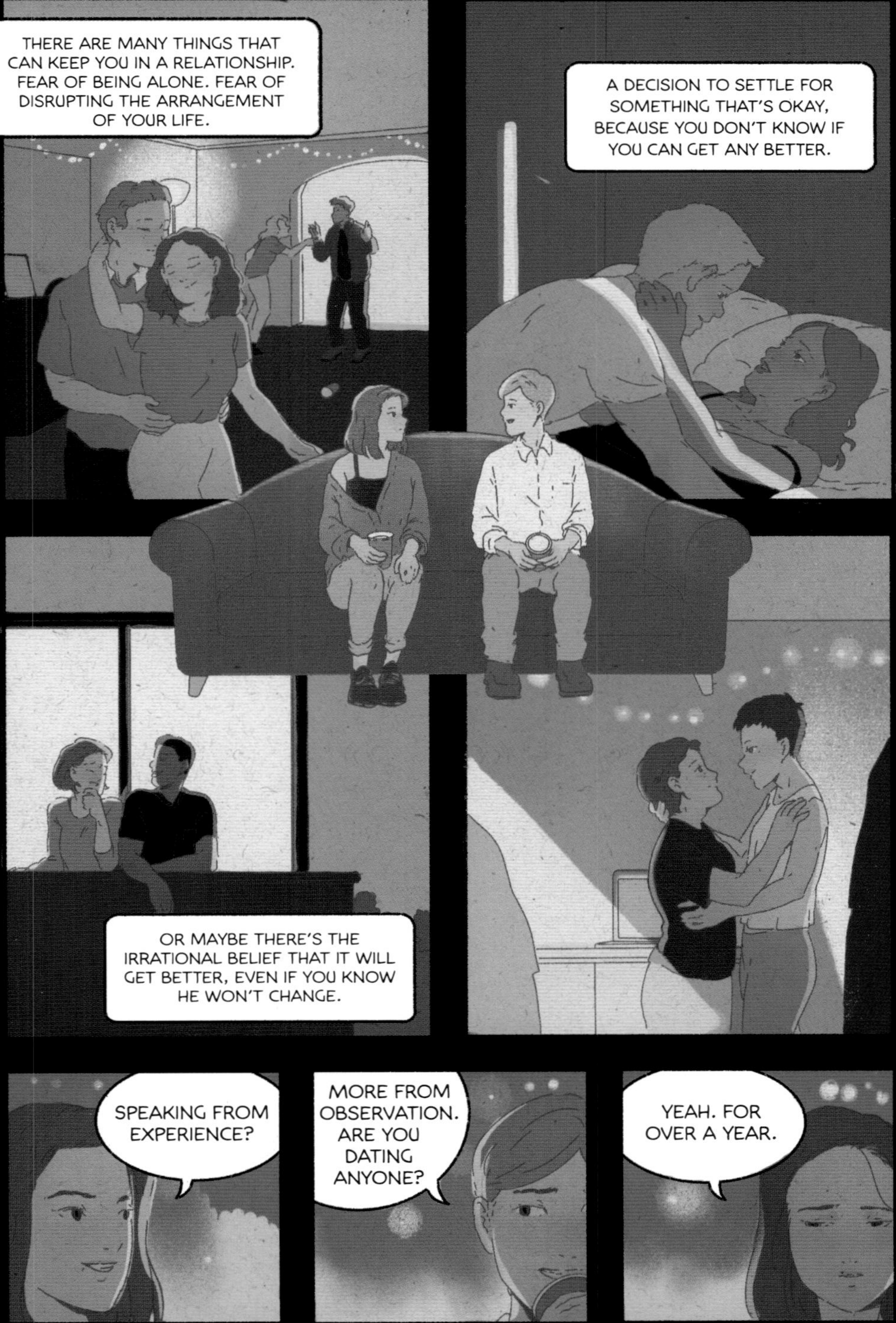
THERE ARE MANY THINGS THAT CAN KEEP YOU IN A RELATIONSHIP. FEAR OF BEING ALONE. FEAR OF DISRUPTING THE ARRANGEMENT OF YOUR LIFE.
A DECISION TO SETTLE FOR SOMETHING THAT'S OKAY, BECAUSE YOU DON'T KNOW IF YOU CAN GET ANY BETTER.
OR MAYBE THERE'S THE IRRATIONAL BELIEF THAT IT WILL GET BETTER, EVEN IF YOU KNOW HE WON'T CHANGE.
SPEAKING FROM EXPERIENCE?
MORE FROM OBSERVATION. ARE YOU DATING ANYONE?
YEAH. FOR OVER A YEAR.

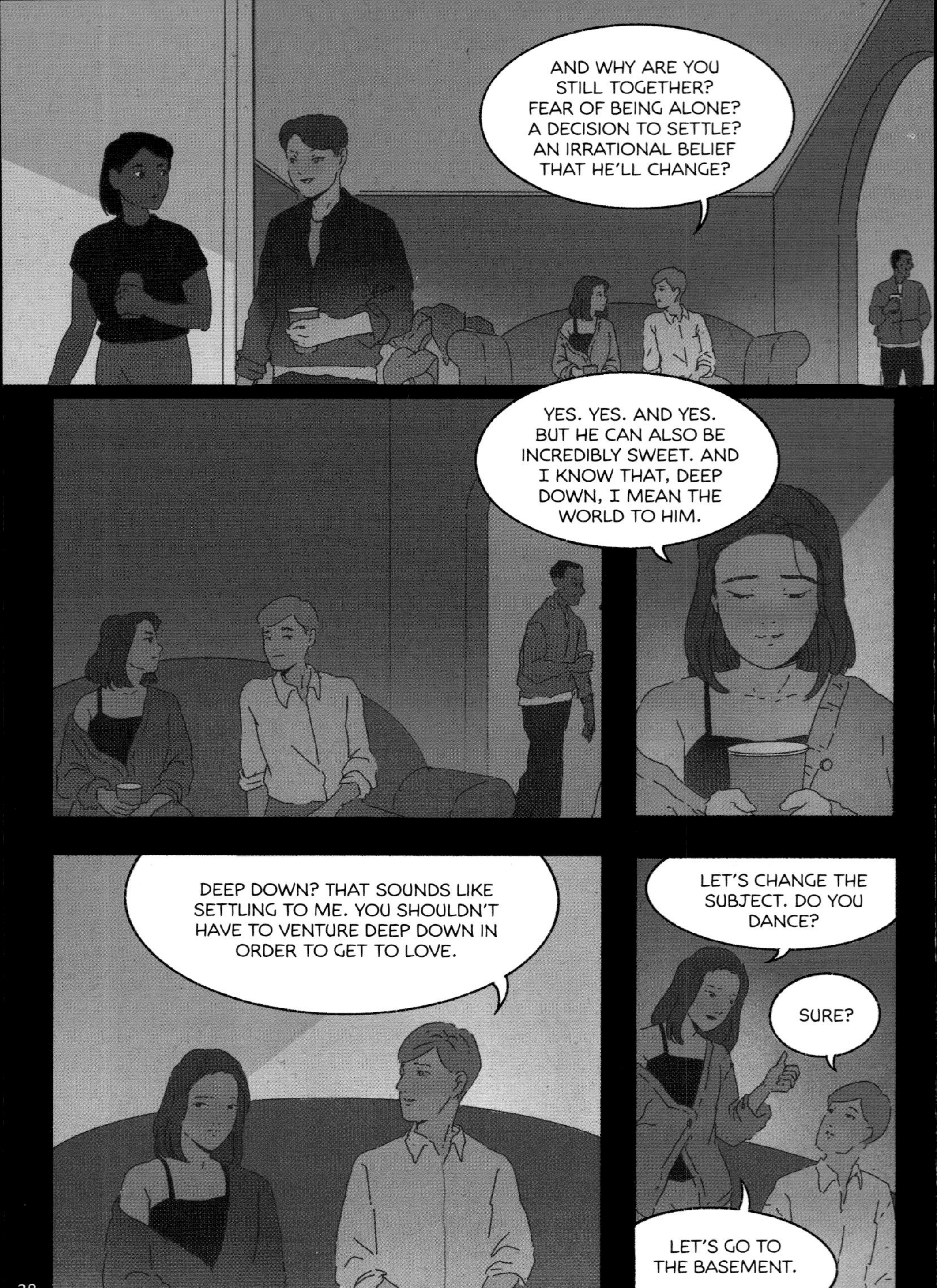
AND WHY ARE YOU STILL TOGETHER? FEAR OF BEING ALONE? A DECISION TO SETTLE? AN IRRATIONAL BELIEF THAT HE'LL CHANGE?
YES. YES. AND YES. BUT HE CAN ALSO BE INCREDIBLY SWEET. AND I KNOW THAT, DEEP DOWN, I MEAN THE WORLD TO HIM.
DEEP DOWN? THAT SOUNDS LIKE SETTLING TO ME. YOU SHOULDN'T HAVE TO VENTURE DEEP DOWN IN ORDER TO GET TO LOVE.
LET'S CHANGE THE SUBJECT. DO YOU DANCE?
SURE?
LET'S GO TO THE BASEMENT.

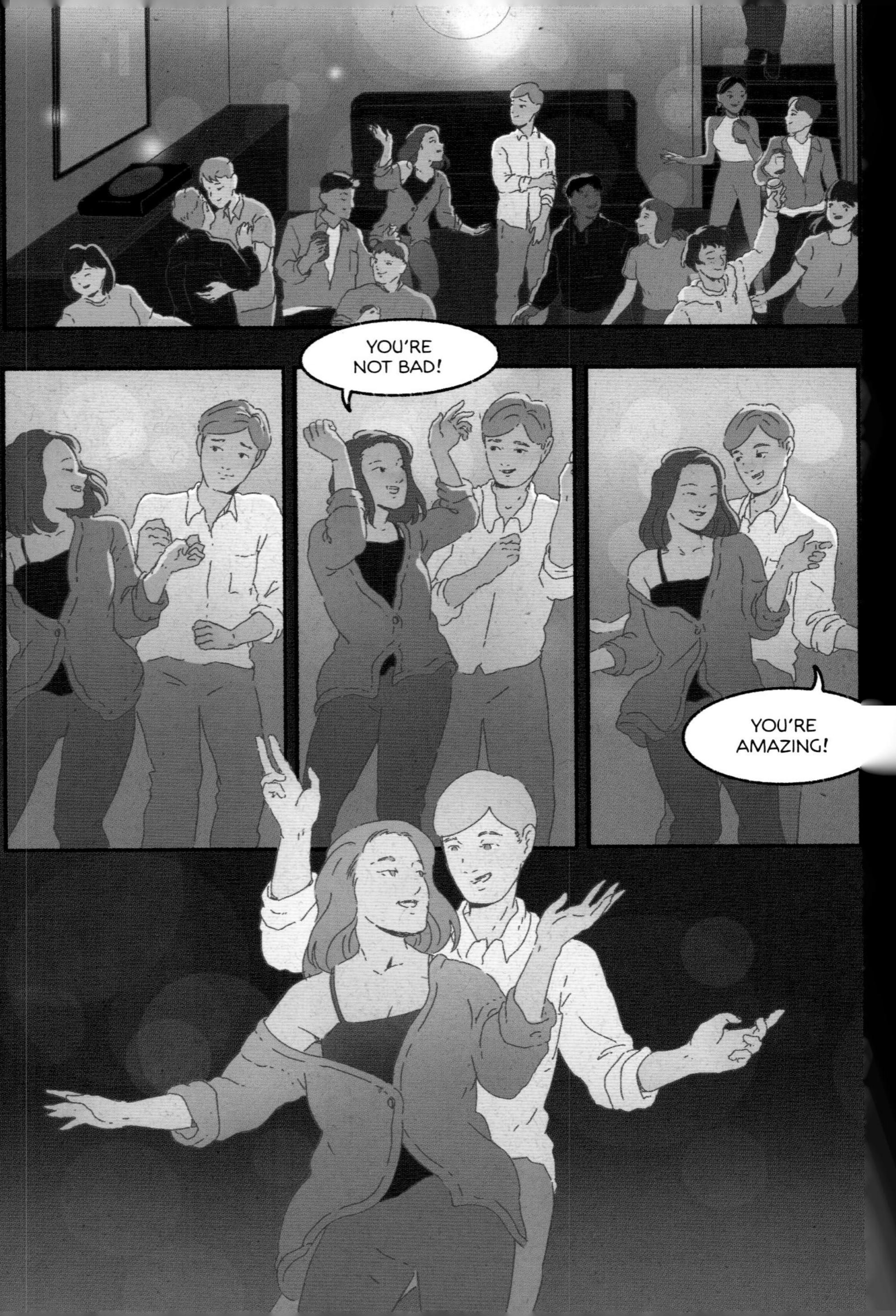
YOU'RE NOT BAD!
YOU'RE AMAZING!

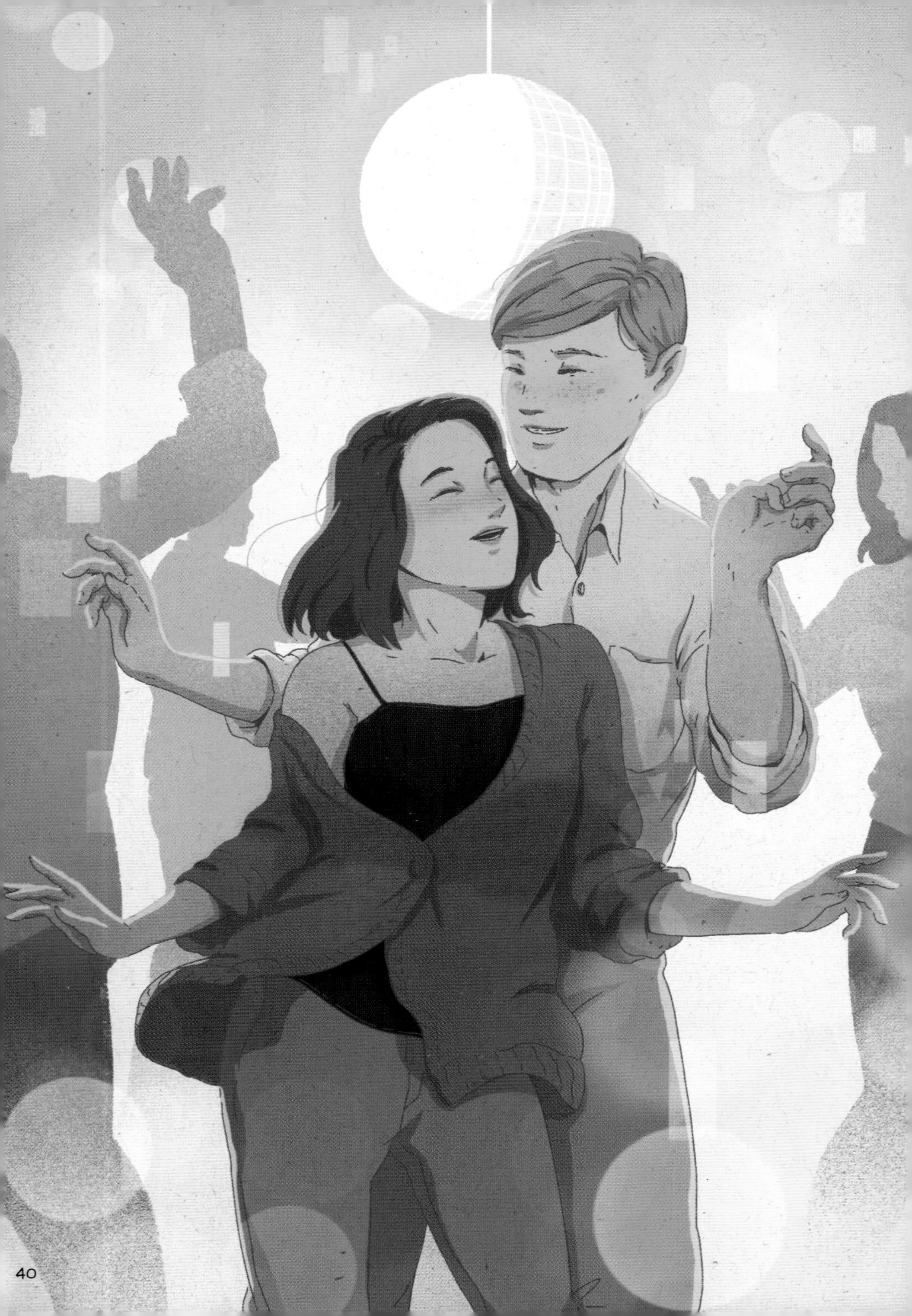

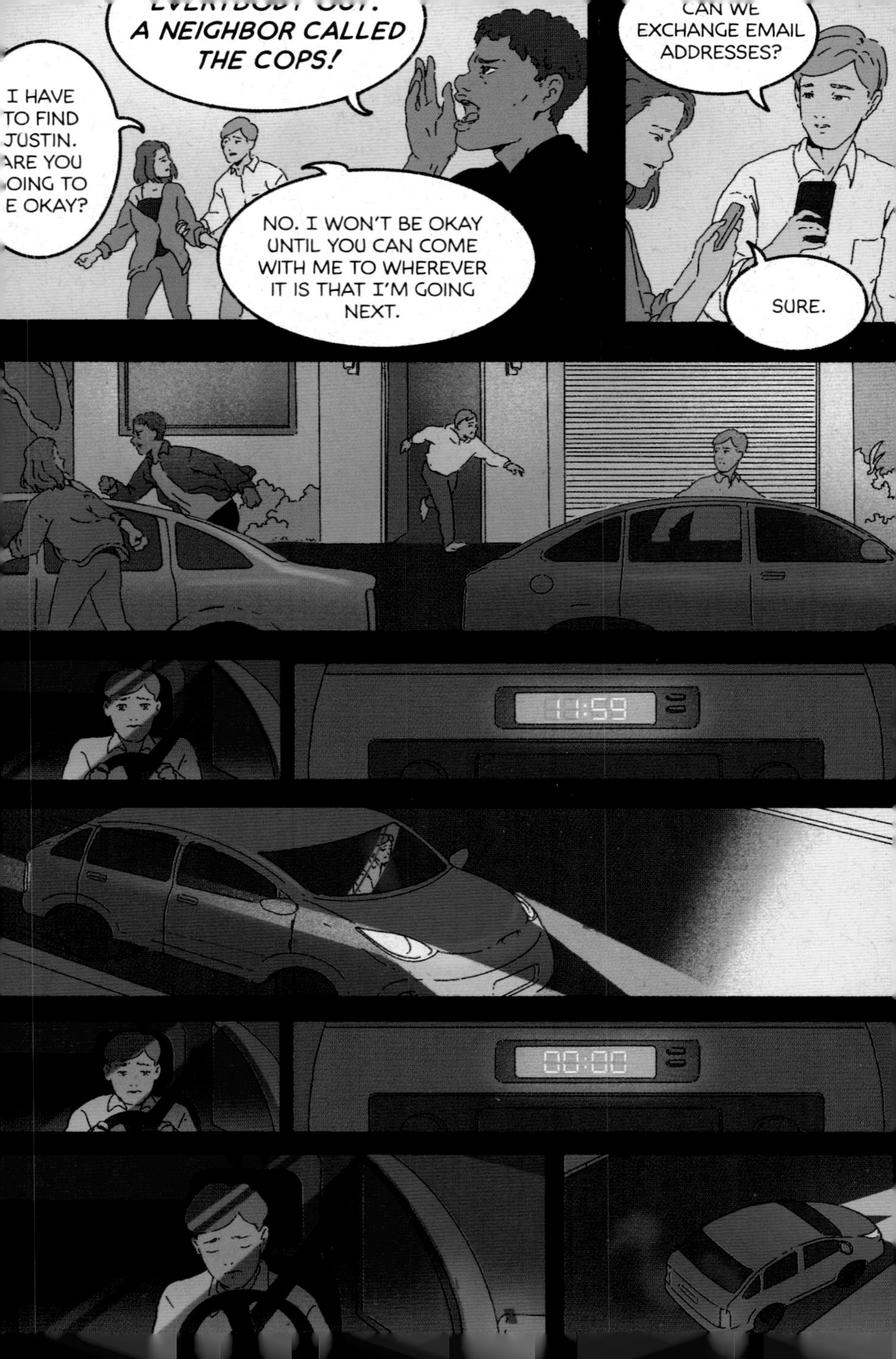
A NEIGHBOR CALLED THE COPS!
I HAVE TO FIND JUSTIN. ARE YOU
NO. I WON'T BE OKAY UNTIL YOU CAN COME WITH ME TO WHEREVER IT IS THAT I'M GOING NEXT.
EXCHANGE EMAIL ADDRESSES?
SURE.
00:00

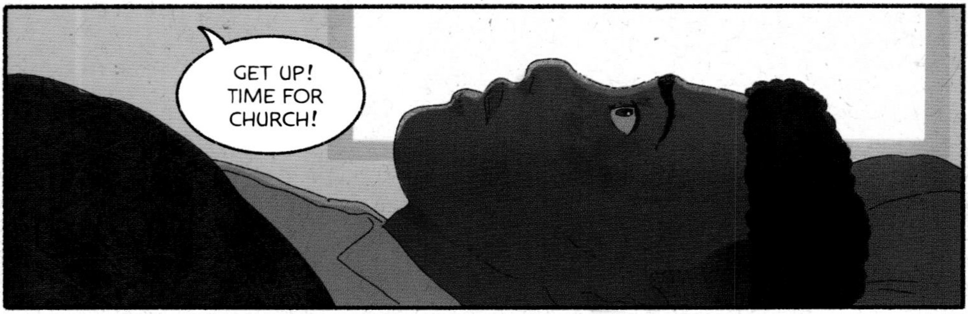
GET UP! TIME FOR CHURCH!

DAY 6000

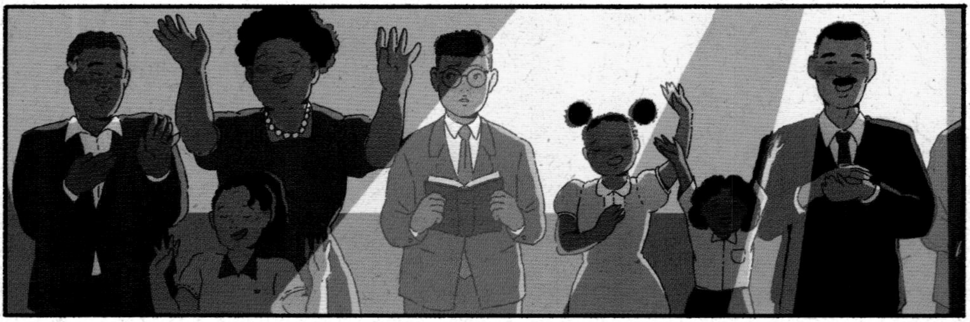

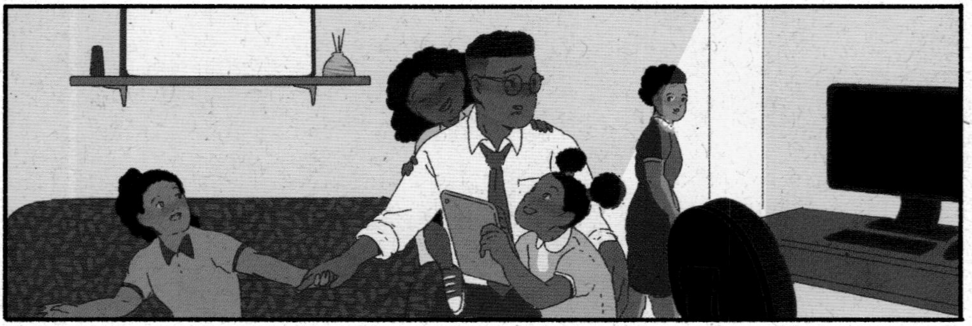

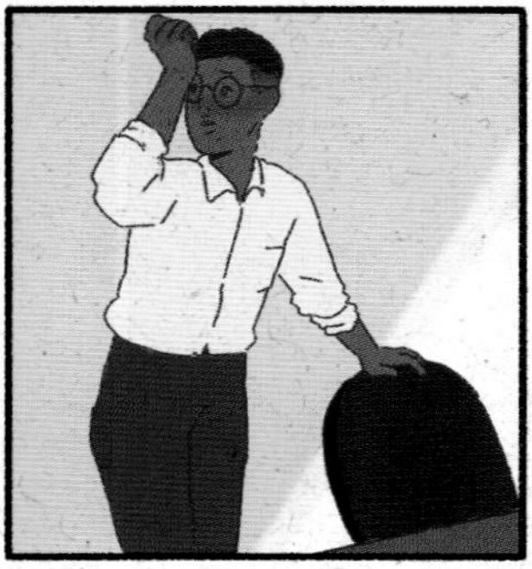

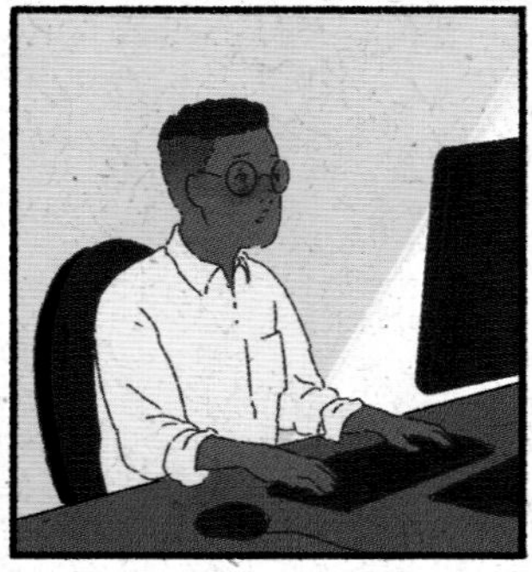

Hi Rhiannon,

I just wanted to say that it was lovely meeting you and dancing with you last night. I'm sorry the police came and separated us. Please keep in touch.

N

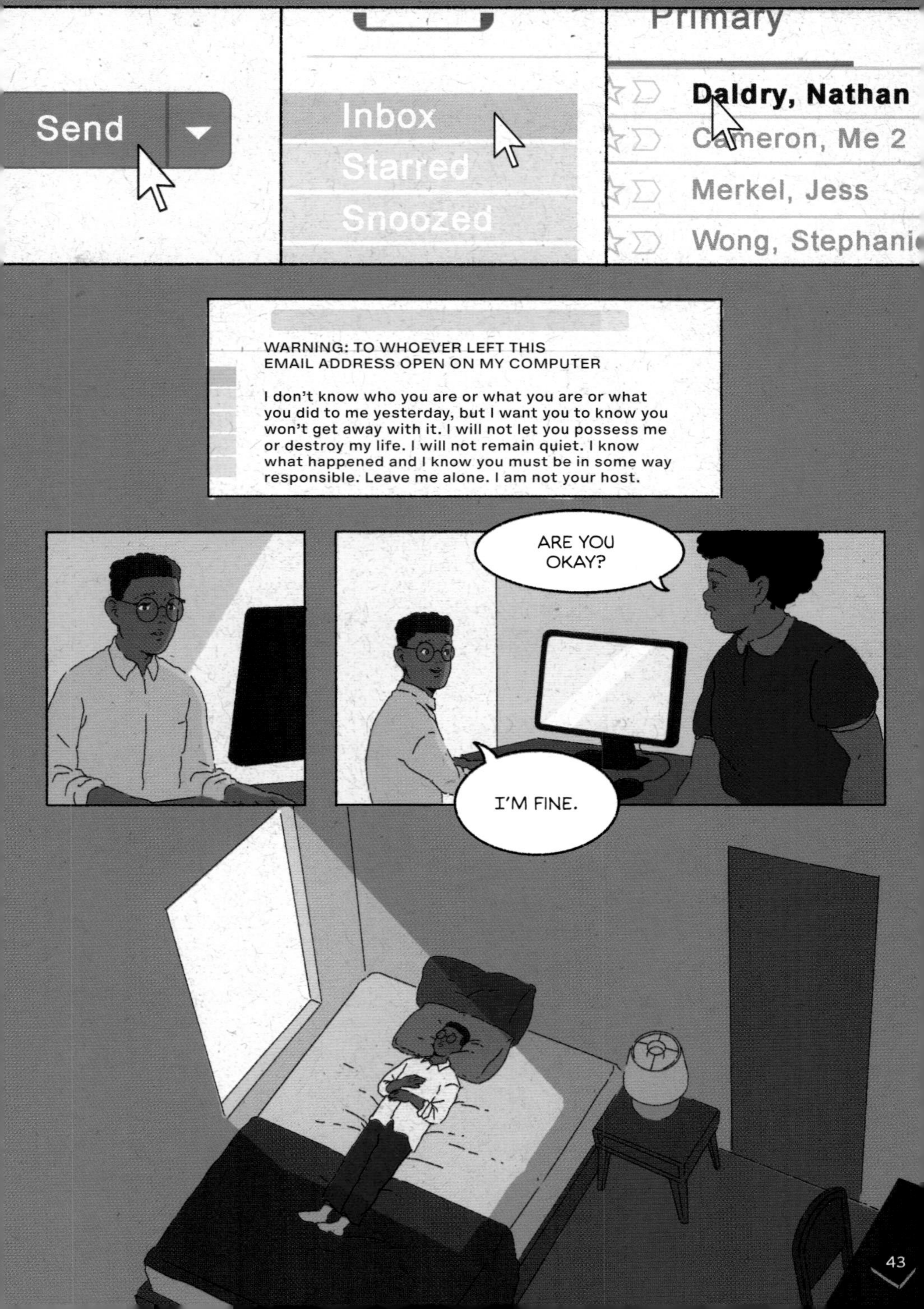
Send
Inbox
Starred
Snoozed
Primary
Daldry, Nathan
Cameron, Me 2
Merkel, Jess
Wong, Stephani
WARNING: TO WHOEVER LEFT THIS
EMAIL ADDRESS OPEN ON MY COMPUTER
I don't know who you are or what you are or what you did to me yesterday, but I want you to know you won't get away with it. I will not let you possess me or destroy my life. I will not remain quiet. I know what happened and I know you must be in some way responsible. Leave me alone. I am not your host.
ARE YOU OKAY?
I'M FINE.

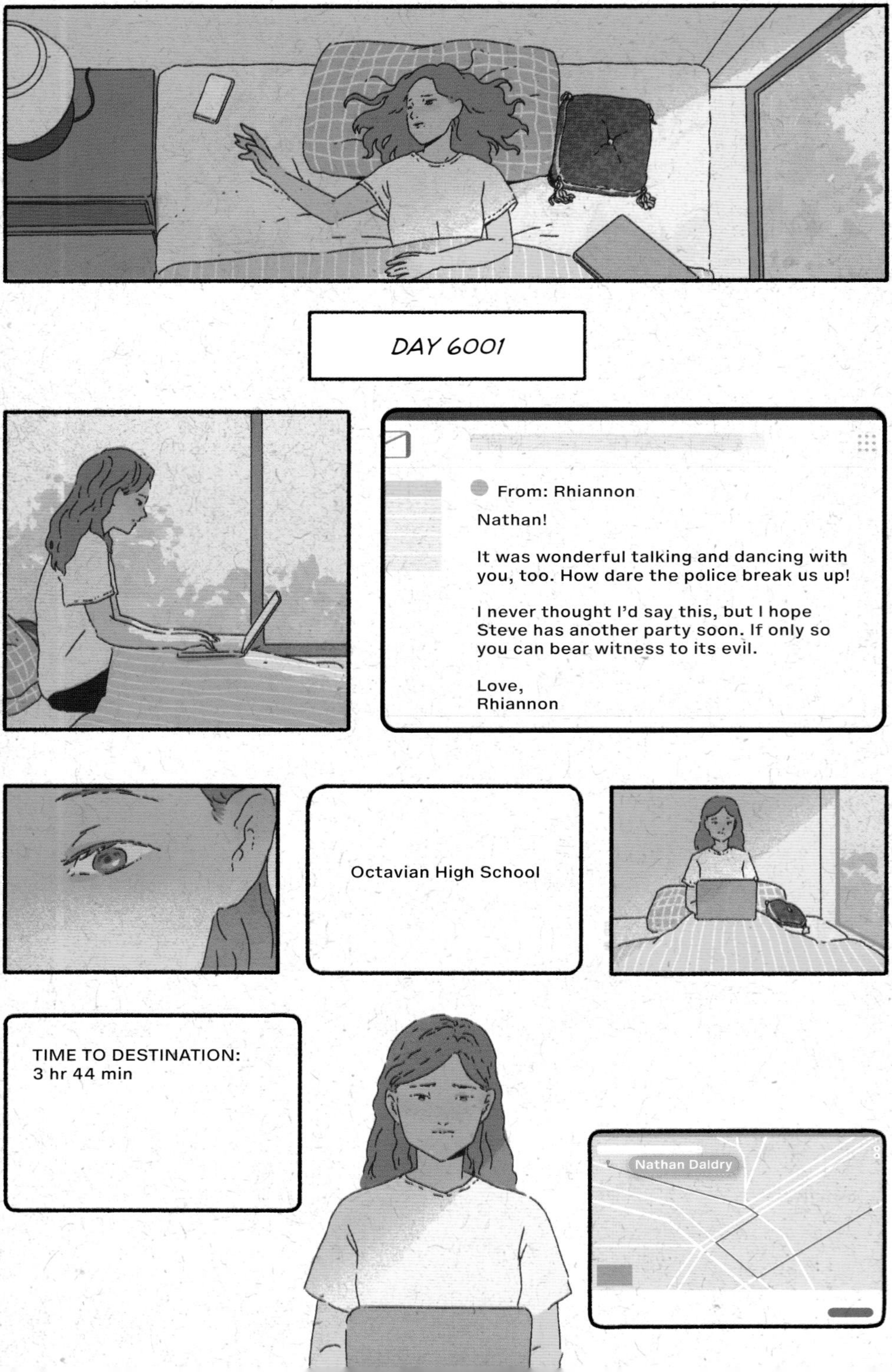
DAY 6001
From: Rhiannon
Nathan!
It was wonderful talking and dancing with you, too. How dare the police break us up!
I never thought I'd say this, but I hope Steve has another party soon. If only so you can bear witness to its evil.
Love,
Rhiannon
Octavian High School
TIME TO DESTINATION:
3 hr 44 min
Nathan Daldry

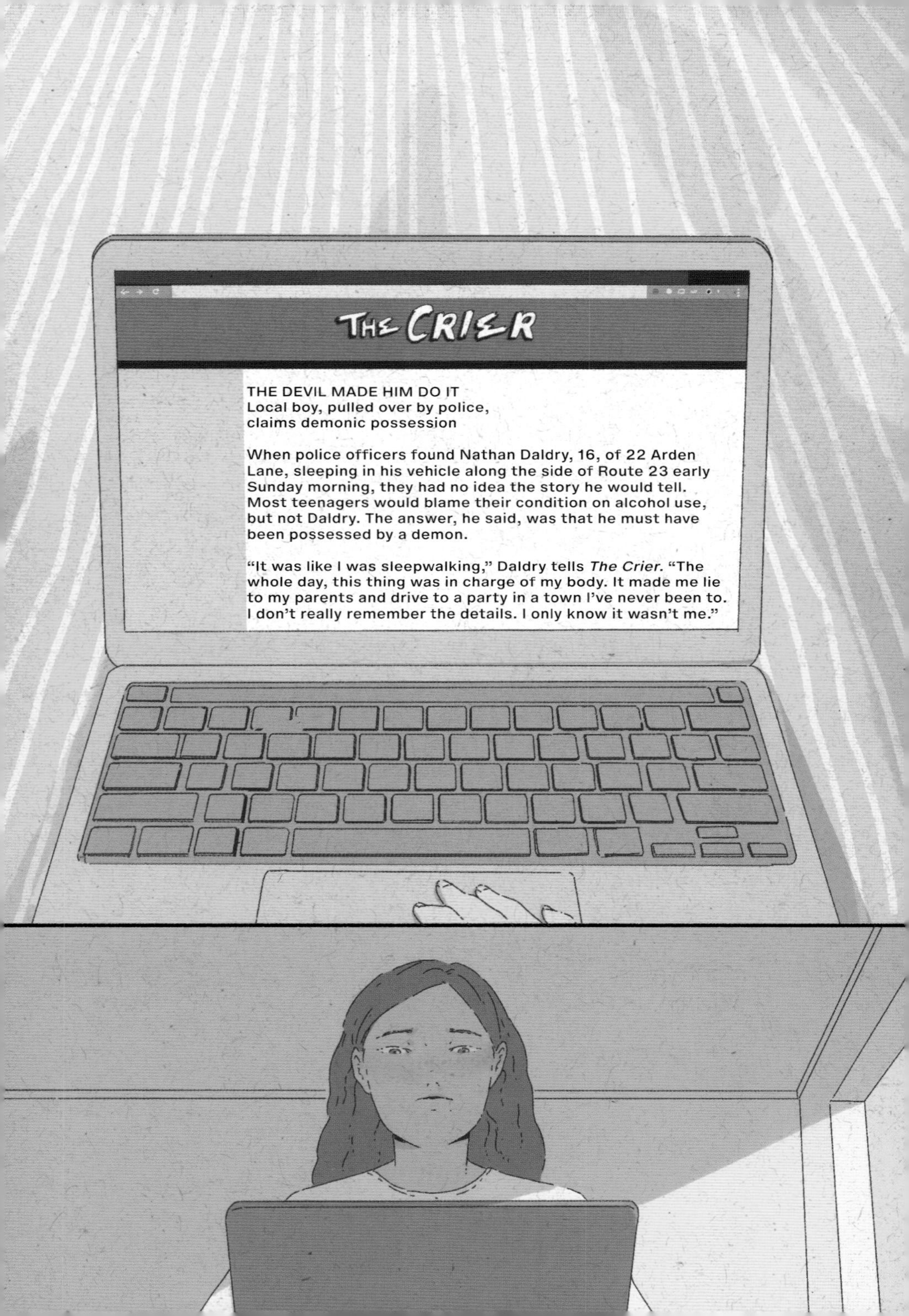
THE CRIER
THE DEVIL MADE HIM DO IT
Local boy, pulled over by police, claims demonic possession
When police officers found Nathan Daldry, 16, of 22 Arden Lane, sleeping in his vehicle along the side of Route 23 early Sunday morning, they had no idea the story he would tell. Most teenagers would blame their condition on alcohol use, but not Daldry. The answer, he said, was that he must have been possessed by a demon.
"It was like I was sleepwalking," Daldry tells *The Crier*. "The whole day, this thing was in charge of my body. It made me lie to my parents and drive to a party in a town I've never been to. I don't really remember the details. I only know it wasn't me."

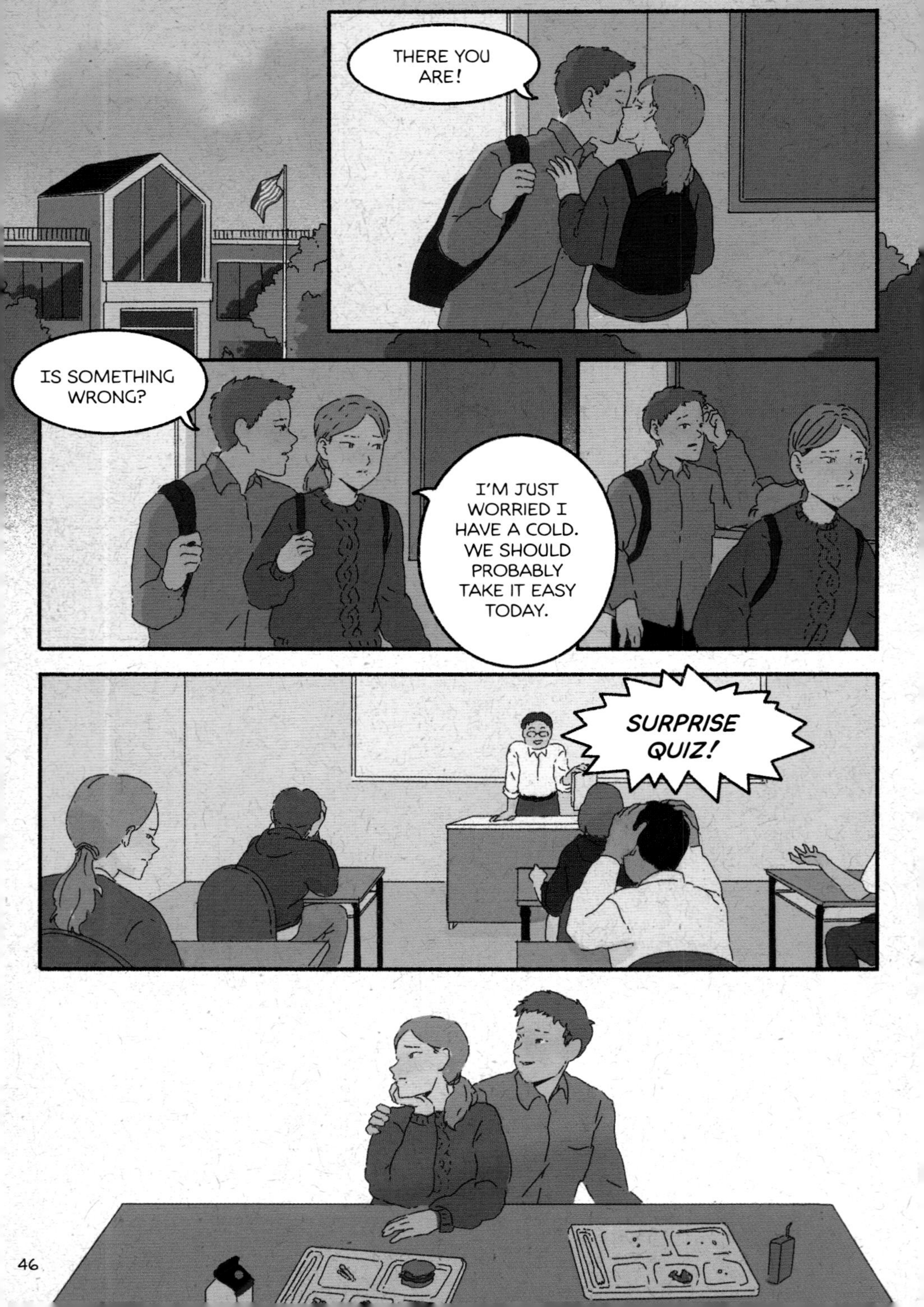
THERE YOU ARE!
IS SOMETHING WRONG?
I'M JUST WORRIED I HAVE A COLD. WE SHOULD PROBABLY TAKE IT EASY TODAY.
SURPRISE QUIZ!

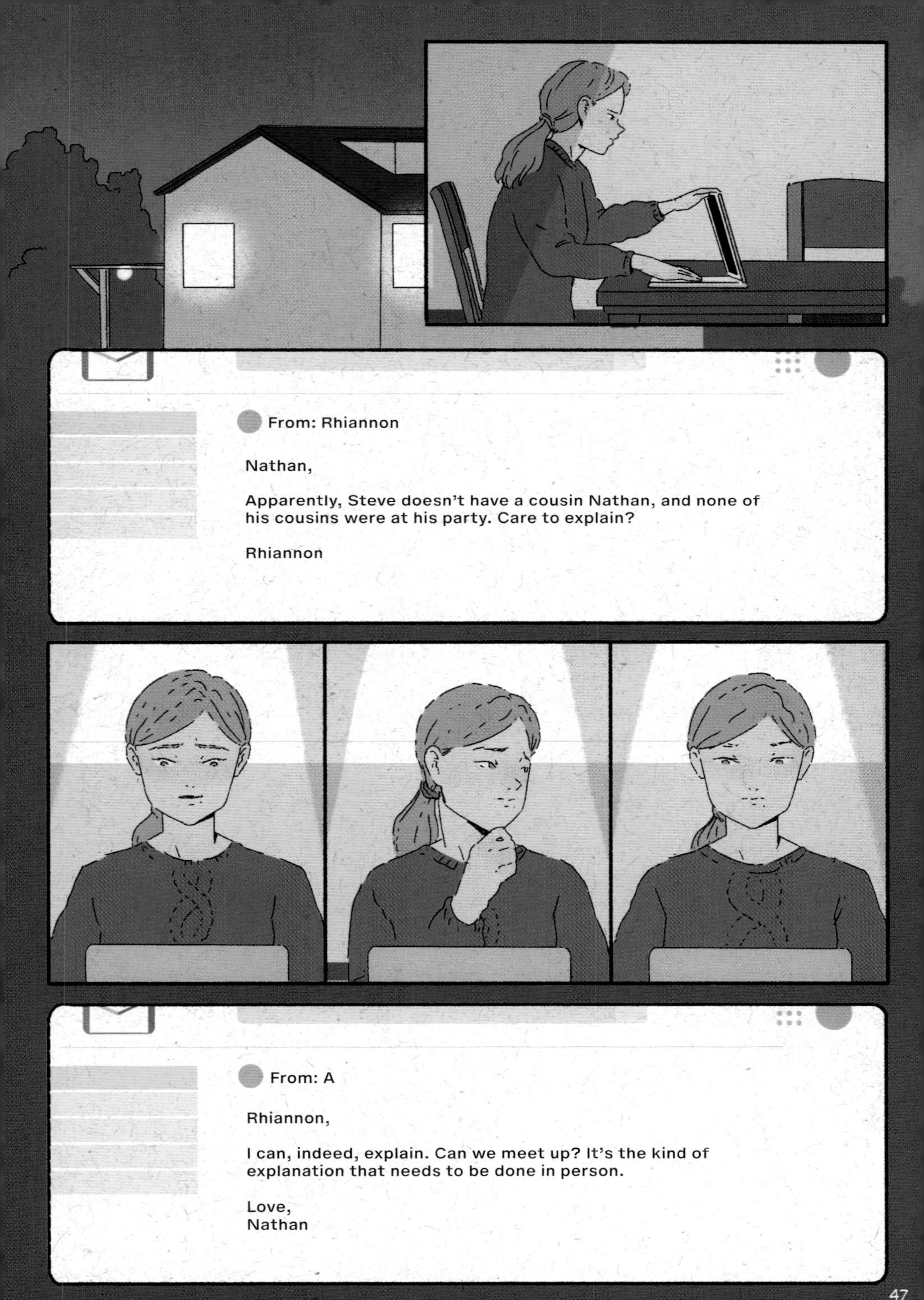
From: Rhiannon
Nathan,
Apparently, Steve doesn't have a cousin Nathan, and none of his cousins were at his party. Care to explain?
Rhiannon
From: A
Rhiannon,
I can, indeed, explain. Can we meet up? It's the kind of explanation that needs to be done in person.
Love,
Nathan

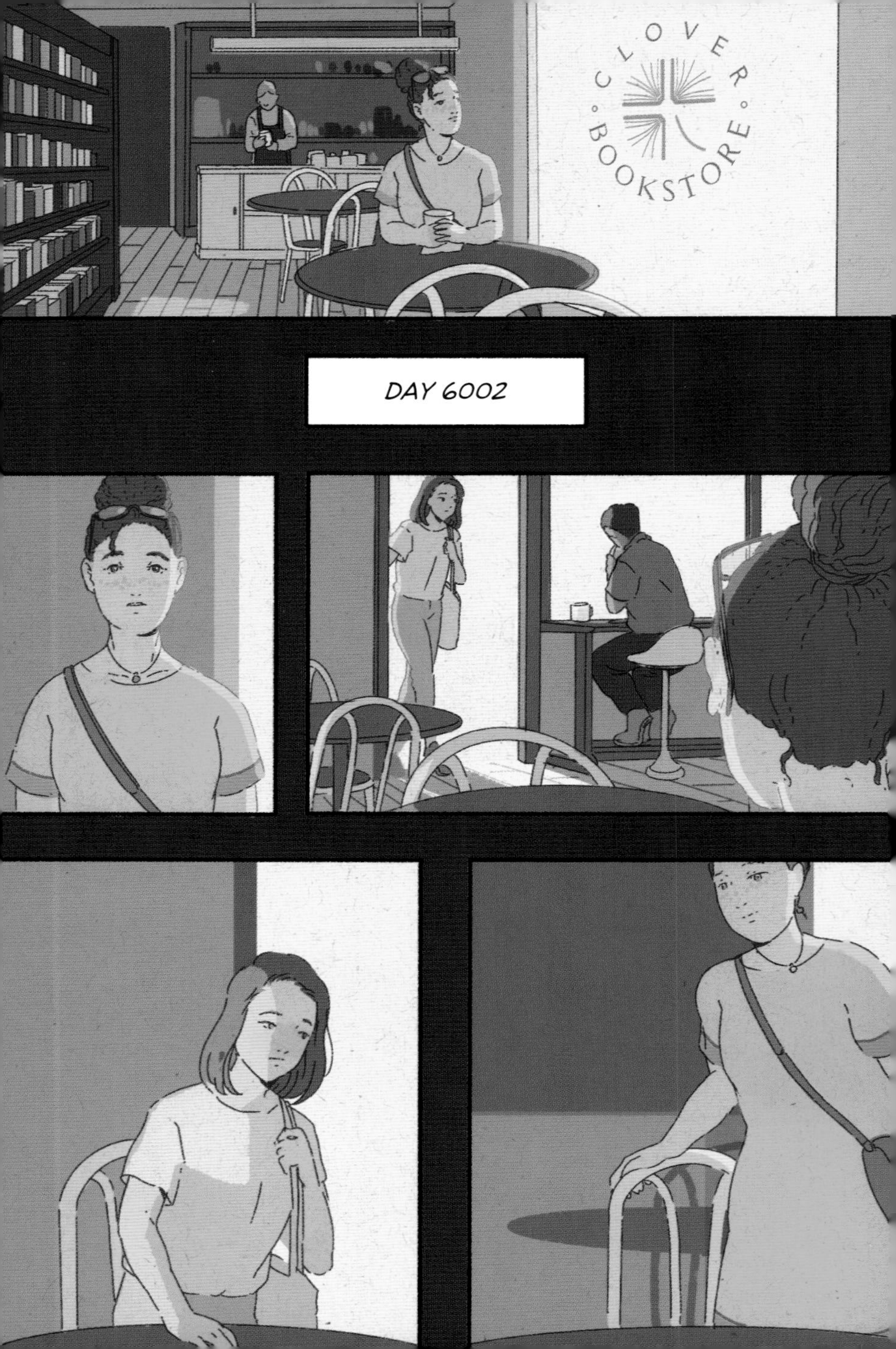
CLOVER BOOKSTORE
DAY 6002

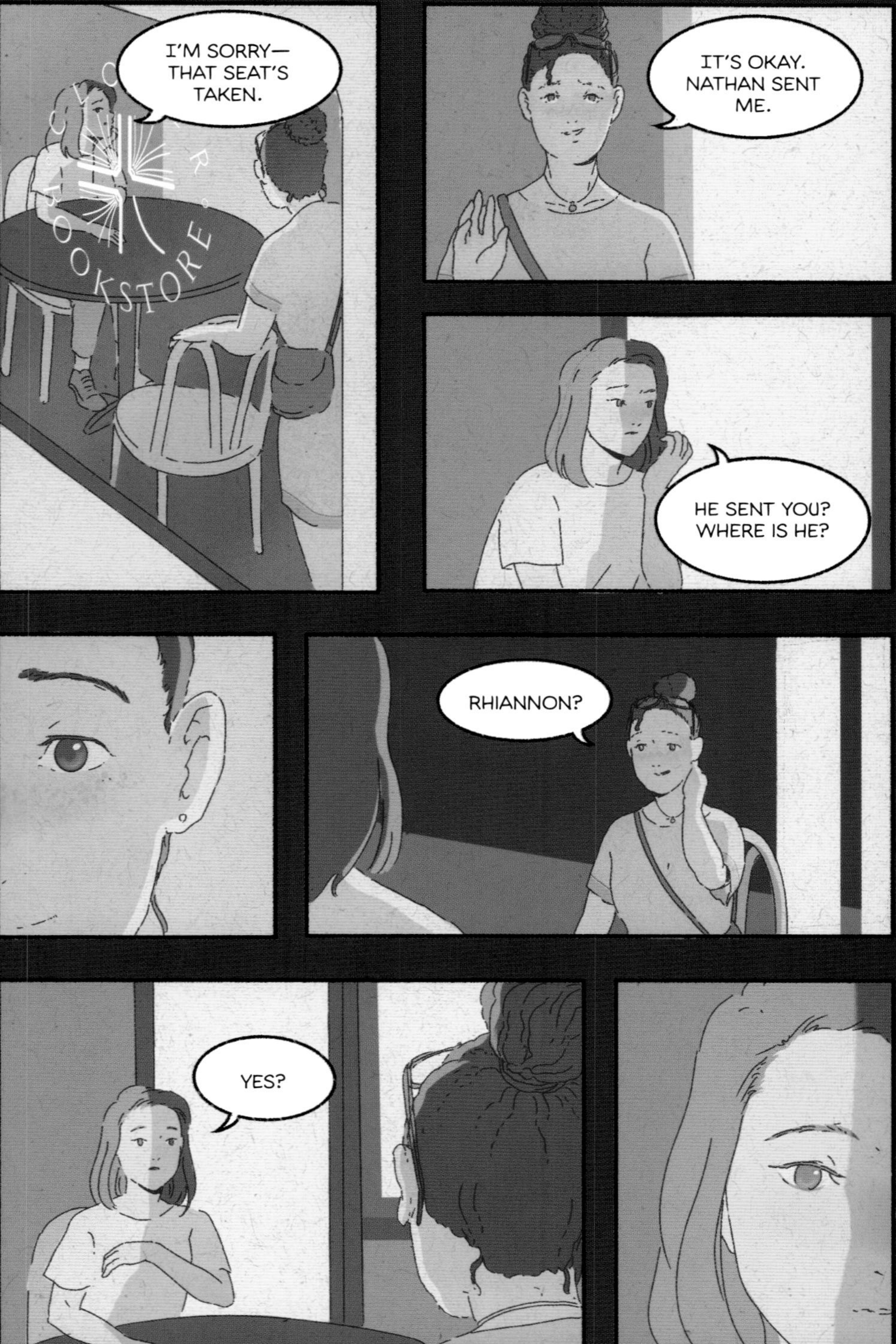
I'M SORRY—
THAT SEAT'S
TAKEN.
IT'S OKAY.
NATHAN SENT
ME.
HE SENT YOU?
WHERE IS HE?
RHIANNON?
YES?

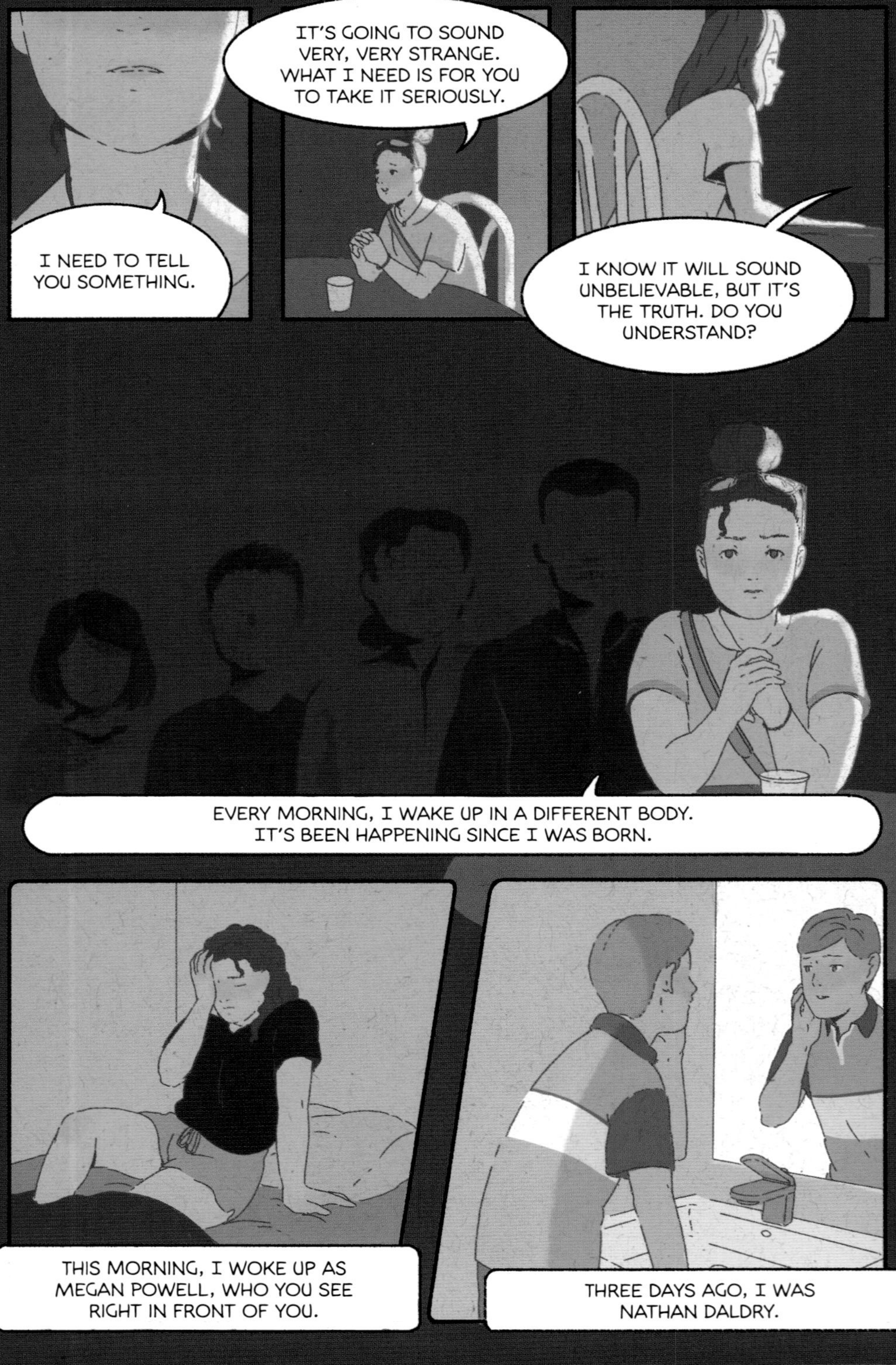
I NEED TO TELL YOU SOMETHING.
IT'S GOING TO SOUND VERY, VERY STRANGE. WHAT I NEED IS FOR YOU TO TAKE IT SERIOUSLY.
I KNOW IT WILL SOUND UNBELIEVABLE, BUT IT'S THE TRUTH. DO YOU UNDERSTAND?
EVERY MORNING, I WAKE UP IN A DIFFERENT BODY. IT'S BEEN HAPPENING SINCE I WAS BORN.
THIS MORNING, I WOKE UP AS MEGAN POWELL, WHO YOU SEE RIGHT IN FRONT OF YOU.
THREE DAYS AGO, I WAS NATHAN DALDRY.

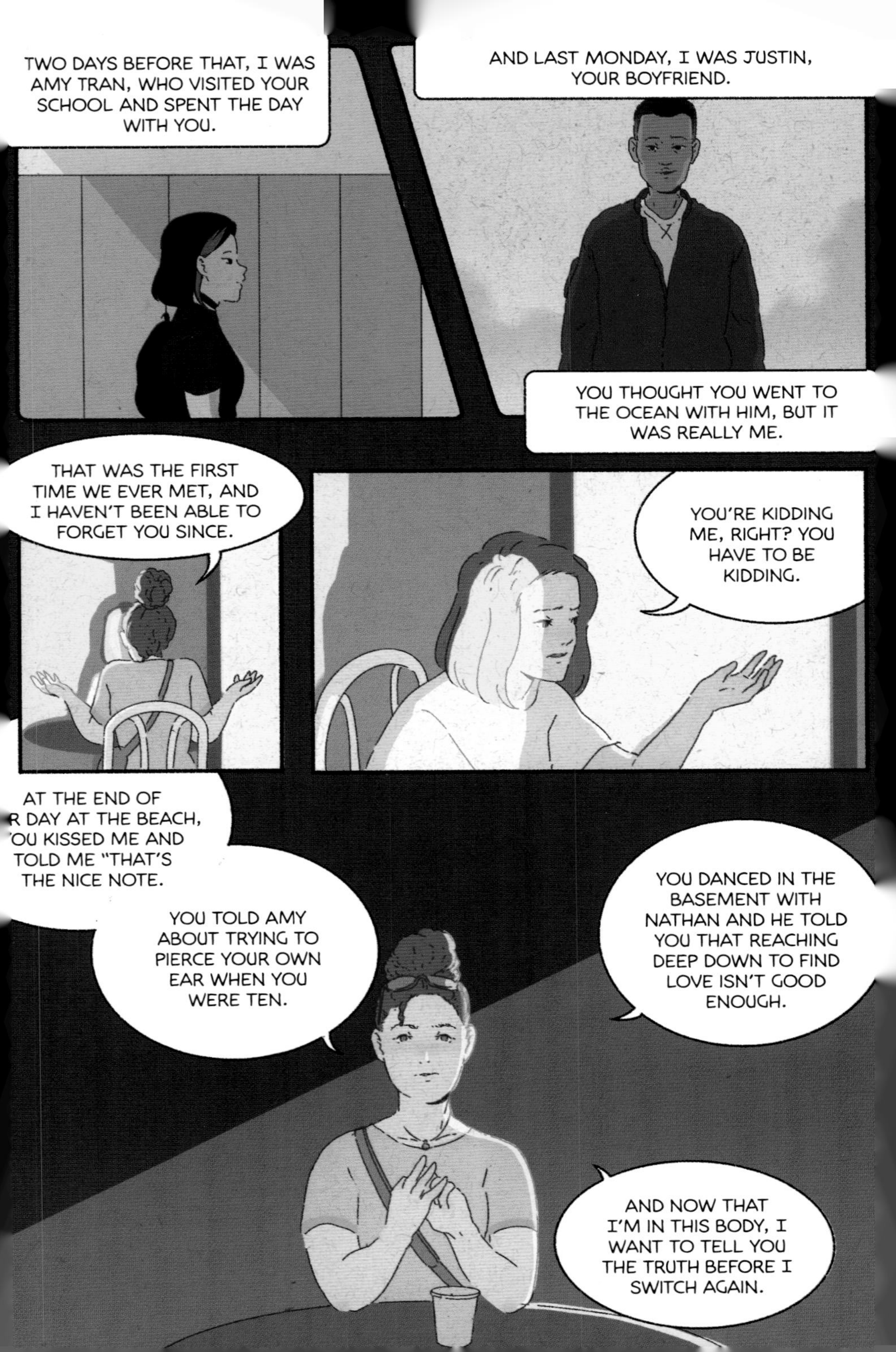
TWO DAYS BEFORE THAT, I WAS AMY TRAN, WHO VISITED YOUR SCHOOL AND SPENT THE DAY WITH YOU.
AND LAST MONDAY, I WAS JUSTIN, YOUR BOYFRIEND.
YOU THOUGHT YOU WENT TO THE OCEAN WITH HIM, BUT IT WAS REALLY ME.
THAT WAS THE FIRST TIME WE EVER MET, AND I HAVEN'T BEEN ABLE TO FORGET YOU SINCE.
YOU'RE KIDDING ME, RIGHT? YOU HAVE TO BE KIDDING.
AT THE END OF R DAY AT THE BEACH, 'OU KISSED ME AND TOLD ME "THAT'S THE NICE NOTE.
YOU TOLD AMY ABOUT TRYING TO PIERCE YOUR OWN EAR WHEN YOU WERE TEN.
YOU DANCED IN THE BASEMENT WITH NATHAN AND HE TOLD YOU THAT REACHING DEEP DOWN TO FIND LOVE ISN'T GOOD ENOUGH.
AND NOW THAT I'M IN THIS BODY, I WANT TO TELL YOU THE TRUTH BEFORE I SWITCH AGAIN.

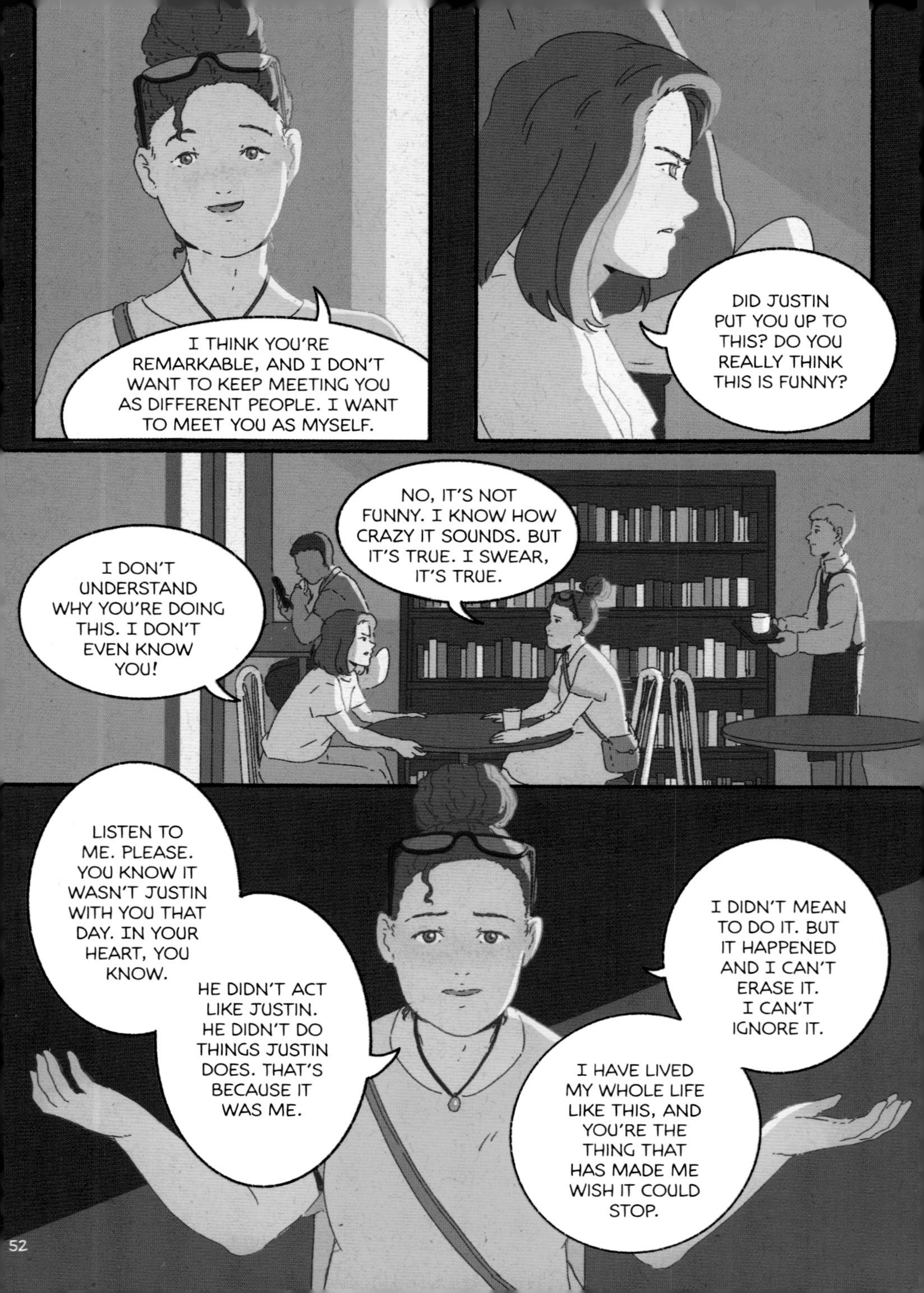
I THINK YOU'RE REMARKABLE, AND I DON'T WANT TO KEEP MEETING YOU AS DIFFERENT PEOPLE. I WANT TO MEET YOU AS MYSELF.
DID JUSTIN PUT YOU UP TO THIS? DO YOU REALLY THINK THIS IS FUNNY?
NO, IT'S NOT FUNNY. I KNOW HOW CRAZY IT SOUNDS. BUT IT'S TRUE. I SWEAR, IT'S TRUE.
I DON'T UNDERSTAND WHY YOU'RE DOING THIS. I DON'T EVEN KNOW YOU!
LISTEN TO ME. PLEASE. YOU KNOW IT WASN'T JUSTIN WITH YOU THAT DAY. IN YOUR HEART, YOU KNOW.
HE DIDN'T ACT LIKE JUSTIN. HE DIDN'T DO THINGS JUSTIN DOES. THAT'S BECAUSE IT WAS ME.
I DIDN'T MEAN TO DO IT. BUT IT HAPPENED AND I CAN'T ERASE IT. I CAN'T IGNORE IT.
I HAVE LIVED MY WHOLE LIFE LIKE THIS, AND YOU'RE THE THING THAT HAS MADE ME WISH IT COULD STOP.

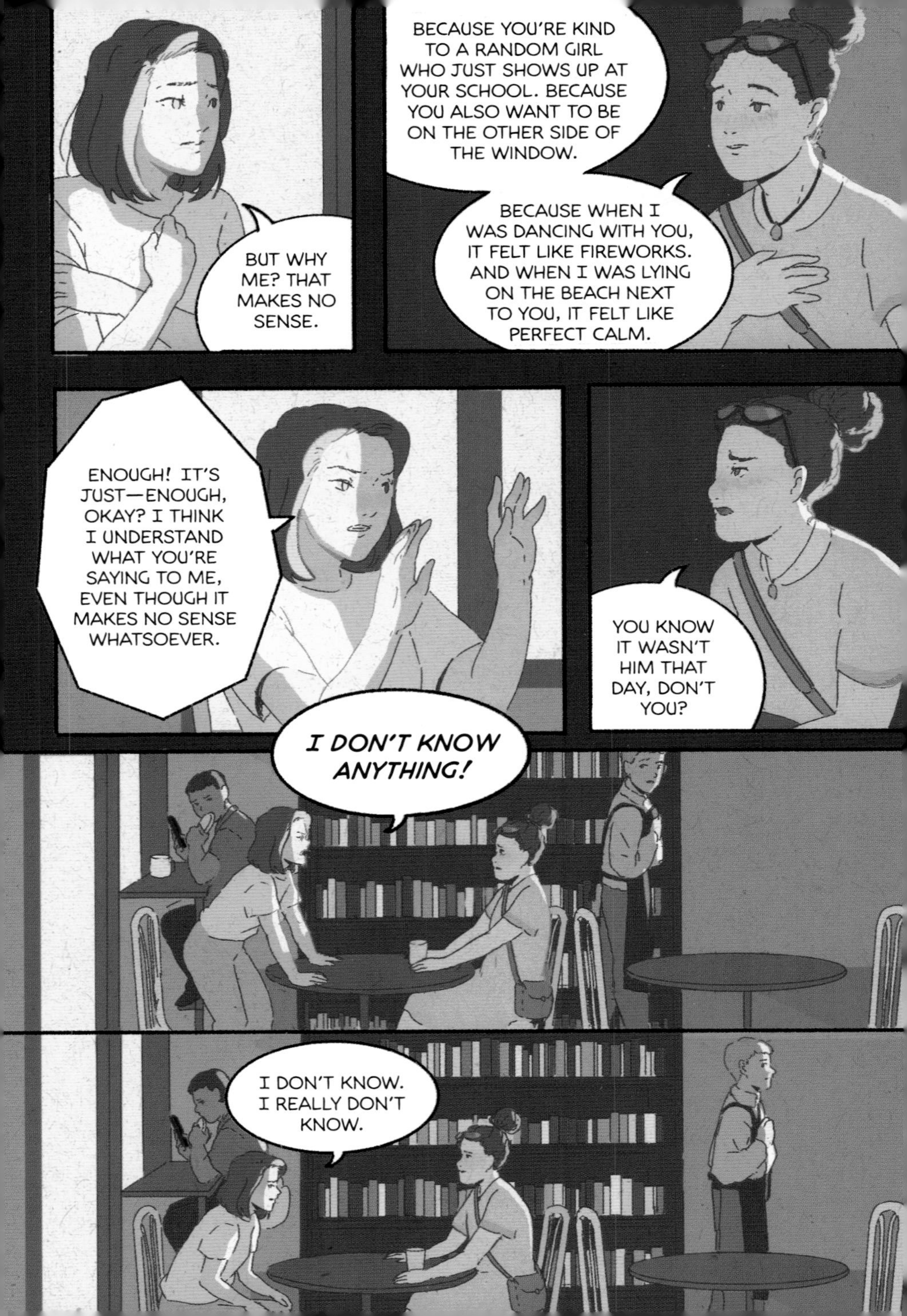
BUT WHY ME? THAT MAKES NO SENSE.
BECAUSE YOU'RE KIND TO A RANDOM GIRL WHO JUST SHOWS UP AT YOUR SCHOOL. BECAUSE YOU ALSO WANT TO BE ON THE OTHER SIDE OF THE WINDOW.
BECAUSE WHEN I WAS DANCING WITH YOU, IT FELT LIKE FIREWORKS. AND WHEN I WAS LYING ON THE BEACH NEXT TO YOU, IT FELT LIKE PERFECT CALM.
ENOUGH! IT'S JUST—ENOUGH, OKAY? I THINK I UNDERSTAND WHAT YOU'RE SAYING TO ME, EVEN THOUGH IT MAKES NO SENSE WHATSOEVER.
YOU KNOW IT WASN'T HIM THAT DAY, DON'T YOU?
I DON'T KNOW ANYTHING!
I DON'T KNOW. I REALLY DON'T KNOW.

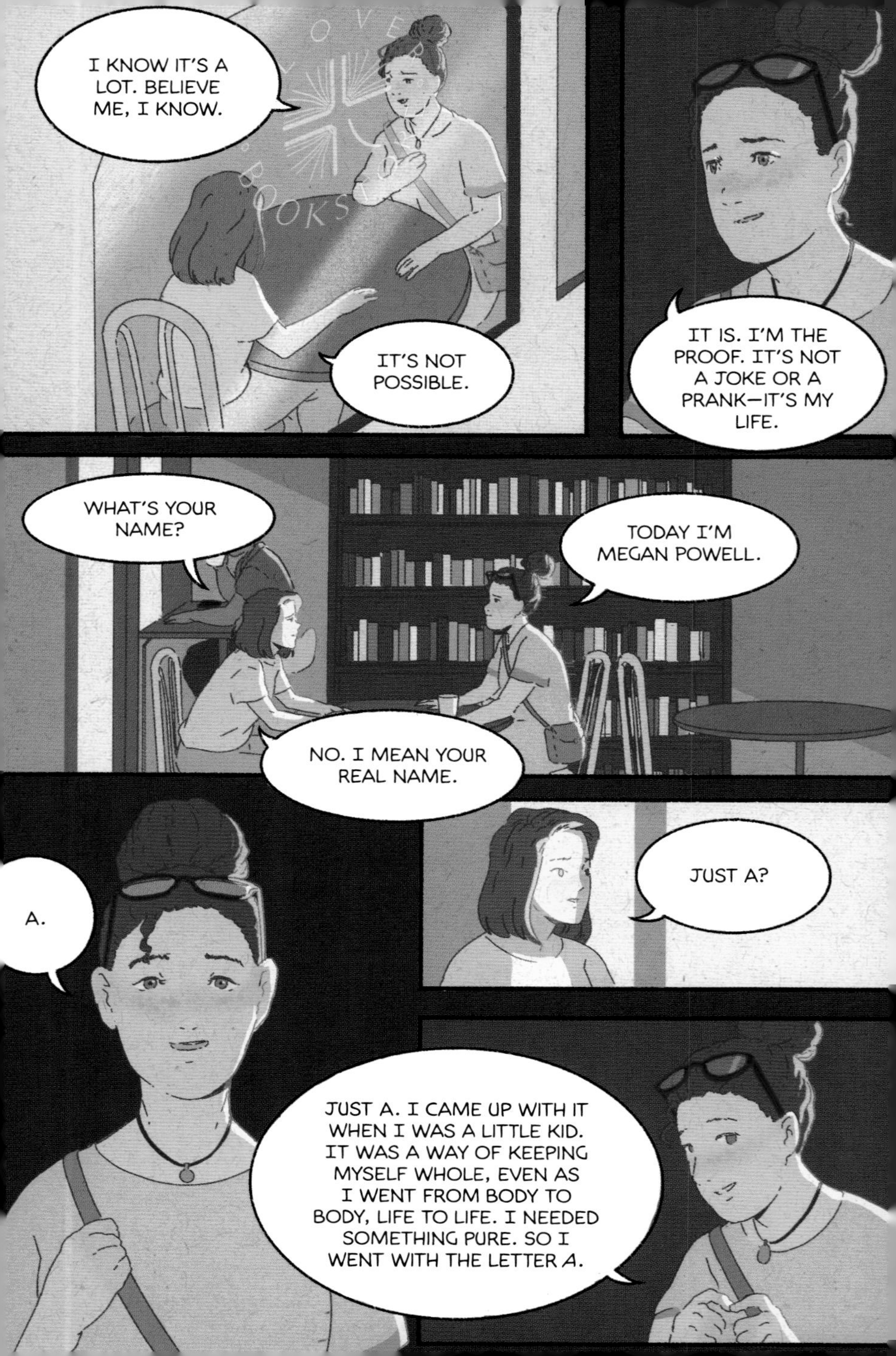
I KNOW IT'S A LOT. BELIEVE ME, I KNOW.
IT'S NOT POSSIBLE.
IT IS. I'M THE PROOF. IT'S NOT A JOKE OR A PRANK—IT'S MY LIFE.
WHAT'S YOUR NAME?
TODAY I'M MEGAN POWELL.
NO. I MEAN YOUR REAL NAME.
A.
JUST A?
JUST A. I CAME UP WITH IT WHEN I WAS A LITTLE KID. IT WAS A WAY OF KEEPING MYSELF WHOLE, EVEN AS I WENT FROM BODY TO BODY, LIFE TO LIFE. I NEEDED SOMETHING PURE. SO I WENT WITH THE LETTER *A*.

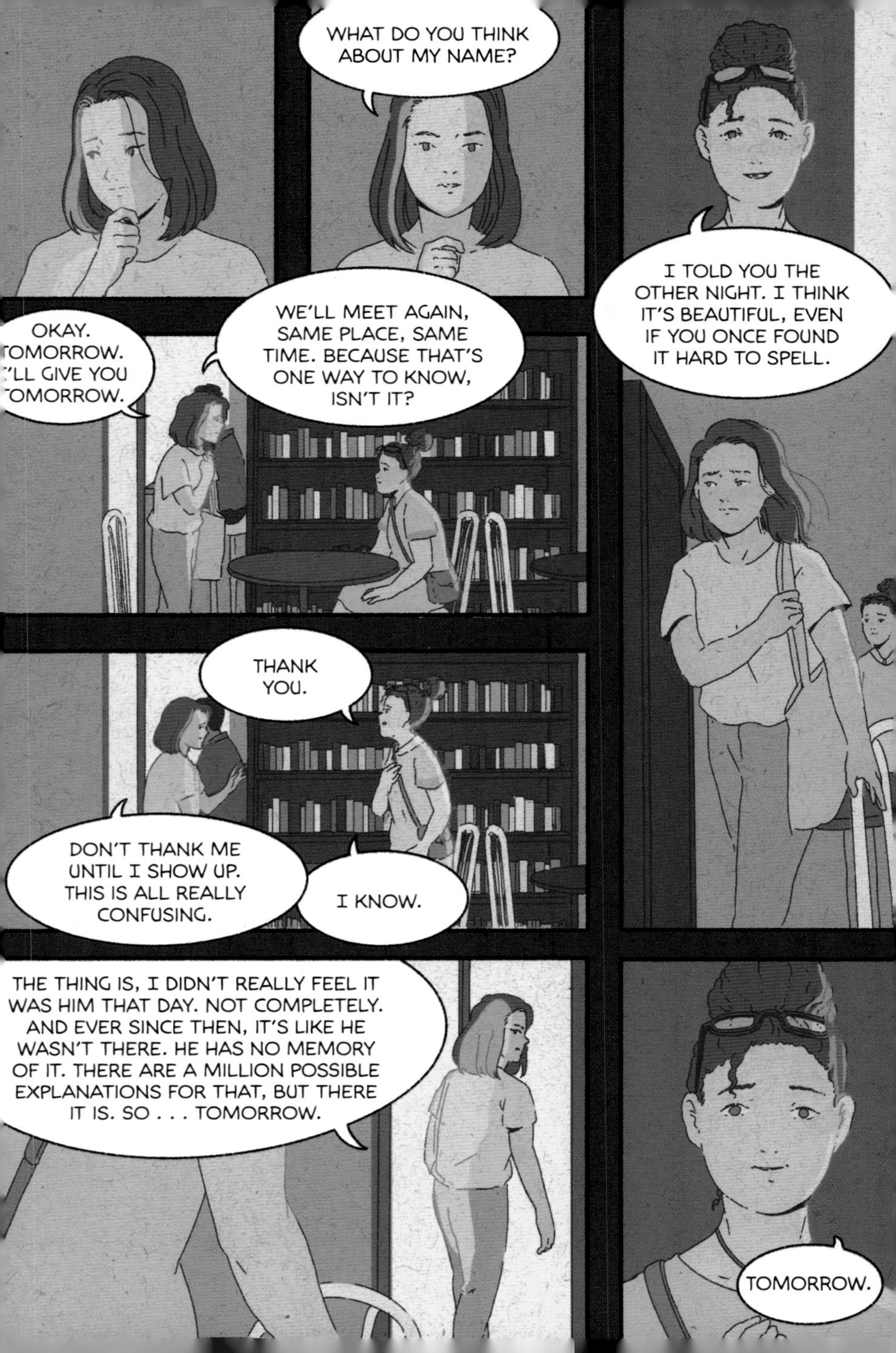
WHAT DO YOU THINK ABOUT MY NAME?
I TOLD YOU THE OTHER NIGHT. I THINK IT'S BEAUTIFUL, EVEN IF YOU ONCE FOUND IT HARD TO SPELL.
OKAY. TOMORROW. 'LL GIVE YOU TOMORROW.
WE'LL MEET AGAIN, SAME PLACE, SAME TIME. BECAUSE THAT'S ONE WAY TO KNOW, ISN'T IT?
THANK YOU.
DON'T THANK ME UNTIL I SHOW UP. THIS IS ALL REALLY CONFUSING.
I KNOW.
THE THING IS, I DIDN'T REALLY FEEL IT WAS HIM THAT DAY. NOT COMPLETELY. AND EVER SINCE THEN, IT'S LIKE HE WASN'T THERE. HE HAS NO MEMORY OF IT. THERE ARE A MILLION POSSIBLE EXPLANATIONS FOR THAT, BUT THERE IT IS. SO . . . TOMORROW.
TOMORROW.

DAY 6003

EVERYBODY UP!

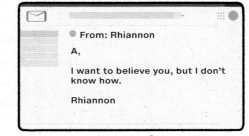

From: Rhiannon

A,

I want to believe you, but I don't know how.

Rhiannon

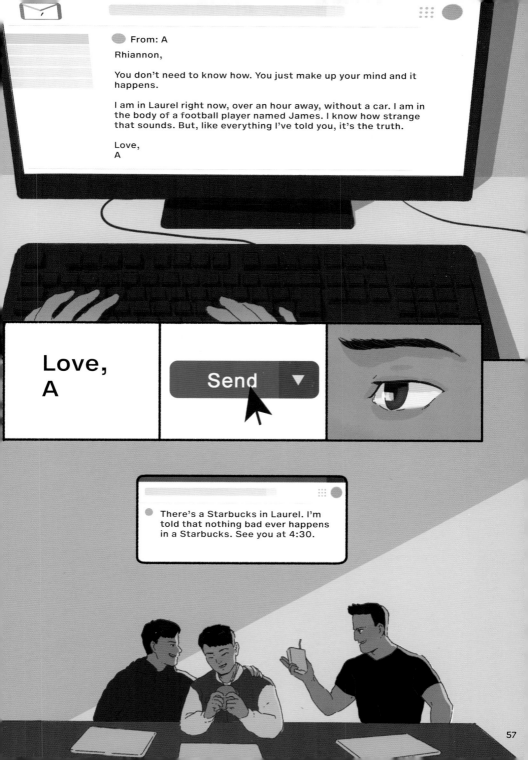

From: A

Rhiannon,

You don't need to know how. You just make up your mind and it happens.

I am in Laurel right now, over an hour away, without a car. I am in the body of a football player named James. I know how strange that sounds. But, like everything I've told you, it's the truth.

Love,
A

Love,
A

Send ▾

There's a Starbucks in Laurel. I'm told that nothing bad ever happens in a Starbucks. See you at 4:30.

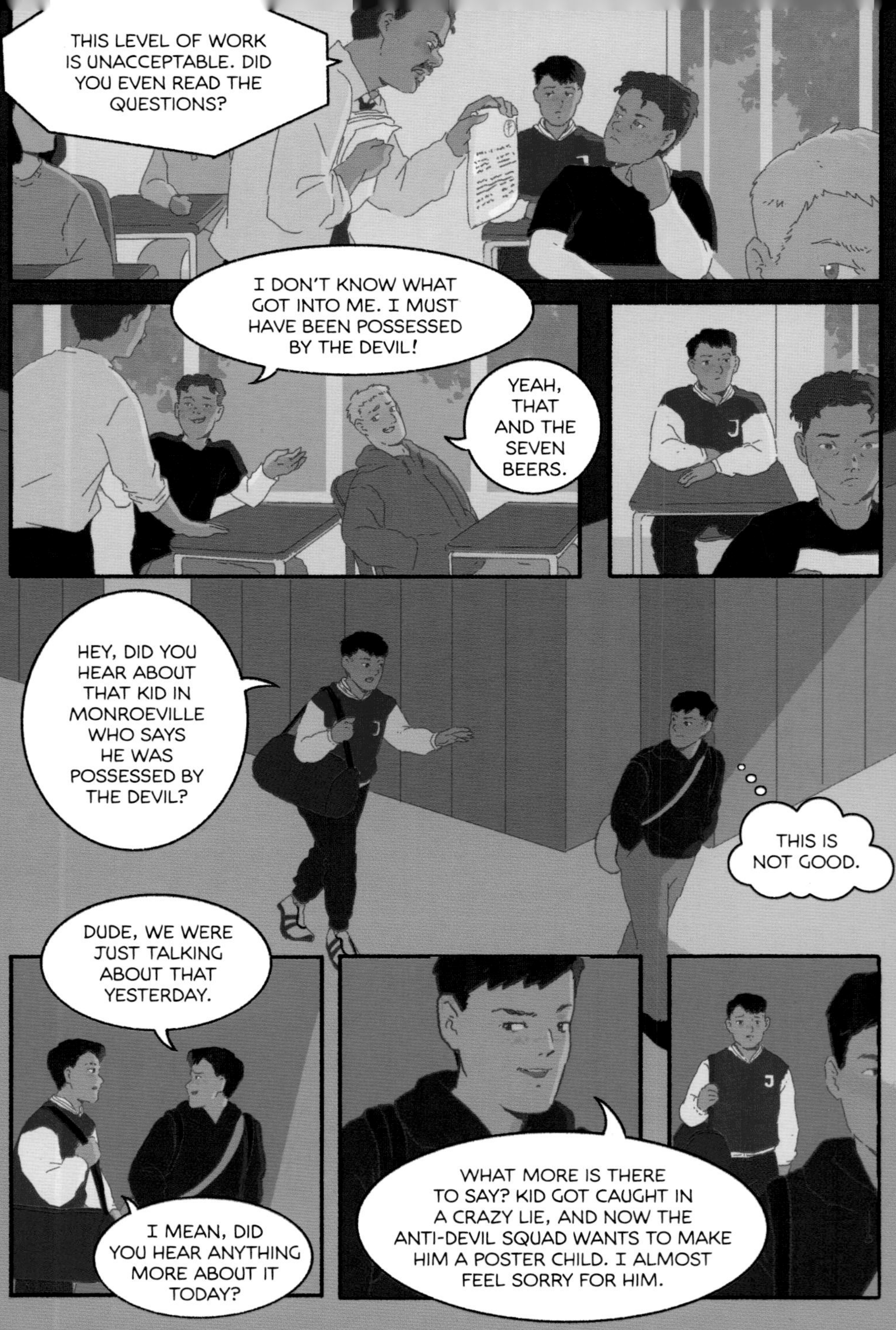

THIS LEVEL OF WORK IS UNACCEPTABLE. DID YOU EVEN READ THE QUESTIONS?
I DON'T KNOW WHAT GOT INTO ME. I MUST HAVE BEEN POSSESSED BY THE DEVIL!
YEAH, THAT AND THE SEVEN BEERS.
HEY, DID YOU HEAR ABOUT THAT KID IN MONROEVILLE WHO SAYS HE WAS POSSESSED BY THE DEVIL?
THIS IS NOT GOOD.
DUDE, WE WERE JUST TALKING ABOUT THAT YESTERDAY.
I MEAN, DID YOU HEAR ANYTHING MORE ABOUT IT TODAY?
WHAT MORE IS THERE TO SAY? KID GOT CAUGHT IN A CRAZY LIE, AND NOW THE ANTI-DEVIL SQUAD WANTS TO MAKE HIM A POSTER CHILD. I ALMOST FEEL SORRY FOR HIM.

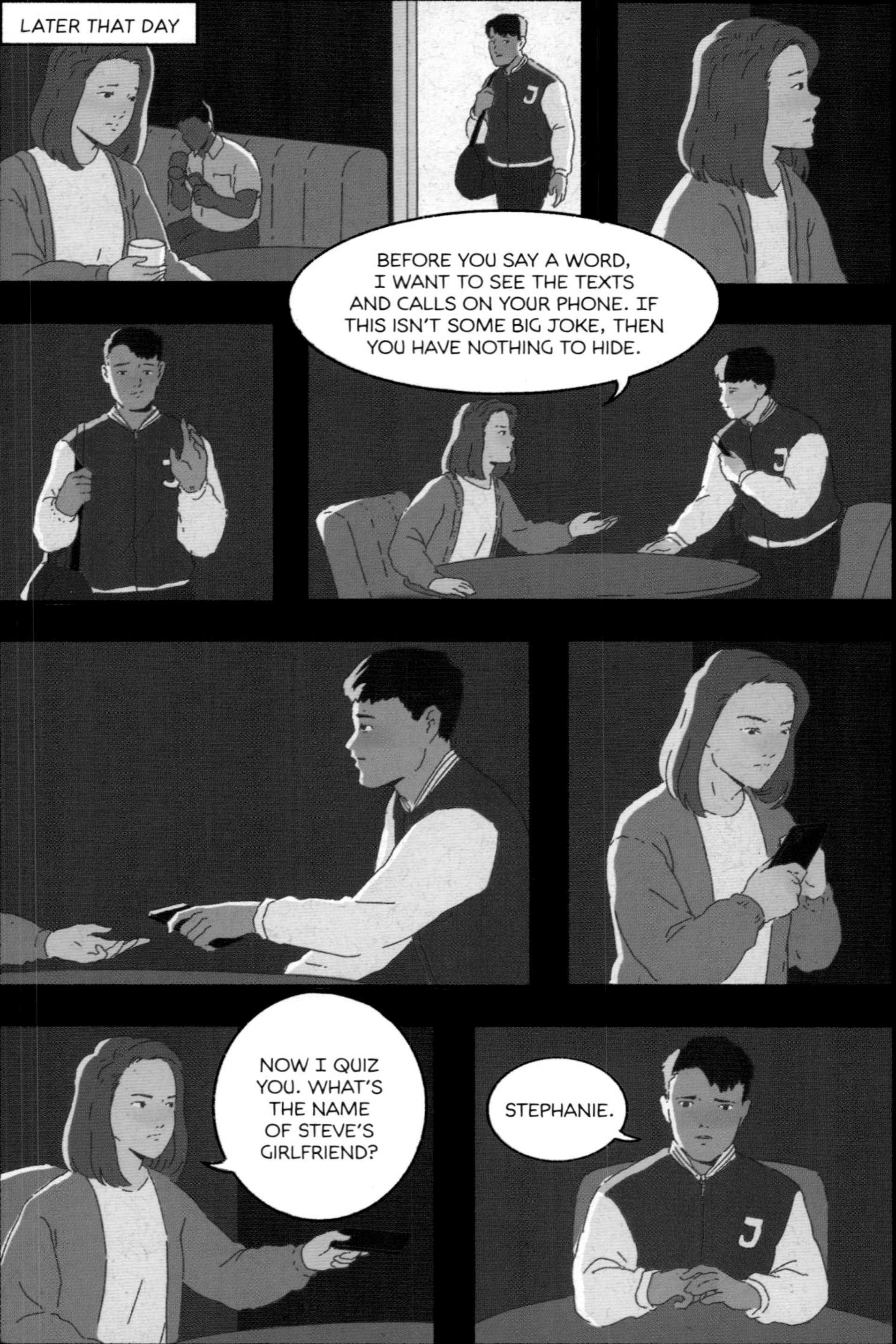
LATER THAT DAY
BEFORE YOU SAY A WORD, I WANT TO SEE THE TEXTS AND CALLS ON YOUR PHONE. IF THIS ISN'T SOME BIG JOKE, THEN YOU HAVE NOTHING TO HIDE.
NOW I QUIZ YOU. WHAT'S THE NAME OF STEVE'S GIRLFRIEND?
STEPHANIE.

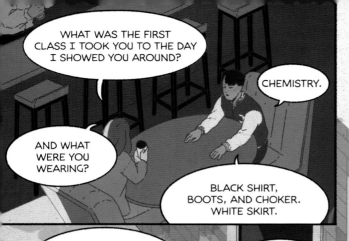

WHAT WAS THE FIRST CLASS I TOOK YOU TO THE DAY I SHOWED YOU AROUND?

CHEMISTRY.

AND WHAT WERE YOU WEARING?

BLACK SHIRT, BOOTS, AND CHOKER. WHITE SKIRT.

WELL, EITHER YOU'RE AN EXCELLENT LIAR, OR YOU SWITCH BODIES EVERY DAY. I HAVE NO IDEA WHICH ONE IS TRUE.

SO YOU SAY YOU'VE BEEN LIKE THIS SINCE THE DAY YOU WERE BORN?

YES. I CAN'T REMEMBER IT BEING ANY DIFFERENT.

SO HOW DID THAT WORK? WEREN'T YOU CONFUSED?

I GUESS I GOT USED TO IT. I'M SURE THAT, AT FIRST, I FIGURED IT WAS JUST HOW EVERYBODY'S LIVES WORKED.

I MEAN, WHEN YOU'RE A BABY, YOU DON'T REALLY CARE MUCH ABOUT WHO'S TAKING CARE OF YOU, AS LONG AS SOMEONE'S TAKING CARE OF YOU.

AND AS A LITTLE KID, I THOUGHT IT WAS SOME KIND OF A GAME, AND MY MIND LEARNED HOW TO ACCESS—YOU KNOW, LOOK AT THE BODY'S MEMORIES— NATURALLY. SO I ALWAYS KNEW WHAT MY NAME WAS, AND WHERE I WAS.

IT WASN'T UNTIL I WAS FOUR OR FIVE THAT I STARTED TO REALIZE I WAS DIFFERENT, AND IT WASN'T UNTIL I WAS NINE OR TEN THAT I REALLY WANTED IT TO STOP.

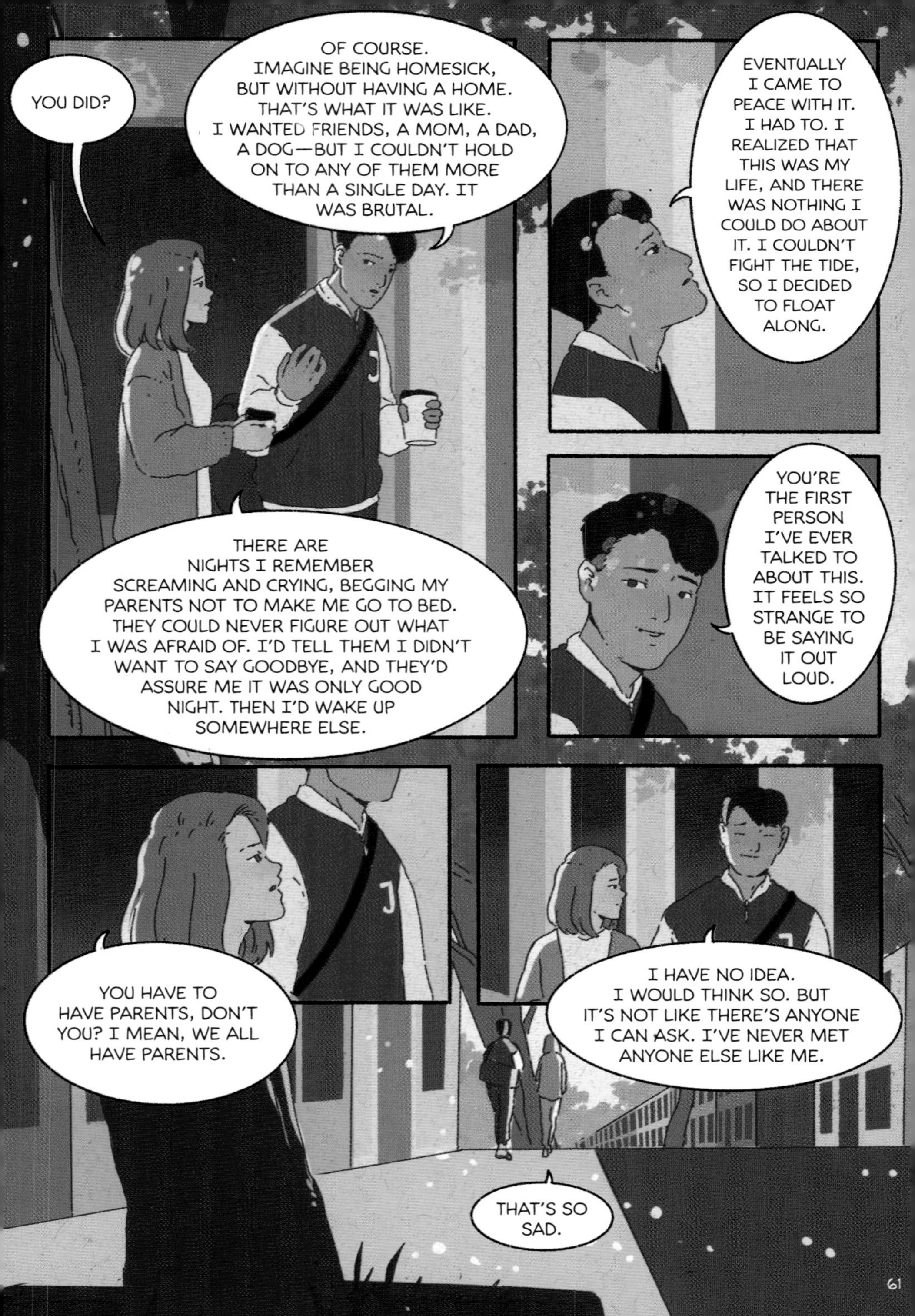
YOU DID?
OF COURSE. IMAGINE BEING HOMESICK, BUT WITHOUT HAVING A HOME. THAT'S WHAT IT WAS LIKE. I WANTED FRIENDS, A MOM, A DAD, A DOG—BUT I COULDN'T HOLD ON TO ANY OF THEM MORE THAN A SINGLE DAY. IT WAS BRUTAL.
THERE ARE NIGHTS I REMEMBER SCREAMING AND CRYING, BEGGING MY PARENTS NOT TO MAKE ME GO TO BED. THEY COULD NEVER FIGURE OUT WHAT I WAS AFRAID OF. I'D TELL THEM I DIDN'T WANT TO SAY GOODBYE, AND THEY'D ASSURE ME IT WAS ONLY GOOD NIGHT. THEN I'D WAKE UP SOMEWHERE ELSE.
EVENTUALLY I CAME TO PEACE WITH IT. I HAD TO. I REALIZED THAT THIS WAS MY LIFE, AND THERE WAS NOTHING I COULD DO ABOUT IT. I COULDN'T FIGHT THE TIDE, SO I DECIDED TO FLOAT ALONG.
YOU'RE THE FIRST PERSON I'VE EVER TALKED TO ABOUT THIS. IT FEELS SO STRANGE TO BE SAYING IT OUT LOUD.
YOU HAVE TO HAVE PARENTS, DON'T YOU? I MEAN, WE ALL HAVE PARENTS.
I HAVE NO IDEA. I WOULD THINK SO. BUT IT'S NOT LIKE THERE'S ANYONE I CAN ASK. I'VE NEVER MET ANYONE ELSE LIKE ME.
THAT'S SO SAD.

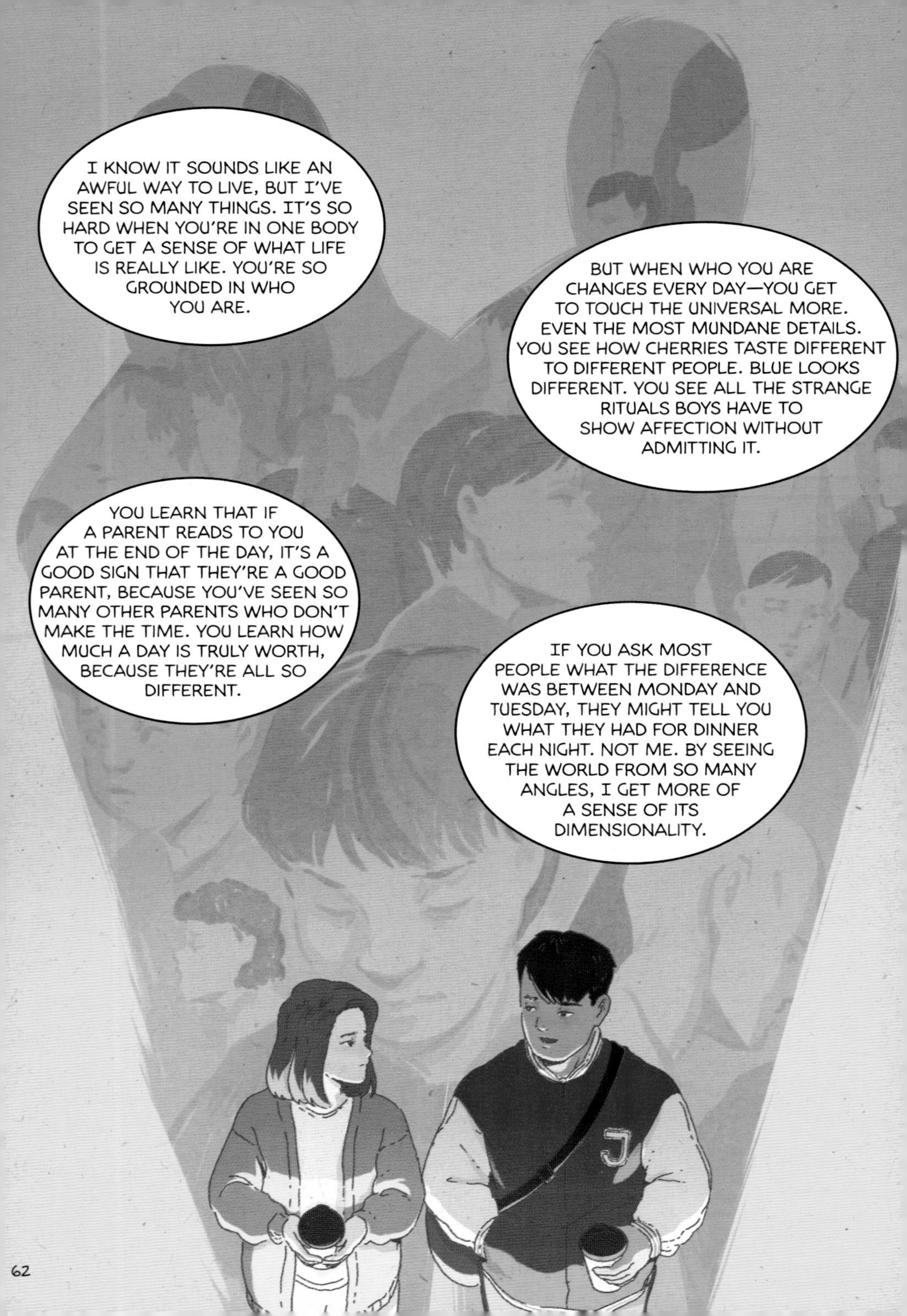
I KNOW IT SOUNDS LIKE AN AWFUL WAY TO LIVE, BUT I'VE SEEN SO MANY THINGS. IT'S SO HARD WHEN YOU'RE IN ONE BODY TO GET A SENSE OF WHAT LIFE IS REALLY LIKE. YOU'RE SO GROUNDED IN WHO YOU ARE.
BUT WHEN WHO YOU ARE CHANGES EVERY DAY—YOU GET TO TOUCH THE UNIVERSAL MORE. EVEN THE MOST MUNDANE DETAILS. YOU SEE HOW CHERRIES TASTE DIFFERENT TO DIFFERENT PEOPLE. BLUE LOOKS DIFFERENT. YOU SEE ALL THE STRANGE RITUALS BOYS HAVE TO SHOW AFFECTION WITHOUT ADMITTING IT.
YOU LEARN THAT IF A PARENT READS TO YOU AT THE END OF THE DAY, IT'S A GOOD SIGN THAT THEY'RE A GOOD PARENT, BECAUSE YOU'VE SEEN SO MANY OTHER PARENTS WHO DON'T MAKE THE TIME. YOU LEARN HOW MUCH A DAY IS TRULY WORTH, BECAUSE THEY'RE ALL SO DIFFERENT.
IF YOU ASK MOST PEOPLE WHAT THE DIFFERENCE WAS BETWEEN MONDAY AND TUESDAY, THEY MIGHT TELL YOU WHAT THEY HAD FOR DINNER EACH NIGHT. NOT ME. BY SEEING THE WORLD FROM SO MANY ANGLES, I GET MORE OF A SENSE OF ITS DIMENSIONALITY.

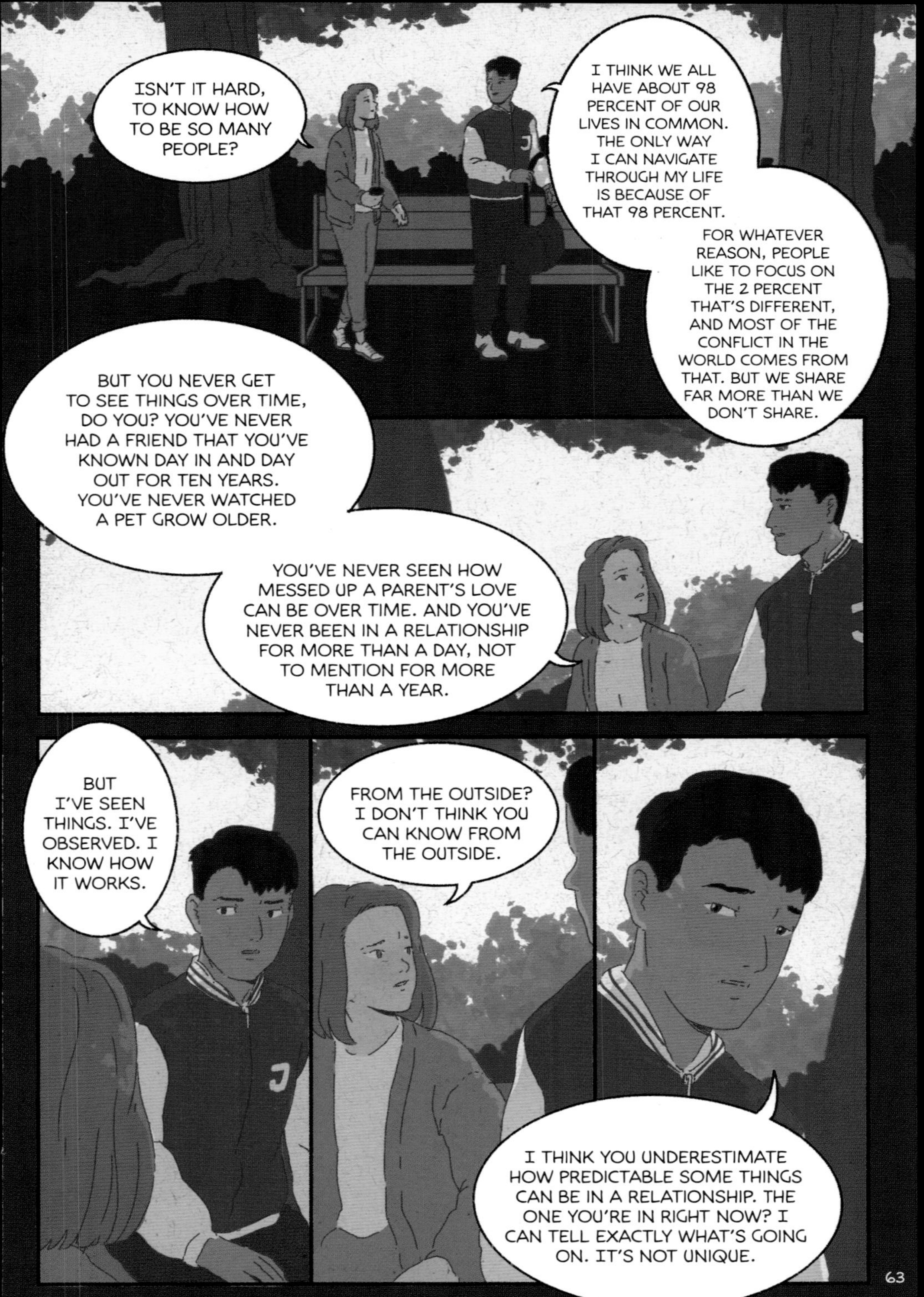
ISN'T IT HARD, TO KNOW HOW TO BE SO MANY PEOPLE?
I THINK WE ALL HAVE ABOUT 98 PERCENT OF OUR LIVES IN COMMON. THE ONLY WAY I CAN NAVIGATE THROUGH MY LIFE IS BECAUSE OF THAT 98 PERCENT.
FOR WHATEVER REASON, PEOPLE LIKE TO FOCUS ON THE 2 PERCENT THAT'S DIFFERENT, AND MOST OF THE CONFLICT IN THE WORLD COMES FROM THAT. BUT WE SHARE FAR MORE THAN WE DON'T SHARE.
BUT YOU NEVER GET TO SEE THINGS OVER TIME, DO YOU? YOU'VE NEVER HAD A FRIEND THAT YOU'VE KNOWN DAY IN AND DAY OUT FOR TEN YEARS. YOU'VE NEVER WATCHED A PET GROW OLDER.
YOU'VE NEVER SEEN HOW MESSED UP A PARENT'S LOVE CAN BE OVER TIME. AND YOU'VE NEVER BEEN IN A RELATIONSHIP FOR MORE THAN A DAY, NOT TO MENTION FOR MORE THAN A YEAR.
BUT I'VE SEEN THINGS. I'VE OBSERVED. I KNOW HOW IT WORKS.
FROM THE OUTSIDE? I DON'T THINK YOU CAN KNOW FROM THE OUTSIDE.
I THINK YOU UNDERESTIMATE HOW PREDICTABLE SOME THINGS CAN BE IN A RELATIONSHIP. THE ONE YOU'RE IN RIGHT NOW? I CAN TELL EXACTLY WHAT'S GOING ON. IT'S NOT UNIQUE.

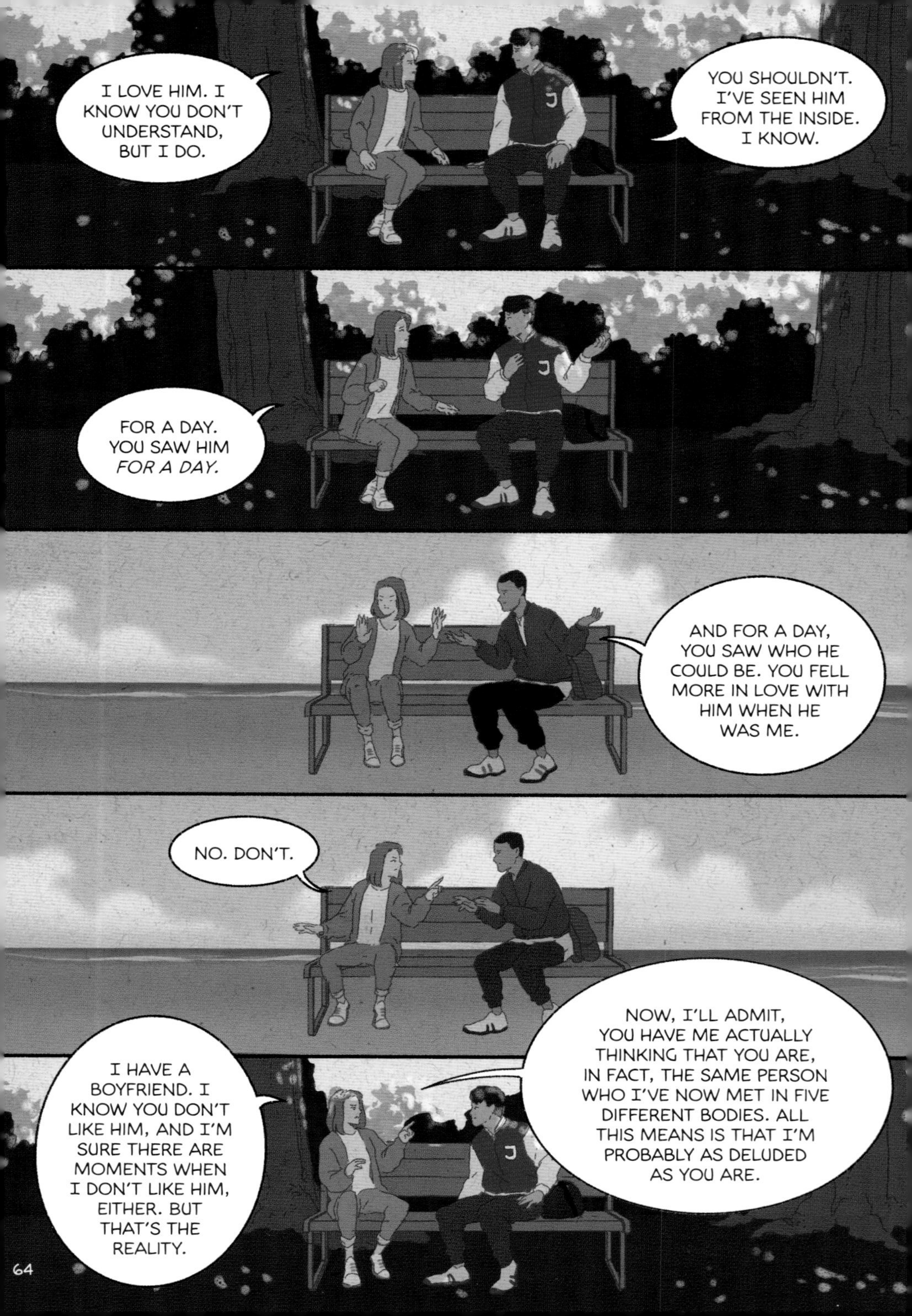

I LOVE HIM. I KNOW YOU DON'T UNDERSTAND, BUT I DO.
YOU SHOULDN'T. I'VE SEEN HIM FROM THE INSIDE. I KNOW.
FOR A DAY. YOU SAW HIM *FOR A DAY.*
AND FOR A DAY, YOU SAW WHO HE COULD BE. YOU FELL MORE IN LOVE WITH HIM WHEN HE WAS ME.
NO. DON'T.
I HAVE A BOYFRIEND. I KNOW YOU DON'T LIKE HIM, AND I'M SURE THERE ARE MOMENTS WHEN I DON'T LIKE HIM, EITHER. BUT THAT'S THE REALITY.
NOW, I'LL ADMIT, YOU HAVE ME ACTUALLY THINKING THAT YOU ARE, IN FACT, THE SAME PERSON WHO I'VE NOW MET IN FIVE DIFFERENT BODIES. ALL THIS MEANS IS THAT I'M PROBABLY AS DELUDED AS YOU ARE.

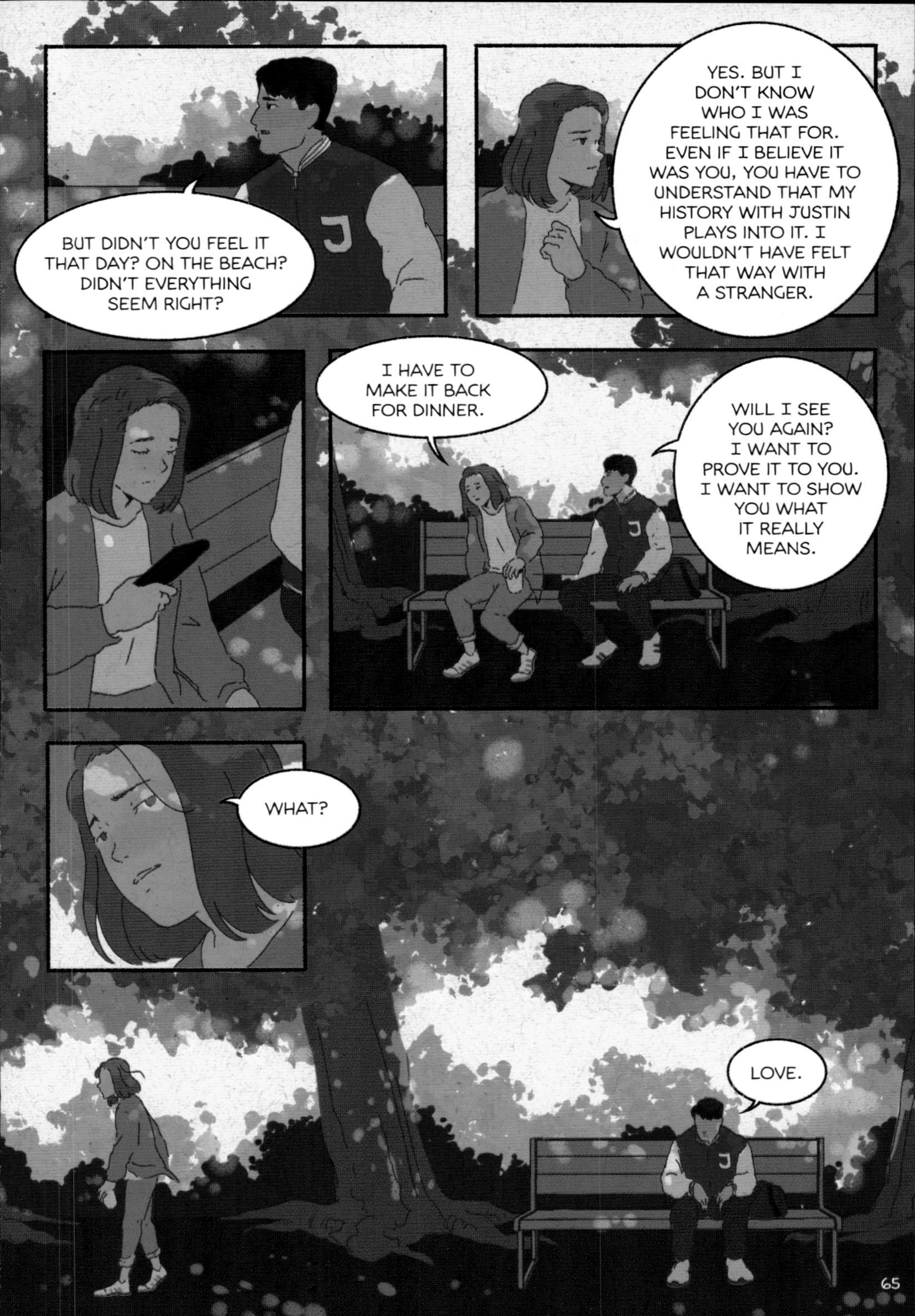
BUT DIDN'T YOU FEEL IT THAT DAY? ON THE BEACH? DIDN'T EVERYTHING SEEM RIGHT?
YES. BUT I DON'T KNOW WHO I WAS FEELING THAT FOR. EVEN IF I BELIEVE IT WAS YOU, YOU HAVE TO UNDERSTAND THAT MY HISTORY WITH JUSTIN PLAYS INTO IT. I WOULDN'T HAVE FELT THAT WAY WITH A STRANGER.
I HAVE TO MAKE IT BACK FOR DINNER.
WILL I SEE YOU AGAIN? I WANT TO PROVE IT TO YOU. I WANT TO SHOW YOU WHAT IT REALLY MEANS.
WHAT?
LOVE.

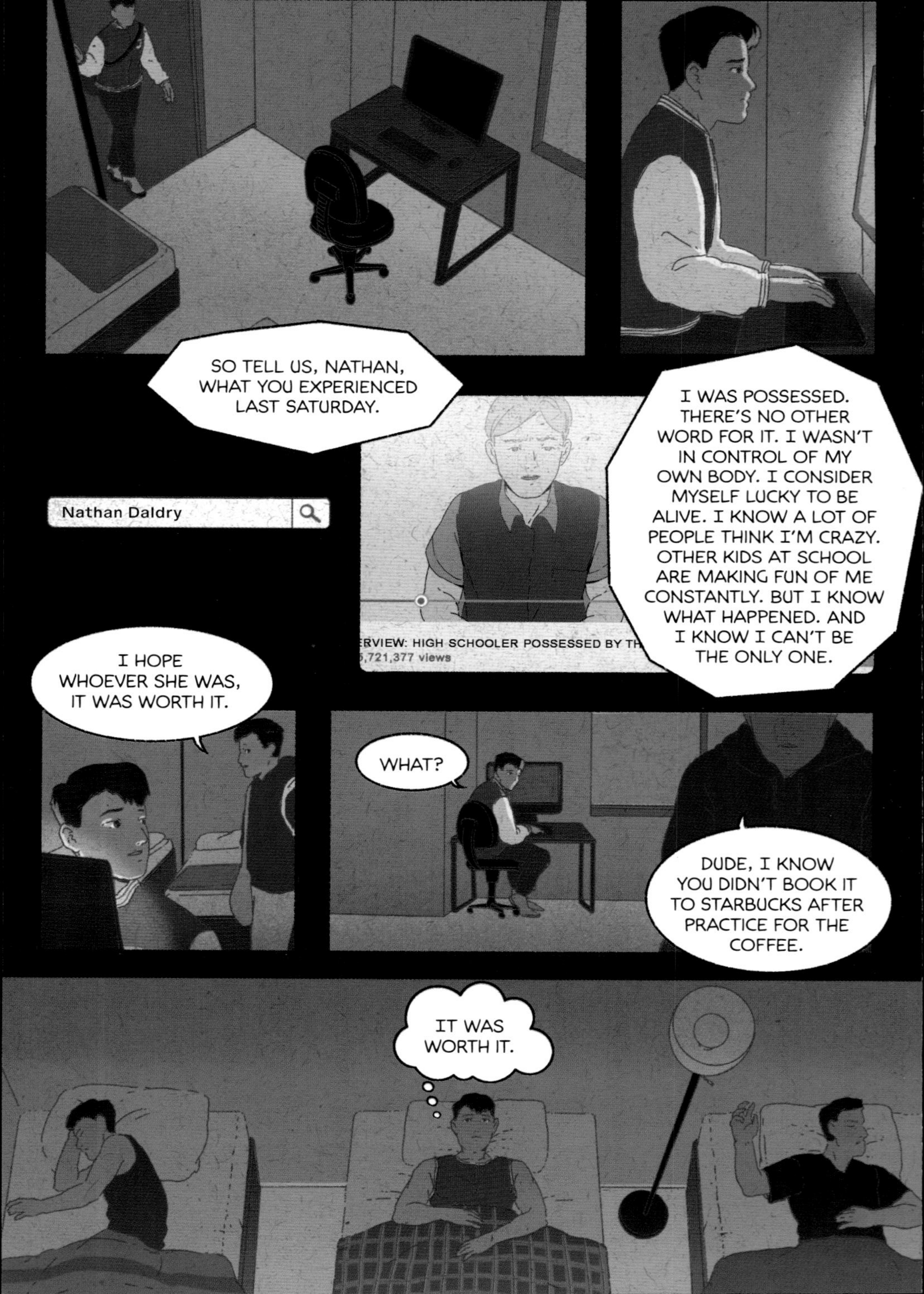
SO TELL US, NATHAN, WHAT YOU EXPERIENCED LAST SATURDAY.
Nathan Daldry
I WAS POSSESSED. THERE'S NO OTHER WORD FOR IT. I WASN'T IN CONTROL OF MY OWN BODY. I CONSIDER MYSELF LUCKY TO BE ALIVE. I KNOW A LOT OF PEOPLE THINK I'M CRAZY. OTHER KIDS AT SCHOOL ARE MAKING FUN OF ME CONSTANTLY. BUT I KNOW WHAT HAPPENED. AND I KNOW I CAN'T BE THE ONLY ONE.
I HOPE WHOEVER SHE WAS, IT WAS WORTH IT.
WHAT?
DUDE, I KNOW YOU DIDN'T BOOK IT TO STARBUCKS AFTER PRACTICE FOR THE COFFEE.
IT WAS WORTH IT.

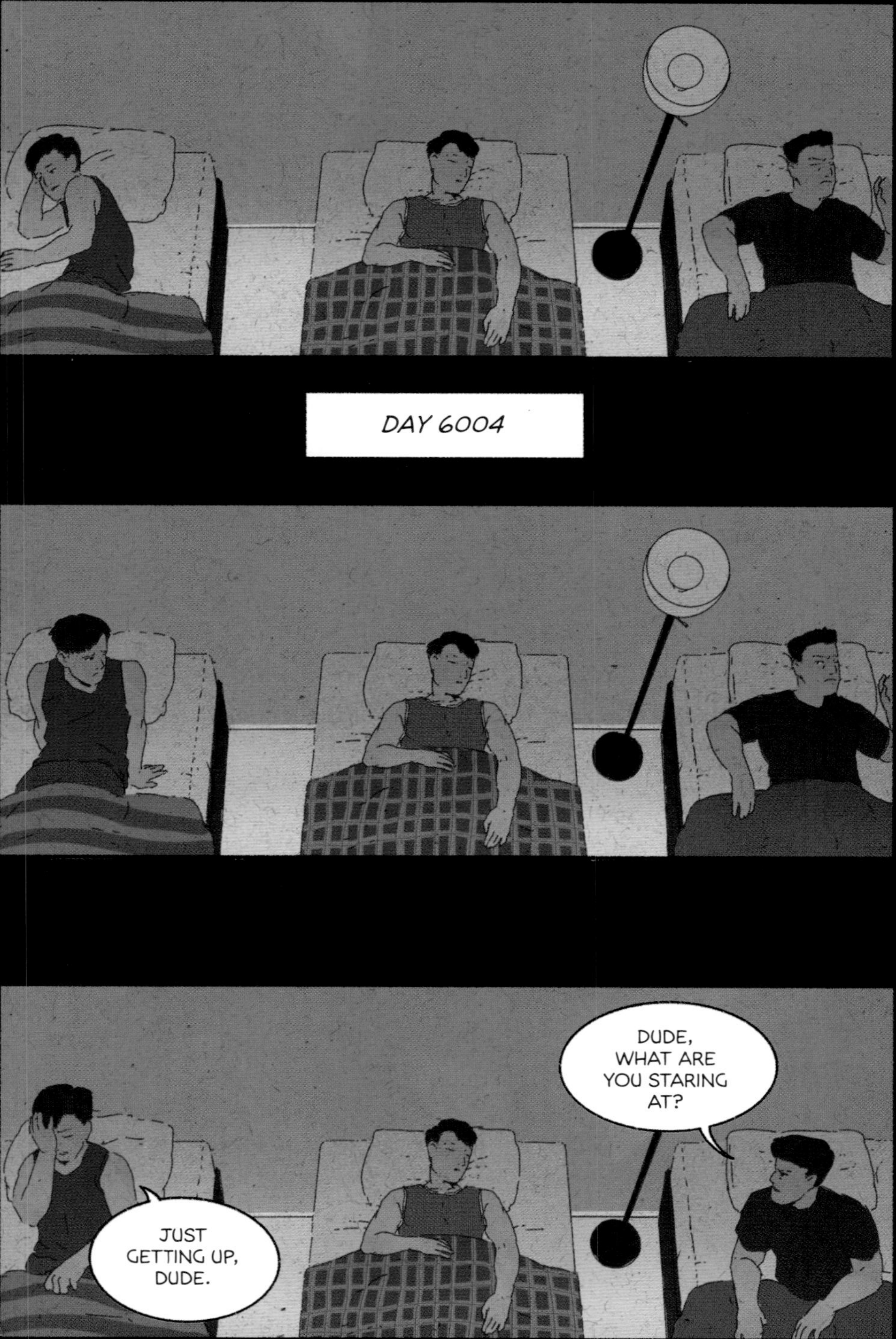
DAY 6004
DUDE, WHAT ARE YOU STARING AT?
JUST GETTING UP, DUDE.

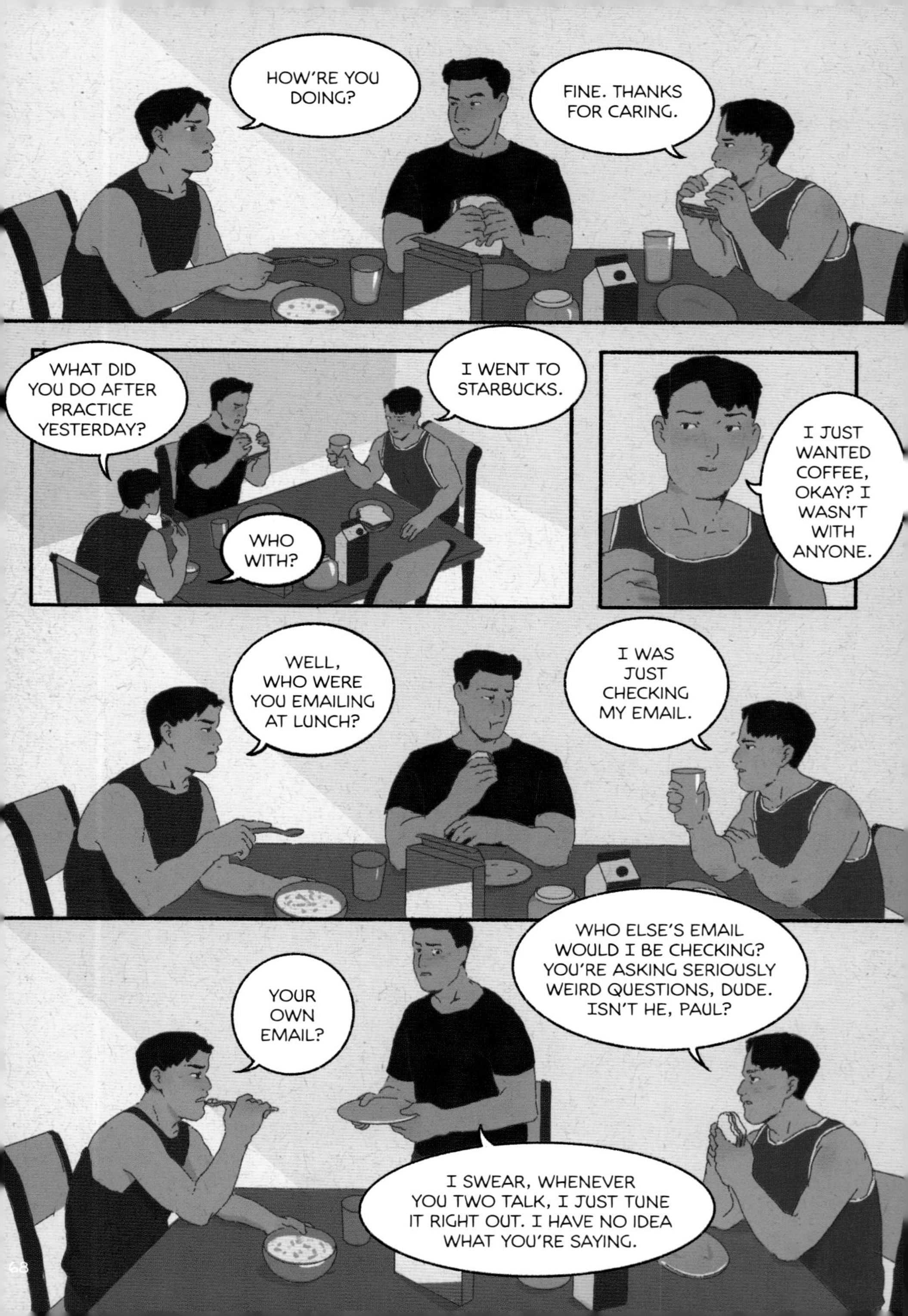
HOW'RE YOU DOING?
FINE. THANKS FOR CARING.
WHAT DID YOU DO AFTER PRACTICE YESTERDAY?
I WENT TO STARBUCKS.
WHO WITH?
I JUST WANTED COFFEE, OKAY? I WASN'T WITH ANYONE.
WELL, WHO WERE YOU EMAILING AT LUNCH?
I WAS JUST CHECKING MY EMAIL.
YOUR OWN EMAIL?
WHO ELSE'S EMAIL WOULD I BE CHECKING? YOU'RE ASKING SERIOUSLY WEIRD QUESTIONS, DUDE. ISN'T HE, PAUL?
I SWEAR, WHENEVER YOU TWO TALK, I JUST TUNE IT RIGHT OUT. I HAVE NO IDEA WHAT YOU'RE SAYING.

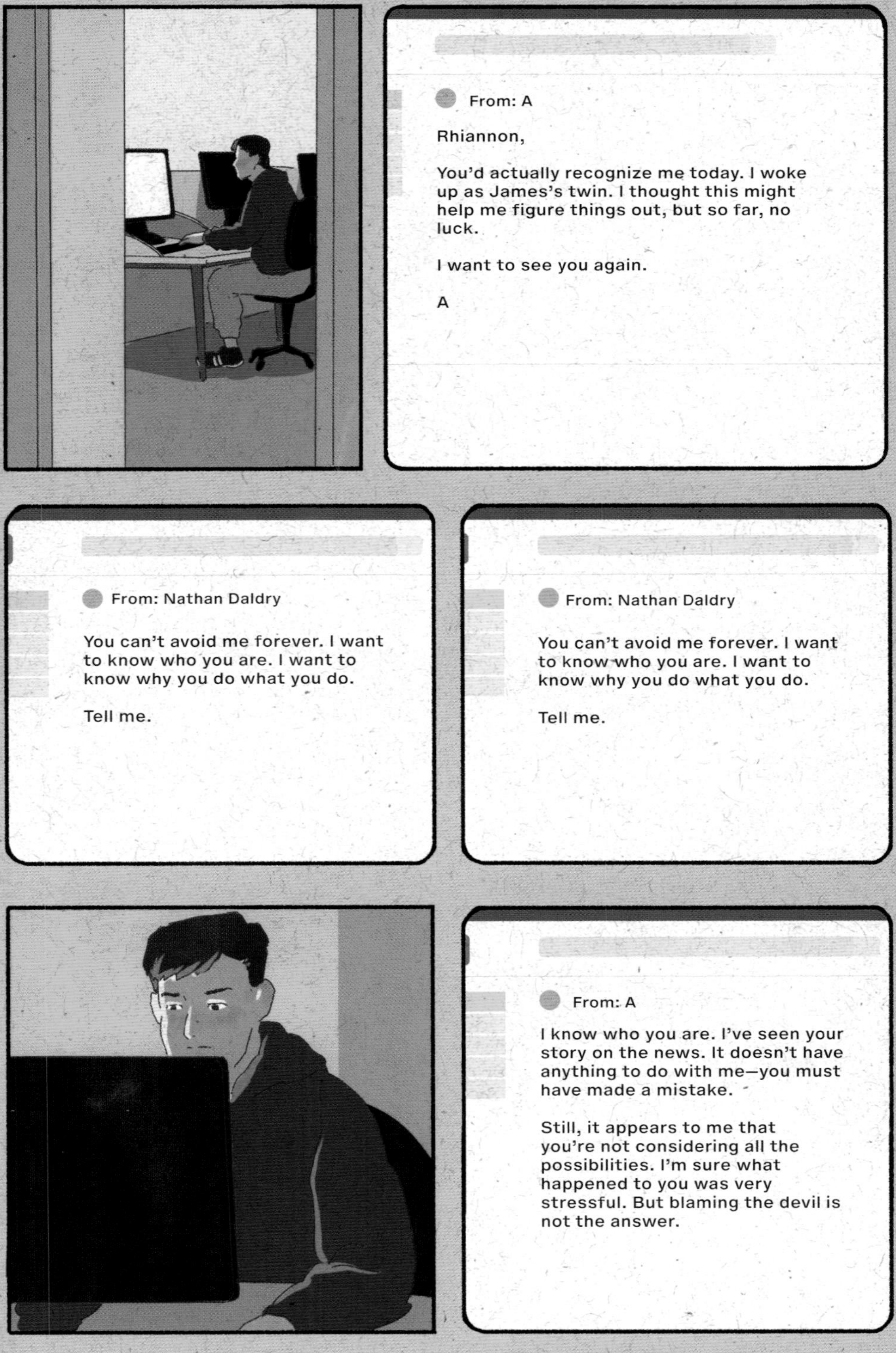
From: A
Rhiannon,
You'd actually recognize me today. I woke up as James's twin. I thought this might help me figure things out, but so far, no luck.
I want to see you again.
A
From: Nathan Daldry
You can't avoid me forever. I want to know who you are. I want to know why you do what you do.
Tell me.
From: Nathan Daldry
You can't avoid me forever. I want to know who you are. I want to know why you do what you do.
Tell me.
From: A
I know who you are. I've seen your story on the news. It doesn't have anything to do with me—you must have made a mistake.
Still, it appears to me that you're not considering all the possibilities. I'm sure what happened to you was very stressful. But blaming the devil is not the answer.

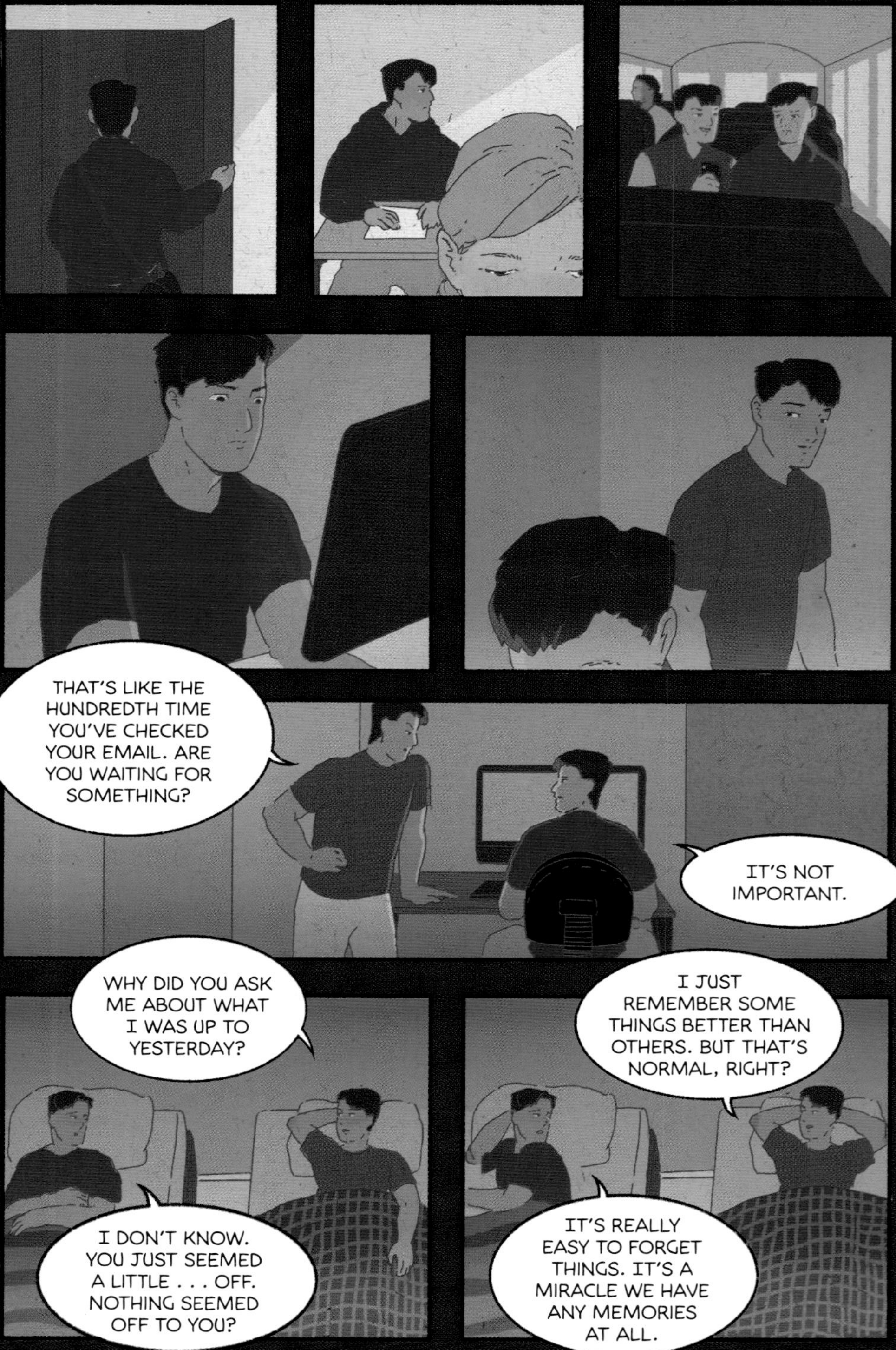
THAT'S LIKE THE HUNDREDTH TIME YOU'VE CHECKED YOUR EMAIL. ARE YOU WAITING FOR SOMETHING?
IT'S NOT IMPORTANT.
WHY DID YOU ASK ME ABOUT WHAT I WAS UP TO YESTERDAY?
I DON'T KNOW. YOU JUST SEEMED A LITTLE . . . OFF. NOTHING SEEMED OFF TO YOU?
I JUST REMEMBER SOME THINGS BETTER THAN OTHERS. BUT THAT'S NORMAL, RIGHT?
IT'S REALLY EASY TO FORGET THINGS. IT'S A MIRACLE WE HAVE ANY MEMORIES AT ALL.

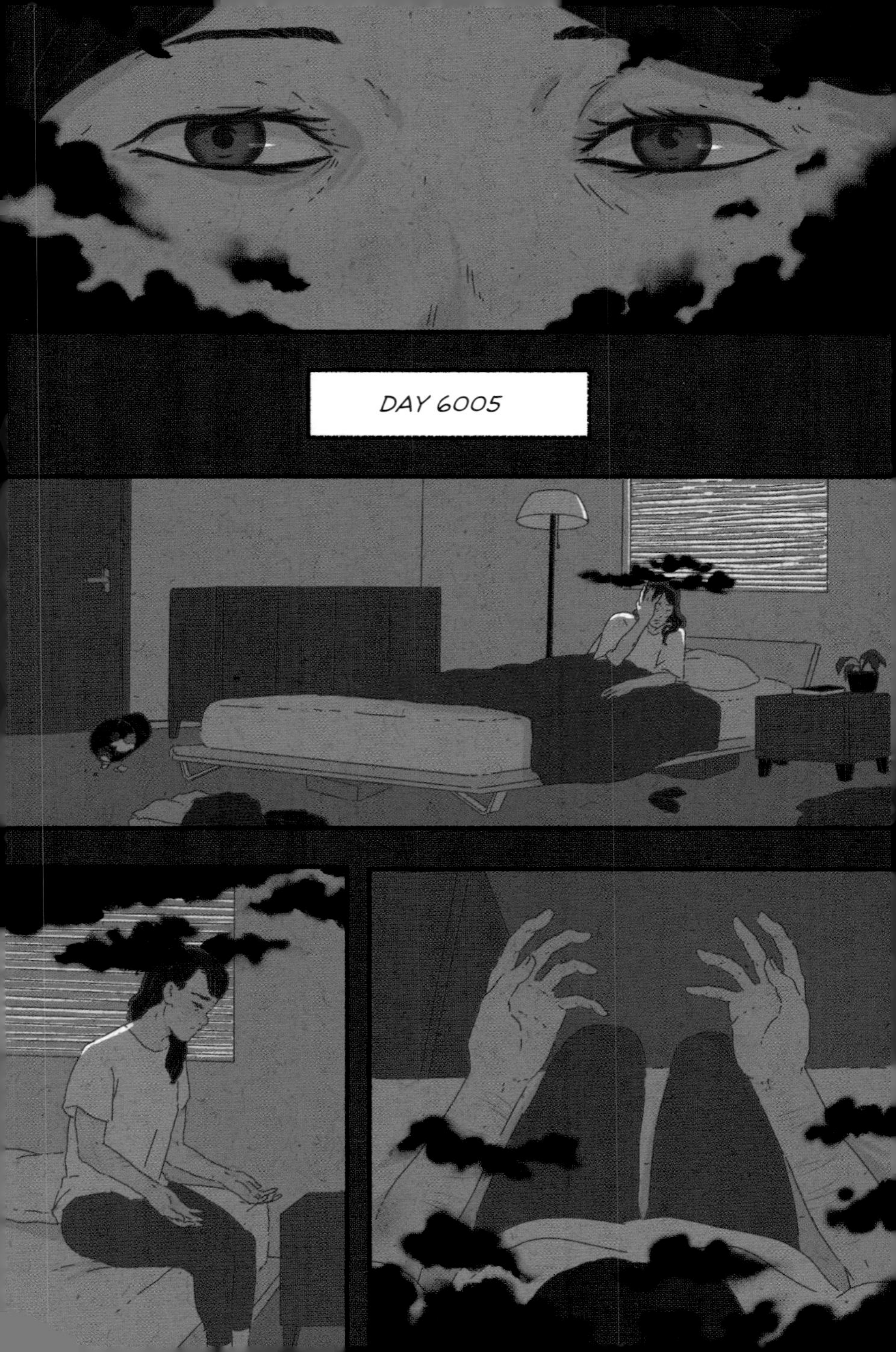
DAY 6005

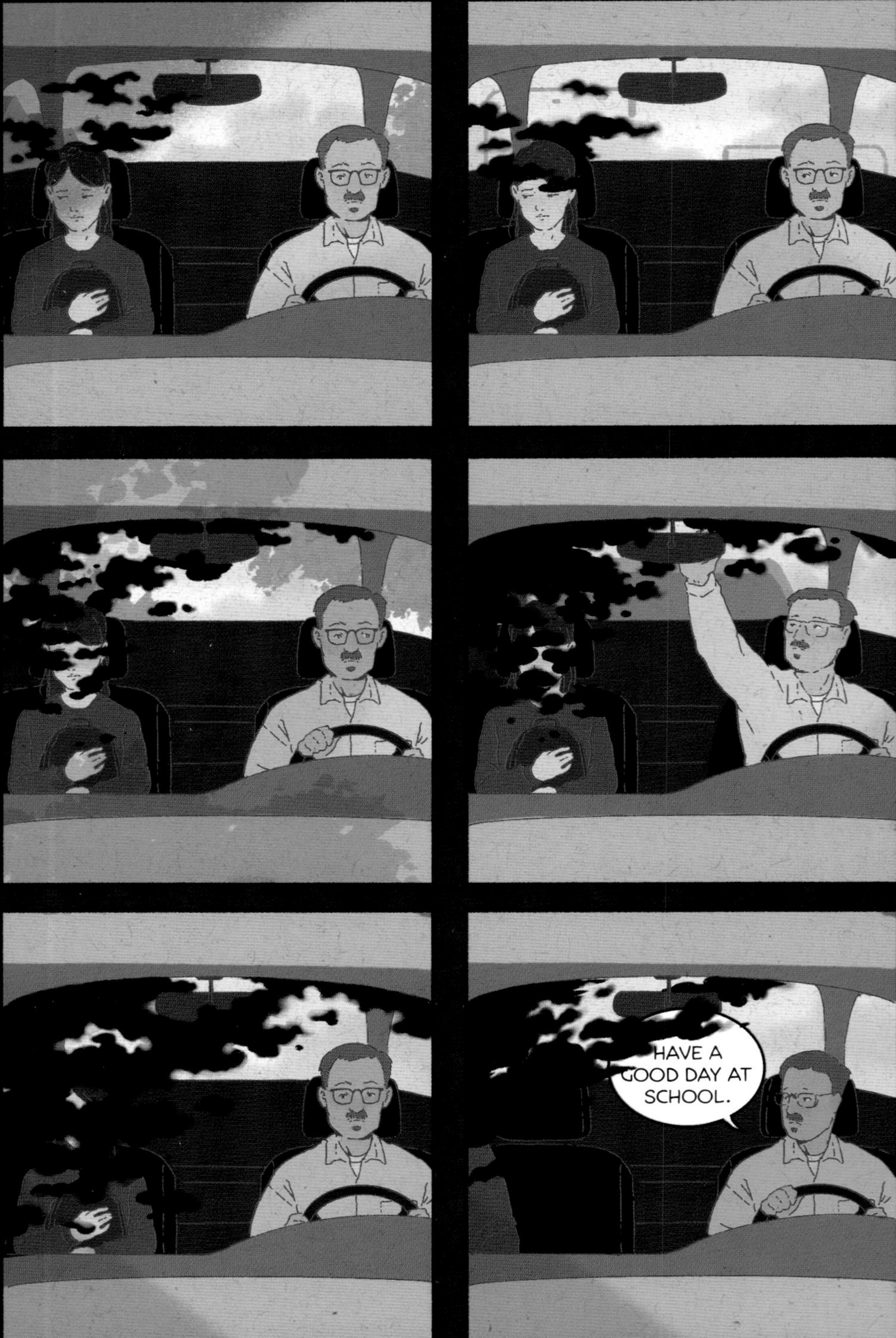
HAVE A GOOD DAY AT SCHOOL.

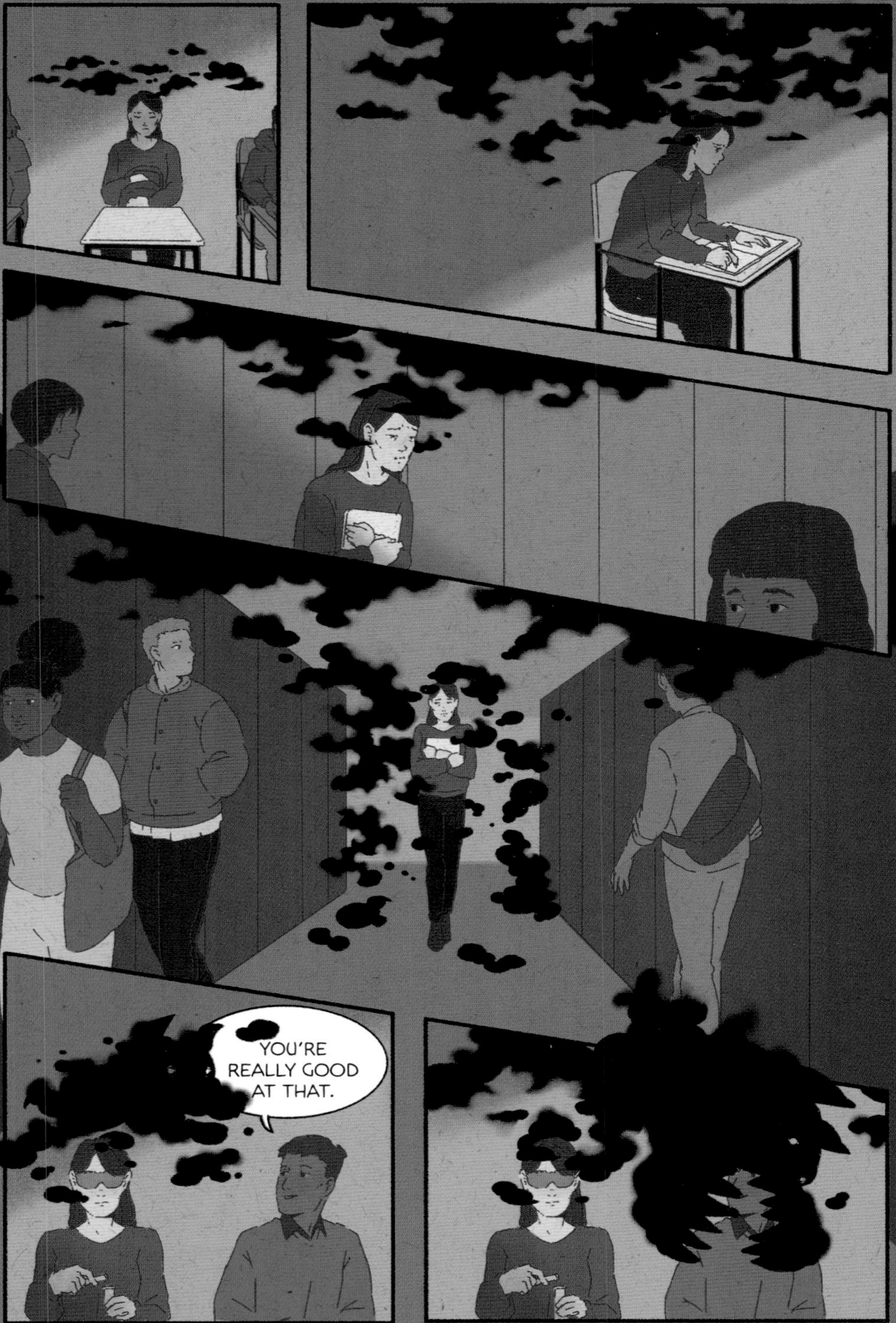
YOU'RE REALLY GOOD AT THAT.

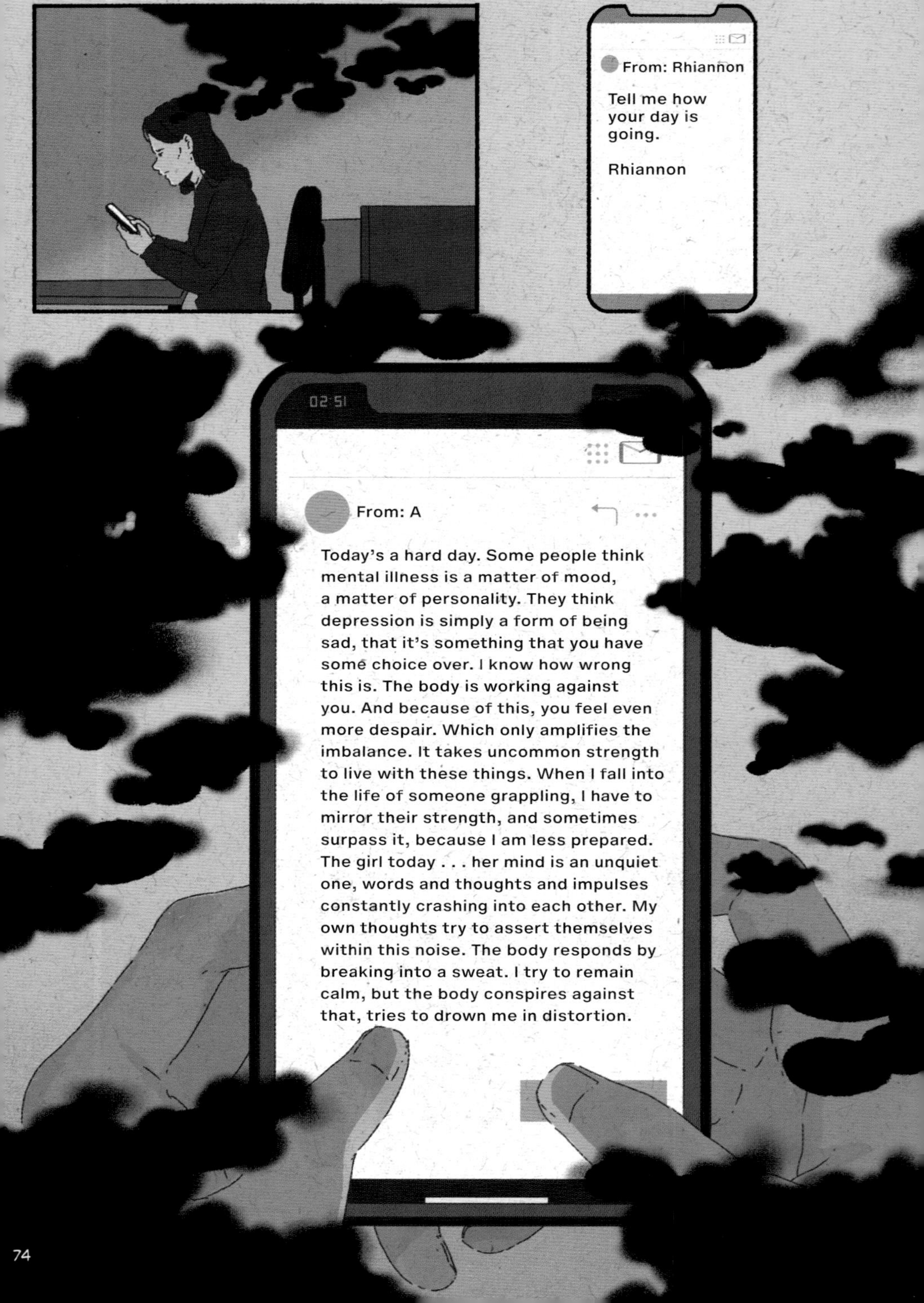
From: Rhiannon
Tell me how your day is going.
Rhiannon
02:51
From: A
Today's a hard day. Some people think mental illness is a matter of mood, a matter of personality. They think depression is simply a form of being sad, that it's something that you have some choice over. I know how wrong this is. The body is working against you. And because of this, you feel even more despair. Which only amplifies the imbalance. It takes uncommon strength to live with these things. When I fall into the life of someone grappling, I have to mirror their strength, and sometimes surpass it, because I am less prepared. The girl today . . . her mind is an unquiet one, words and thoughts and impulses constantly crashing into each other. My own thoughts try to assert themselves within this noise. The body responds by breaking into a sweat. I try to remain calm, but the body conspires against that, tries to drown me in distortion.

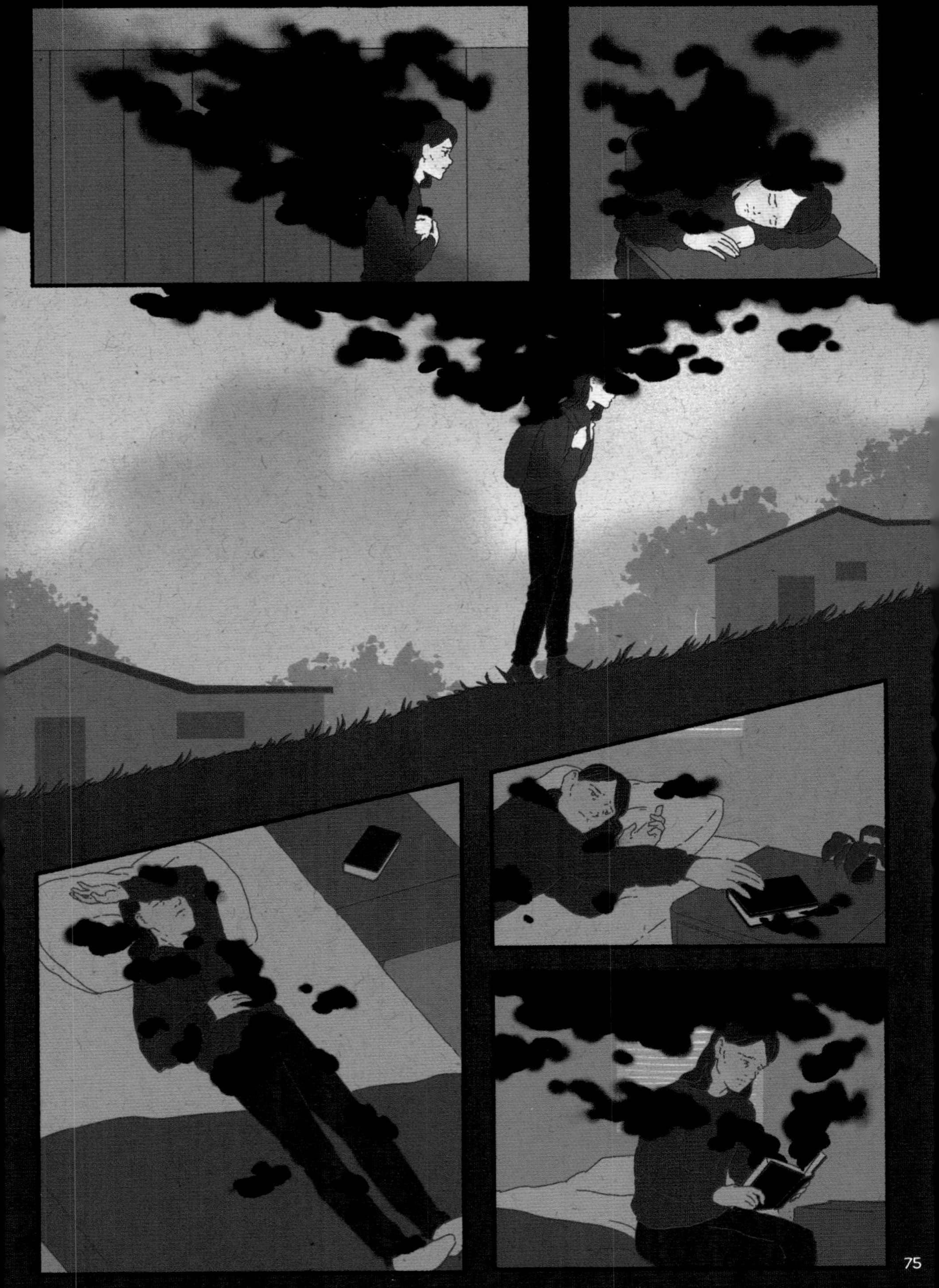

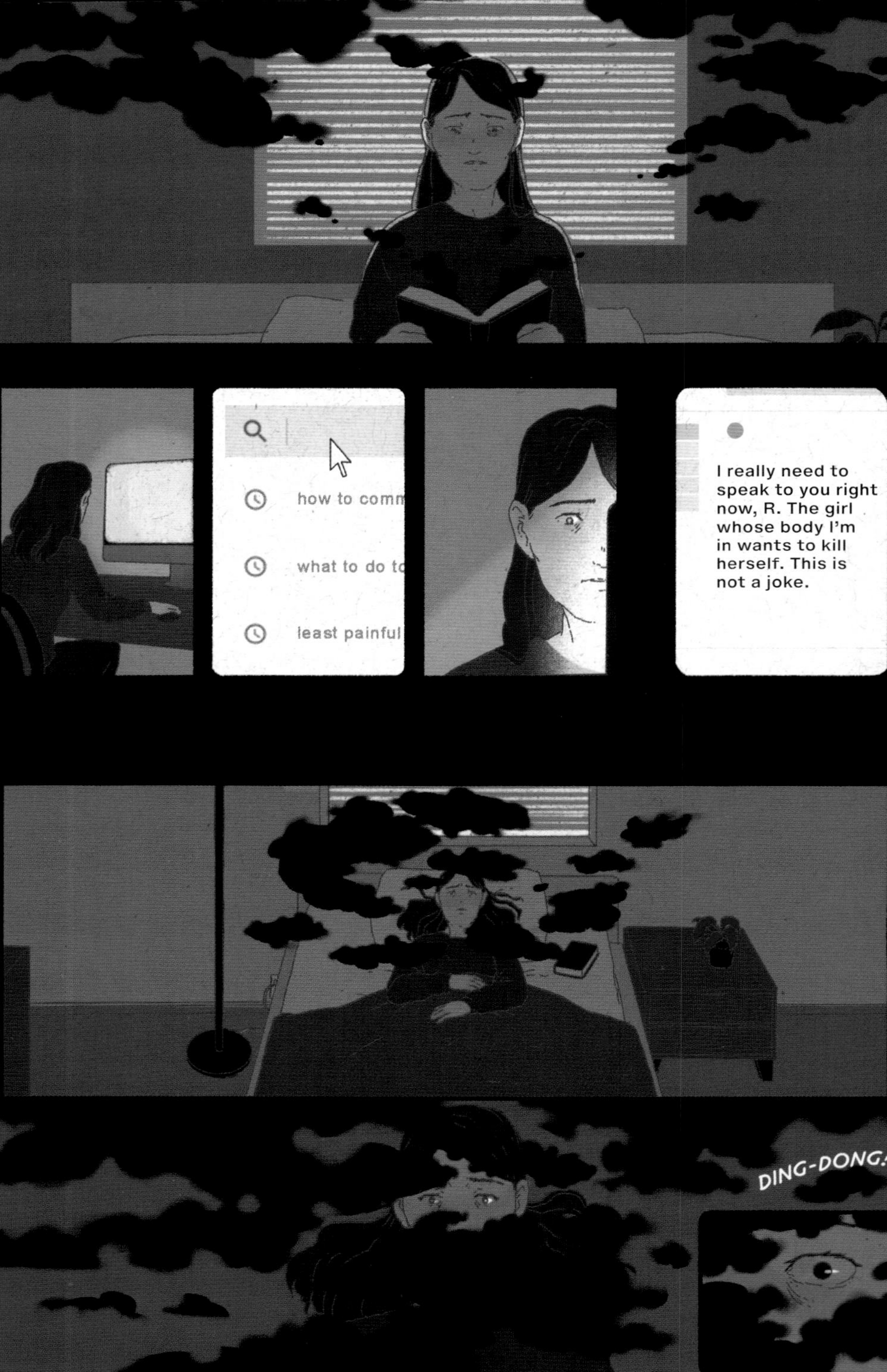
how to comm
what to do to
least painful
I really need to speak to you right now, R. The girl whose body I'm in wants to kill herself. This is not a joke.
DING-DONG!

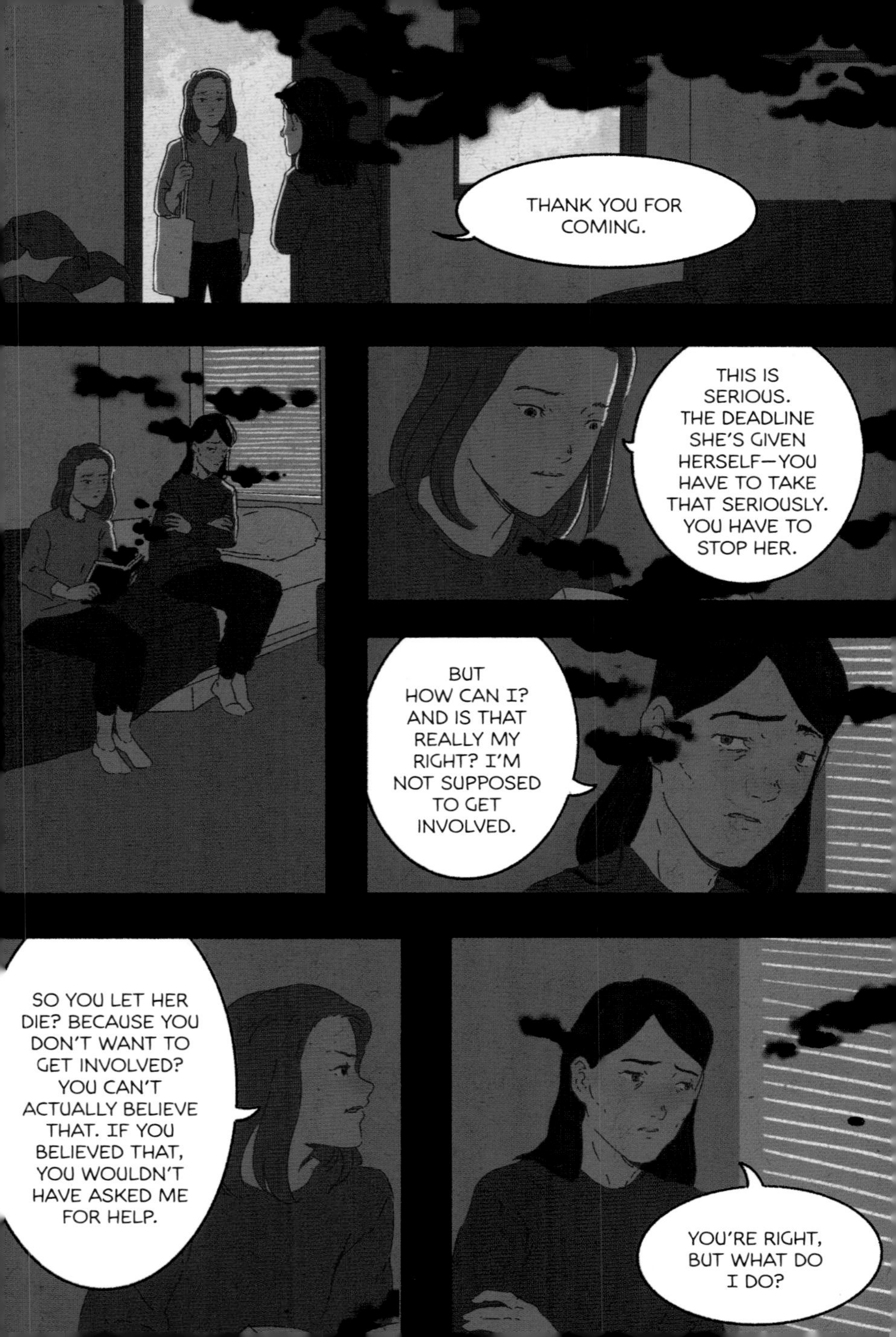
THANK YOU FOR COMING.
THIS IS SERIOUS. THE DEADLINE SHE'S GIVEN HERSELF—YOU HAVE TO TAKE THAT SERIOUSLY. YOU HAVE TO STOP HER.
BUT HOW CAN I? AND IS THAT REALLY MY RIGHT? I'M NOT SUPPOSED TO GET INVOLVED.
SO YOU LET HER DIE? BECAUSE YOU DON'T WANT TO GET INVOLVED? YOU CAN'T ACTUALLY BELIEVE THAT. IF YOU BELIEVED THAT, YOU WOULDN'T HAVE ASKED ME FOR HELP.
YOU'RE RIGHT, BUT WHAT DO I DO?

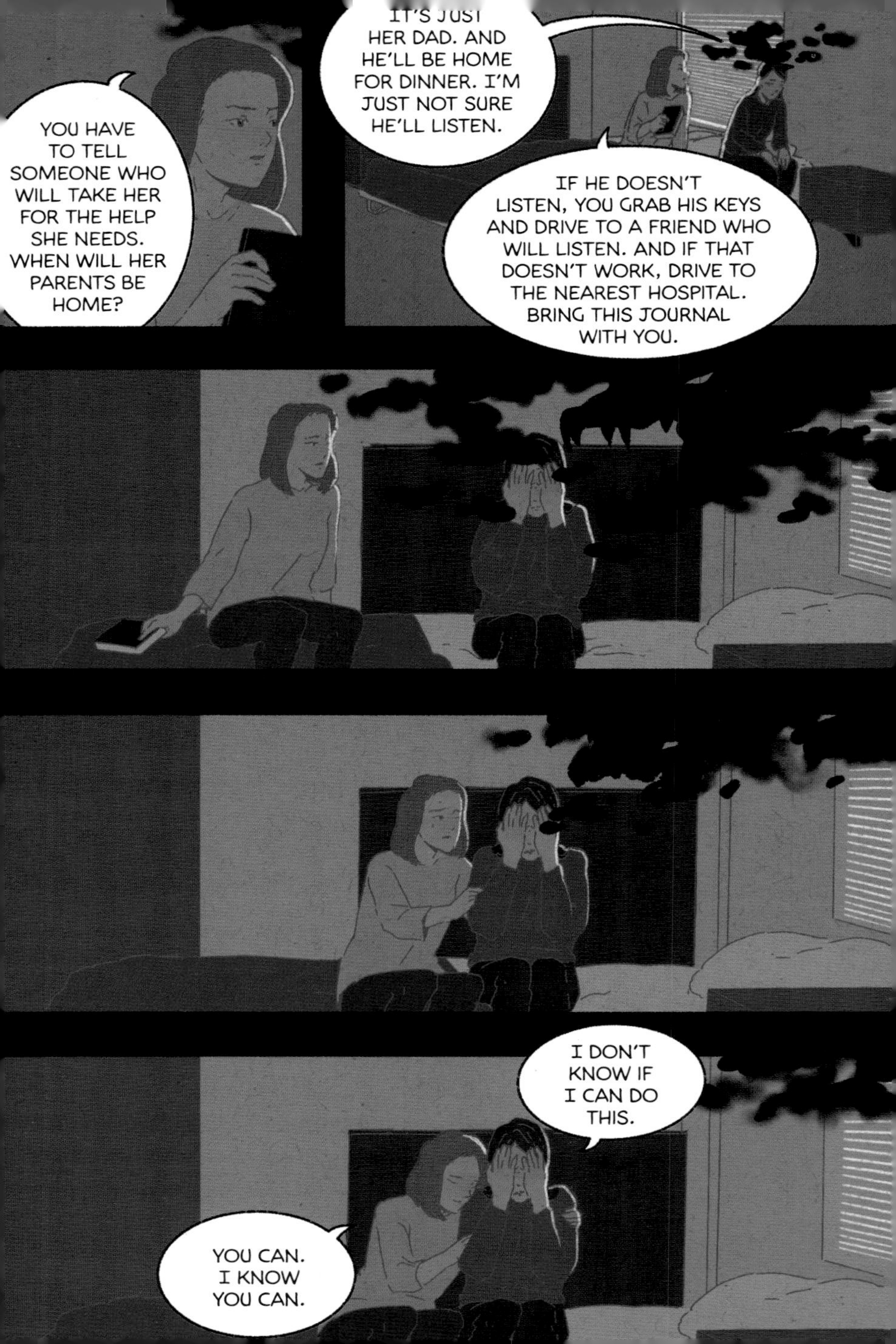
YOU HAVE TO TELL SOMEONE WHO WILL TAKE HER FOR THE HELP SHE NEEDS. WHEN WILL HER PARENTS BE HOME?
IT'S JUST HER DAD. AND HE'LL BE HOME FOR DINNER. I'M JUST NOT SURE HE'LL LISTEN.
IF HE DOESN'T LISTEN, YOU GRAB HIS KEYS AND DRIVE TO A FRIEND WHO WILL LISTEN. AND IF THAT DOESN'T WORK, DRIVE TO THE NEAREST HOSPITAL. BRING THIS JOURNAL WITH YOU.
I DON'T KNOW IF I CAN DO THIS.
YOU CAN. I KNOW YOU CAN.

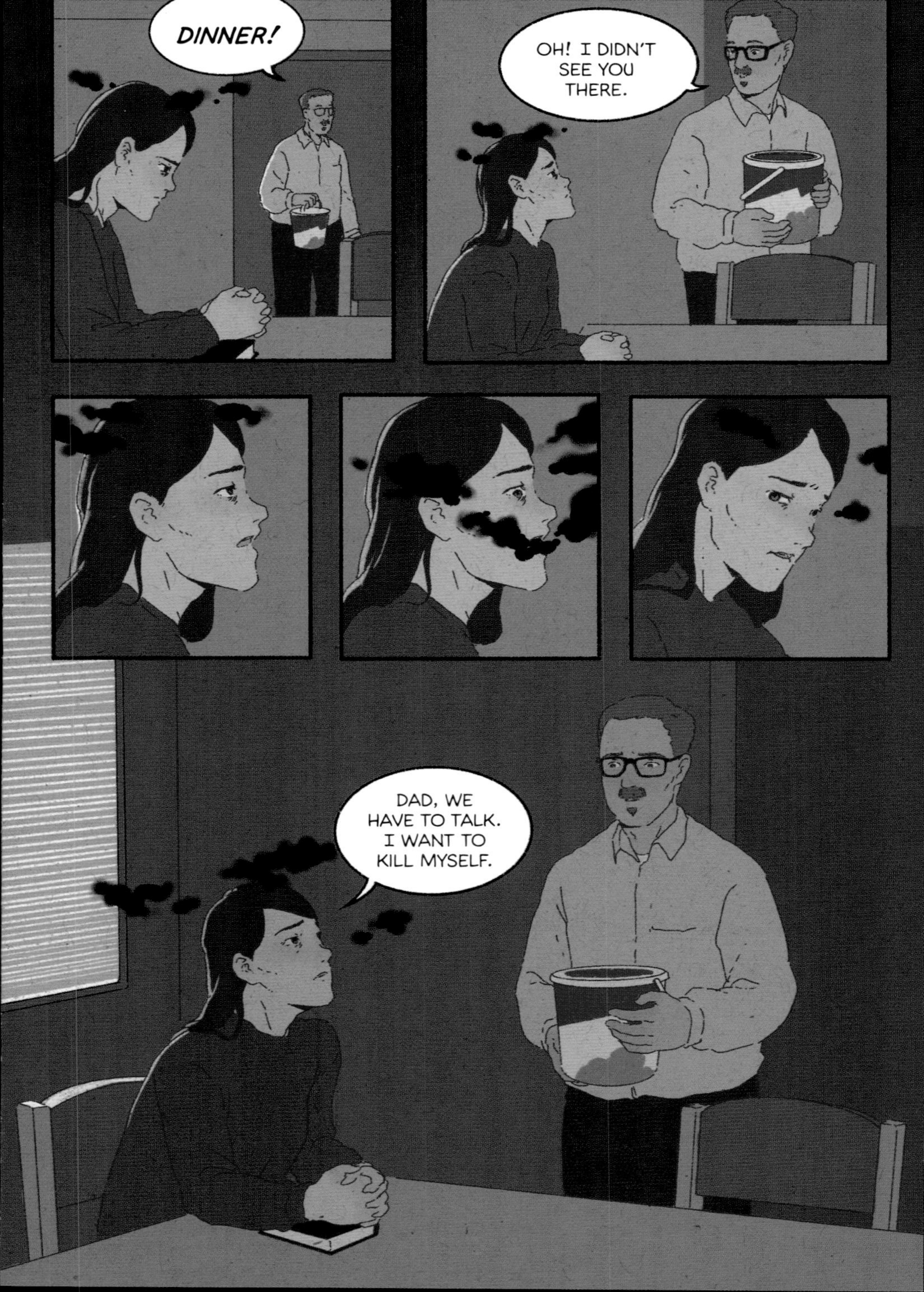
DINNER!
OH! I DIDN'T SEE YOU THERE.
DAD, WE HAVE TO TALK. I WANT TO KILL MYSELF.

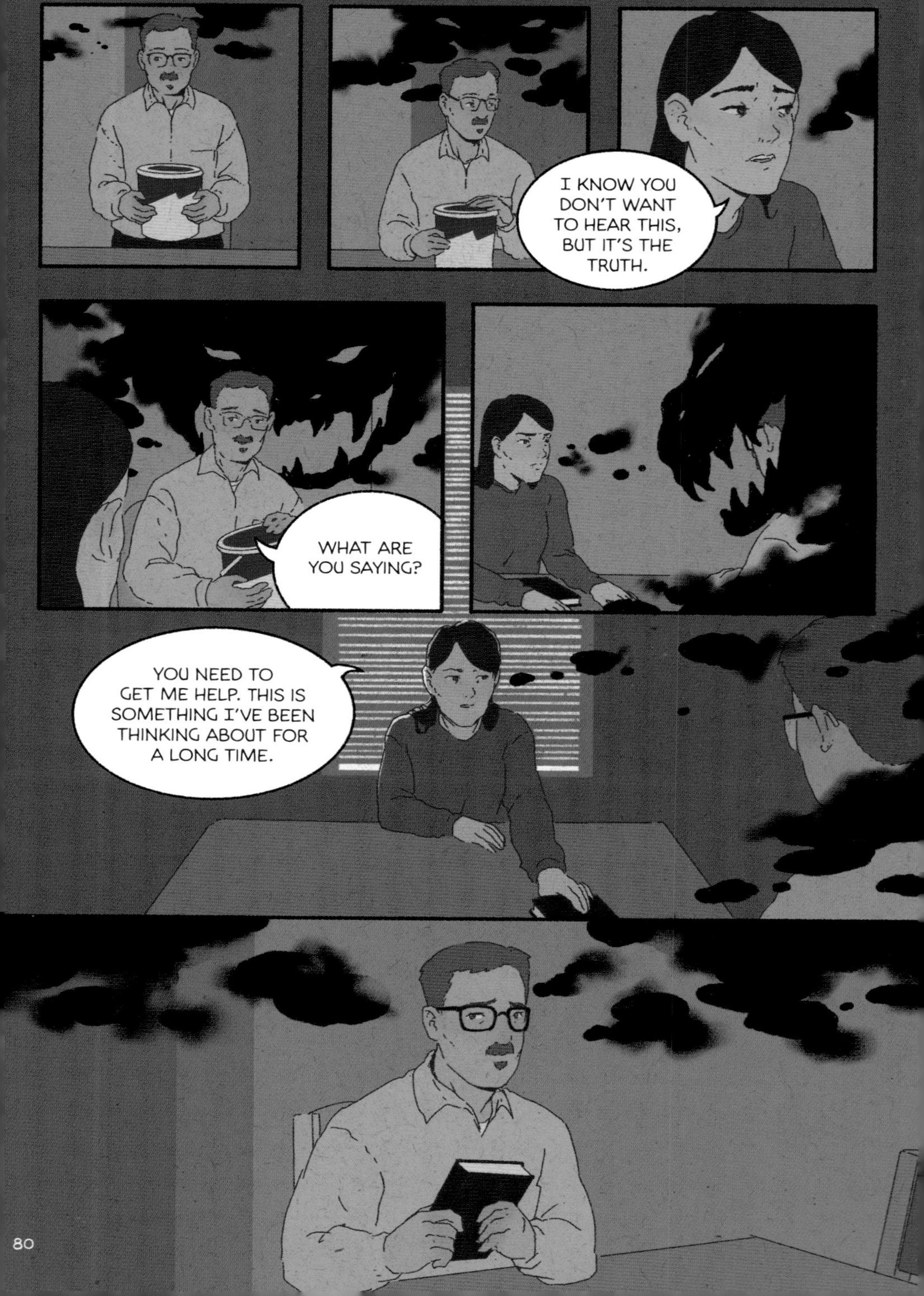
I KNOW YOU DON'T WANT TO HEAR THIS, BUT IT'S THE TRUTH.
WHAT ARE YOU SAYING?
YOU NEED TO GET ME HELP. THIS IS SOMETHING I'VE BEEN THINKING ABOUT FOR A LONG TIME.

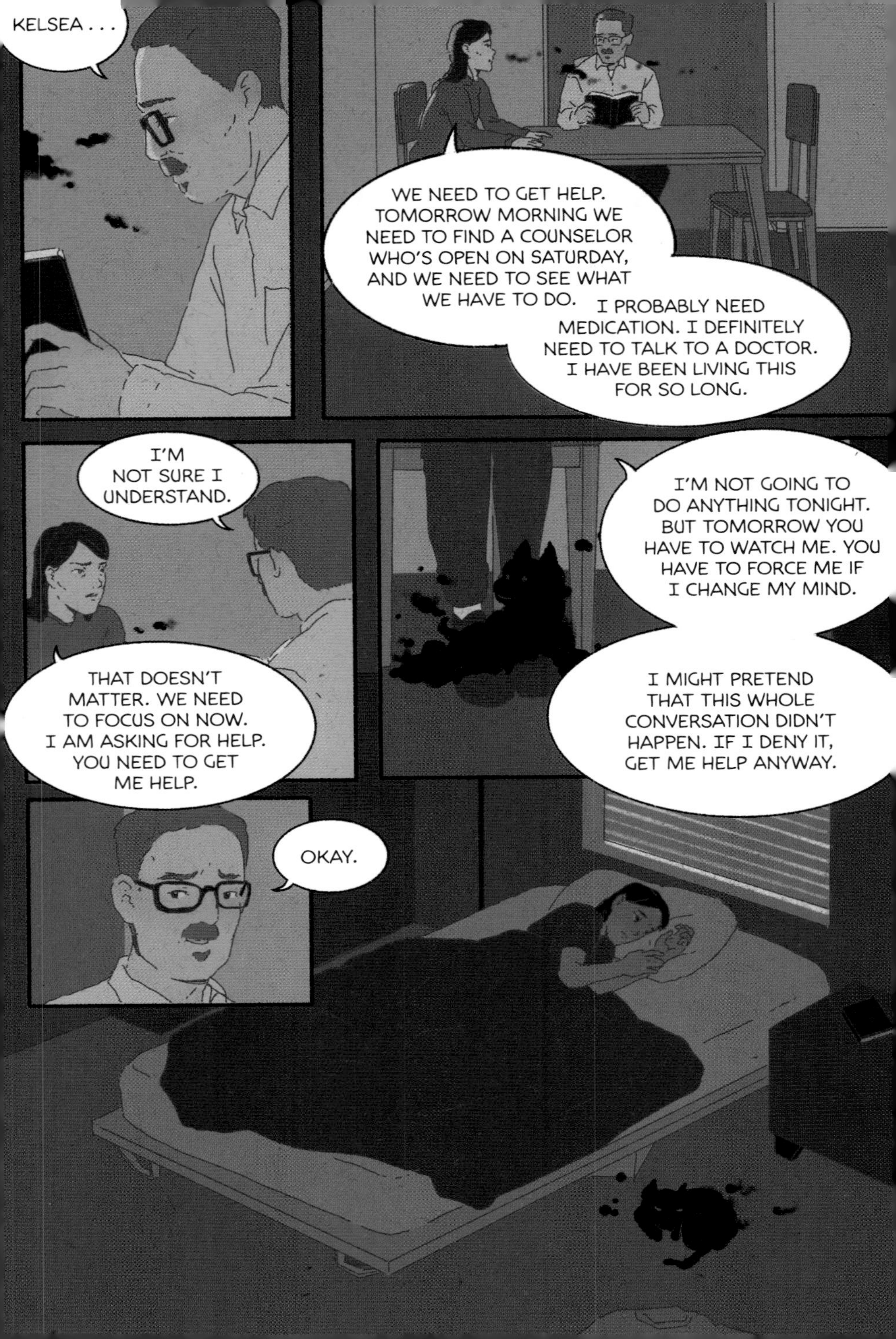
KELSEA . . .
WE NEED TO GET HELP. TOMORROW MORNING WE NEED TO FIND A COUNSELOR WHO'S OPEN ON SATURDAY, AND WE NEED TO SEE WHAT WE HAVE TO DO.
I PROBABLY NEED MEDICATION. I DEFINITELY NEED TO TALK TO A DOCTOR. I HAVE BEEN LIVING THIS FOR SO LONG.
I'M NOT SURE I UNDERSTAND.
THAT DOESN'T MATTER. WE NEED TO FOCUS ON NOW. I AM ASKING FOR HELP. YOU NEED TO GET ME HELP.
I'M NOT GOING TO DO ANYTHING TONIGHT. BUT TOMORROW YOU HAVE TO WATCH ME. YOU HAVE TO FORCE ME IF I CHANGE MY MIND.
I MIGHT PRETEND THAT THIS WHOLE CONVERSATION DIDN'T HAPPEN. IF I DENY IT, GET ME HELP ANYWAY.
OKAY.

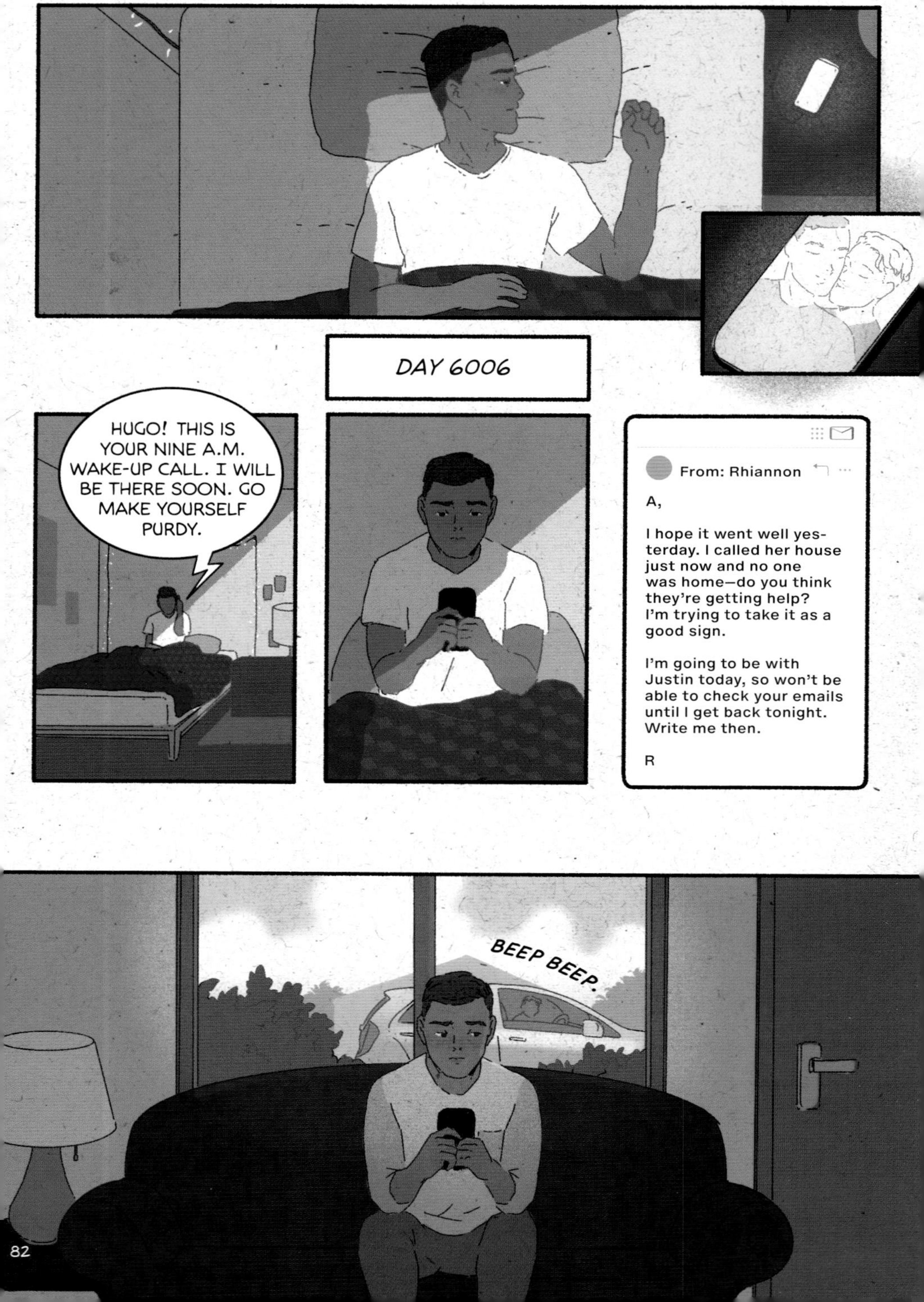
DAY 6006
HUGO! THIS IS YOUR NINE A.M. WAKE-UP CALL. I WILL BE THERE SOON. GO MAKE YOURSELF PURDY.
From: Rhiannon
A,
I hope it went well yesterday. I called her house just now and no one was home—do you think they're getting help? I'm trying to take it as a good sign.
I'm going to be with Justin today, so won't be able to check your emails until I get back tonight. Write me then.
R
BEEP BEEP.

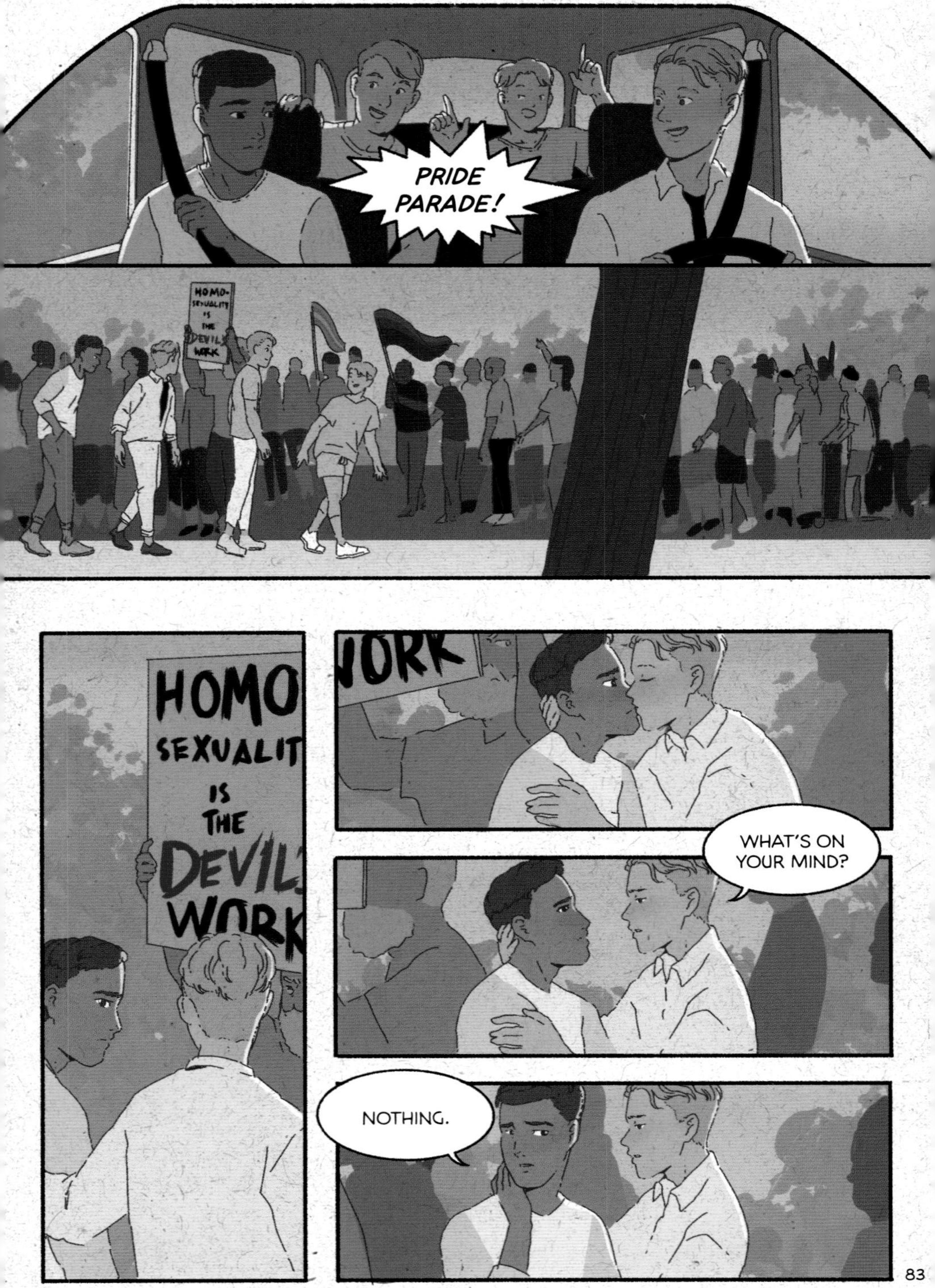
PRIDE PARADE!
HOMOSEXUALITY IS THE DEVIL'S WORK
HOMO SEXUALIT IS THE DEVIL WORK
WHAT'S ON YOUR MIND?
NOTHING.

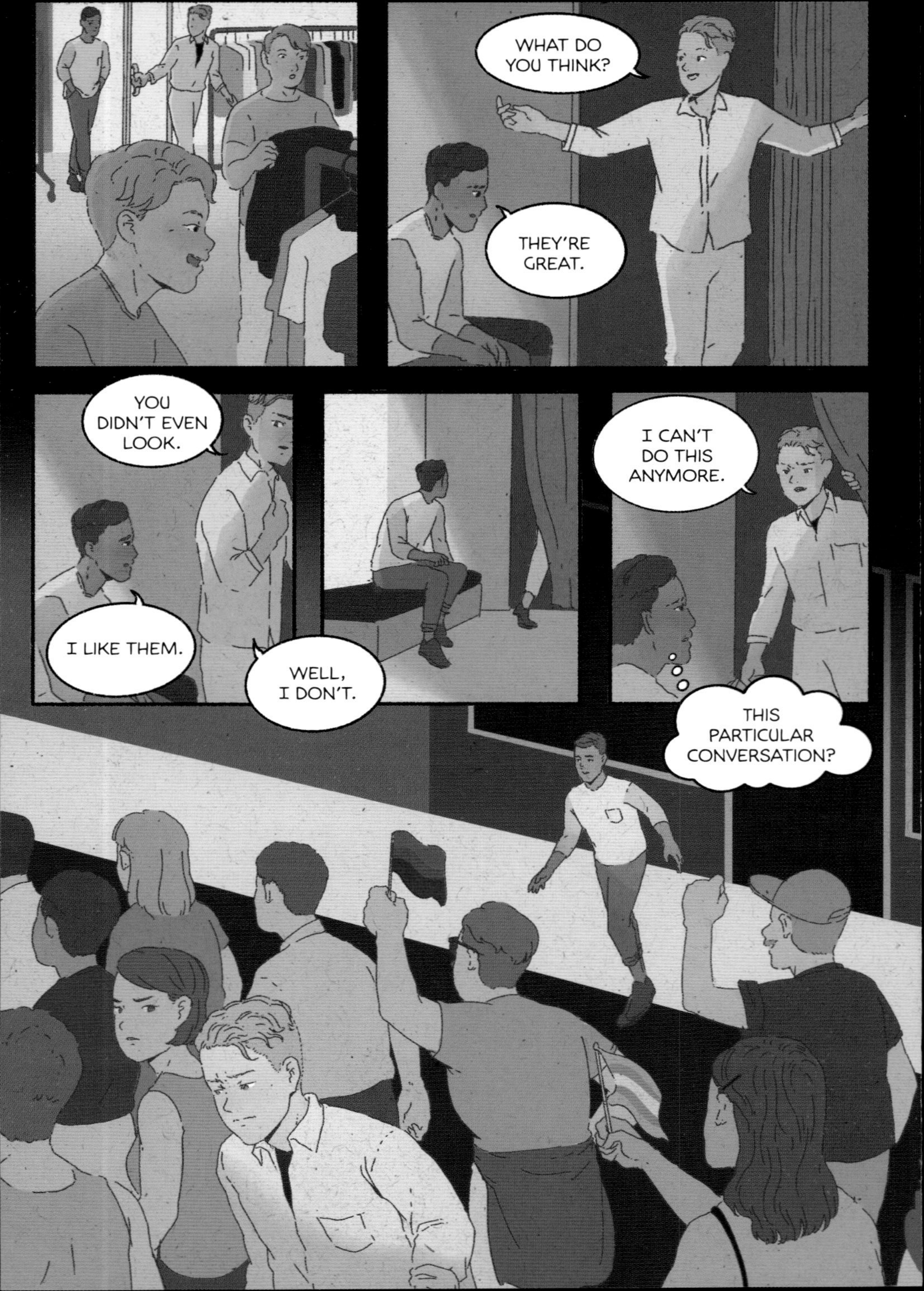
WHAT DO YOU THINK?
THEY'RE GREAT.
YOU DIDN'T EVEN LOOK.
I LIKE THEM.
WELL, I DON'T.
I CAN'T DO THIS ANYMORE.
THIS PARTICULAR CONVERSATION?

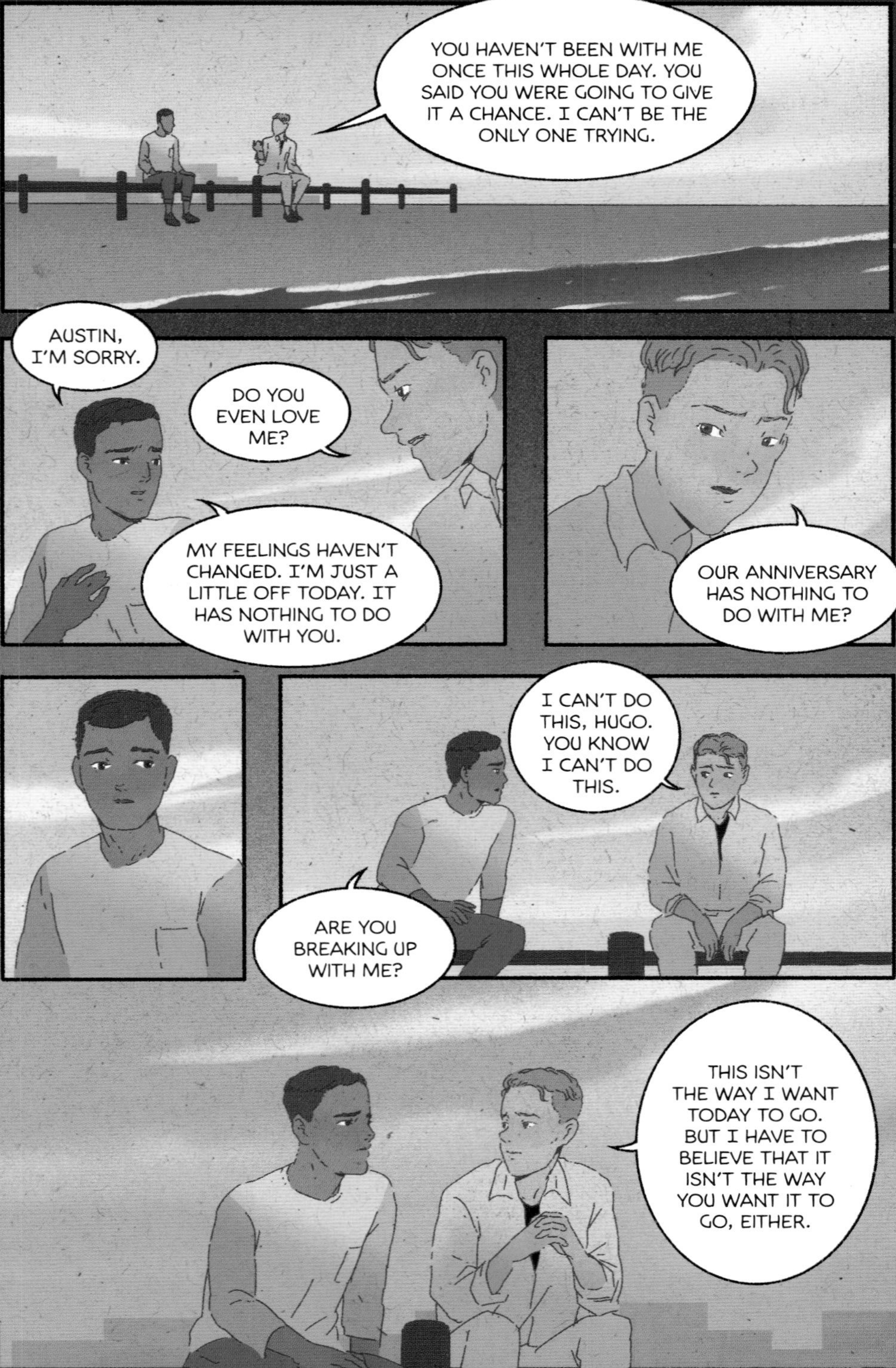
YOU HAVEN'T BEEN WITH ME ONCE THIS WHOLE DAY. YOU SAID YOU WERE GOING TO GIVE IT A CHANCE. I CAN'T BE THE ONLY ONE TRYING.
AUSTIN, I'M SORRY.
DO YOU EVEN LOVE ME?
MY FEELINGS HAVEN'T CHANGED. I'M JUST A LITTLE OFF TODAY. IT HAS NOTHING TO DO WITH YOU.
OUR ANNIVERSARY HAS NOTHING TO DO WITH ME?
I CAN'T DO THIS, HUGO. YOU KNOW I CAN'T DO THIS.
ARE YOU BREAKING UP WITH ME?
THIS ISN'T THE WAY I WANT TODAY TO GO. BUT I HAVE TO BELIEVE THAT IT ISN'T THE WAY YOU WANT IT TO GO, EITHER.

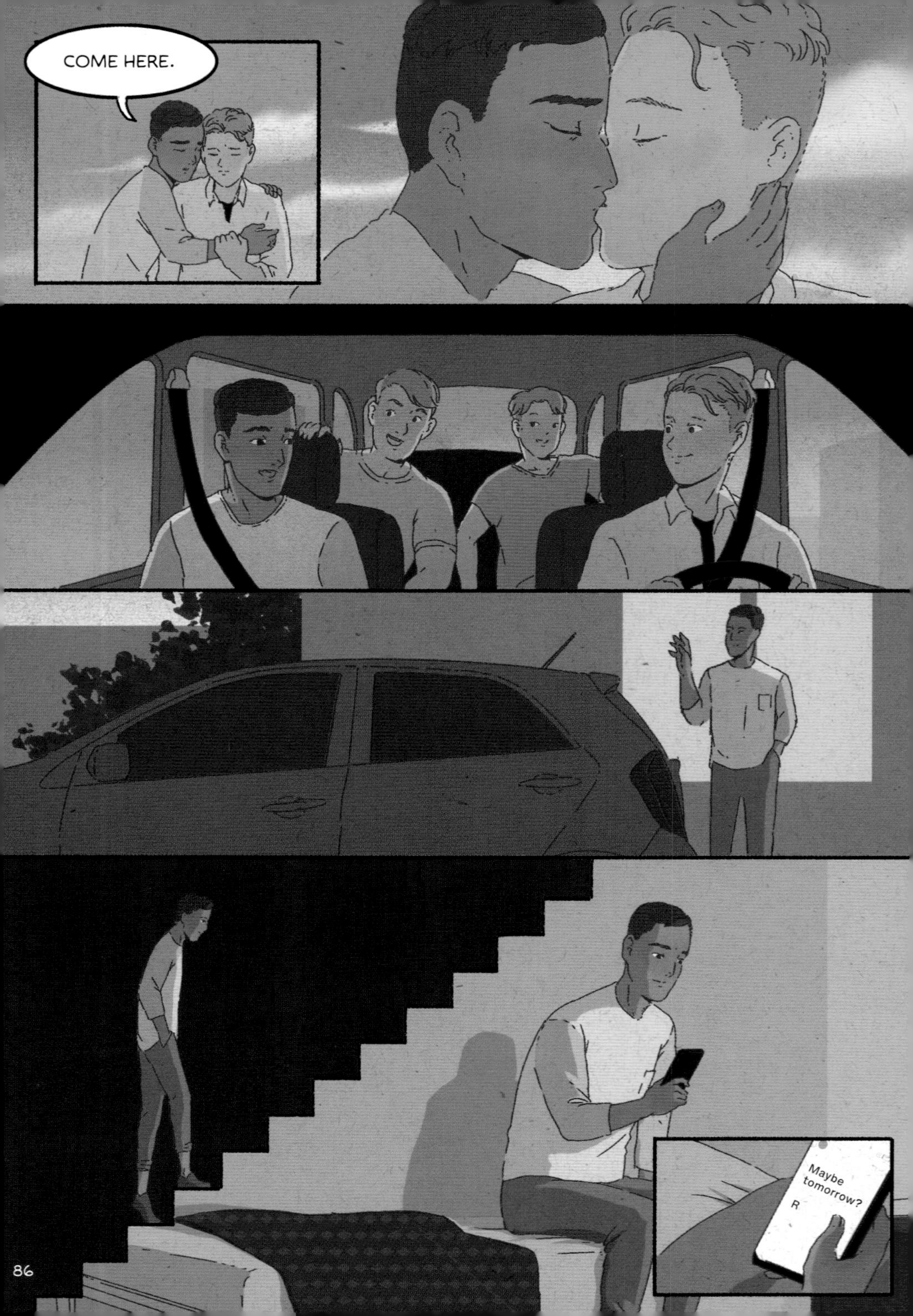
COME HERE.
Maybe tomorrow?
R

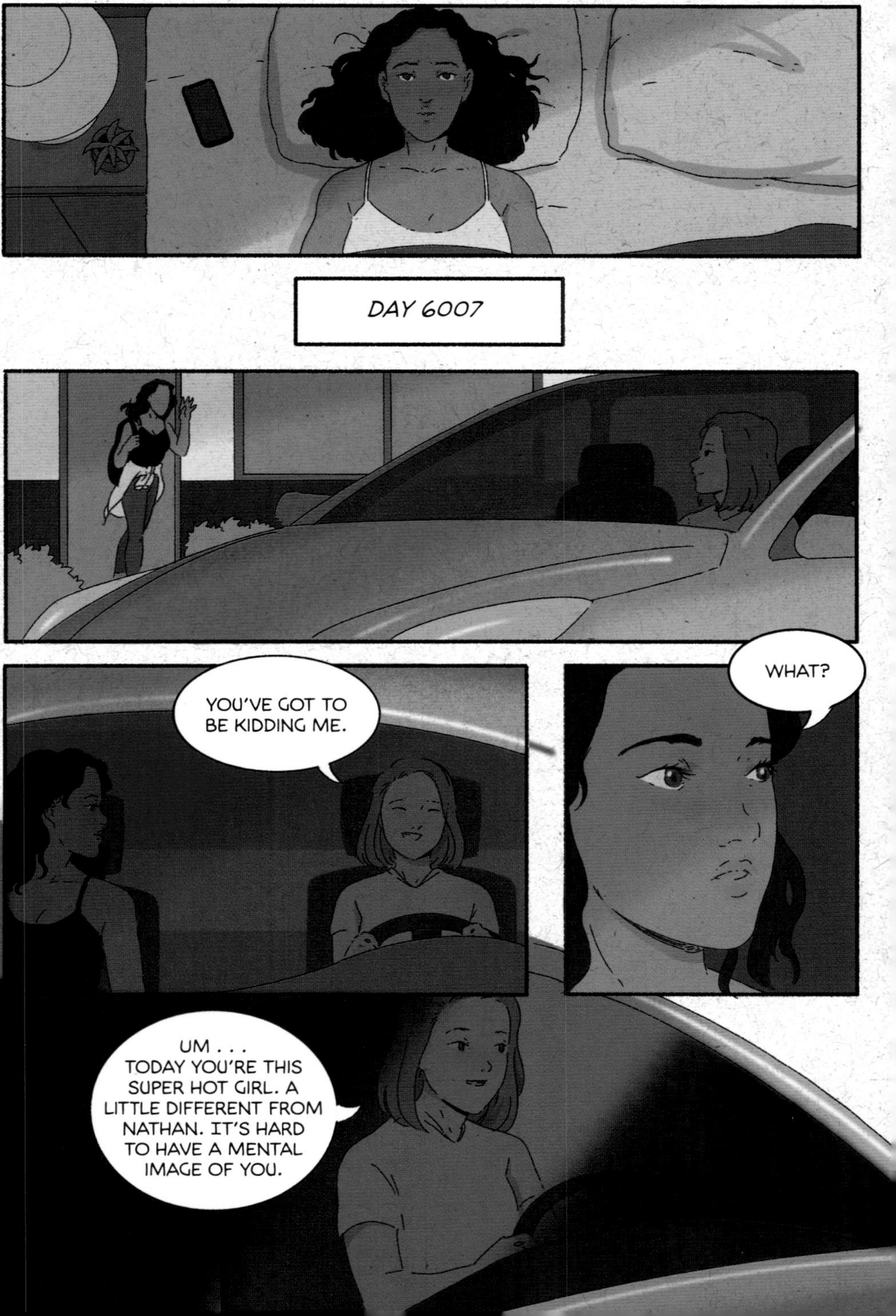
DAY 6007
YOU'VE GOT TO BE KIDDING ME.
WHAT?
UM . . . TODAY YOU'RE THIS SUPER HOT GIRL. A LITTLE DIFFERENT FROM NATHAN. IT'S HARD TO HAVE A MENTAL IMAGE OF YOU.

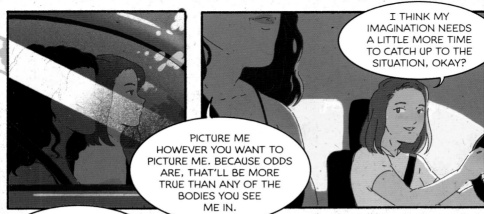

I THINK MY IMAGINATION NEEDS A LITTLE MORE TIME TO CATCH UP TO THE SITUATION, OKAY?

PICTURE ME HOWEVER YOU WANT TO PICTURE ME. BECAUSE ODDS ARE, THAT'LL BE MORE TRUE THAN ANY OF THE BODIES YOU SEE ME IN.

SINCE WE'VE ALREADY BEEN TO THE OCEAN, I FIGURED TODAY WE'D GO TO A FOREST.

I CALLED KELSEA'S HOUSE AGAIN. THIS TIME HER FATHER ANSWERED. I TOLD HIM I WAS A FRIEND OF KELSEA'S AND HE TOLD ME SHE'D GONE AWAY TO GET SOME HELP WITH SOME THINGS. I FIGURE THAT'S A GOOD SIGN, RIGHT?

I THINK SO.

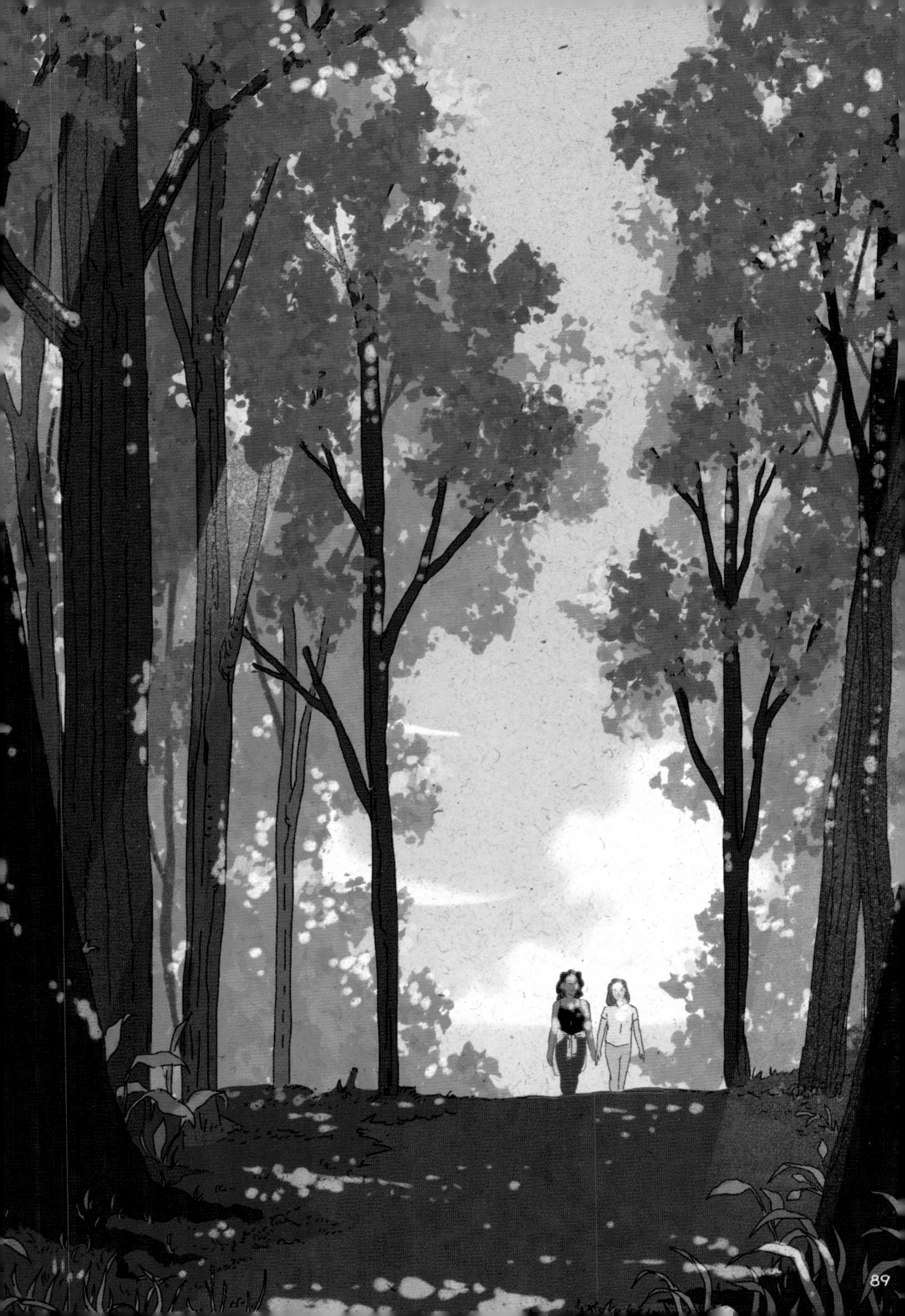

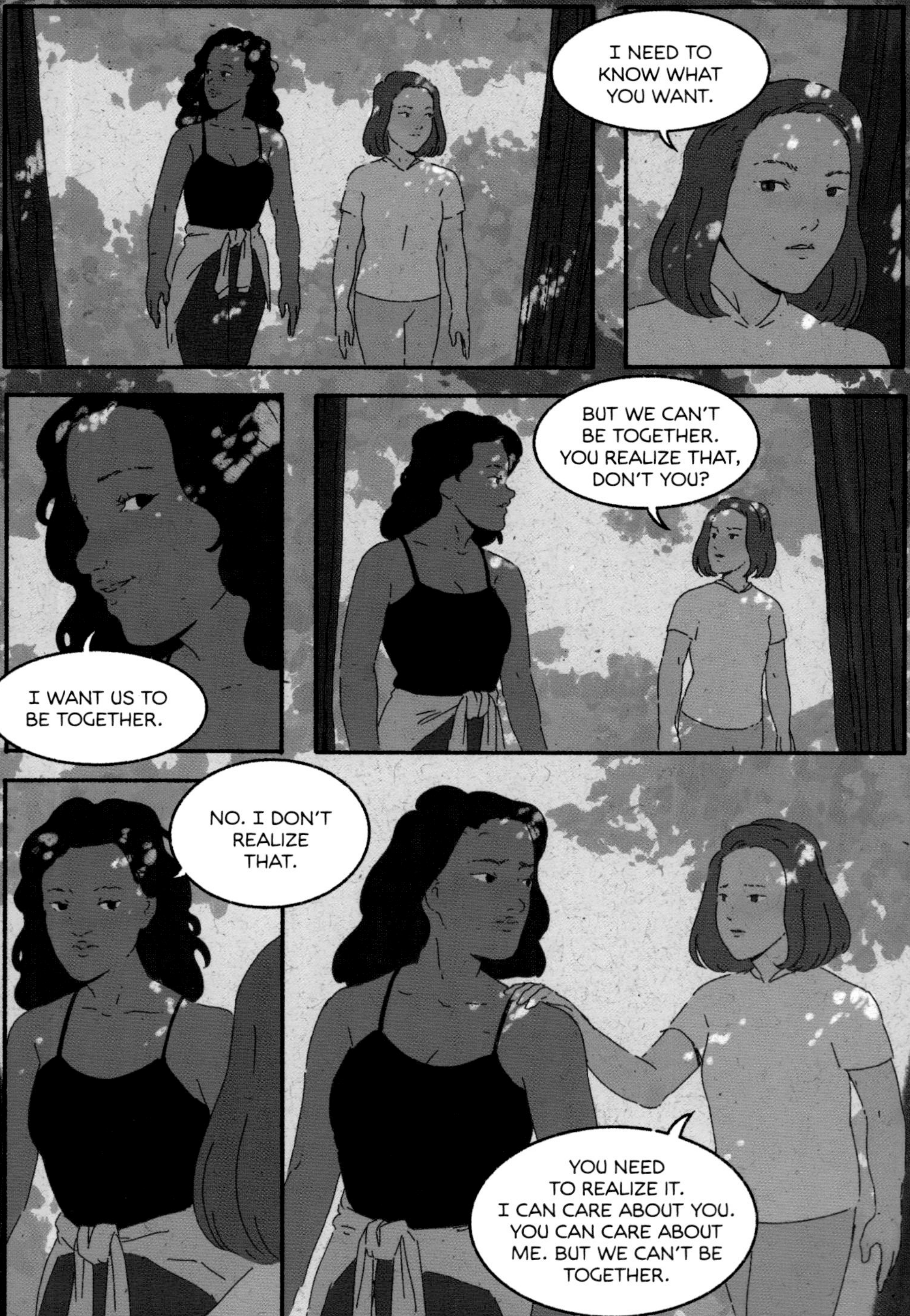
I NEED TO KNOW WHAT YOU WANT.
I WANT US TO BE TOGETHER.
BUT WE CAN'T BE TOGETHER. YOU REALIZE THAT, DON'T YOU?
NO. I DON'T REALIZE THAT.
YOU NEED TO REALIZE IT. I CAN CARE ABOUT YOU. YOU CAN CARE ABOUT ME. BUT WE CAN'T BE TOGETHER.

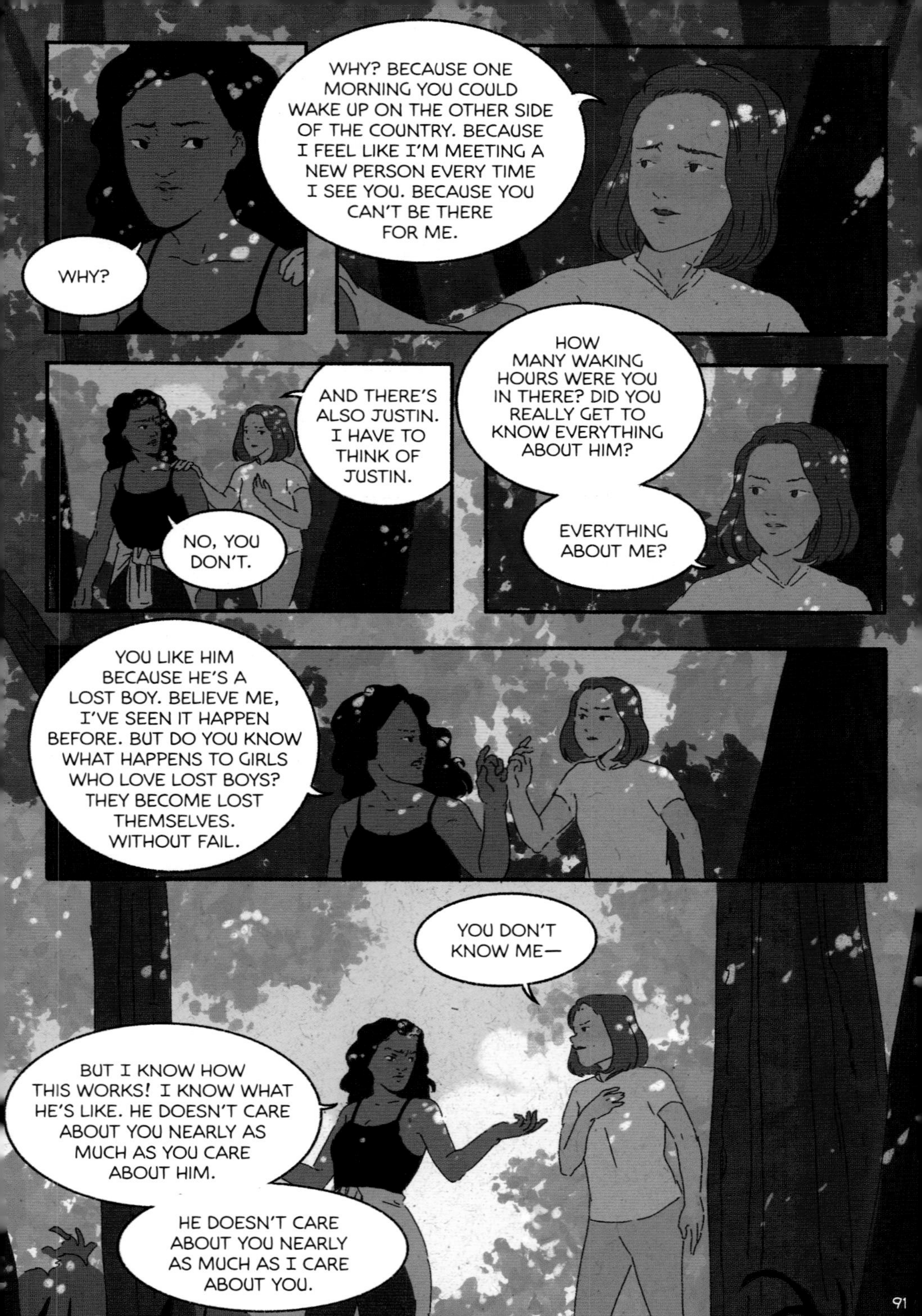
WHY?
WHY? BECAUSE ONE MORNING YOU COULD WAKE UP ON THE OTHER SIDE OF THE COUNTRY. BECAUSE I FEEL LIKE I'M MEETING A NEW PERSON EVERY TIME I SEE YOU. BECAUSE YOU CAN'T BE THERE FOR ME.
AND THERE'S ALSO JUSTIN. I HAVE TO THINK OF JUSTIN.
NO, YOU DON'T.
HOW MANY WAKING HOURS WERE YOU IN THERE? DID YOU REALLY GET TO KNOW EVERYTHING ABOUT HIM?
EVERYTHING ABOUT ME?
YOU LIKE HIM BECAUSE HE'S A LOST BOY. BELIEVE ME, I'VE SEEN IT HAPPEN BEFORE. BUT DO YOU KNOW WHAT HAPPENS TO GIRLS WHO LOVE LOST BOYS? THEY BECOME LOST THEMSELVES. WITHOUT FAIL.
YOU DON'T KNOW ME—
BUT I KNOW HOW THIS WORKS! I KNOW WHAT HE'S LIKE. HE DOESN'T CARE ABOUT YOU NEARLY AS MUCH AS YOU CARE ABOUT HIM.
HE DOESN'T CARE ABOUT YOU NEARLY AS MUCH AS I CARE ABOUT YOU.

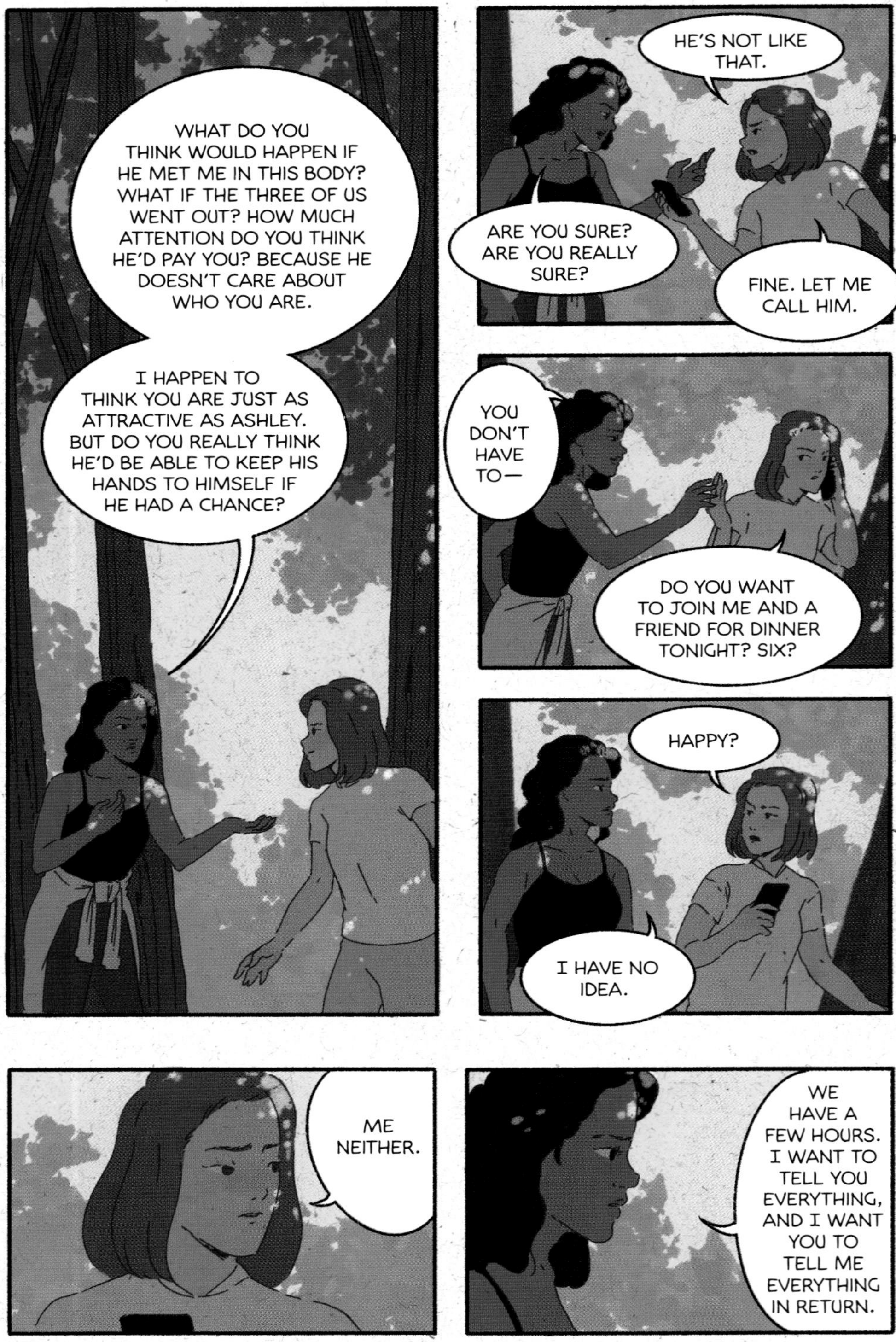
WHAT DO YOU THINK WOULD HAPPEN IF HE MET ME IN THIS BODY? WHAT IF THE THREE OF US WENT OUT? HOW MUCH ATTENTION DO YOU THINK HE'D PAY YOU? BECAUSE HE DOESN'T CARE ABOUT WHO YOU ARE.
I HAPPEN TO THINK YOU ARE JUST AS ATTRACTIVE AS ASHLEY. BUT DO YOU REALLY THINK HE'D BE ABLE TO KEEP HIS HANDS TO HIMSELF IF HE HAD A CHANCE?
HE'S NOT LIKE THAT.
ARE YOU SURE? ARE YOU REALLY SURE?
FINE. LET ME CALL HIM.
YOU DON'T HAVE TO—
DO YOU WANT TO JOIN ME AND A FRIEND FOR DINNER TONIGHT? SIX?
HAPPY?
I HAVE NO IDEA.
ME NEITHER.
WE HAVE A FEW HOURS. I WANT TO TELL YOU EVERYTHING, AND I WANT YOU TO TELL ME EVERYTHING IN RETURN.

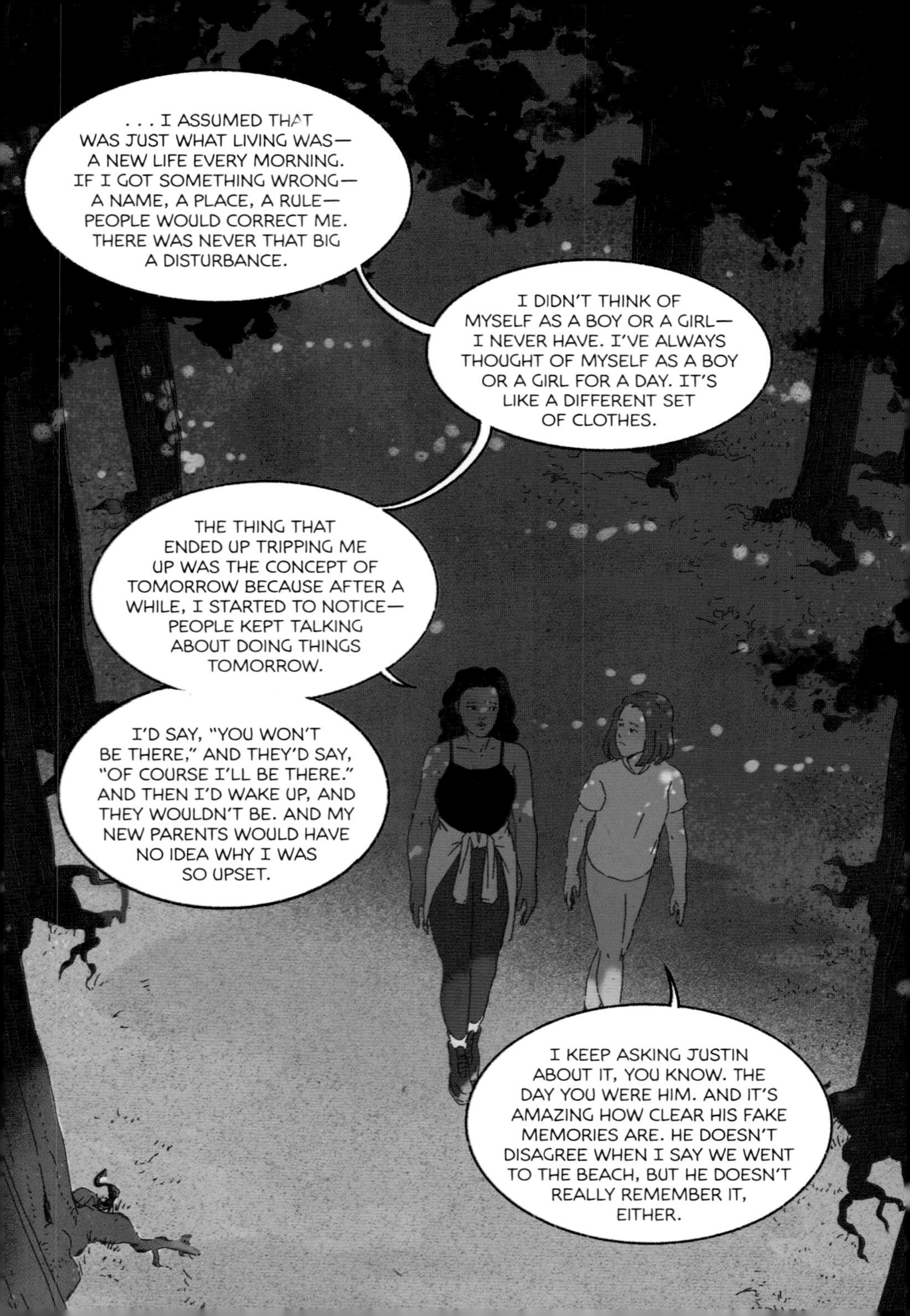
. . . I ASSUMED THAT WAS JUST WHAT LIVING WAS— A NEW LIFE EVERY MORNING. IF I GOT SOMETHING WRONG— A NAME, A PLACE, A RULE— PEOPLE WOULD CORRECT ME. THERE WAS NEVER THAT BIG A DISTURBANCE.
I DIDN'T THINK OF MYSELF AS A BOY OR A GIRL— I NEVER HAVE. I'VE ALWAYS THOUGHT OF MYSELF AS A BOY OR A GIRL FOR A DAY. IT'S LIKE A DIFFERENT SET OF CLOTHES.
THE THING THAT ENDED UP TRIPPING ME UP WAS THE CONCEPT OF TOMORROW BECAUSE AFTER A WHILE, I STARTED TO NOTICE— PEOPLE KEPT TALKING ABOUT DOING THINGS TOMORROW.
I'D SAY, "YOU WON'T BE THERE," AND THEY'D SAY, "OF COURSE I'LL BE THERE." AND THEN I'D WAKE UP, AND THEY WOULDN'T BE. AND MY NEW PARENTS WOULD HAVE NO IDEA WHY I WAS SO UPSET.
I KEEP ASKING JUSTIN ABOUT IT, YOU KNOW. THE DAY YOU WERE HIM. AND IT'S AMAZING HOW CLEAR HIS FAKE MEMORIES ARE. HE DOESN'T DISAGREE WHEN I SAY WE WENT TO THE BEACH, BUT HE DOESN'T REALLY REMEMBER IT, EITHER.

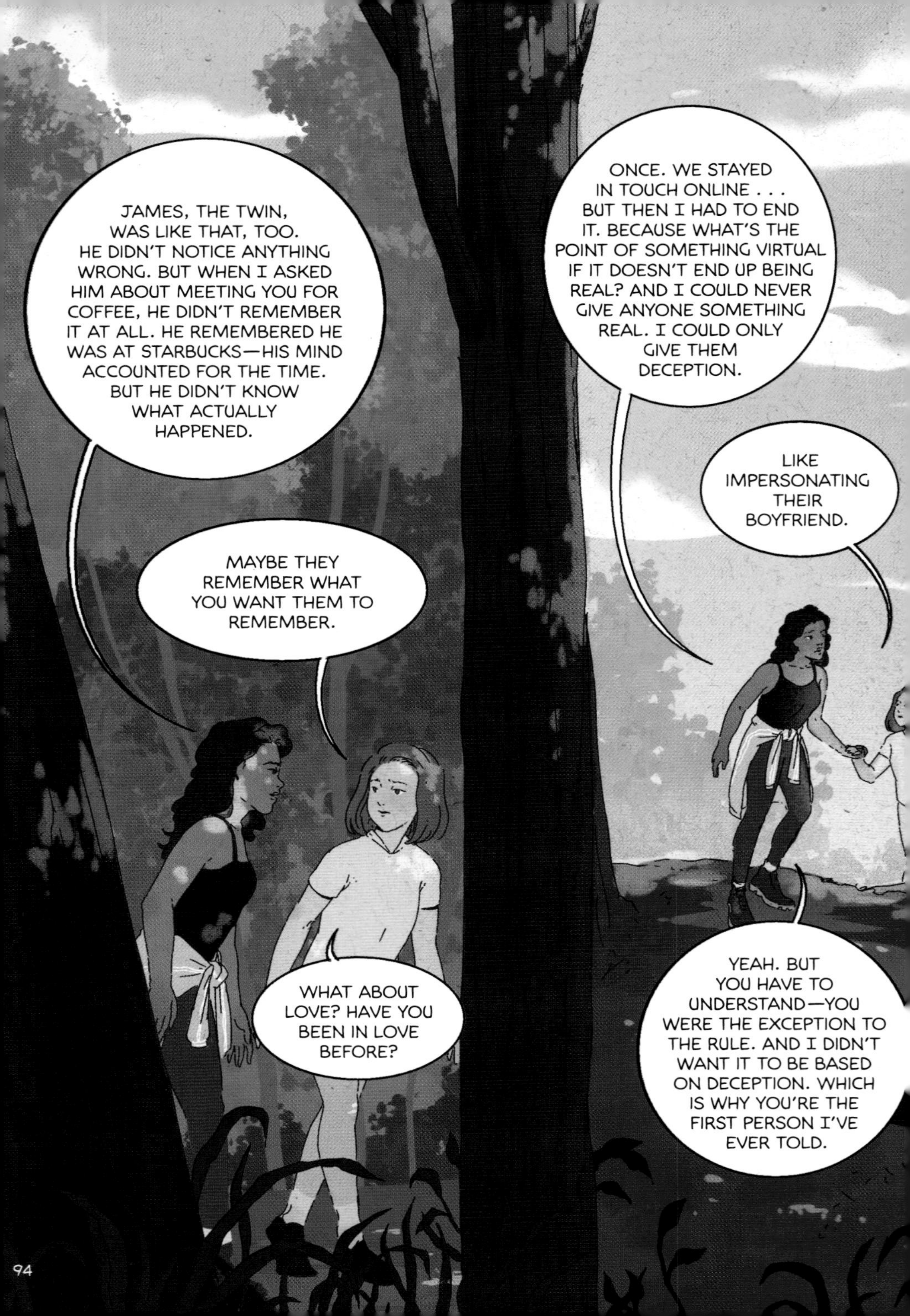
JAMES, THE TWIN, WAS LIKE THAT, TOO. HE DIDN'T NOTICE ANYTHING WRONG. BUT WHEN I ASKED HIM ABOUT MEETING YOU FOR COFFEE, HE DIDN'T REMEMBER IT AT ALL. HE REMEMBERED HE WAS AT STARBUCKS—HIS MIND ACCOUNTED FOR THE TIME. BUT HE DIDN'T KNOW WHAT ACTUALLY HAPPENED.
MAYBE THEY REMEMBER WHAT YOU WANT THEM TO REMEMBER.
WHAT ABOUT LOVE? HAVE YOU BEEN IN LOVE BEFORE?
ONCE. WE STAYED IN TOUCH ONLINE . . . BUT THEN I HAD TO END IT. BECAUSE WHAT'S THE POINT OF SOMETHING VIRTUAL IF IT DOESN'T END UP BEING REAL? AND I COULD NEVER GIVE ANYONE SOMETHING REAL. I COULD ONLY GIVE THEM DECEPTION.
LIKE IMPERSONATING THEIR BOYFRIEND.
YEAH. BUT YOU HAVE TO UNDERSTAND—YOU WERE THE EXCEPTION TO THE RULE. AND I DIDN'T WANT IT TO BE BASED ON DECEPTION. WHICH IS WHY YOU'RE THE FIRST PERSON I'VE EVER TOLD.

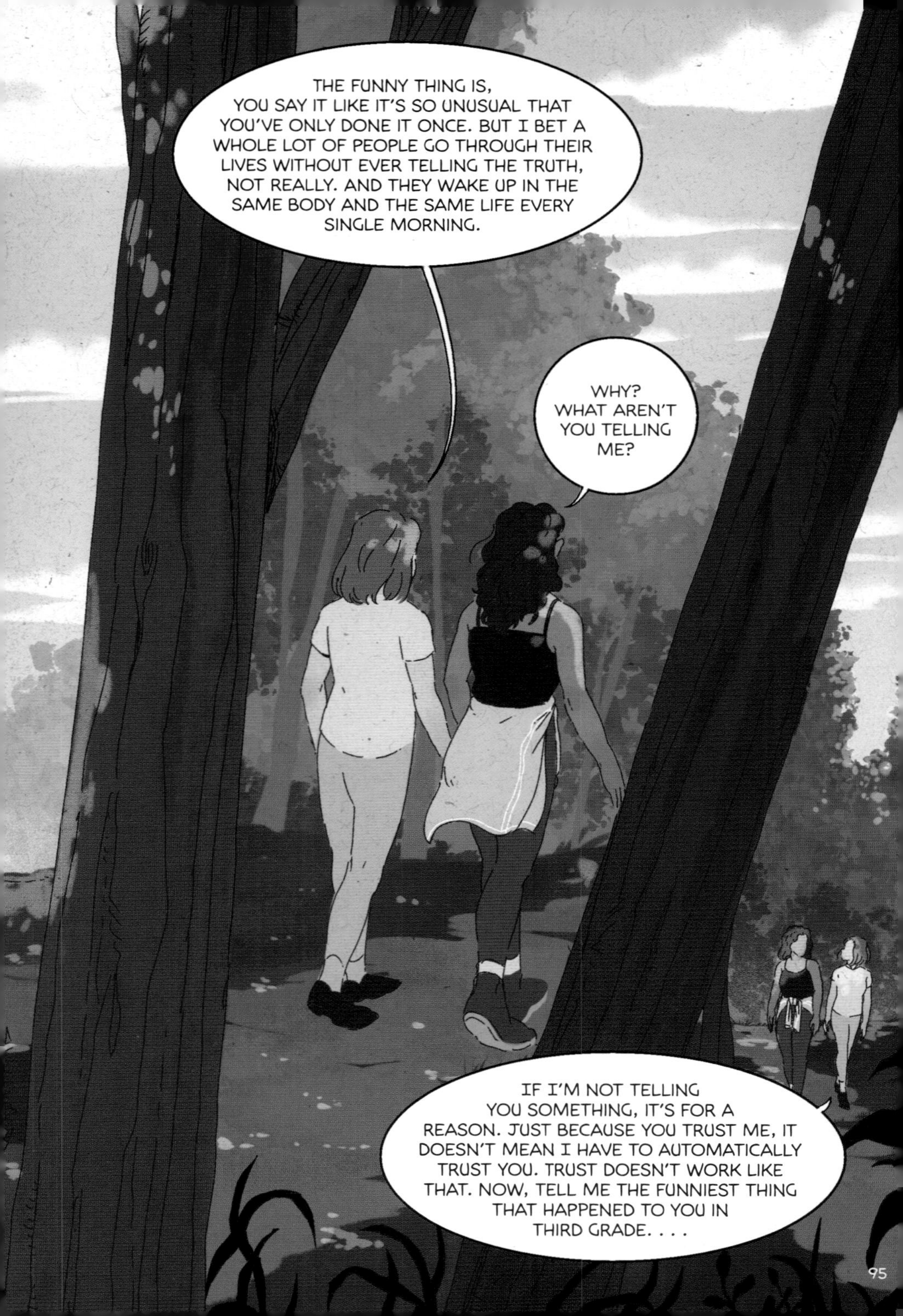
THE FUNNY THING IS, YOU SAY IT LIKE IT'S SO UNUSUAL THAT YOU'VE ONLY DONE IT ONCE. BUT I BET A WHOLE LOT OF PEOPLE GO THROUGH THEIR LIVES WITHOUT EVER TELLING THE TRUTH, NOT REALLY. AND THEY WAKE UP IN THE SAME BODY AND THE SAME LIFE EVERY SINGLE MORNING.
WHY? WHAT AREN'T YOU TELLING ME?
IF I'M NOT TELLING YOU SOMETHING, IT'S FOR A REASON. JUST BECAUSE YOU TRUST ME, IT DOESN'T MEAN I HAVE TO AUTOMATICALLY TRUST YOU. TRUST DOESN'T WORK LIKE THAT. NOW, TELL ME THE FUNNIEST THING THAT HAPPENED TO YOU IN THIRD GRADE. . . .

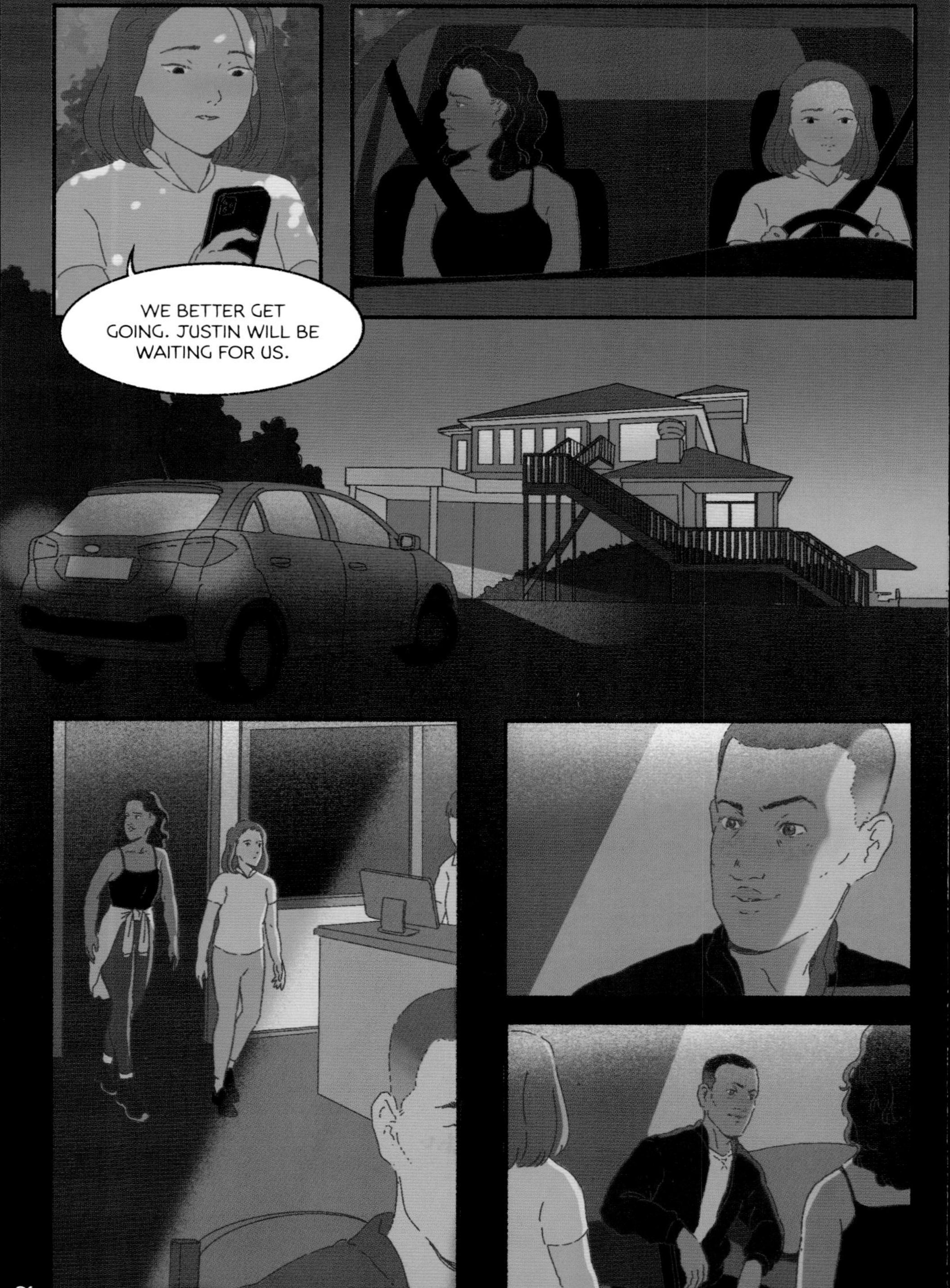
WE BETTER GET GOING. JUSTIN WILL BE WAITING FOR US.

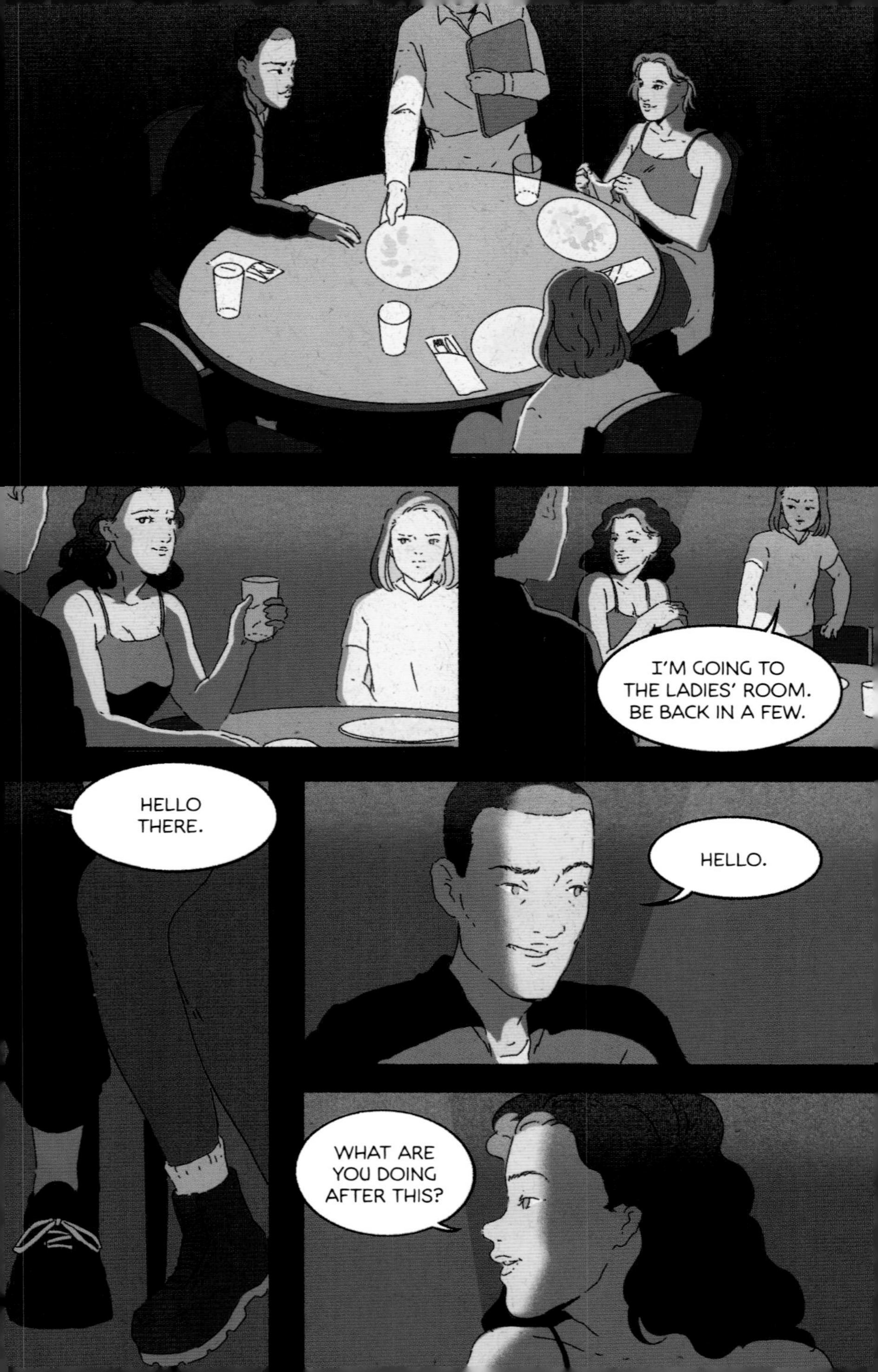
I'M GOING TO THE LADIES' ROOM. BE BACK IN A FEW.
HELLO THERE.
HELLO.
WHAT ARE YOU DOING AFTER THIS?

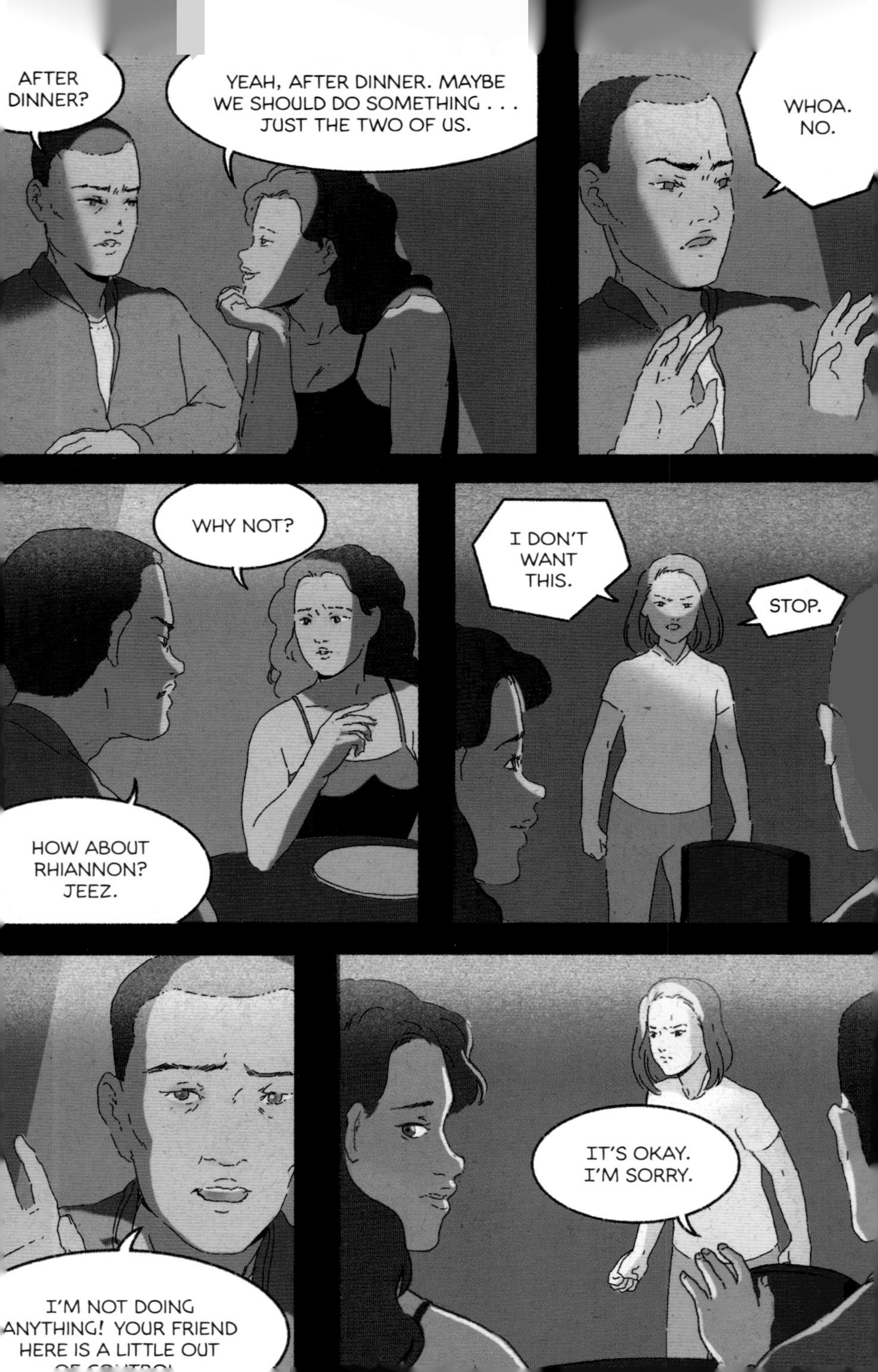
AFTER DINNER?
YEAH, AFTER DINNER. MAYBE WE SHOULD DO SOMETHING . . . JUST THE TWO OF US.
WHOA. NO.
WHY NOT?
HOW ABOUT RHIANNON? JEEZ.
I DON'T WANT THIS.
STOP.
I'M NOT DOING ANYTHING! YOUR FRIEND HERE IS A LITTLE OUT
IT'S OKAY. I'M SORRY.

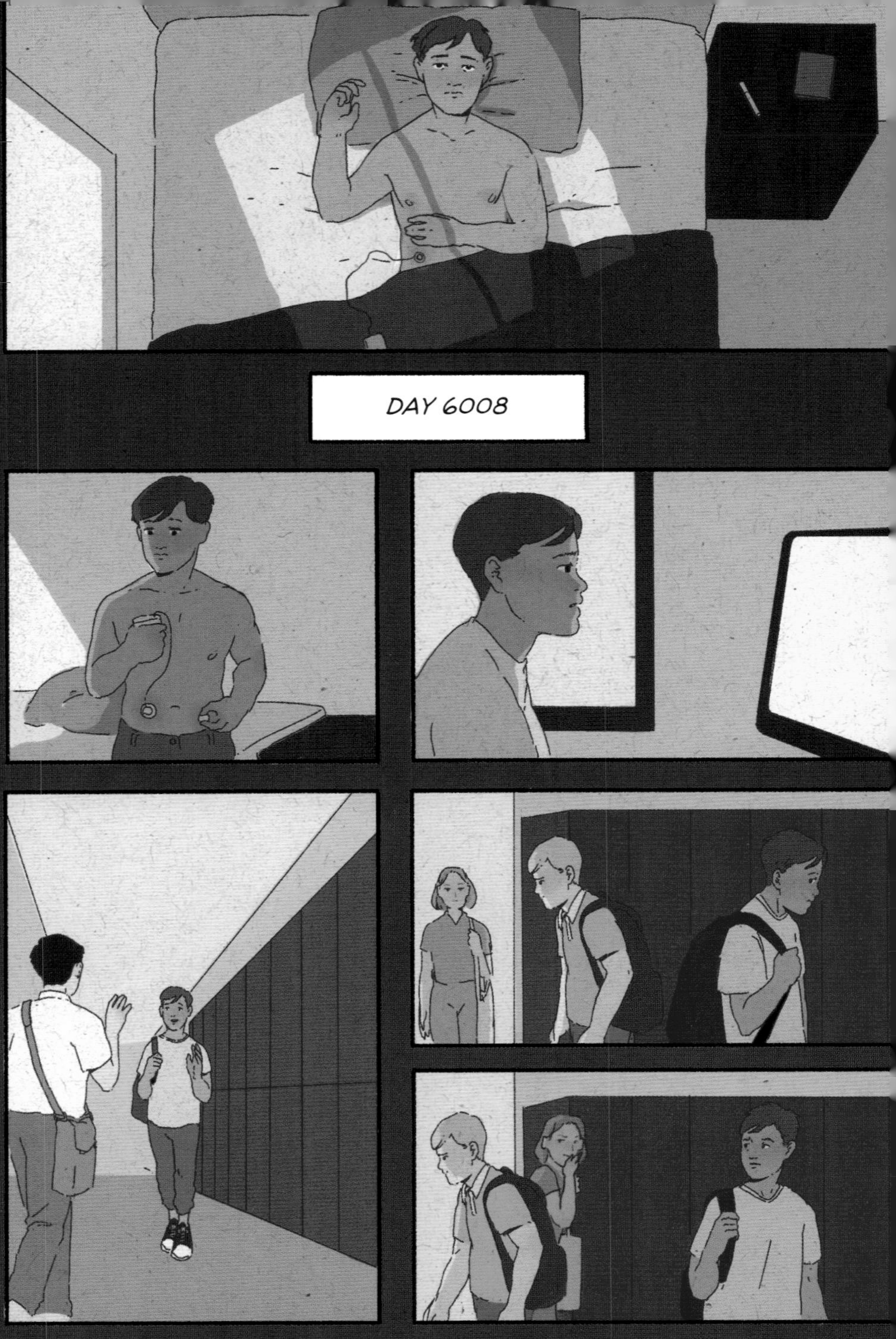
DAY 6008

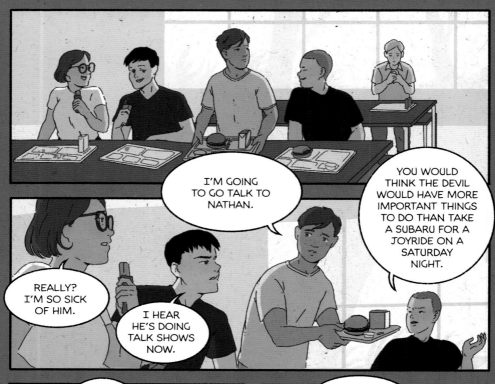

I'M GOING TO GO TALK TO NATHAN.

YOU WOULD THINK THE DEVIL WOULD HAVE MORE IMPORTANT THINGS TO DO THAN TAKE A SUBARU FOR A JOYRIDE ON A SATURDAY NIGHT.

REALLY? I'M SO SICK OF HIM.

I HEAR HE'S DOING TALK SHOWS NOW.

DO YOU MIND?

HOW ARE YOU DOING?

OKAY, I GUESS.

NO. NOT AT ALL.

YOUR FRIENDS ARE LOOKING AT US.

WHATEVER. DON'T PAY ATTENTION TO THEM. TO ANY OF THEM.

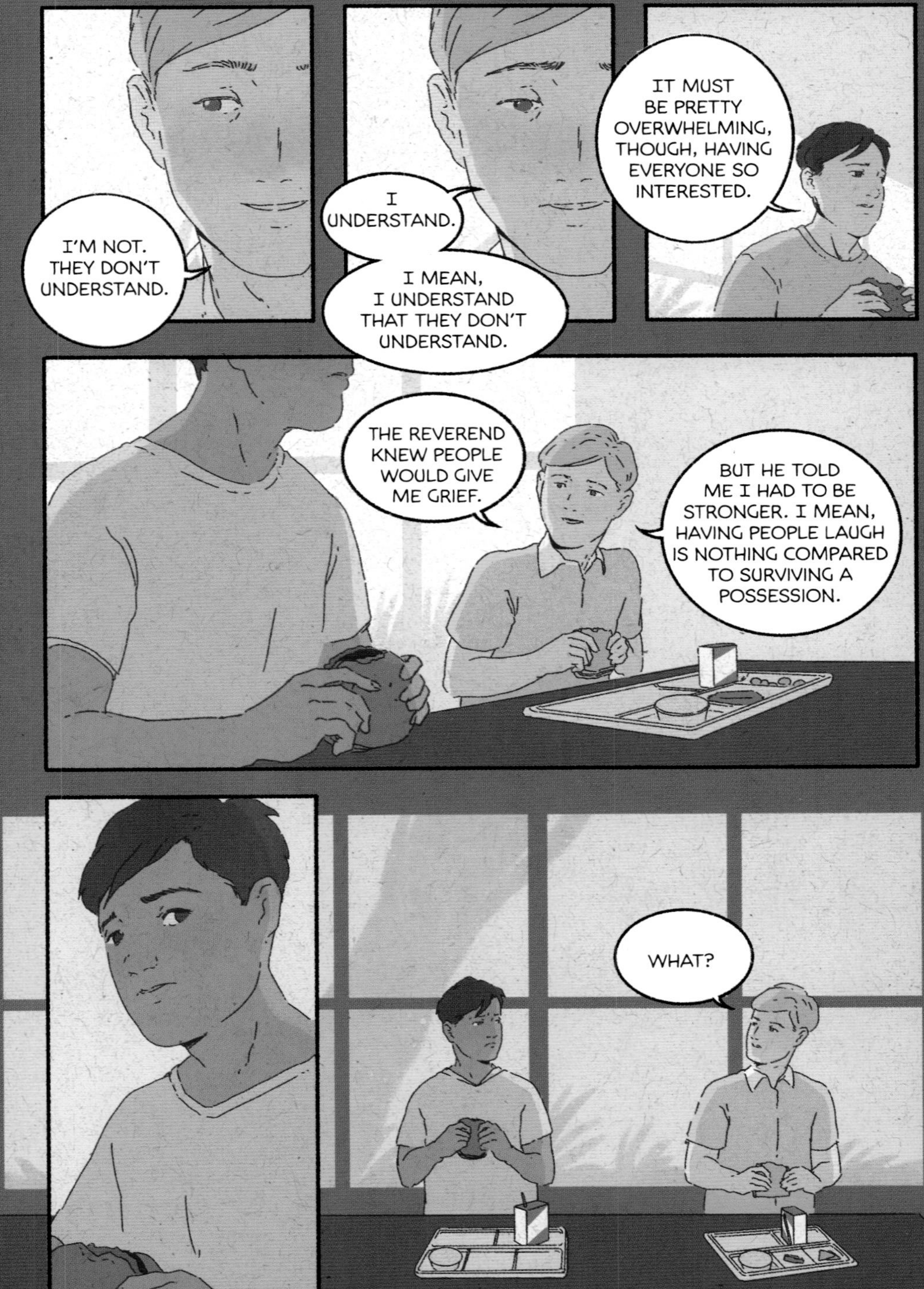
I'M NOT. THEY DON'T UNDERSTAND.
I UNDERSTAND.
I MEAN, I UNDERSTAND THAT THEY DON'T UNDERSTAND.
IT MUST BE PRETTY OVERWHELMING, THOUGH, HAVING EVERYONE SO INTERESTED.
THE REVEREND KNEW PEOPLE WOULD GIVE ME GRIEF.
BUT HE TOLD ME I HAD TO BE STRONGER. I MEAN, HAVING PEOPLE LAUGH IS NOTHING COMPARED TO SURVIVING A POSSESSION.
WHAT?

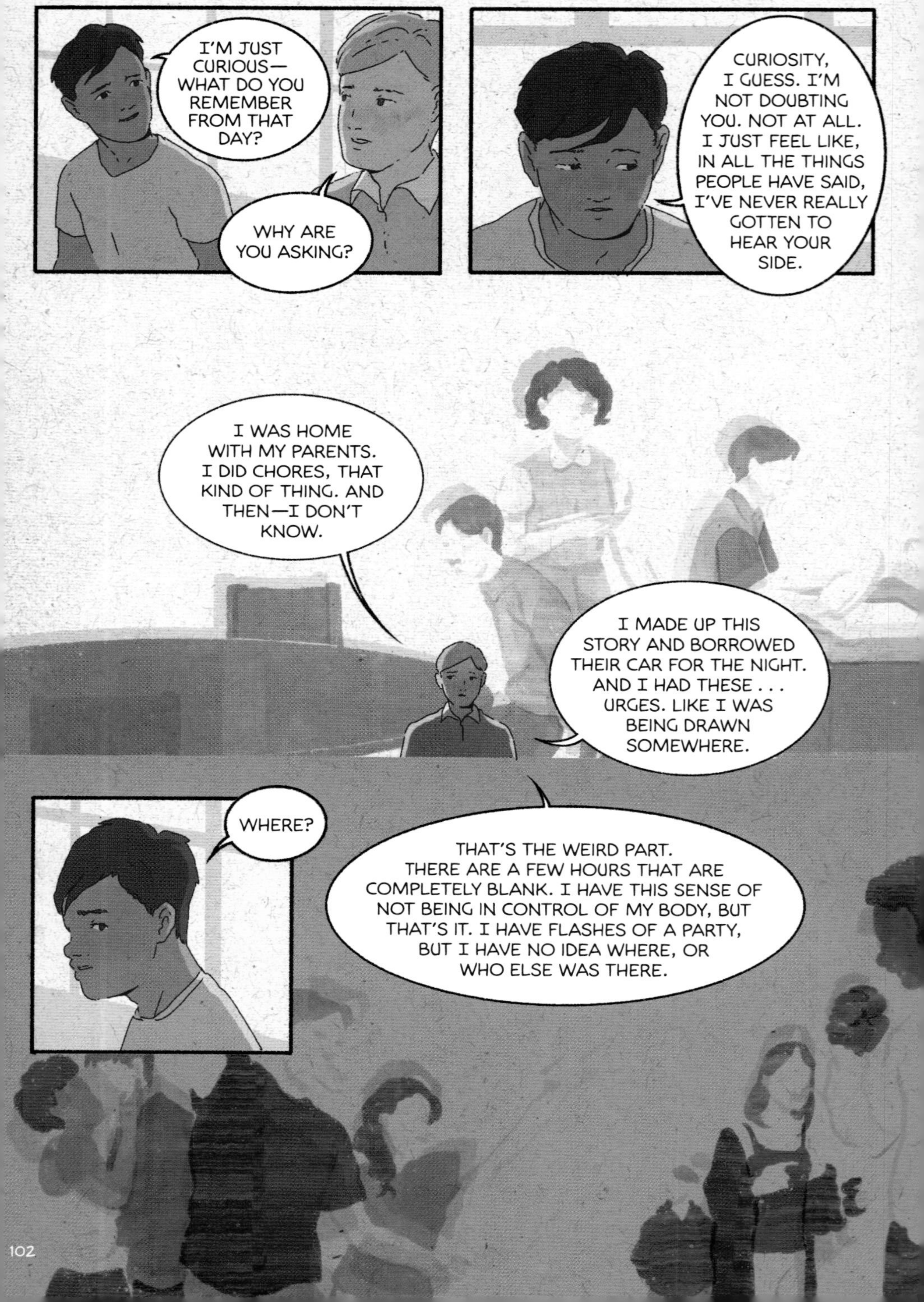
I'M JUST CURIOUS— WHAT DO YOU REMEMBER FROM THAT DAY?
WHY ARE YOU ASKING?
CURIOSITY, I GUESS. I'M NOT DOUBTING YOU. NOT AT ALL. I JUST FEEL LIKE, IN ALL THE THINGS PEOPLE HAVE SAID, I'VE NEVER REALLY GOTTEN TO HEAR YOUR SIDE.
I WAS HOME WITH MY PARENTS. I DID CHORES, THAT KIND OF THING. AND THEN—I DON'T KNOW.
I MADE UP THIS STORY AND BORROWED THEIR CAR FOR THE NIGHT. AND I HAD THESE . . . URGES. LIKE I WAS BEING DRAWN SOMEWHERE.
WHERE?
THAT'S THE WEIRD PART. THERE ARE A FEW HOURS THAT ARE COMPLETELY BLANK. I HAVE THIS SENSE OF NOT BEING IN CONTROL OF MY BODY, BUT THAT'S IT. I HAVE FLASHES OF A PARTY, BUT I HAVE NO IDEA WHERE, OR WHO ELSE WAS THERE.

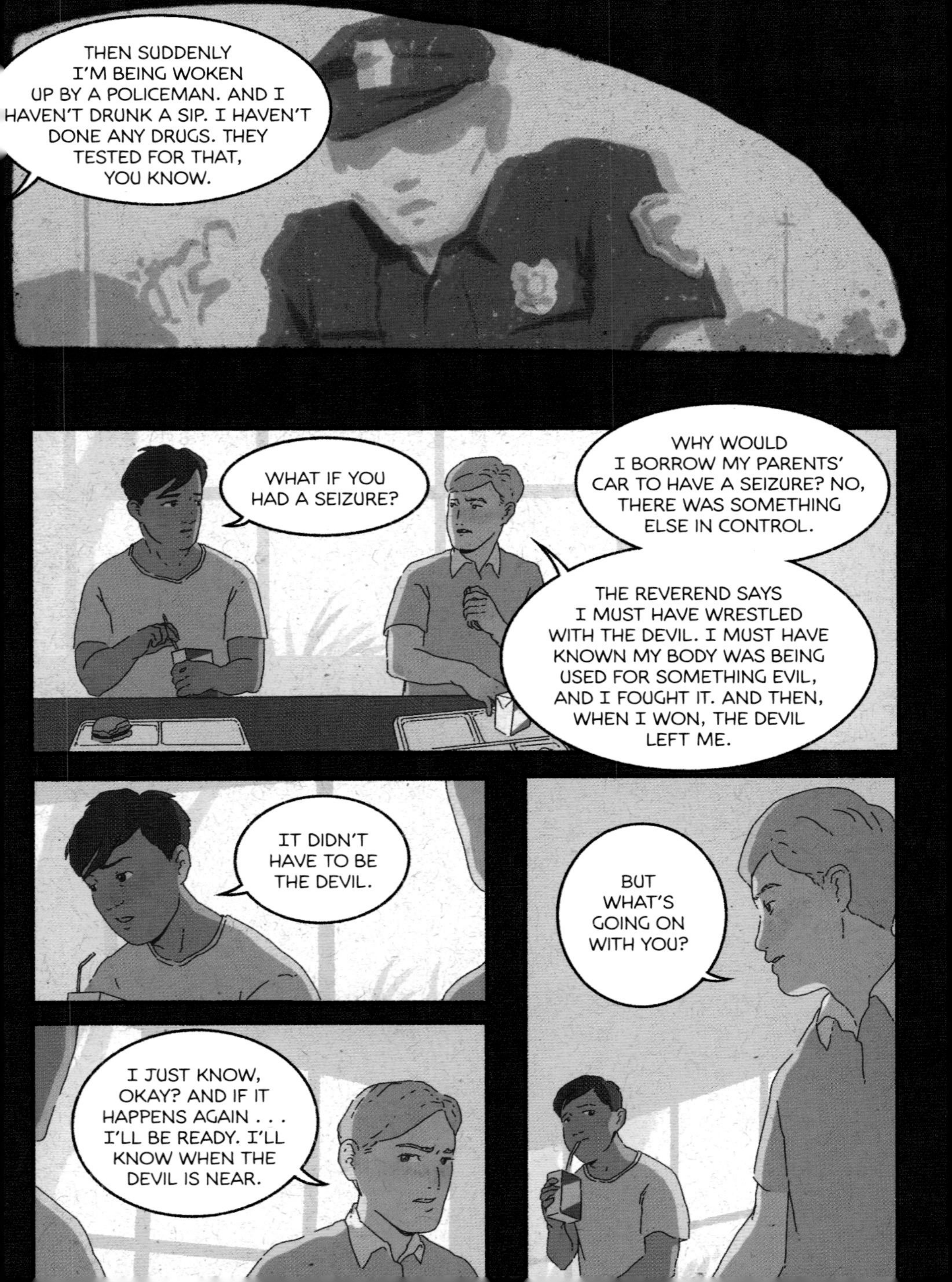
THEN SUDDENLY I'M BEING WOKEN UP BY A POLICEMAN. AND I HAVEN'T DRUNK A SIP. I HAVEN'T DONE ANY DRUGS. THEY TESTED FOR THAT, YOU KNOW.
WHAT IF YOU HAD A SEIZURE?
WHY WOULD I BORROW MY PARENTS' CAR TO HAVE A SEIZURE? NO, THERE WAS SOMETHING ELSE IN CONTROL.
THE REVEREND SAYS I MUST HAVE WRESTLED WITH THE DEVIL. I MUST HAVE KNOWN MY BODY WAS BEING USED FOR SOMETHING EVIL, AND I FOUGHT IT. AND THEN, WHEN I WON, THE DEVIL LEFT ME.
IT DIDN'T HAVE TO BE THE DEVIL.
BUT WHAT'S GOING ON WITH YOU?
I JUST KNOW, OKAY? AND IF IT HAPPENS AGAIN . . . I'LL BE READY. I'LL KNOW WHEN THE DEVIL IS NEAR.

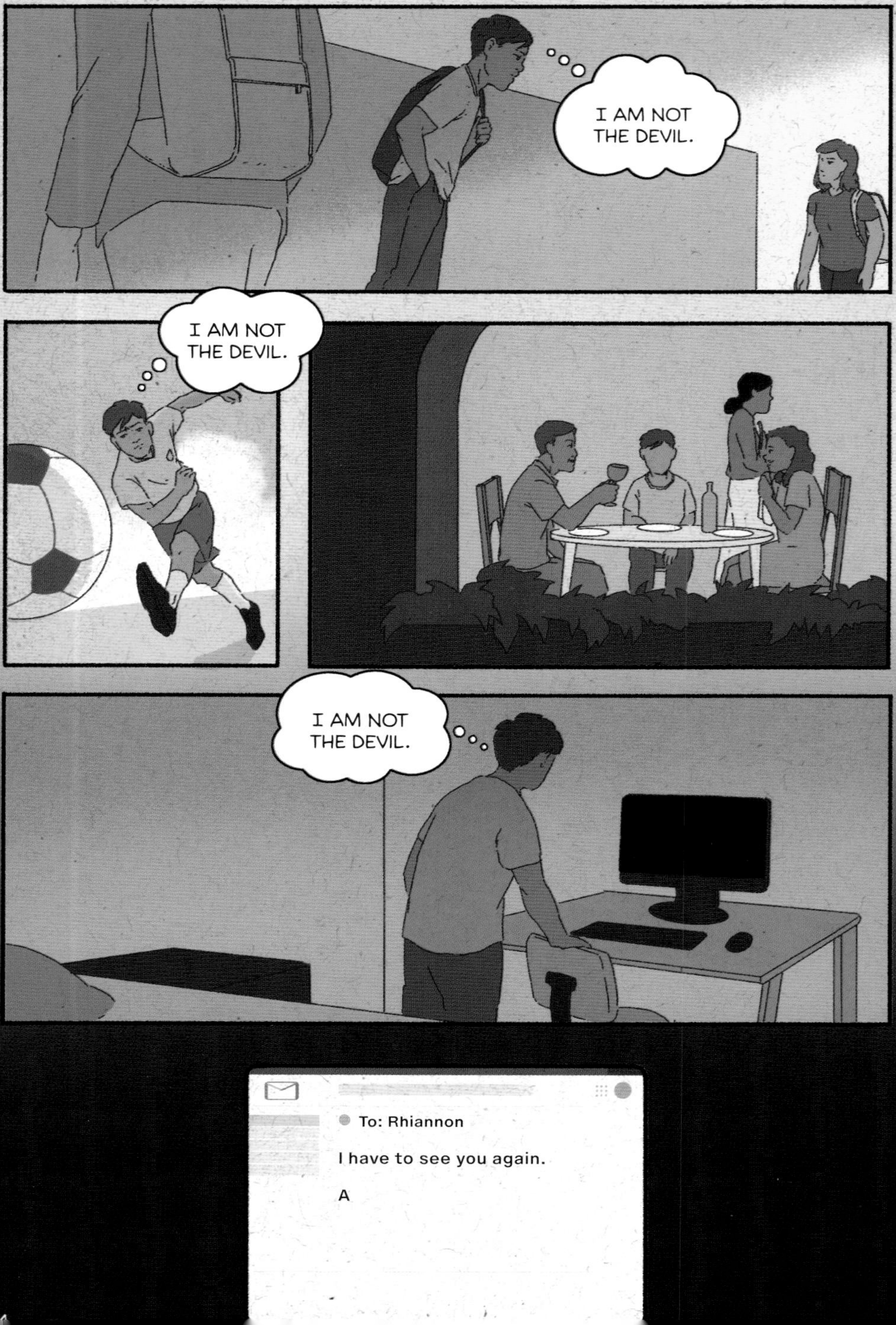
I AM NOT THE DEVIL.
I AM NOT THE DEVIL.
I AM NOT THE DEVIL.
To: Rhiannon
I have to see you again.
A

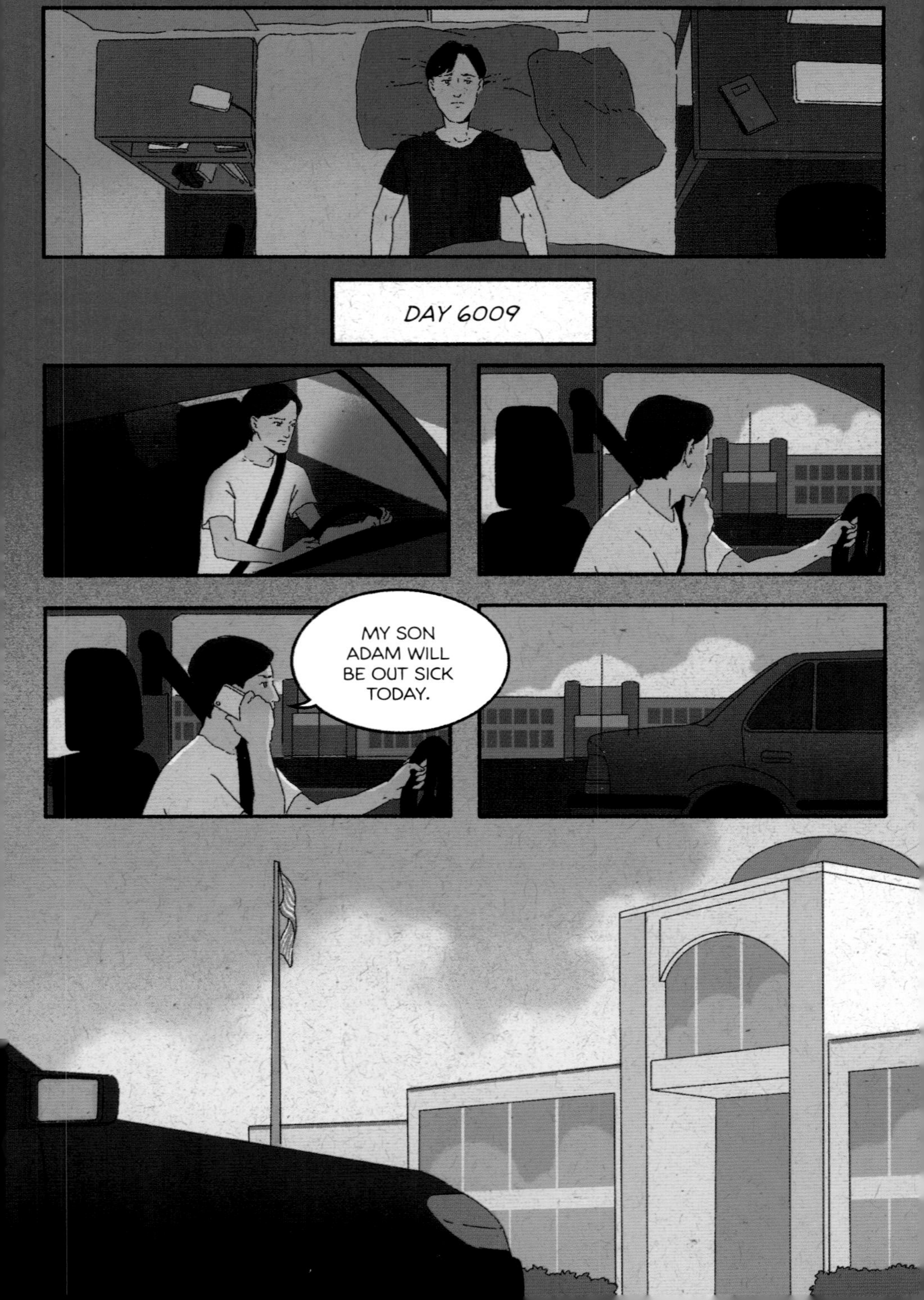
DAY 6009
MY SON ADAM WILL BE OUT SICK TODAY.

HEY.
HEY.
I THOUGHT YOU MIGHT COME.
ARE YOU MAD?

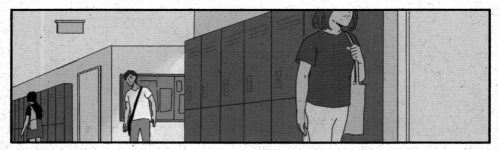

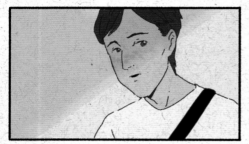

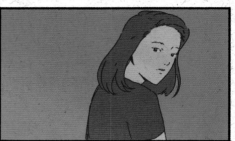

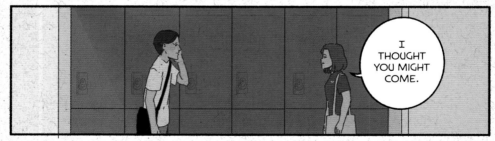

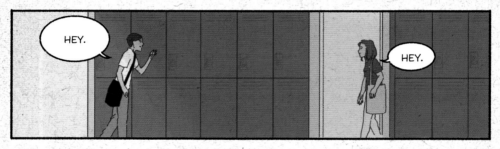

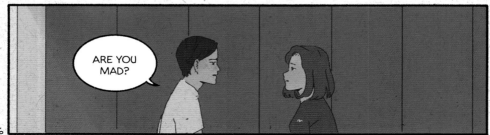

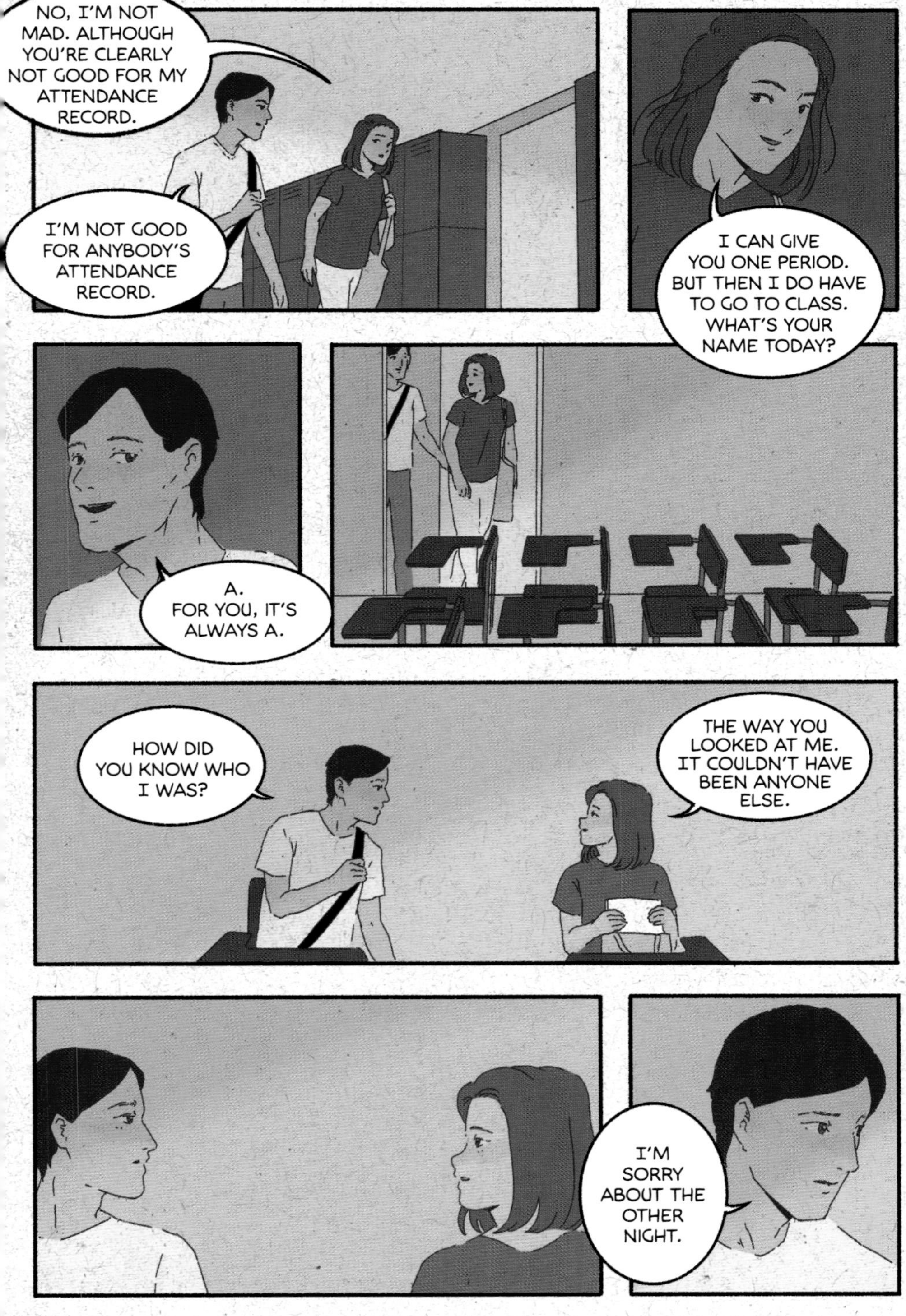
NO, I'M NOT MAD. ALTHOUGH YOU'RE CLEARLY NOT GOOD FOR MY ATTENDANCE RECORD.
I'M NOT GOOD FOR ANYBODY'S ATTENDANCE RECORD.
I CAN GIVE YOU ONE PERIOD. BUT THEN I DO HAVE TO GO TO CLASS. WHAT'S YOUR NAME TODAY?
A. FOR YOU, IT'S ALWAYS A.
HOW DID YOU KNOW WHO I WAS?
THE WAY YOU LOOKED AT ME. IT COULDN'T HAVE BEEN ANYONE ELSE.
I'M SORRY ABOUT THE OTHER NIGHT.

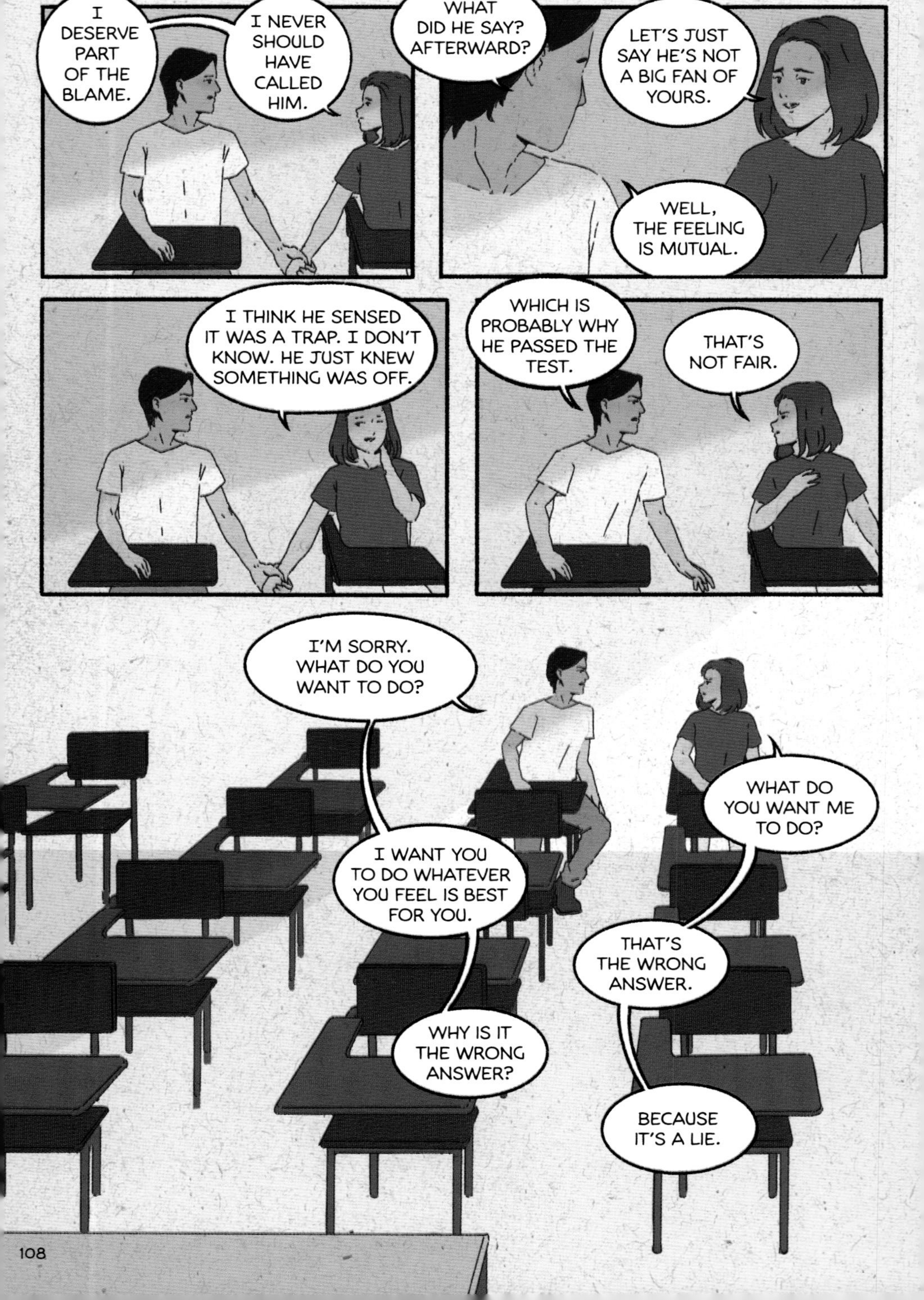
I DESERVE PART OF THE BLAME.
I NEVER SHOULD HAVE CALLED HIM.
WHAT DID HE SAY? AFTERWARD?
LET'S JUST SAY HE'S NOT A BIG FAN OF YOURS.
WELL, THE FEELING IS MUTUAL.
I THINK HE SENSED IT WAS A TRAP. I DON'T KNOW. HE JUST KNEW SOMETHING WAS OFF.
WHICH IS PROBABLY WHY HE PASSED THE TEST.
THAT'S NOT FAIR.
I'M SORRY. WHAT DO YOU WANT TO DO?
WHAT DO YOU WANT ME TO DO?
I WANT YOU TO DO WHATEVER YOU FEEL IS BEST FOR YOU.
THAT'S THE WRONG ANSWER.
WHY IS IT THE WRONG ANSWER?
BECAUSE IT'S A LIE.

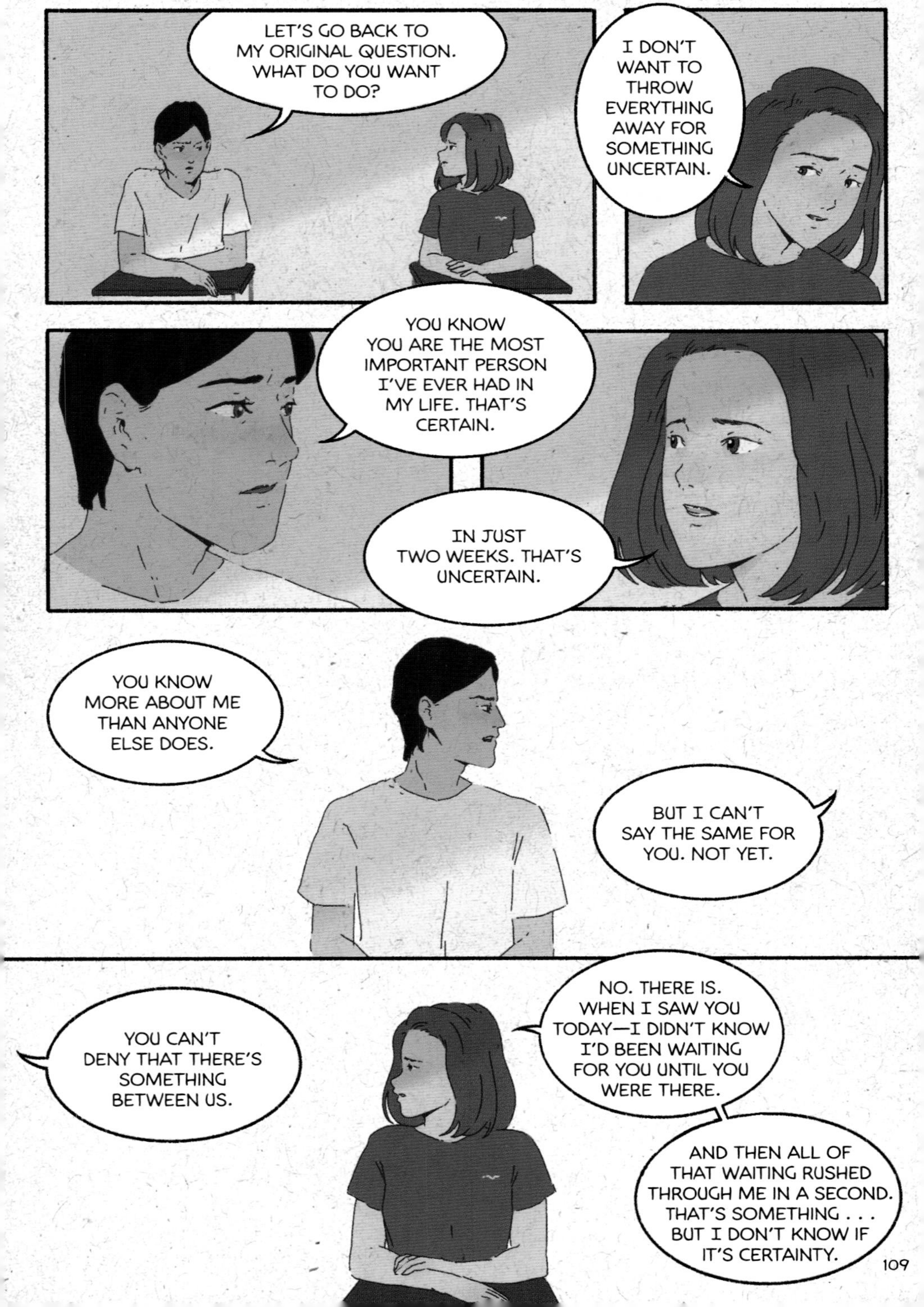
LET'S GO BACK TO MY ORIGINAL QUESTION. WHAT DO YOU WANT TO DO?
I DON'T WANT TO THROW EVERYTHING AWAY FOR SOMETHING UNCERTAIN.
YOU KNOW YOU ARE THE MOST IMPORTANT PERSON I'VE EVER HAD IN MY LIFE. THAT'S CERTAIN.
IN JUST TWO WEEKS. THAT'S UNCERTAIN.
YOU KNOW MORE ABOUT ME THAN ANYONE ELSE DOES.
BUT I CAN'T SAY THE SAME FOR YOU. NOT YET.
YOU CAN'T DENY THAT THERE'S SOMETHING BETWEEN US.
NO. THERE IS. WHEN I SAW YOU TODAY—I DIDN'T KNOW I'D BEEN WAITING FOR YOU UNTIL YOU WERE THERE.
AND THEN ALL OF THAT WAITING RUSHED THROUGH ME IN A SECOND. THAT'S SOMETHING . . . BUT I DON'T KNOW IF IT'S CERTAINTY.

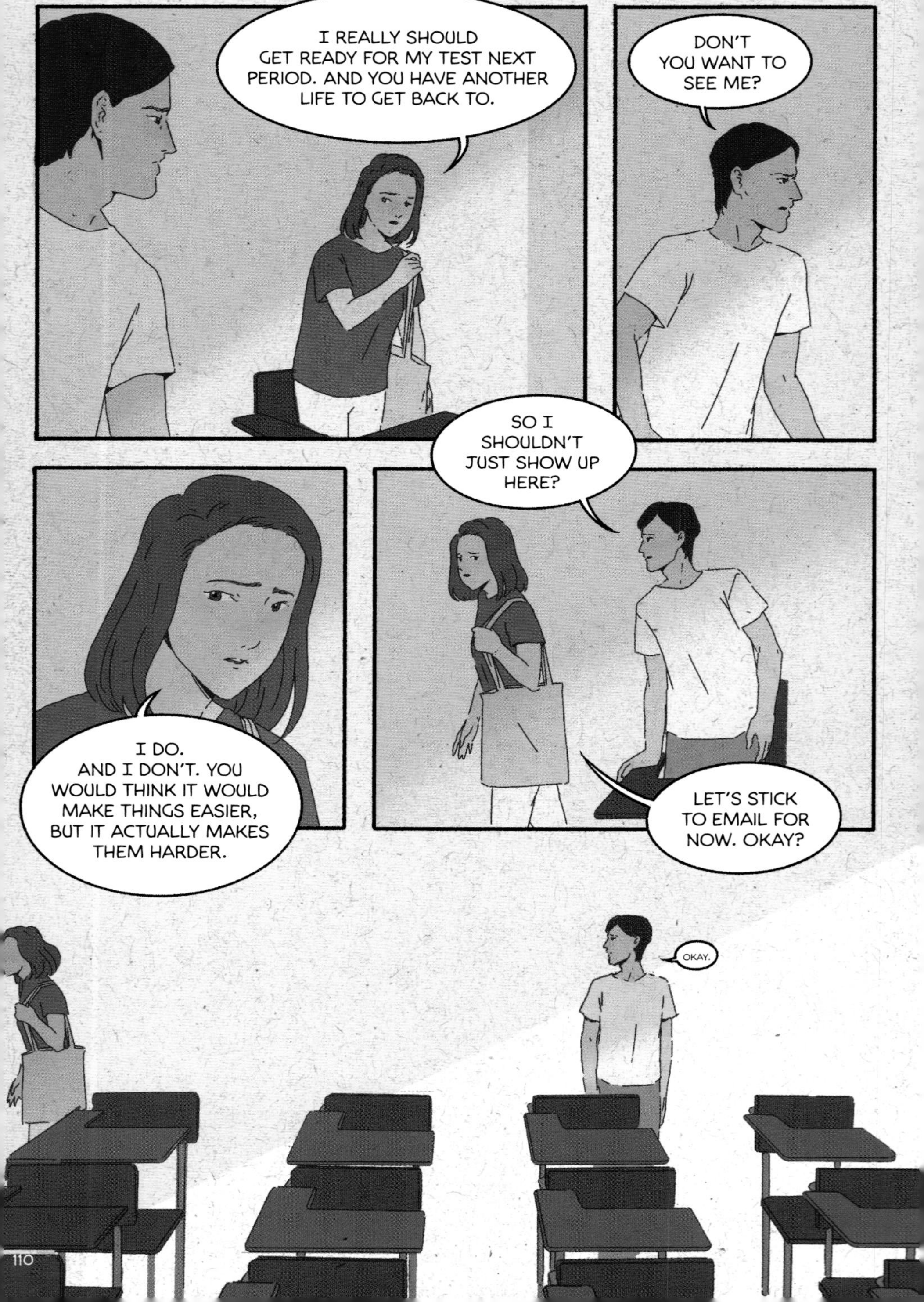
I REALLY SHOULD GET READY FOR MY TEST NEXT PERIOD. AND YOU HAVE ANOTHER LIFE TO GET BACK TO.
DON'T YOU WANT TO SEE ME?
I DO. AND I DON'T. YOU WOULD THINK IT WOULD MAKE THINGS EASIER, BUT IT ACTUALLY MAKES THEM HARDER.
SO I SHOULDN'T JUST SHOW UP HERE?
LET'S STICK TO EMAIL FOR NOW. OKAY?
OKAY.

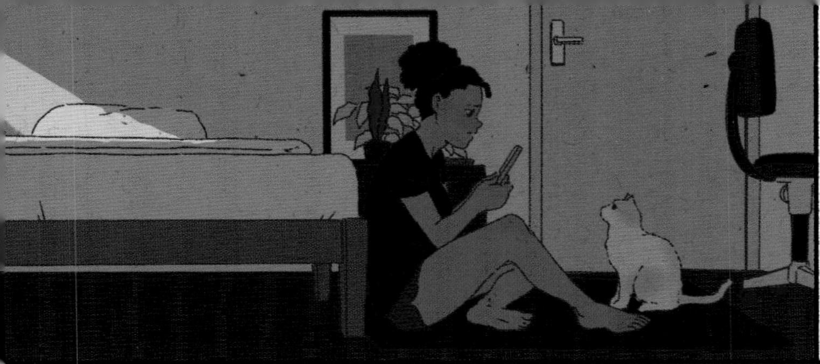

DAY 6010

DAY 6011

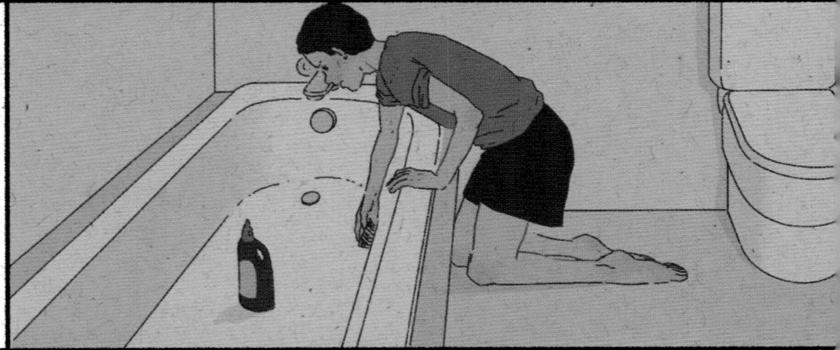

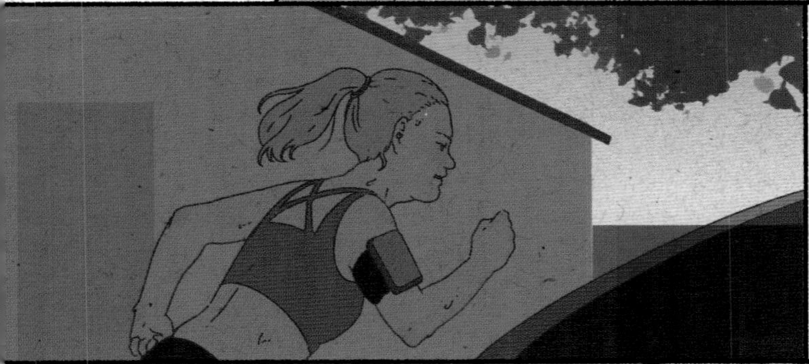

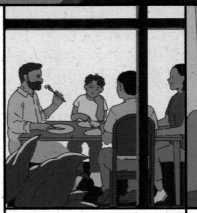

DAY 6012

From: Rhiannon

A,

I'm sorry I didn't get to write to you earlier. I meant to, but then all these other things happened (none of them important, just time-consuming). Even though it was hard to see you, it was good to see you. I mean it. But taking a break and thinking things out makes sense.

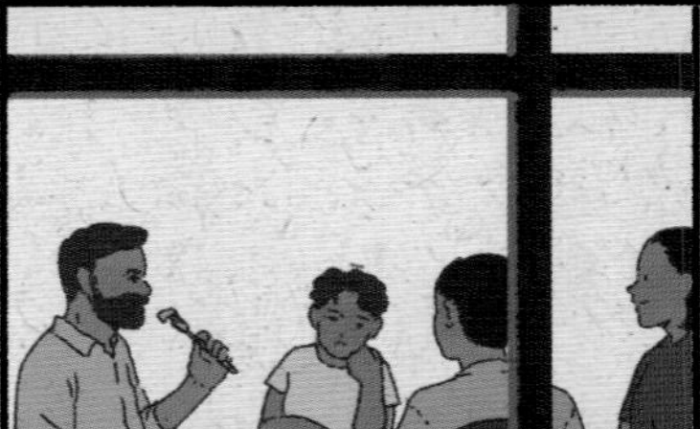

DAY 6013

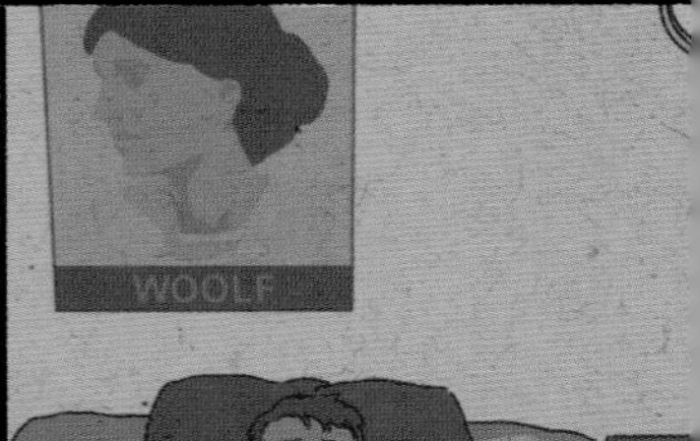
WOOLF

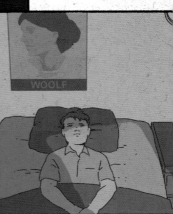

DAY 6014

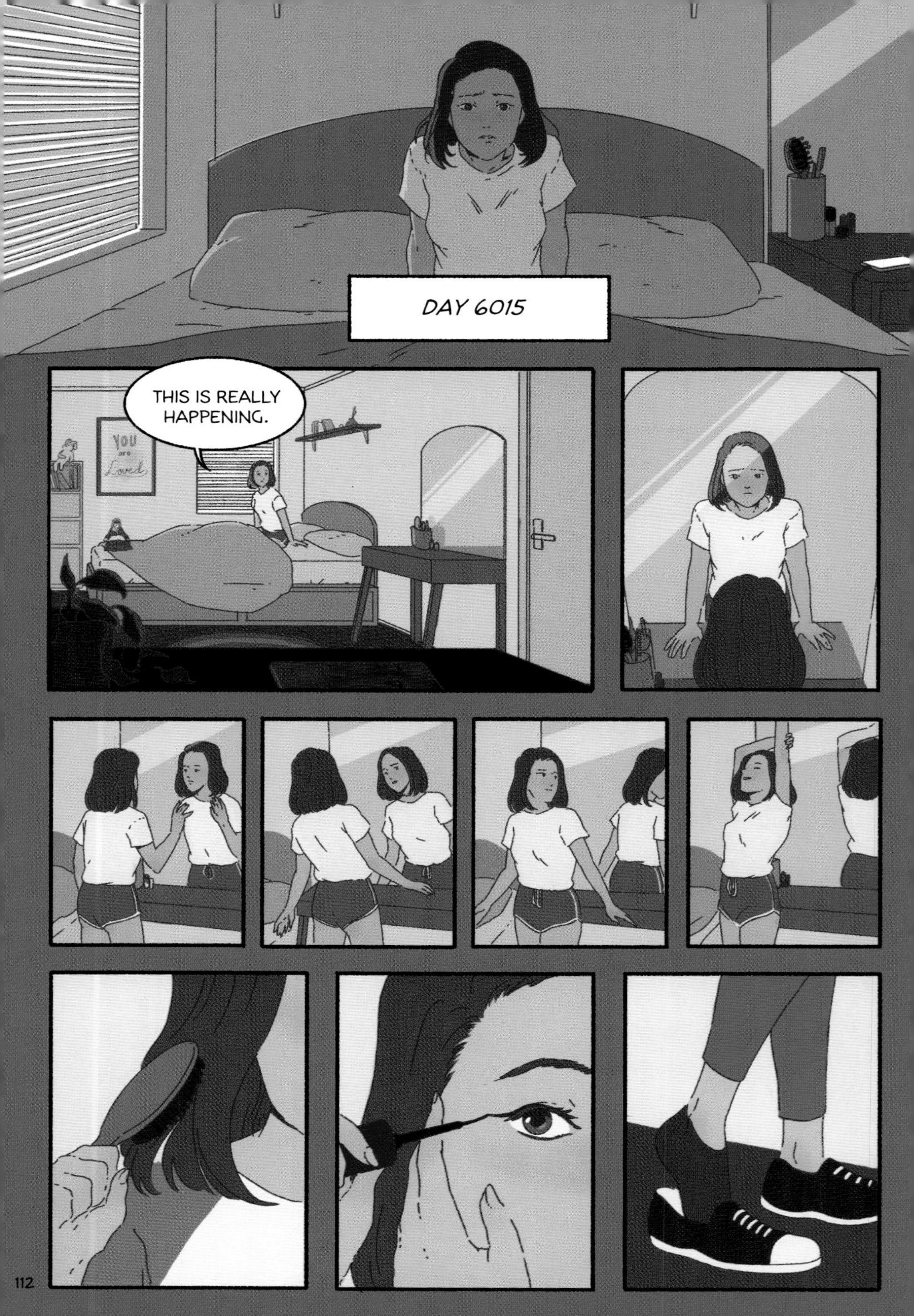
DAY 6015
THIS IS REALLY HAPPENING.
YOU are Loved

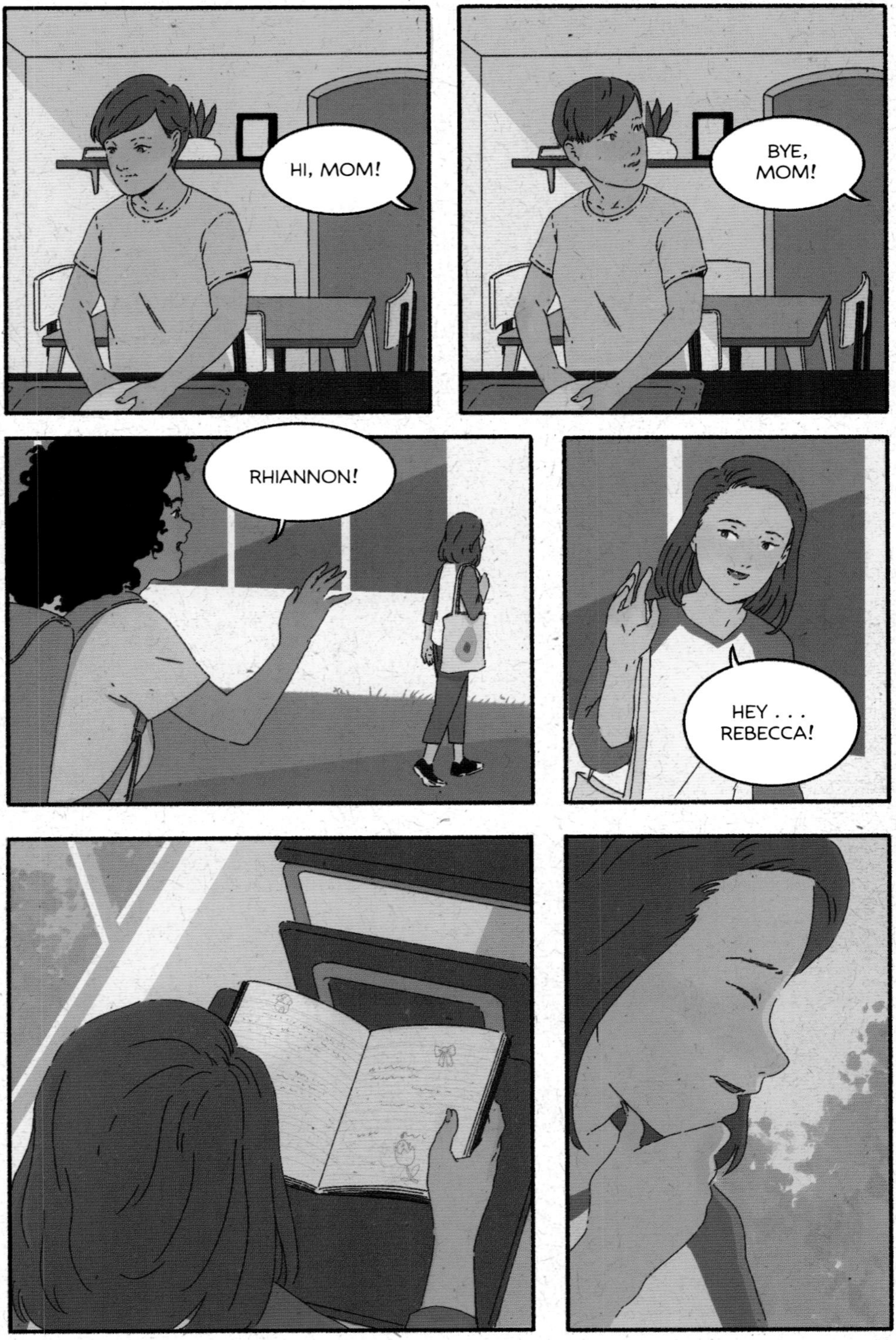
HI, MOM!
BYE, MOM!
RHIANNON!
HEY . . . REBECCA!

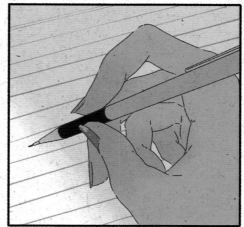

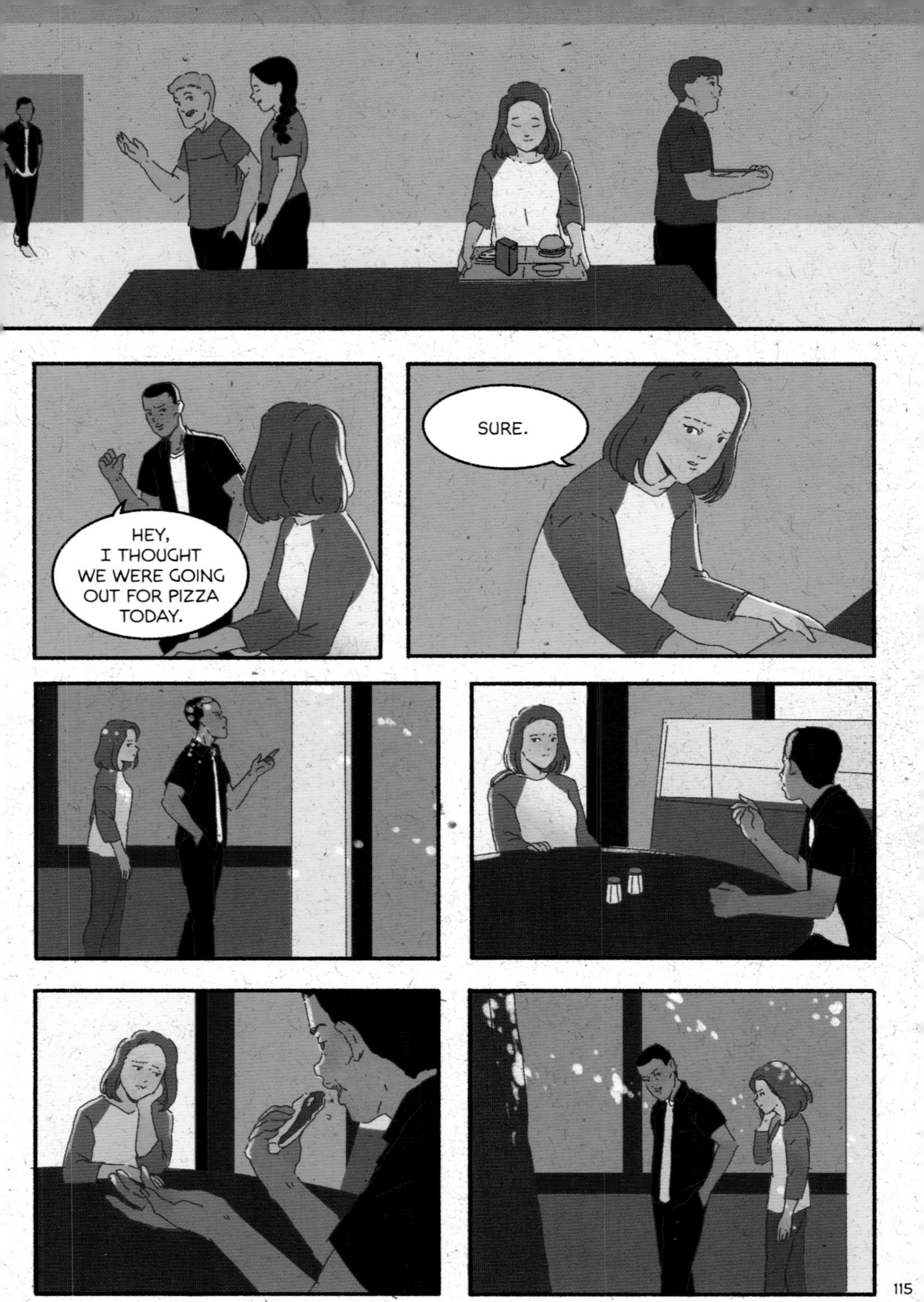
HEY, I THOUGHT WE WERE GOING OUT FOR PIZZA TODAY.
SURE.

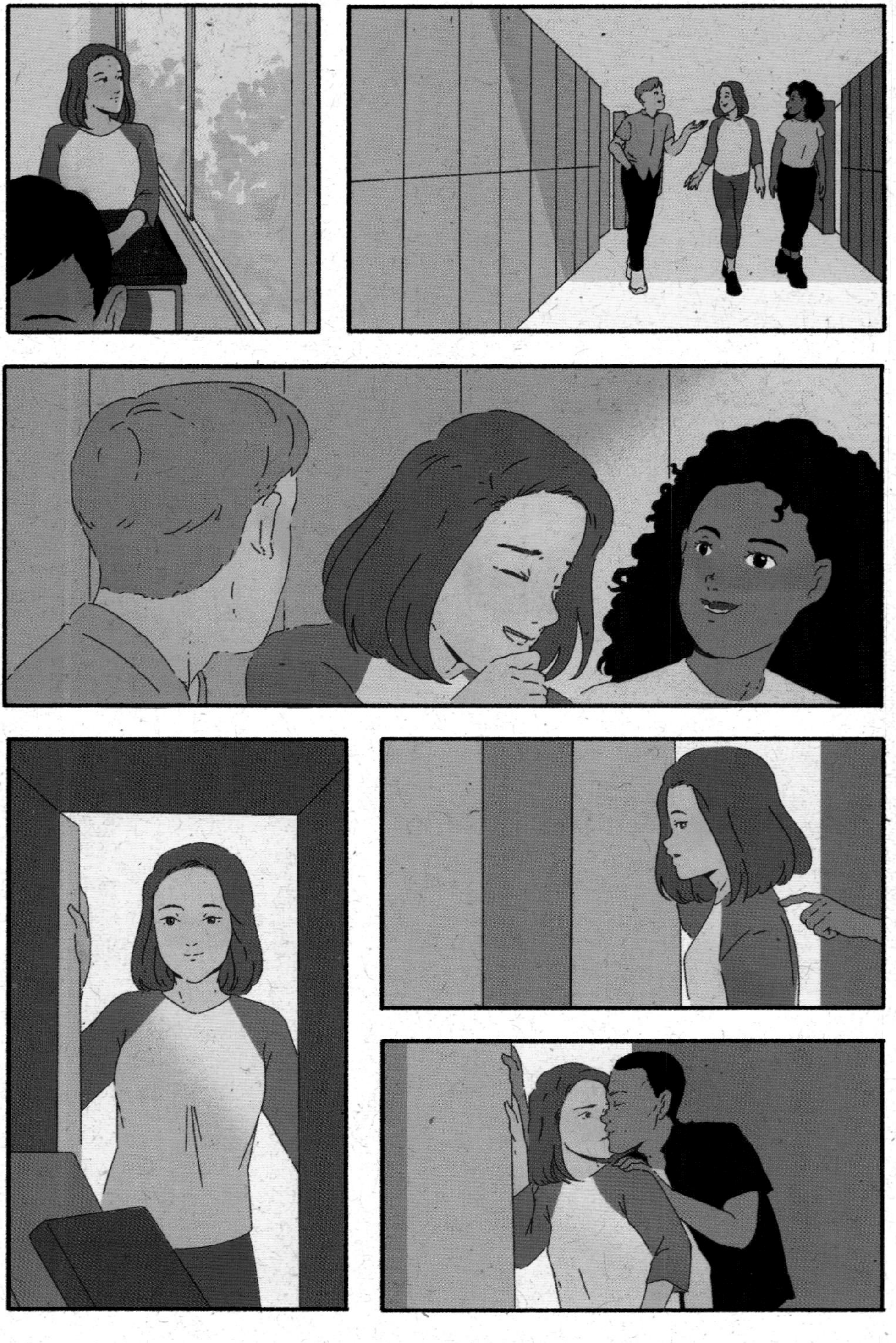

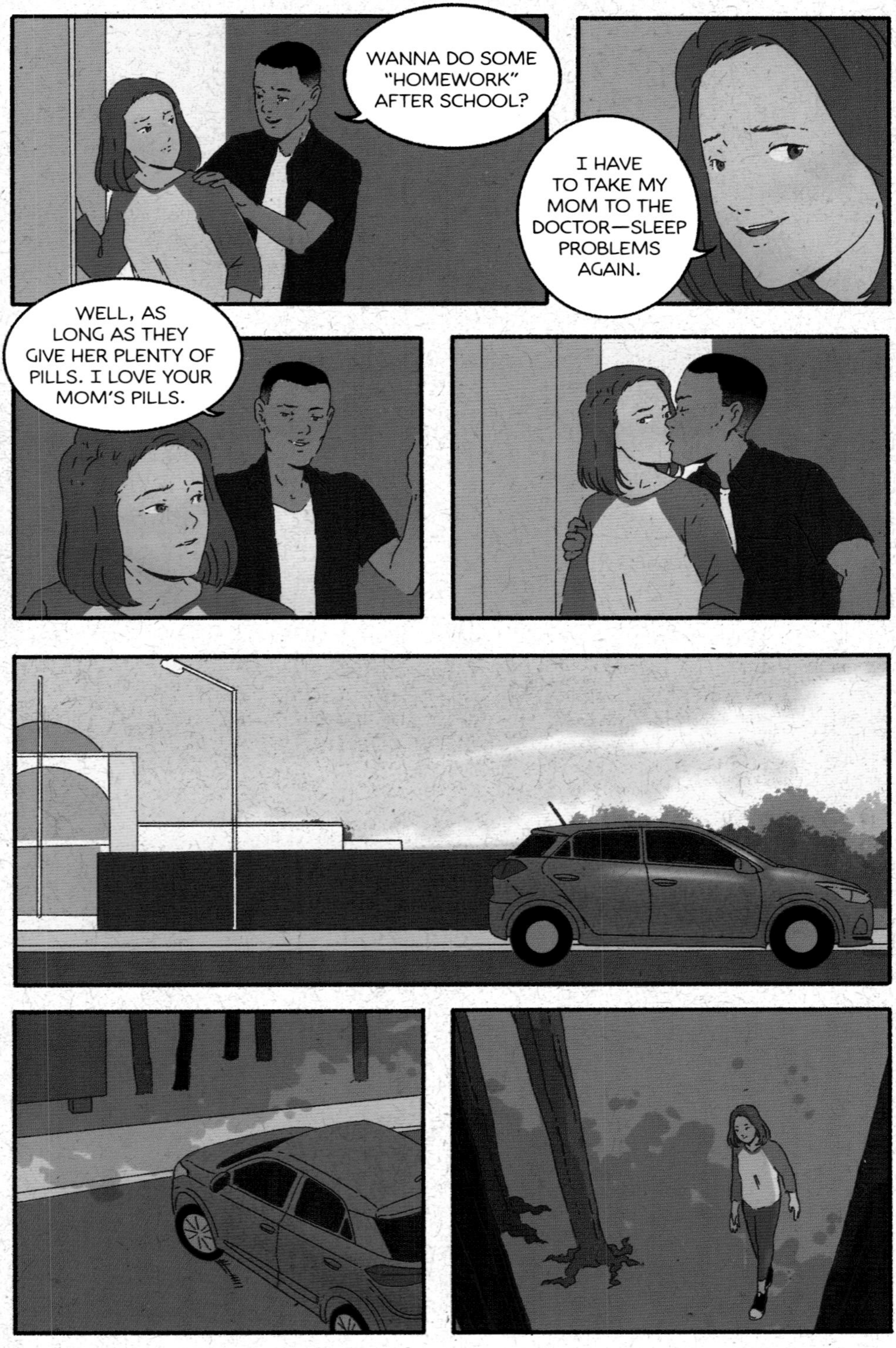
WANNA DO SOME "HOMEWORK" AFTER SCHOOL?
I HAVE TO TAKE MY MOM TO THE DOCTOR—SLEEP PROBLEMS AGAIN.
WELL, AS LONG AS THEY GIVE HER PLENTY OF PILLS. I LOVE YOUR MOM'S PILLS.

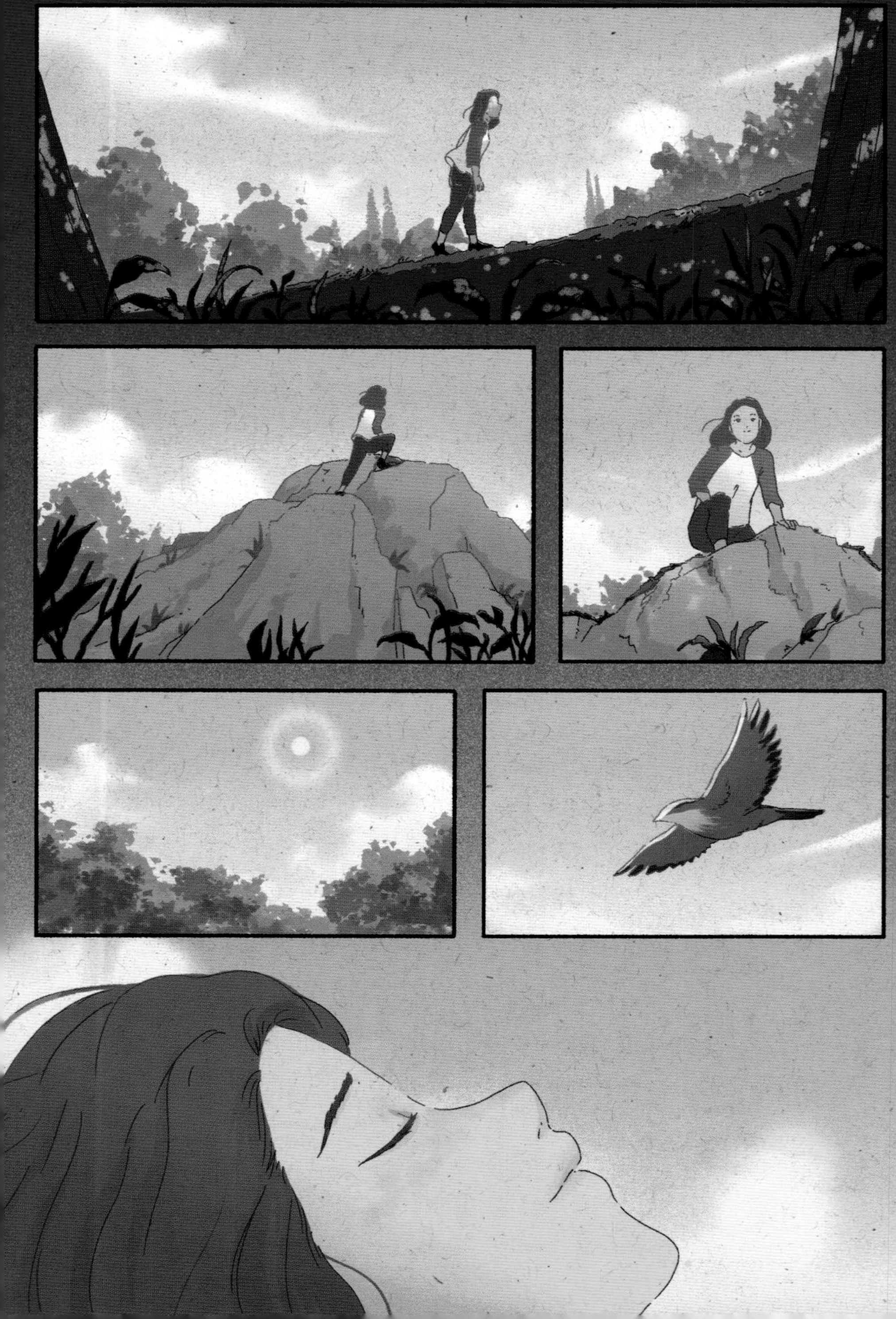

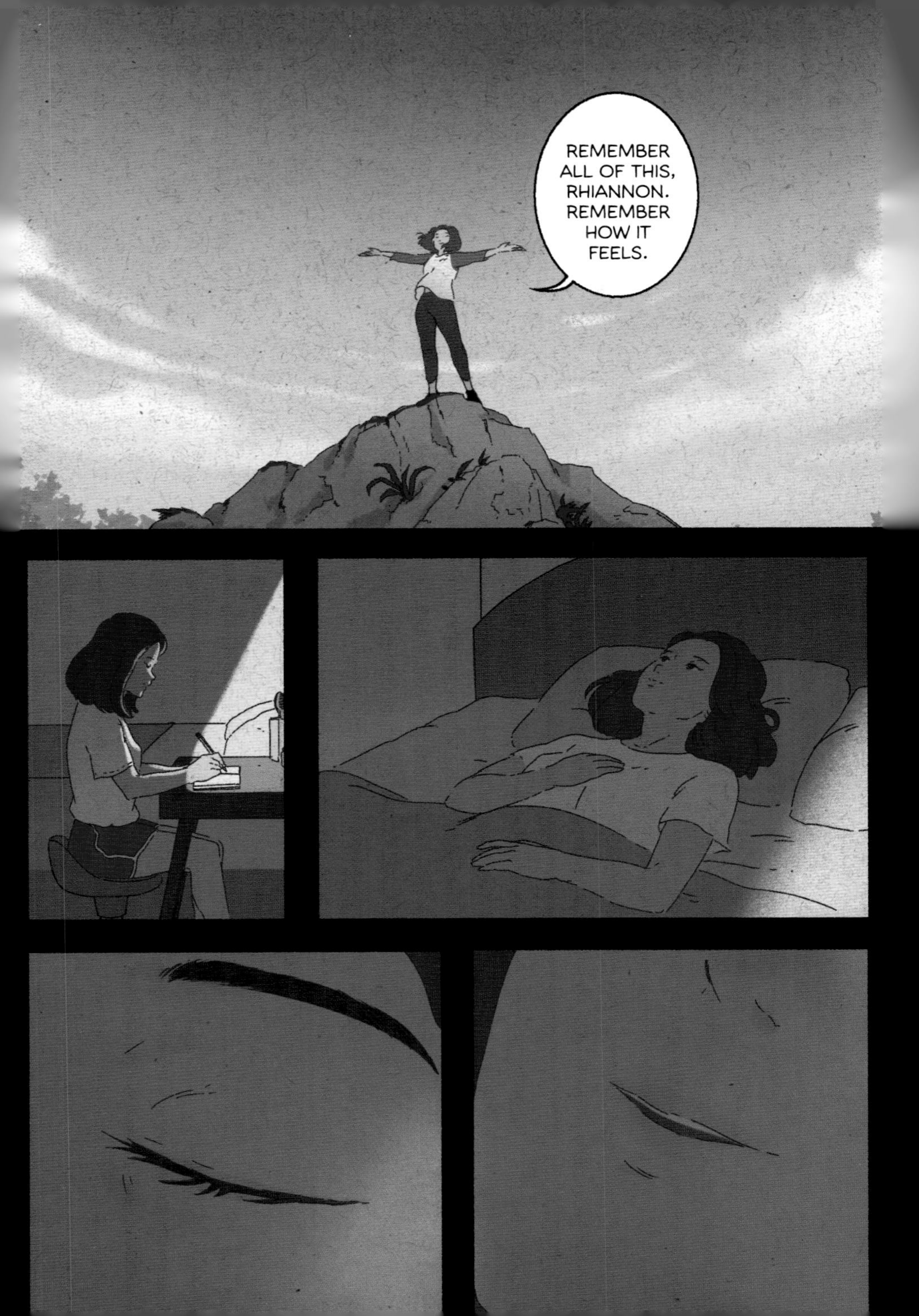
REMEMBER ALL OF THIS, RHIANNON. REMEMBER HOW IT FEELS.

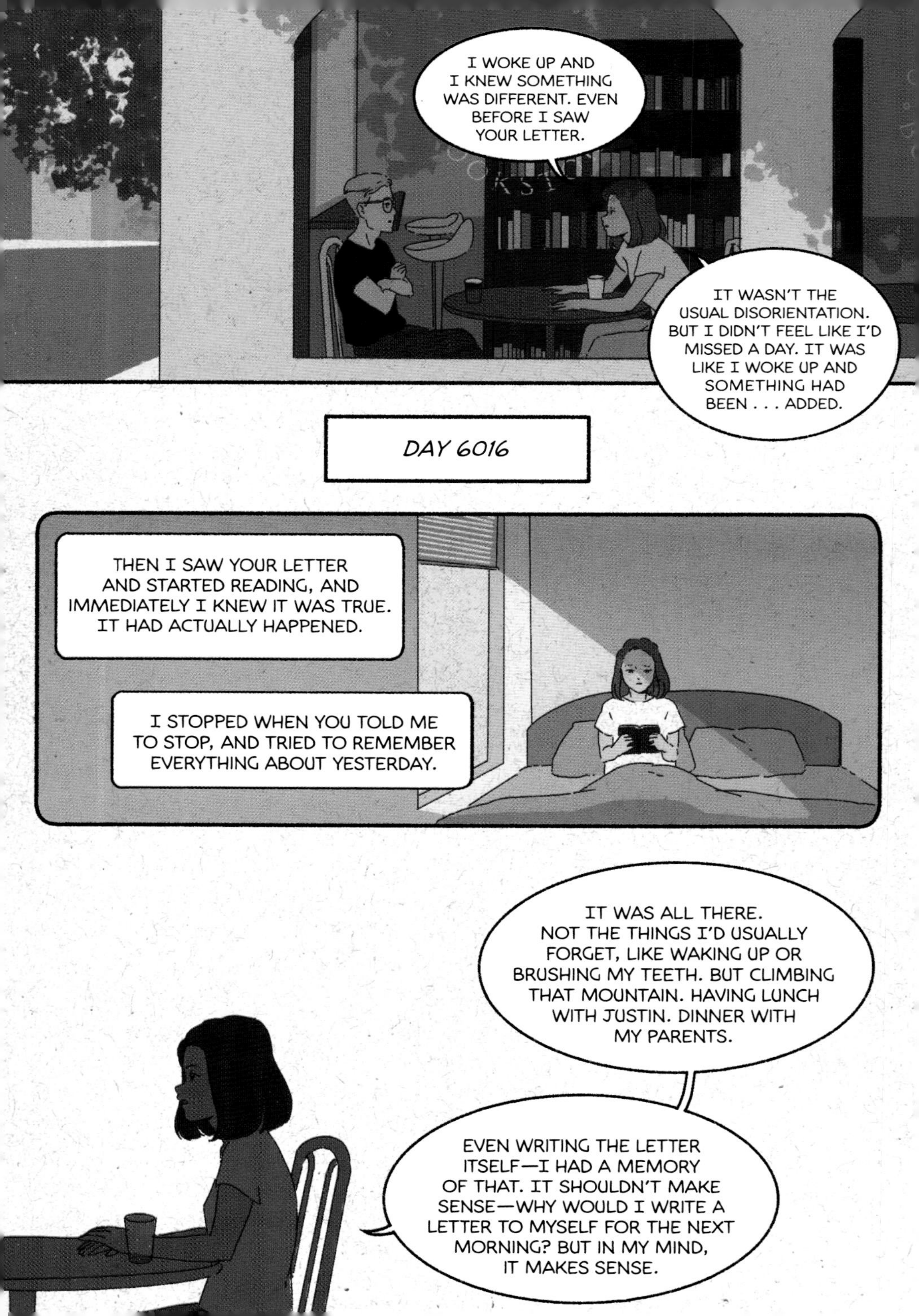
I WOKE UP AND I KNEW SOMETHING WAS DIFFERENT. EVEN BEFORE I SAW YOUR LETTER.
IT WASN'T THE USUAL DISORIENTATION. BUT I DIDN'T FEEL LIKE I'D MISSED A DAY. IT WAS LIKE I WOKE UP AND SOMETHING HAD BEEN . . . ADDED.
DAY 6016
THEN I SAW YOUR LETTER AND STARTED READING, AND IMMEDIATELY I KNEW IT WAS TRUE. IT HAD ACTUALLY HAPPENED.
I STOPPED WHEN YOU TOLD ME TO STOP, AND TRIED TO REMEMBER EVERYTHING ABOUT YESTERDAY.
IT WAS ALL THERE. NOT THE THINGS I'D USUALLY FORGET, LIKE WAKING UP OR BRUSHING MY TEETH. BUT CLIMBING THAT MOUNTAIN. HAVING LUNCH WITH JUSTIN. DINNER WITH MY PARENTS.
EVEN WRITING THE LETTER ITSELF—I HAD A MEMORY OF THAT. IT SHOULDN'T MAKE SENSE—WHY WOULD I WRITE A LETTER TO MYSELF FOR THE NEXT MORNING? BUT IN MY MIND, IT MAKES SENSE.

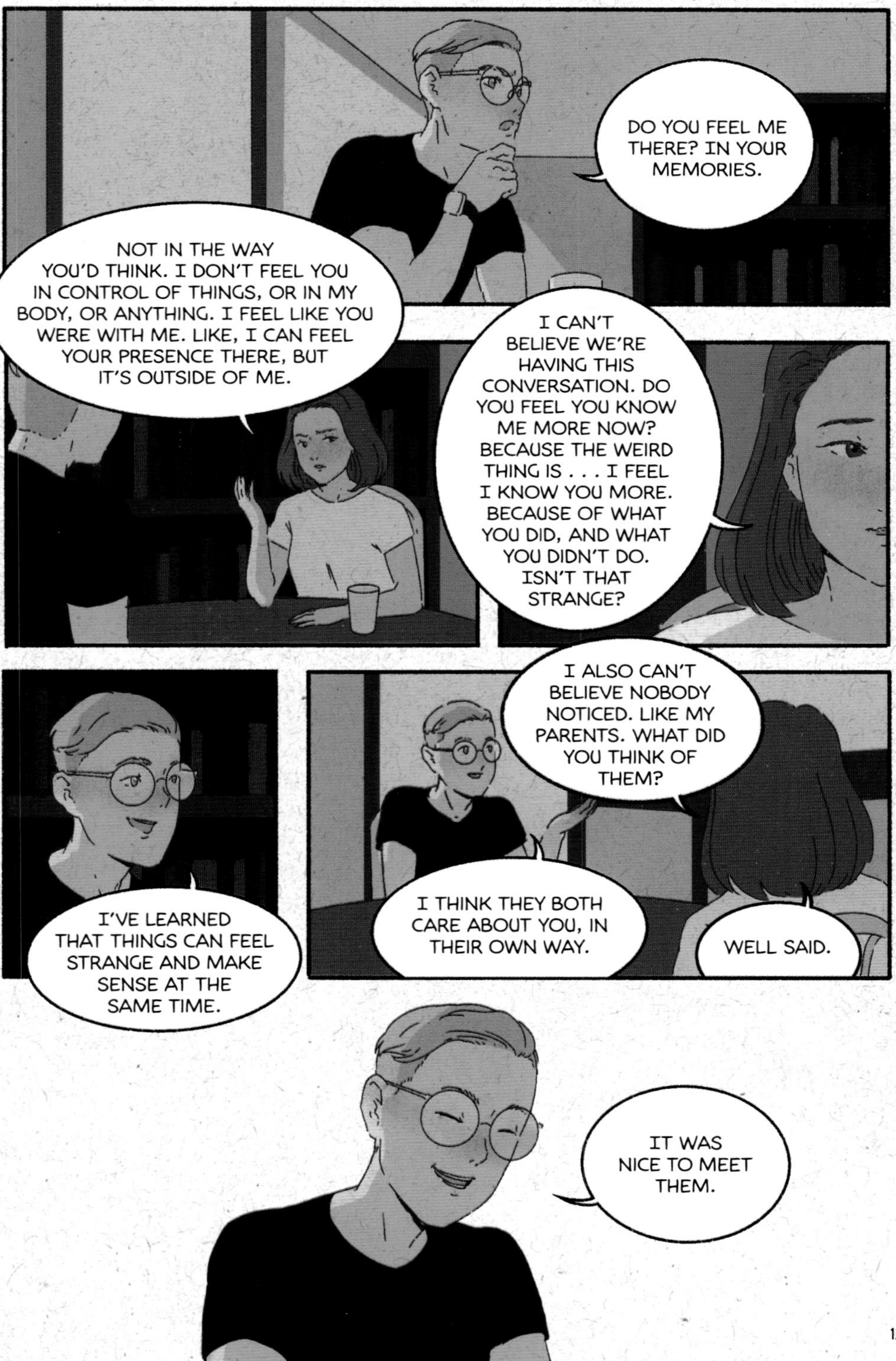
DO YOU FEEL ME THERE? IN YOUR MEMORIES.
NOT IN THE WAY YOU'D THINK. I DON'T FEEL YOU IN CONTROL OF THINGS, OR IN MY BODY, OR ANYTHING. I FEEL LIKE YOU WERE WITH ME. LIKE, I CAN FEEL YOUR PRESENCE THERE, BUT IT'S OUTSIDE OF ME.
I CAN'T BELIEVE WE'RE HAVING THIS CONVERSATION. DO YOU FEEL YOU KNOW ME MORE NOW? BECAUSE THE WEIRD THING IS . . . I FEEL I KNOW YOU MORE. BECAUSE OF WHAT YOU DID, AND WHAT YOU DIDN'T DO. ISN'T THAT STRANGE?
I'VE LEARNED THAT THINGS CAN FEEL STRANGE AND MAKE SENSE AT THE SAME TIME.
I ALSO CAN'T BELIEVE NOBODY NOTICED. LIKE MY PARENTS. WHAT DID YOU THINK OF THEM?
I THINK THEY BOTH CARE ABOUT YOU, IN THEIR OWN WAY.
WELL SAID.
IT WAS NICE TO MEET THEM.

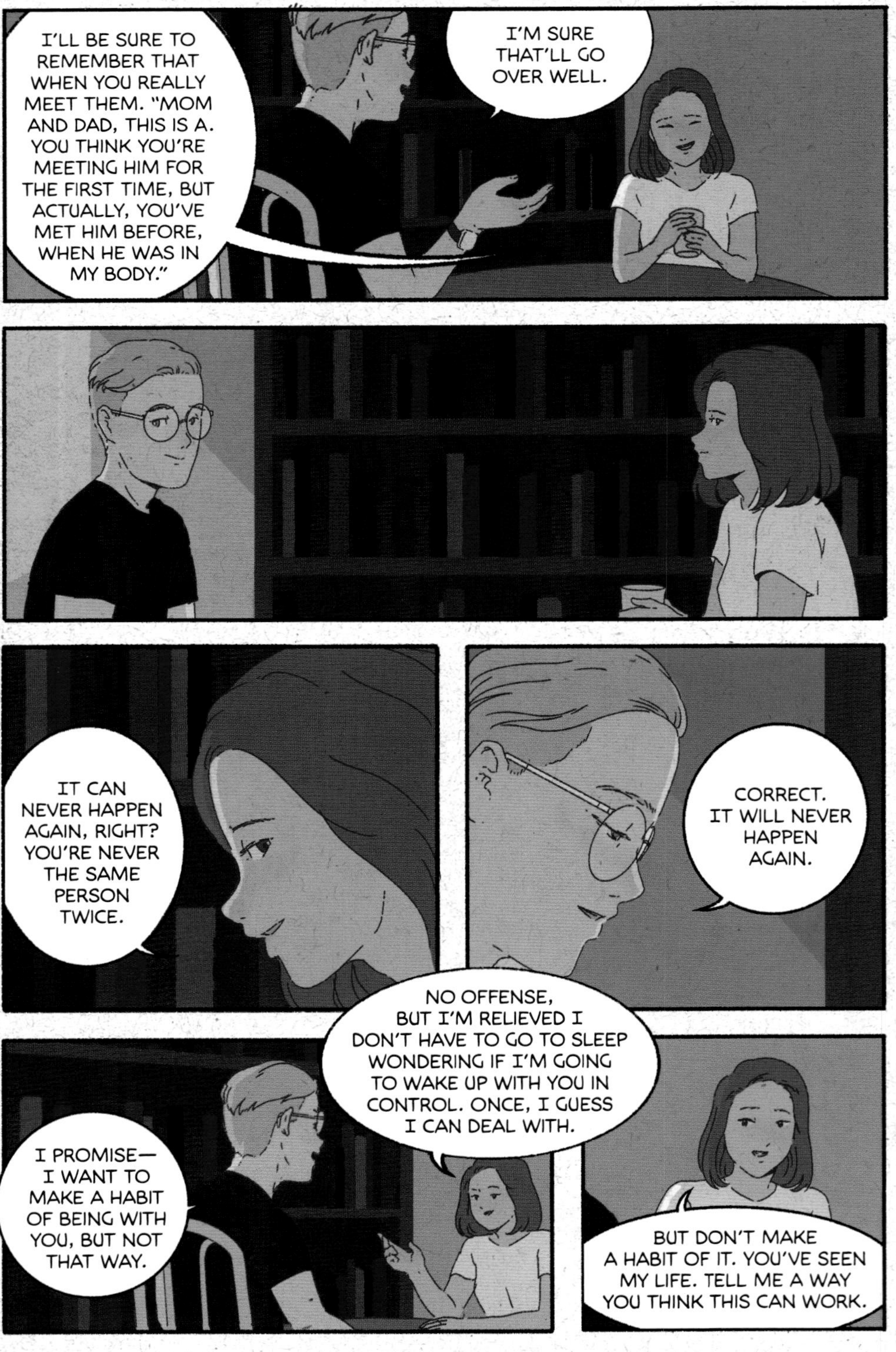
I'LL BE SURE TO REMEMBER THAT WHEN YOU REALLY MEET THEM. "MOM AND DAD, THIS IS A. YOU THINK YOU'RE MEETING HIM FOR THE FIRST TIME, BUT ACTUALLY, YOU'VE MET HIM BEFORE, WHEN HE WAS IN MY BODY."
I'M SURE THAT'LL GO OVER WELL.
IT CAN NEVER HAPPEN AGAIN, RIGHT? YOU'RE NEVER THE SAME PERSON TWICE.
CORRECT. IT WILL NEVER HAPPEN AGAIN.
NO OFFENSE, BUT I'M RELIEVED I DON'T HAVE TO GO TO SLEEP WONDERING IF I'M GOING TO WAKE UP WITH YOU IN CONTROL. ONCE, I GUESS I CAN DEAL WITH.
I PROMISE— I WANT TO MAKE A HABIT OF BEING WITH YOU, BUT NOT THAT WAY.
BUT DON'T MAKE A HABIT OF IT. YOU'VE SEEN MY LIFE. TELL ME A WAY YOU THINK THIS CAN WORK.

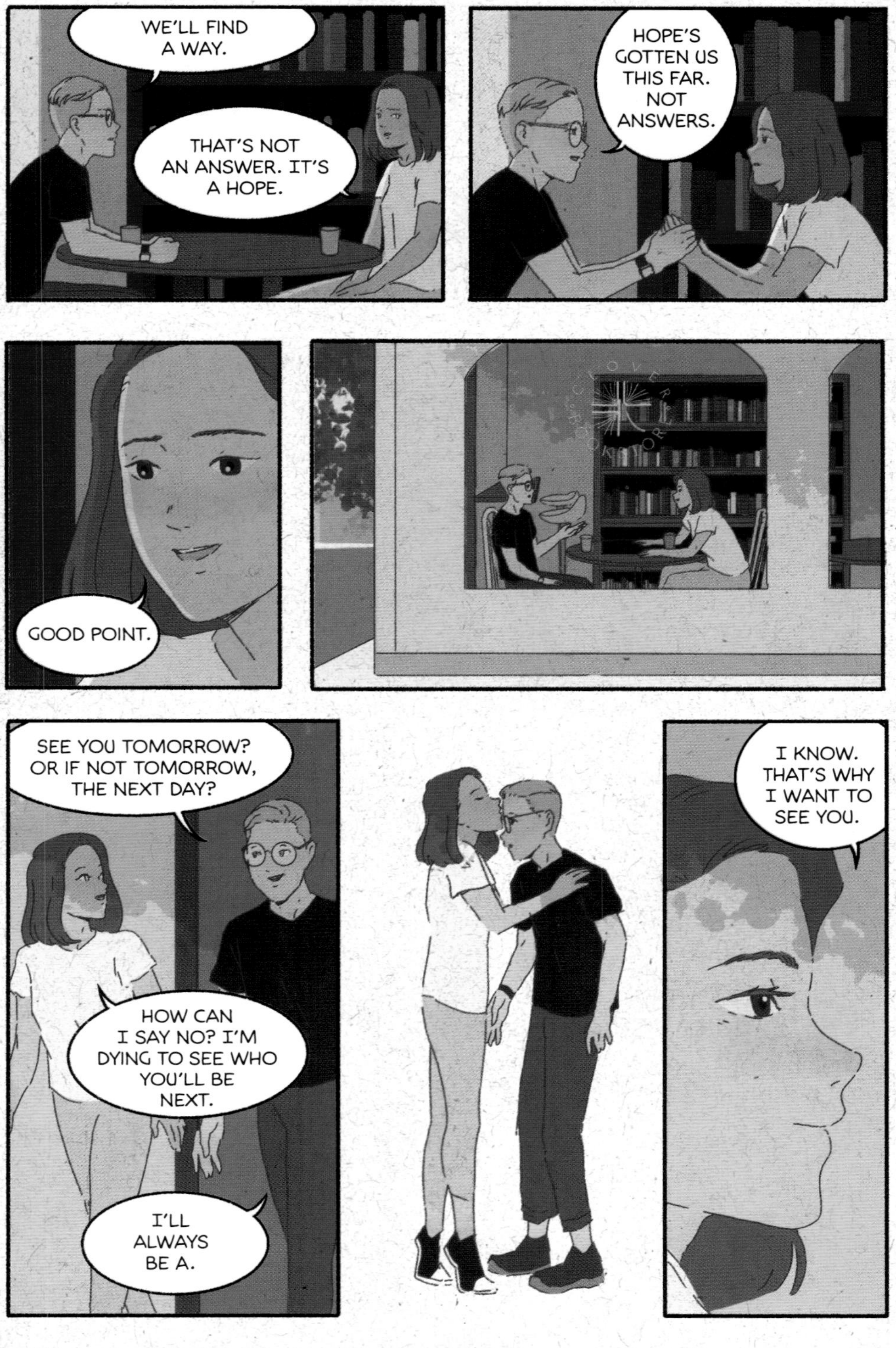
WE'LL FIND A WAY.
THAT'S NOT AN ANSWER. IT'S A HOPE.
HOPE'S GOTTEN US THIS FAR. NOT ANSWERS.
GOOD POINT.
SEE YOU TOMORROW? OR IF NOT TOMORROW, THE NEXT DAY?
HOW CAN I SAY NO? I'M DYING TO SEE WHO YOU'LL BE NEXT.
I'LL ALWAYS BE A.
I KNOW. THAT'S WHY I WANT TO SEE YOU.

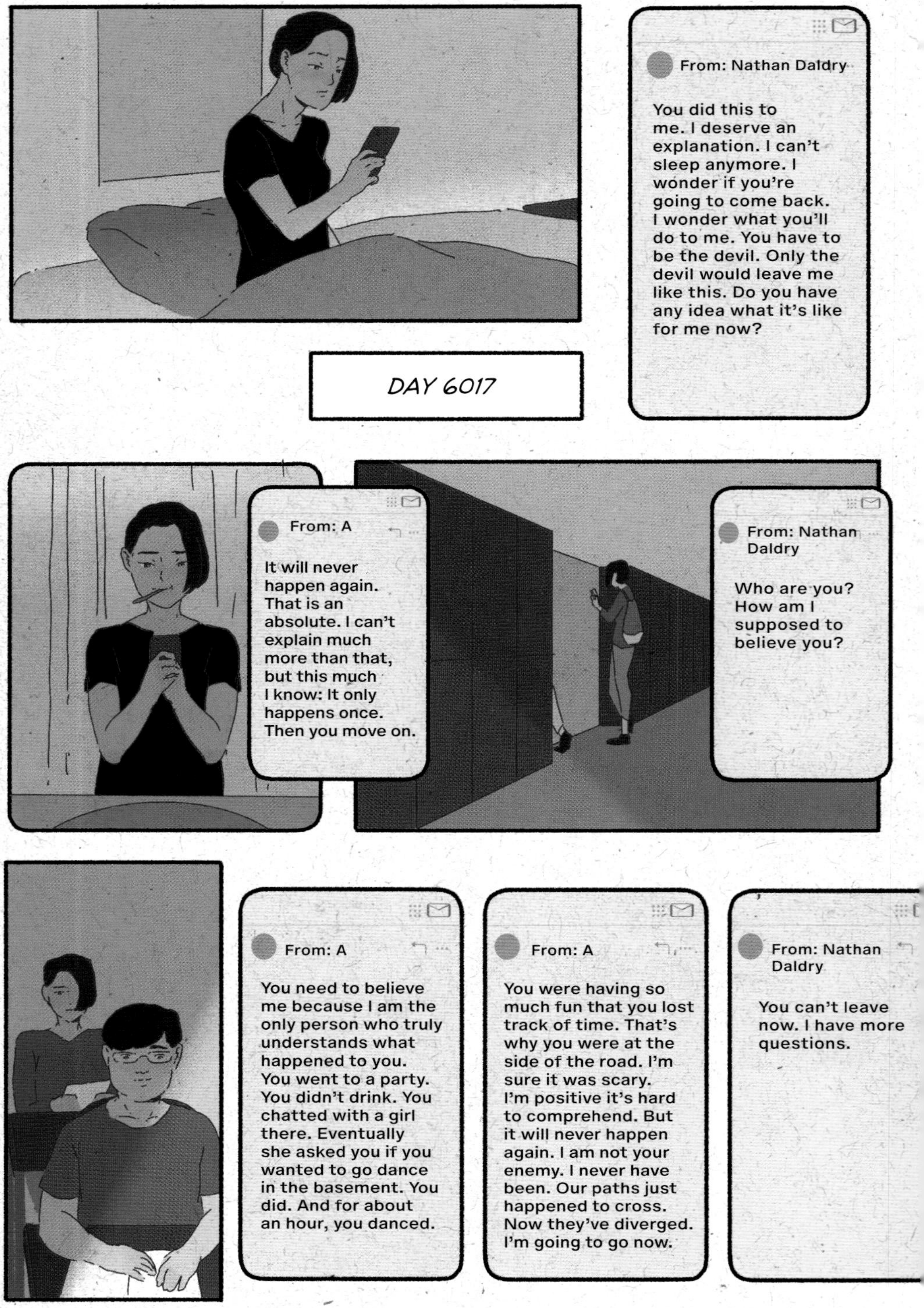
From: Nathan Daldry
You did this to me. I deserve an explanation. I can't sleep anymore. I wonder if you're going to come back. I wonder what you'll do to me. You have to be the devil. Only the devil would leave me like this. Do you have any idea what it's like for me now?
DAY 6017
From: A
It will never happen again. That is an absolute. I can't explain much more than that, but this much I know: It only happens once. Then you move on.
From: Nathan Daldry
Who are you? How am I supposed to believe you?
From: A
You need to believe me because I am the only person who truly understands what happened to you. You went to a party. You didn't drink. You chatted with a girl there. Eventually she asked you if you wanted to go dance in the basement. You did. And for about an hour, you danced.
From: A
You were having so much fun that you lost track of time. That's why you were at the side of the road. I'm sure it was scary. I'm positive it's hard to comprehend. But it will never happen again. I am not your enemy. I never have been. Our paths just happened to cross. Now they've diverged. I'm going to go now.
From: Nathan Daldry
You can't leave now. I have more questions.

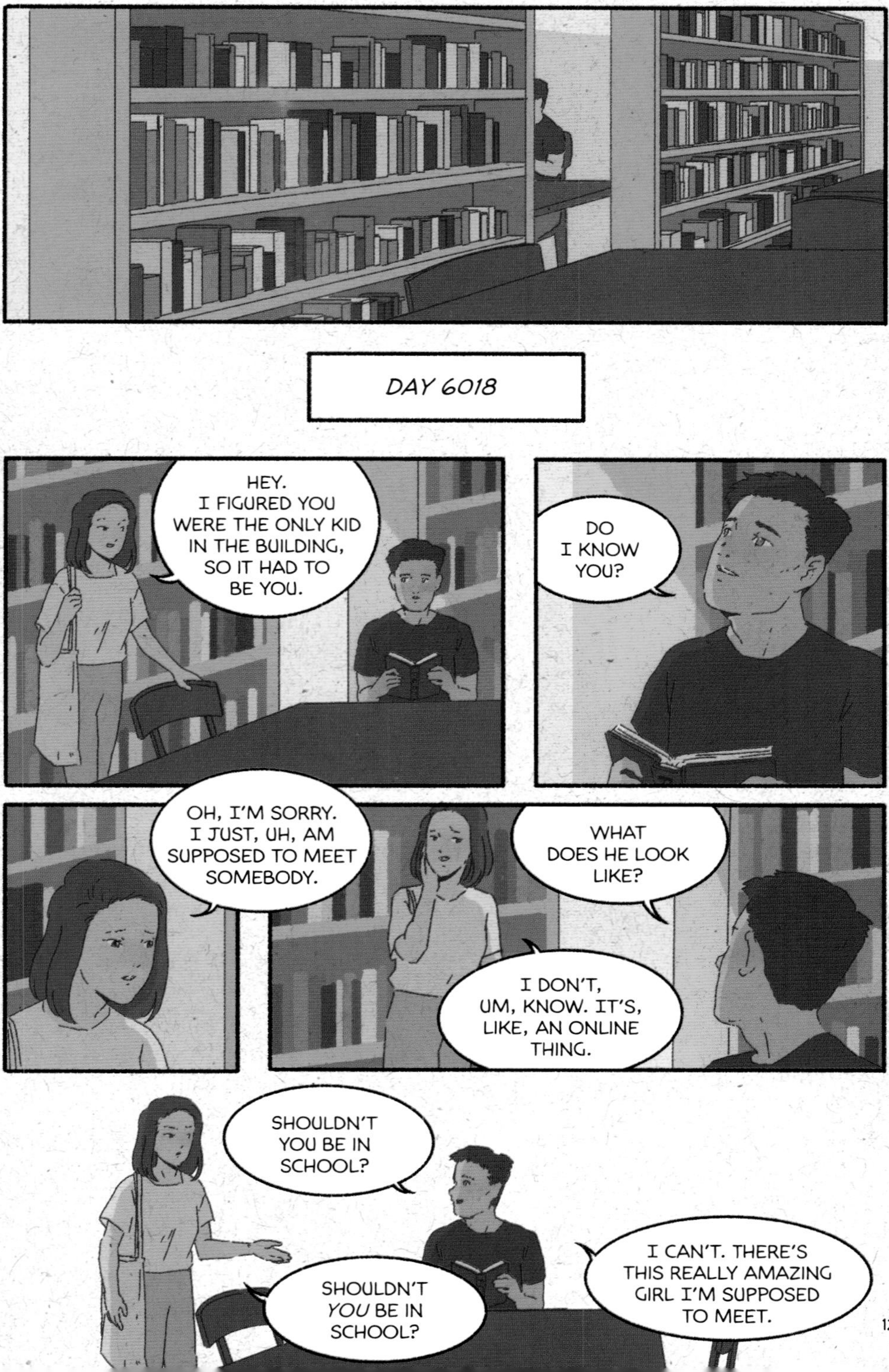
DAY 6018
HEY. I FIGURED YOU WERE THE ONLY KID IN THE BUILDING, SO IT HAD TO BE YOU.
DO I KNOW YOU?
OH, I'M SORRY. I JUST, UH, AM SUPPOSED TO MEET SOMEBODY.
WHAT DOES HE LOOK LIKE?
I DON'T, UM, KNOW. IT'S, LIKE, AN ONLINE THING.
SHOULDN'T YOU BE IN SCHOOL?
SHOULDN'T *YOU* BE IN SCHOOL?
I CAN'T. THERE'S THIS REALLY AMAZING GIRL I'M SUPPOSED TO MEET.

YOU CAN'T DO THAT. IT'S NOT FAIR.

YOU JERK.

RHIANNON, I'M SORRY.

I BELIEVE YOU. BUT YOU'RE STILL A JERK UNTIL YOU PROVE OTHERWISE.

I WILL NEVER DO IT AGAIN. I PROMISE.

NOW, LET'S GET LUNCH, BECAUSE I HAVE TO BE BACK IN AN HOUR. HOW ABOUT YOU?

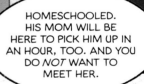

HOMESCHOOLED. HIS MOM WILL BE HERE TO PICK HIM UP IN AN HOUR, TOO. AND YOU DO *NOT* WANT TO MEET HER.

WHAT ARE YOU DOING?

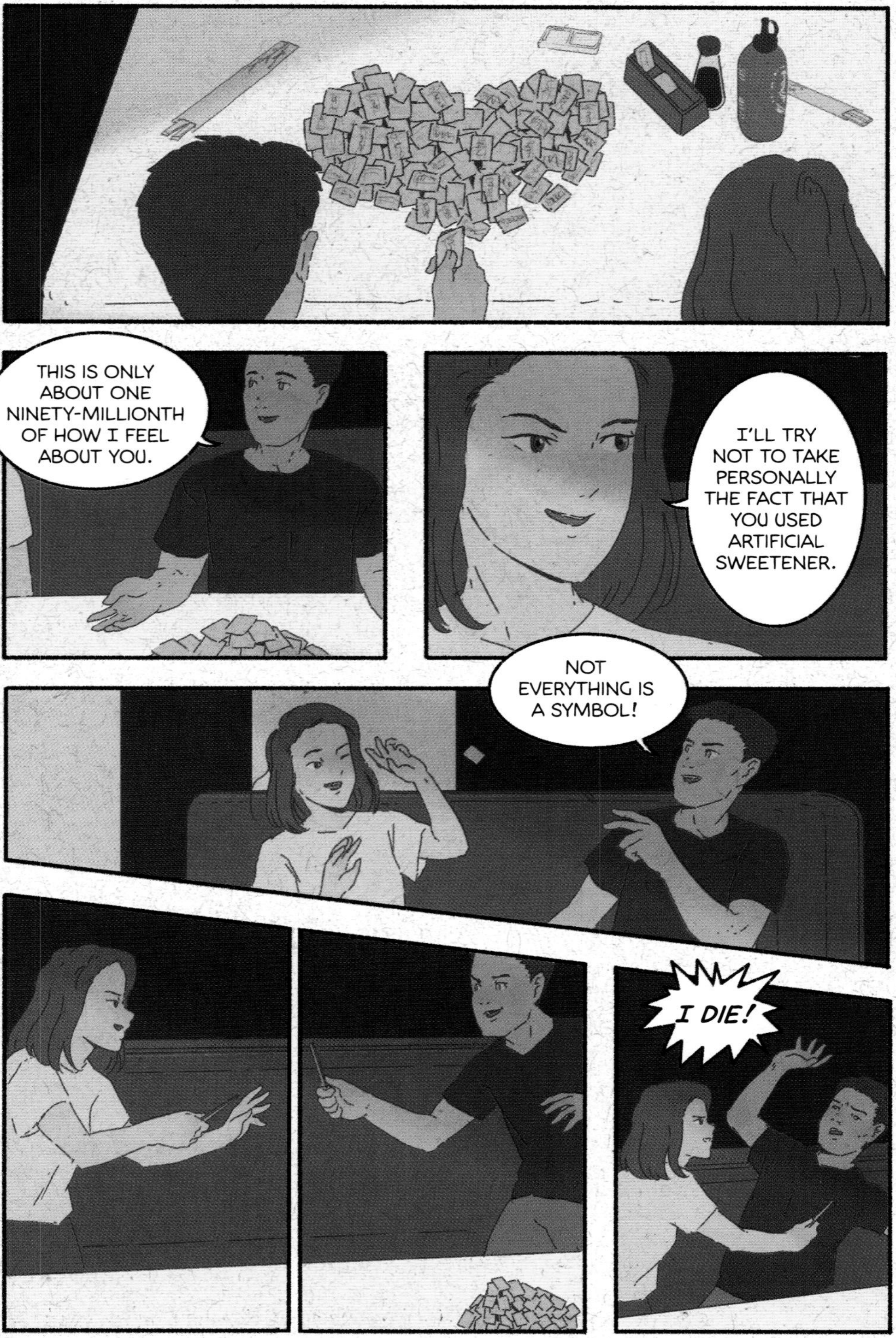
THIS IS ONLY ABOUT ONE NINETY-MILLIONTH OF HOW I FEEL ABOUT YOU.
I'LL TRY NOT TO TAKE PERSONALLY THE FACT THAT YOU USED ARTIFICIAL SWEETENER.
NOT EVERYTHING IS A SYMBOL!
I DIE!

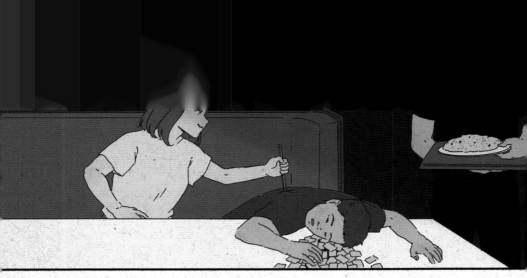

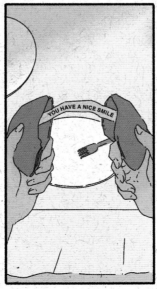

YOU HAVE A NICE SMILE

THIS ISN'T A FORTUNE.

NO. "YOU WILL HAVE A NICE SMILE"— THAT WOULD BE A FORTUNE.

I'M GOING TO SEND IT BACK.

I ONLY NEED ONE.

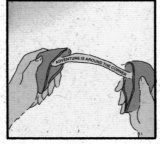

ADVENTURE IS AROUND THE CORNER

WELL DONE, SIR.

129

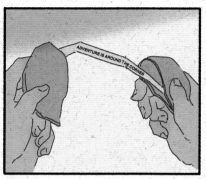

ADVENTURE IS AROUND THE CORNER

SO WHAT SHOULD I READ NEXT?

IT'S A COMFORT TO ME THAT NO MATTER WHAT LIFE I'M IN, I CAN RETURN TO BOOKS AND THEY'RE STILL THE SAME.

WHAT'S YOUR FAVORITE?

NO! NOT THAT ONE!

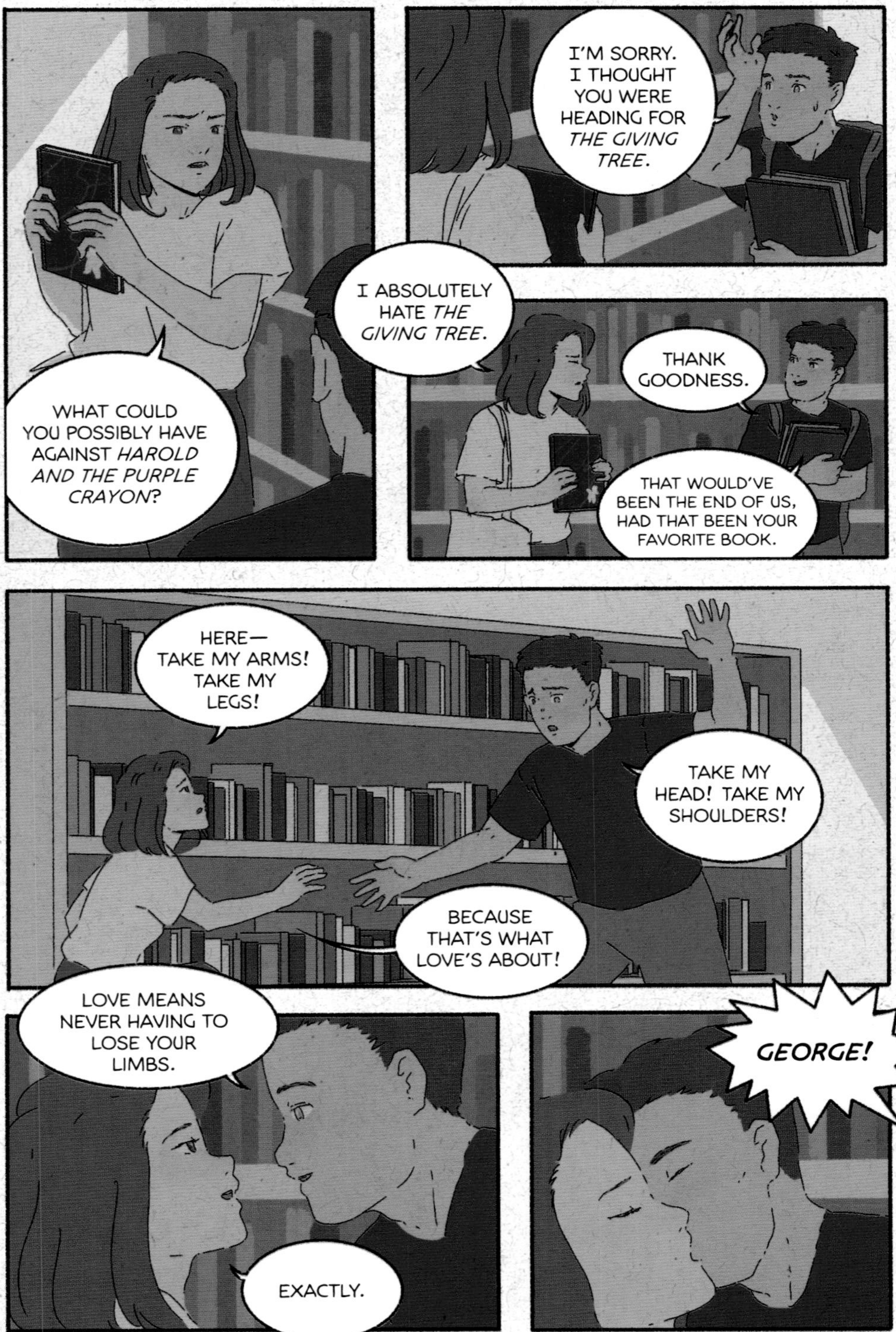
WHAT COULD YOU POSSIBLY HAVE AGAINST *HAROLD AND THE PURPLE CRAYON*?
I'M SORRY. I THOUGHT YOU WERE HEADING FOR *THE GIVING TREE*.
I ABSOLUTELY HATE *THE GIVING TREE*.
THANK GOODNESS.
THAT WOULD'VE BEEN THE END OF US, HAD THAT BEEN YOUR FAVORITE BOOK.
HERE— TAKE MY ARMS! TAKE MY LEGS!
TAKE MY HEAD! TAKE MY SHOULDERS!
BECAUSE THAT'S WHAT LOVE'S ABOUT!
LOVE MEANS NEVER HAVING TO LOSE YOUR LIMBS.
EXACTLY.
GEORGE!

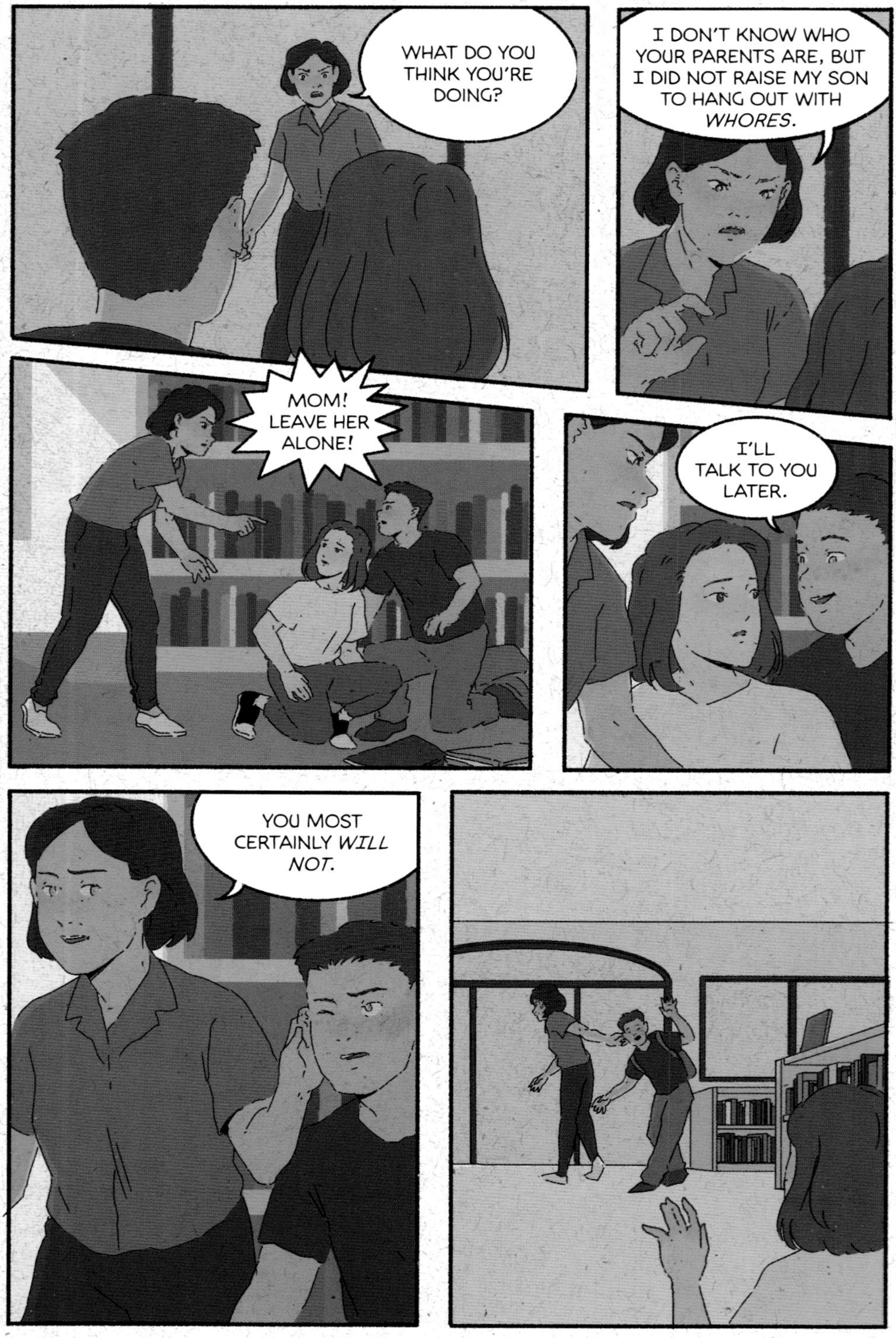
WHAT DO YOU THINK YOU'RE DOING?
I DON'T KNOW WHO YOUR PARENTS ARE, BUT I DID NOT RAISE MY SON TO HANG OUT WITH *WHORES*.
MOM! LEAVE HER ALONE!
I'LL TALK TO YOU LATER.
YOU MOST CERTAINLY *WILL NOT*.

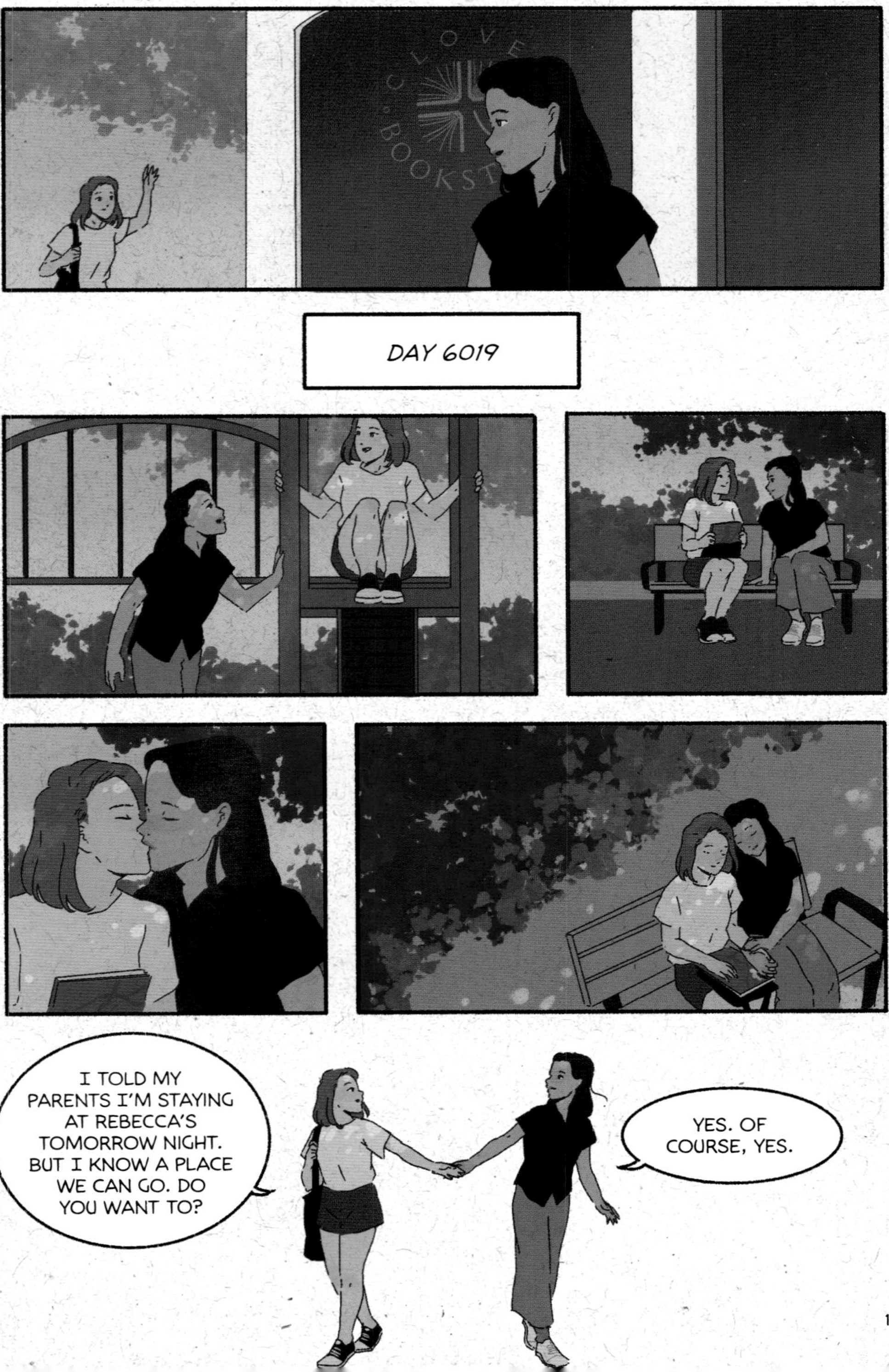
DAY 6019
I TOLD MY PARENTS I'M STAYING AT REBECCA'S TOMORROW NIGHT. BUT I KNOW A PLACE WE CAN GO. DO YOU WANT TO?
YES. OF COURSE, YES.

DAY 6020

NOPE.

YOU'RE REALLY CUTE TODAY. YOUR MOM ISN'T GOING TO SHOW UP THIS TIME, IS SHE?

GOOD, THEN I CAN DO THIS WITHOUT BEING KILLED.

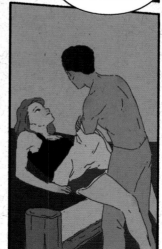

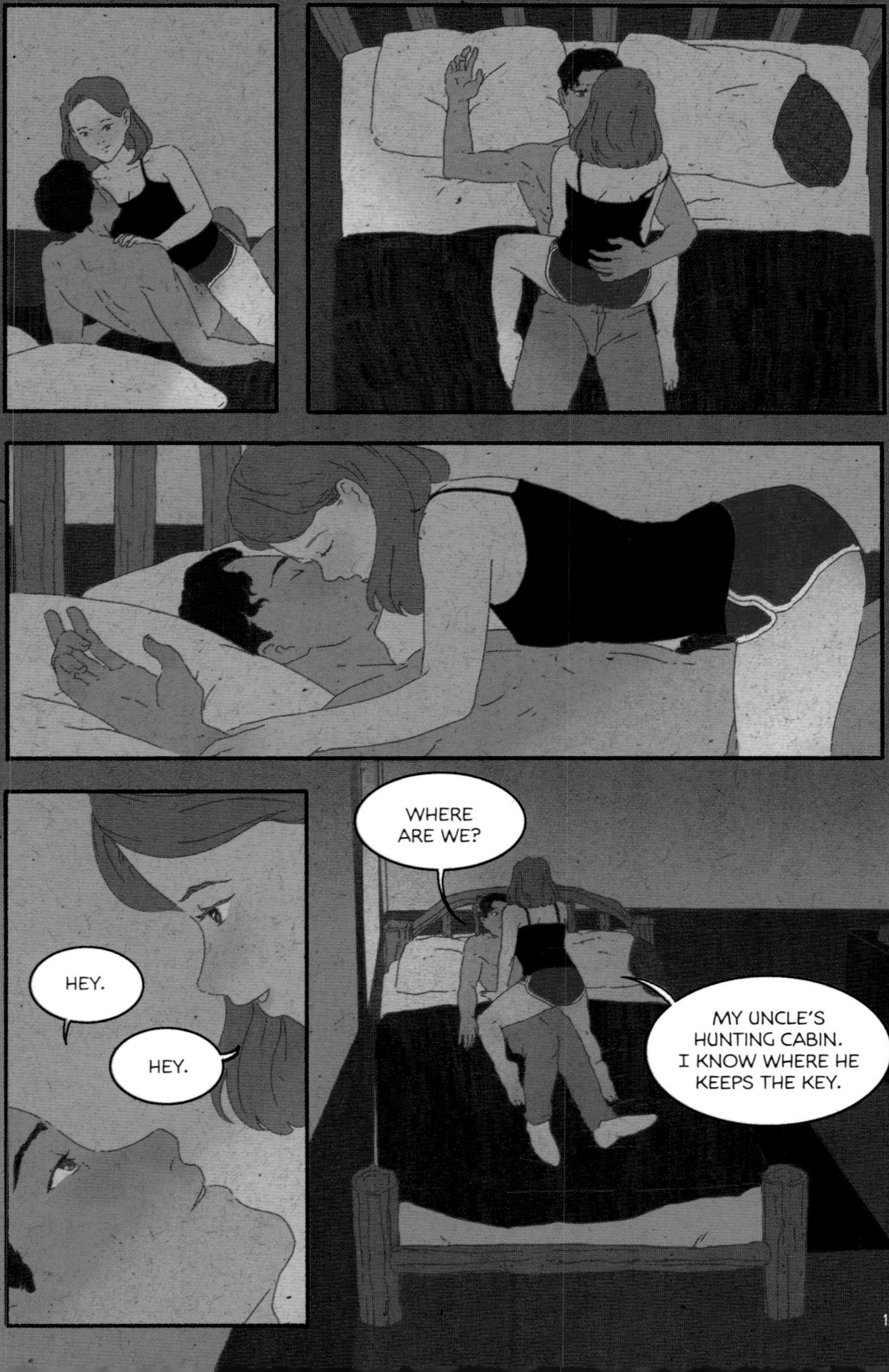
HEY.
HEY.
WHERE ARE WE?
MY UNCLE'S HUNTING CABIN. I KNOW WHERE HE KEEPS THE KEY.

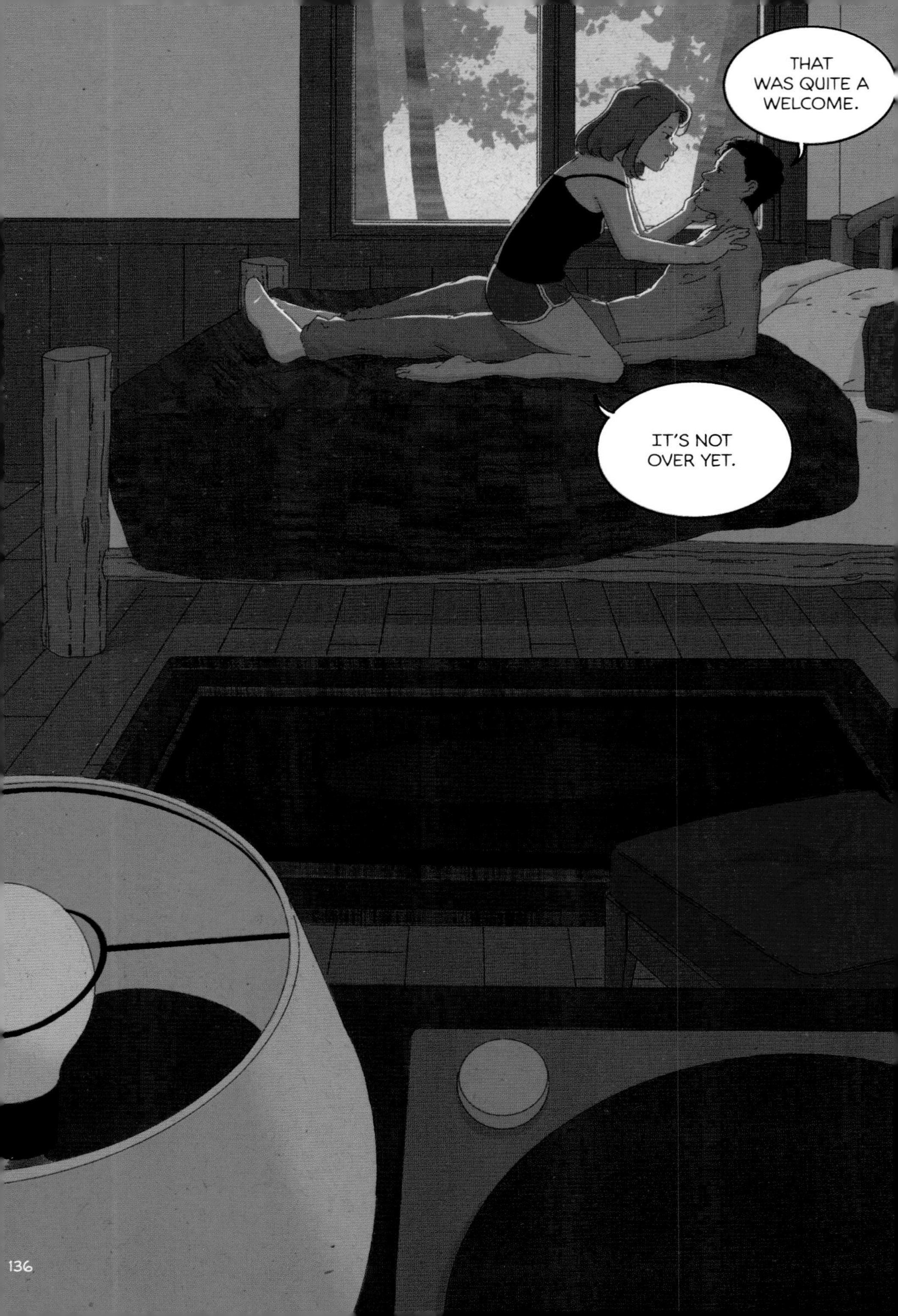
THAT WAS QUITE A WELCOME.
IT'S NOT OVER YET.

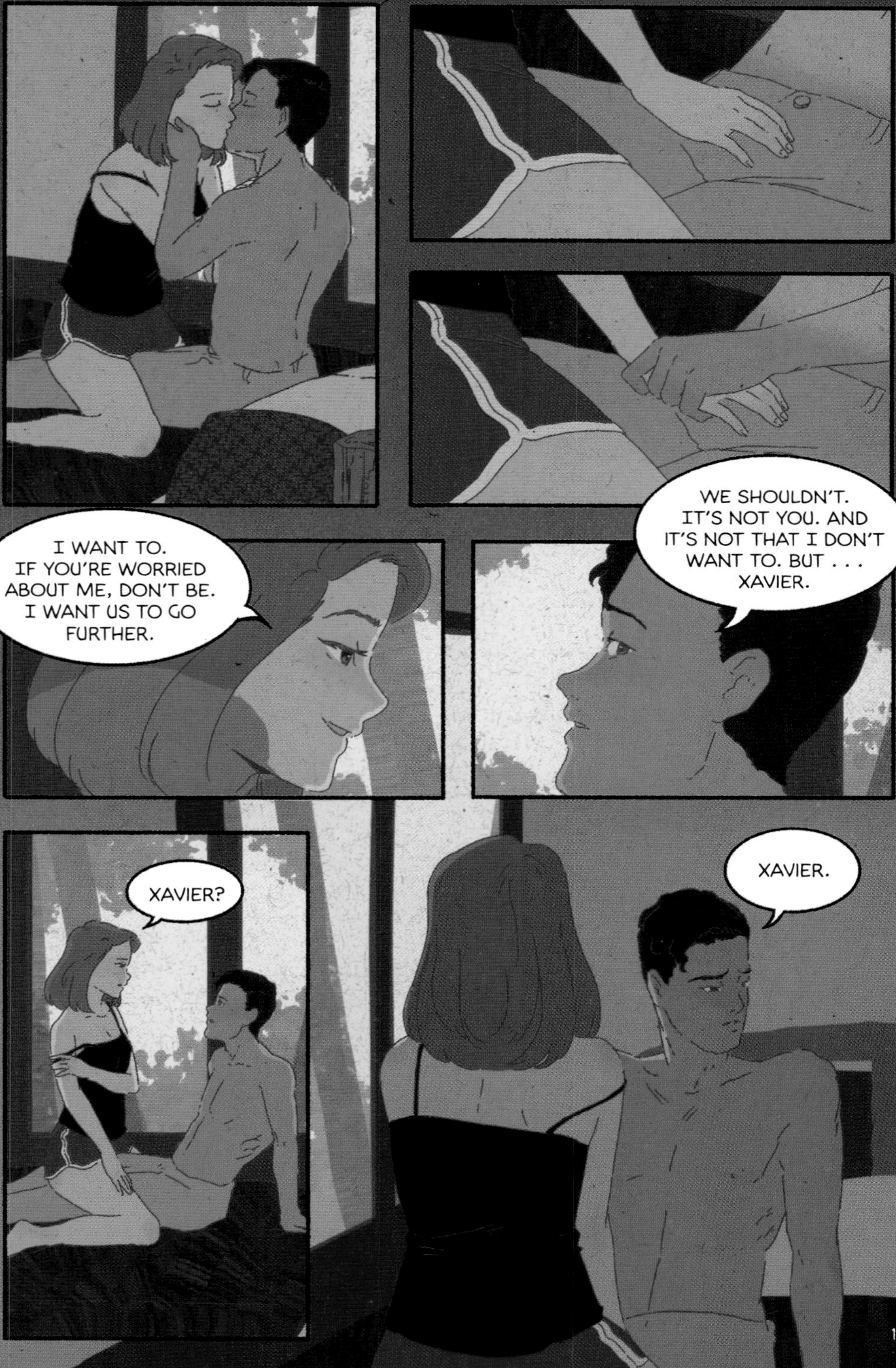
WE SHOULDN'T. IT'S NOT YOU. AND IT'S NOT THAT I DON'T WANT TO. BUT . . . XAVIER.
I WANT TO. IF YOU'RE WORRIED ABOUT ME, DON'T BE. I WANT US TO GO FURTHER.
XAVIER?
XAVIER.

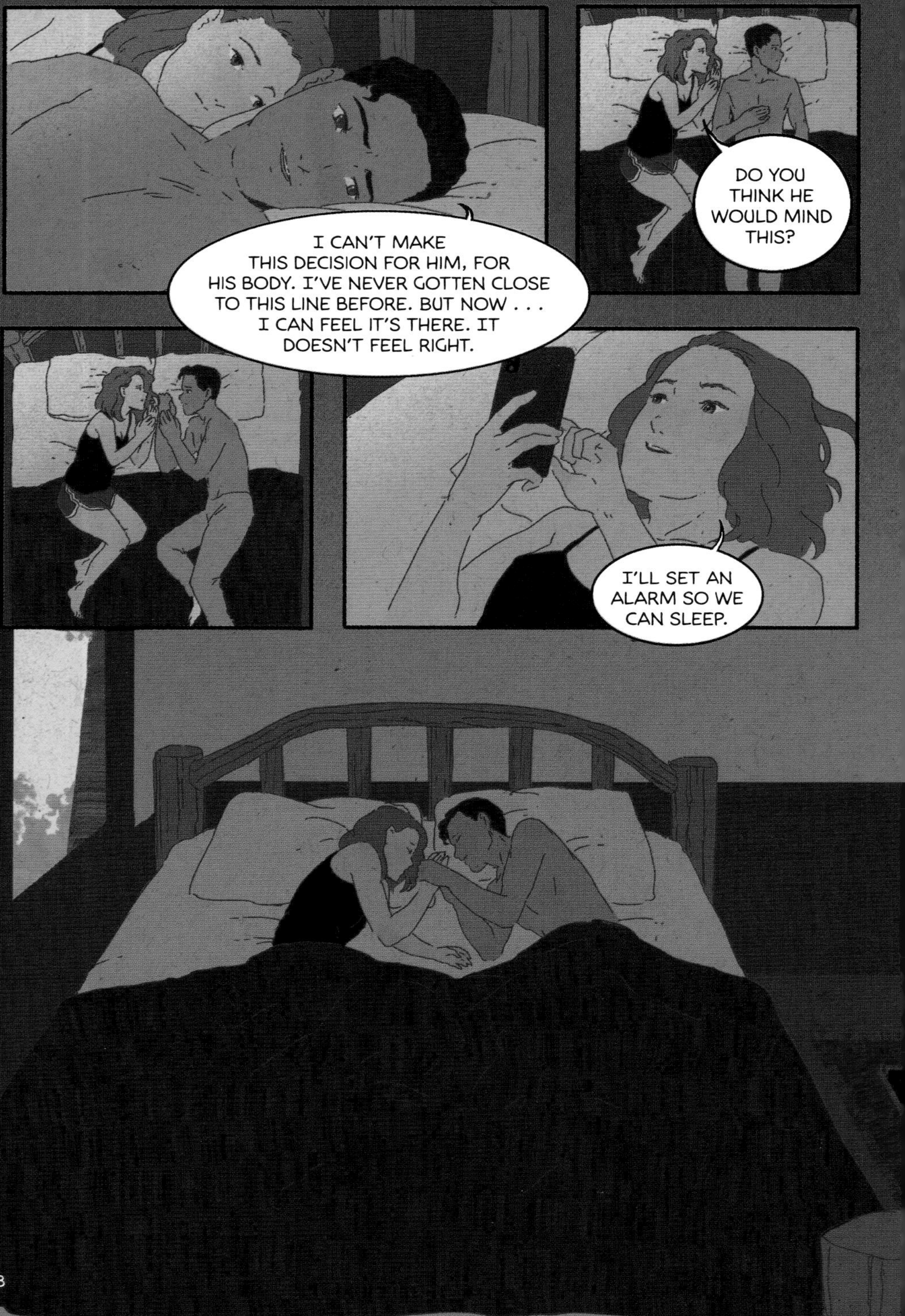
I CAN'T MAKE THIS DECISION FOR HIM, FOR HIS BODY. I'VE NEVER GOTTEN CLOSE TO THIS LINE BEFORE. BUT NOW . . . I CAN FEEL IT'S THERE. IT DOESN'T FEEL RIGHT.
DO YOU THINK HE WOULD MIND THIS?
I'LL SET AN ALARM SO WE CAN SLEEP.

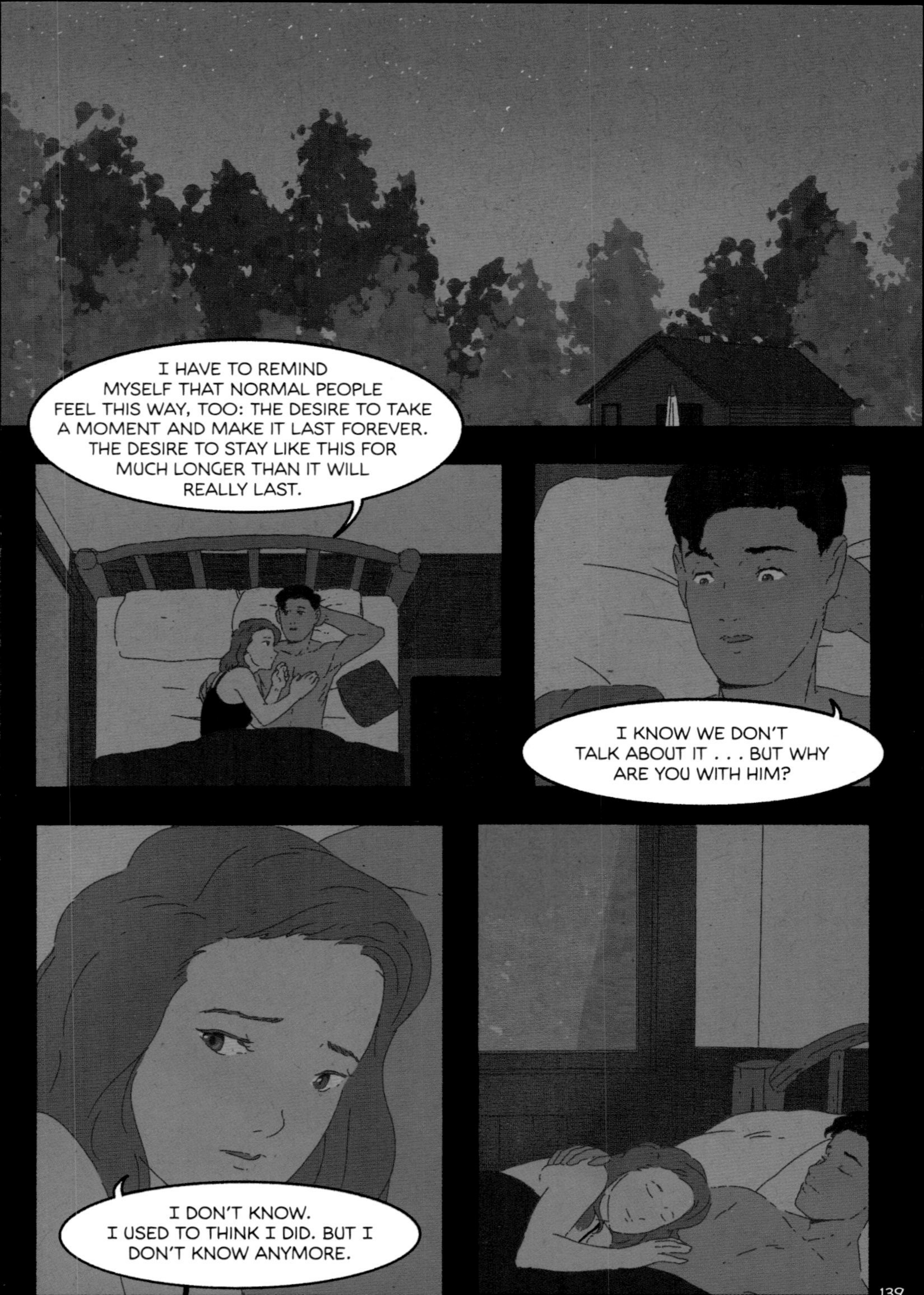
I HAVE TO REMIND MYSELF THAT NORMAL PEOPLE FEEL THIS WAY, TOO: THE DESIRE TO TAKE A MOMENT AND MAKE IT LAST FOREVER. THE DESIRE TO STAY LIKE THIS FOR MUCH LONGER THAN IT WILL REALLY LAST.
I KNOW WE DON'T TALK ABOUT IT . . . BUT WHY ARE YOU WITH HIM?
I DON'T KNOW. I USED TO THINK I DID. BUT I DON'T KNOW ANYMORE.

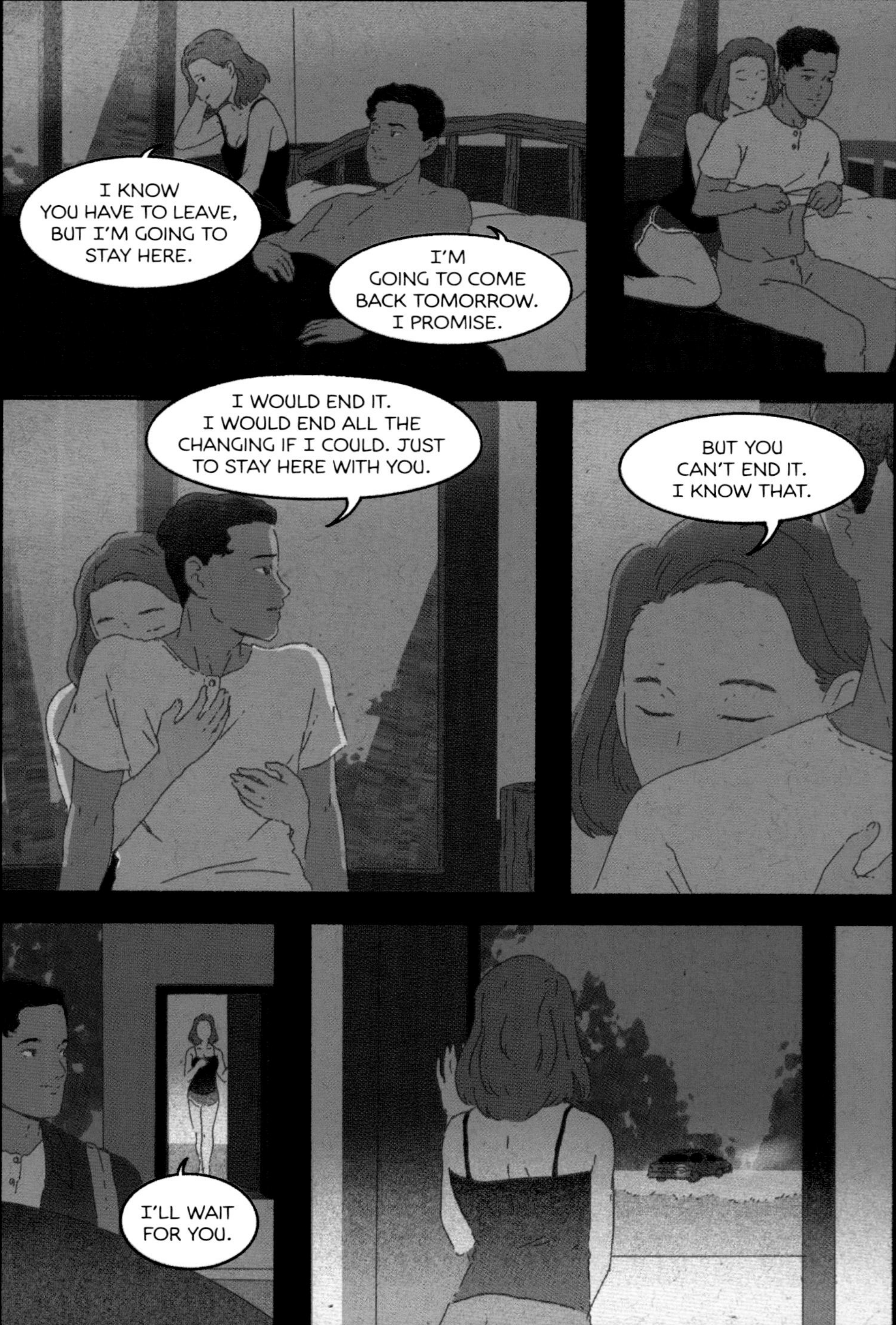

I KNOW YOU HAVE TO LEAVE, BUT I'M GOING TO STAY HERE.
I'M GOING TO COME BACK TOMORROW. I PROMISE.
I WOULD END IT. I WOULD END ALL THE CHANGING IF I COULD. JUST TO STAY HERE WITH YOU.
BUT YOU CAN'T END IT. I KNOW THAT.
I'LL WAIT FOR YOU.

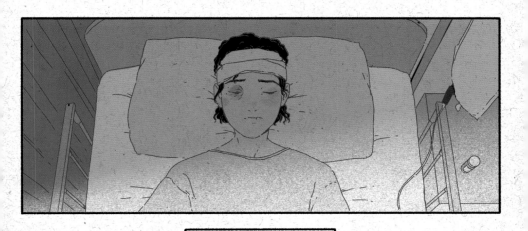

DAY 6021

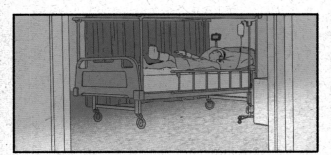

RHIANNON . . .

DO YOU NEED SOMETHING?

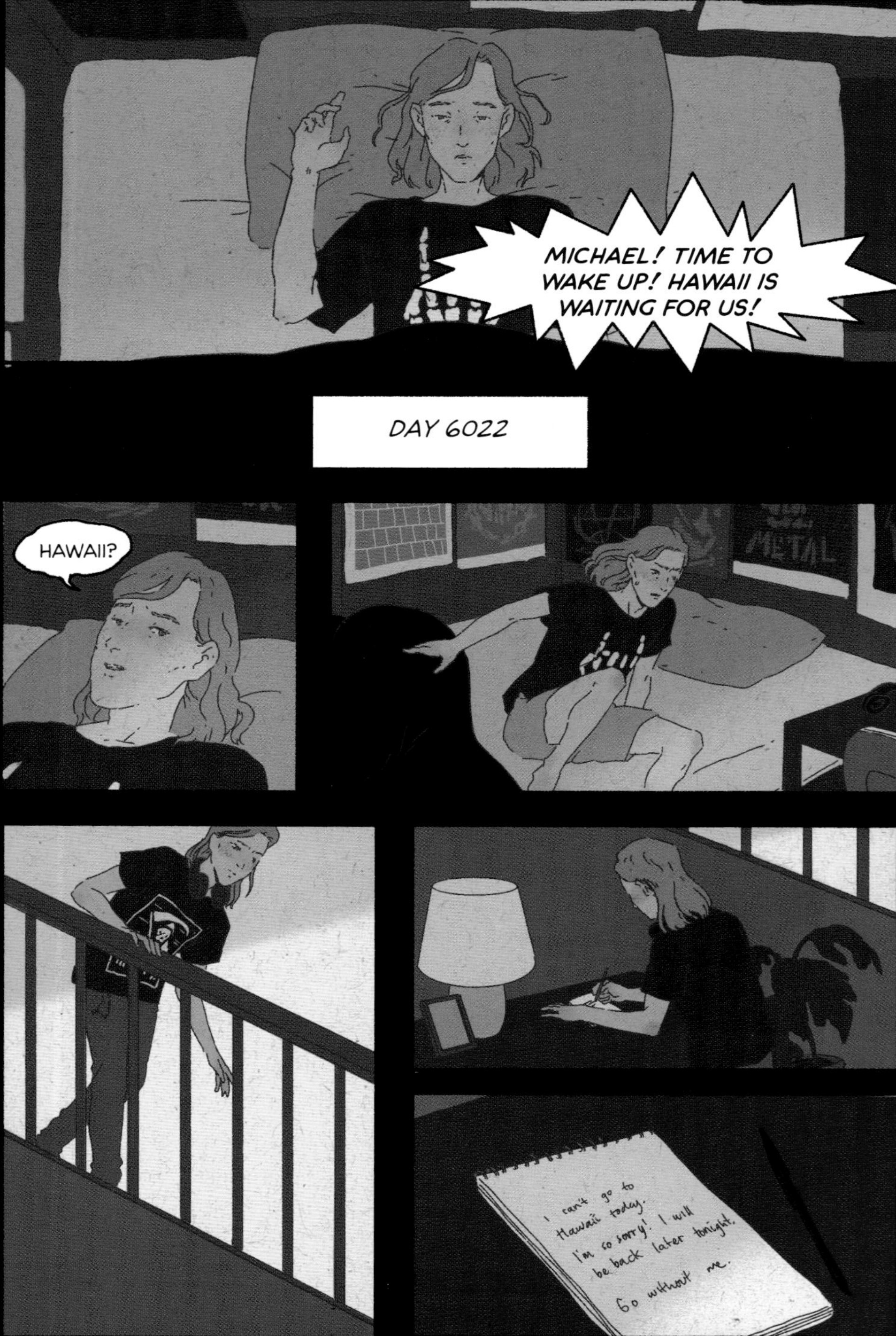
MICHAEL! TIME TO WAKE UP! HAWAII IS WAITING FOR US!
DAY 6022
HAWAII?
I can't go to Hawaii today.
I'm so sorry! I will be back later tonight.
Go without me.

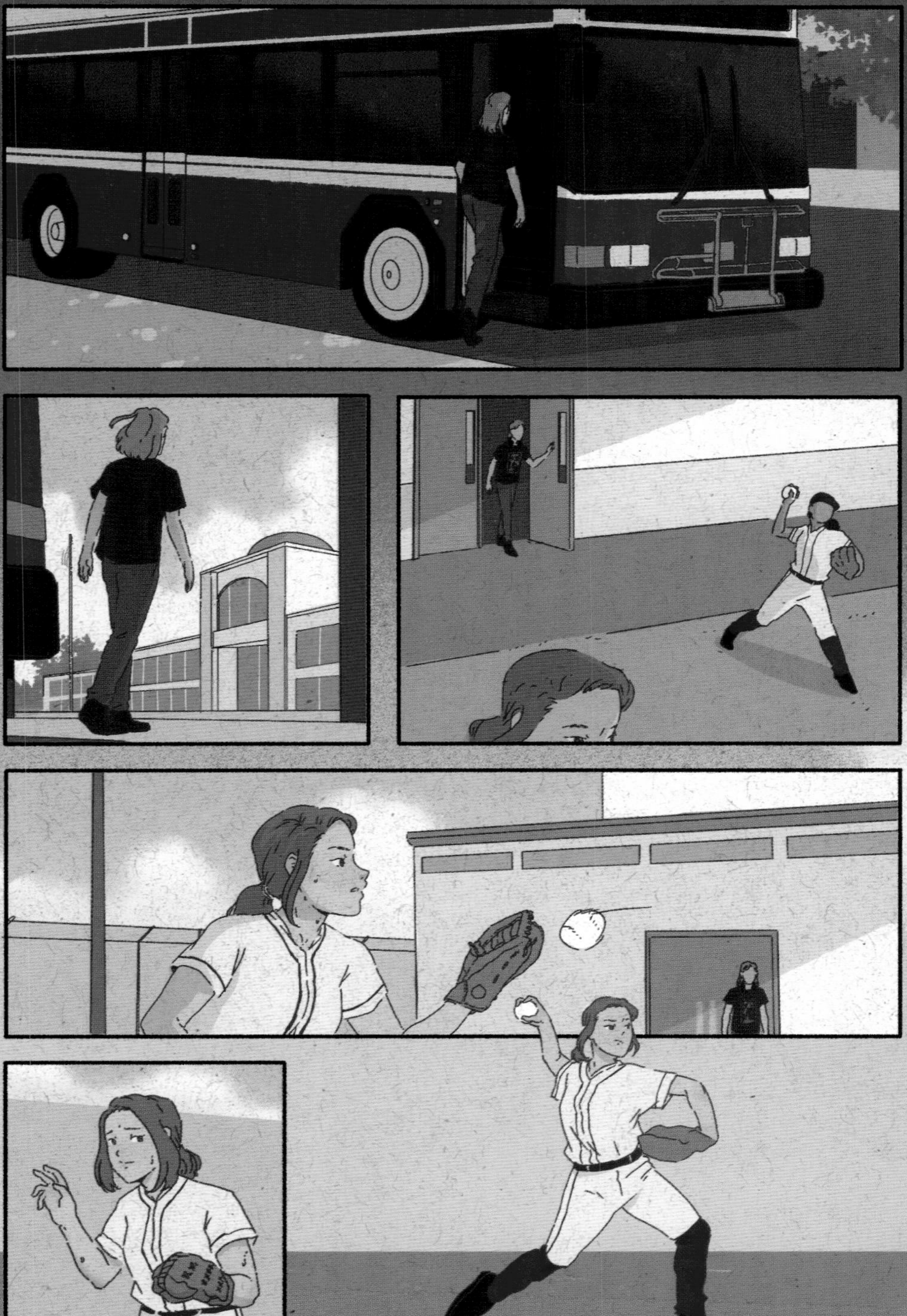

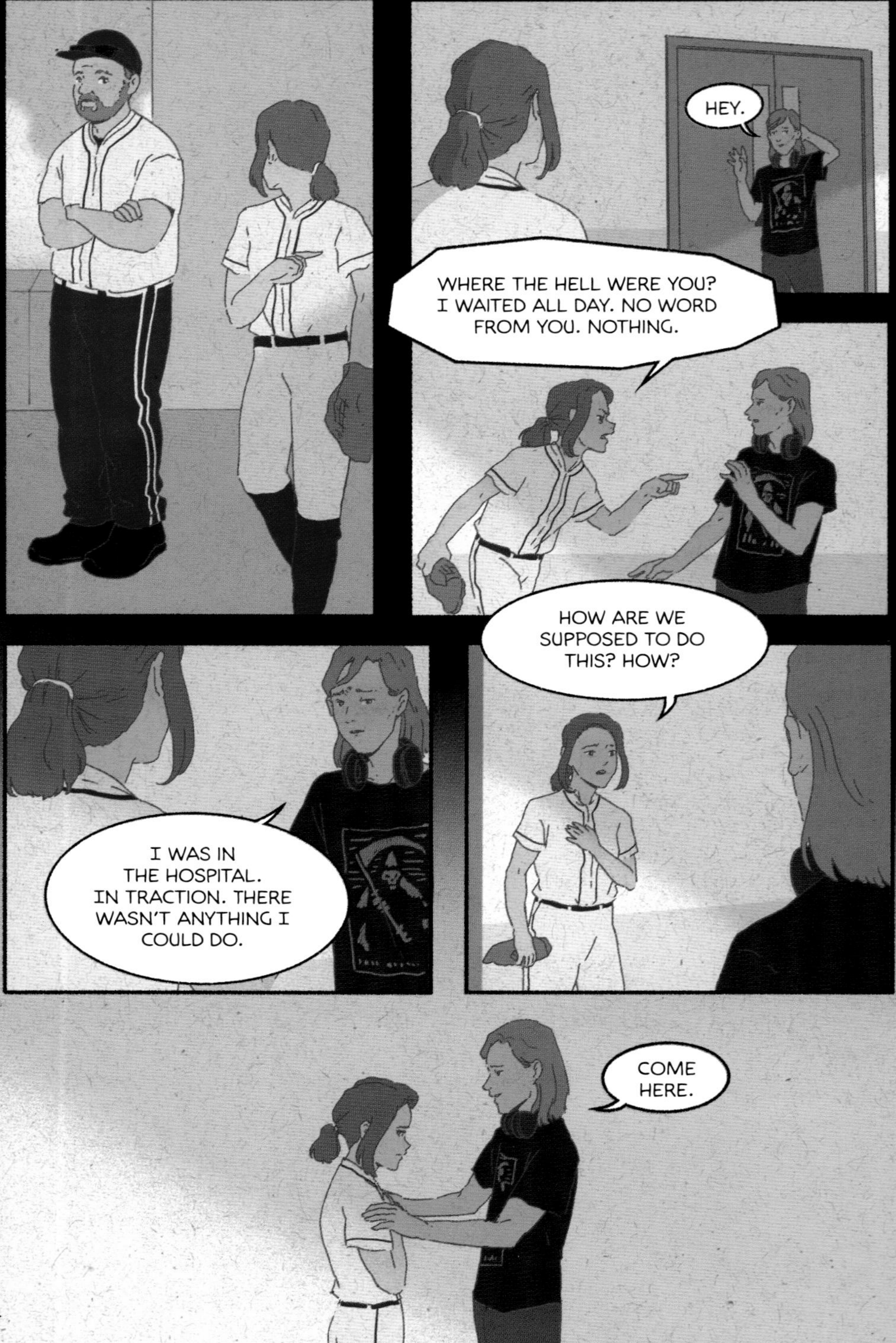
HEY.
WHERE THE HELL WERE YOU? I WAITED ALL DAY. NO WORD FROM YOU. NOTHING.
HOW ARE WE SUPPOSED TO DO THIS? HOW?
I WAS IN THE HOSPITAL. IN TRACTION. THERE WASN'T ANYTHING I COULD DO.
COME HERE.

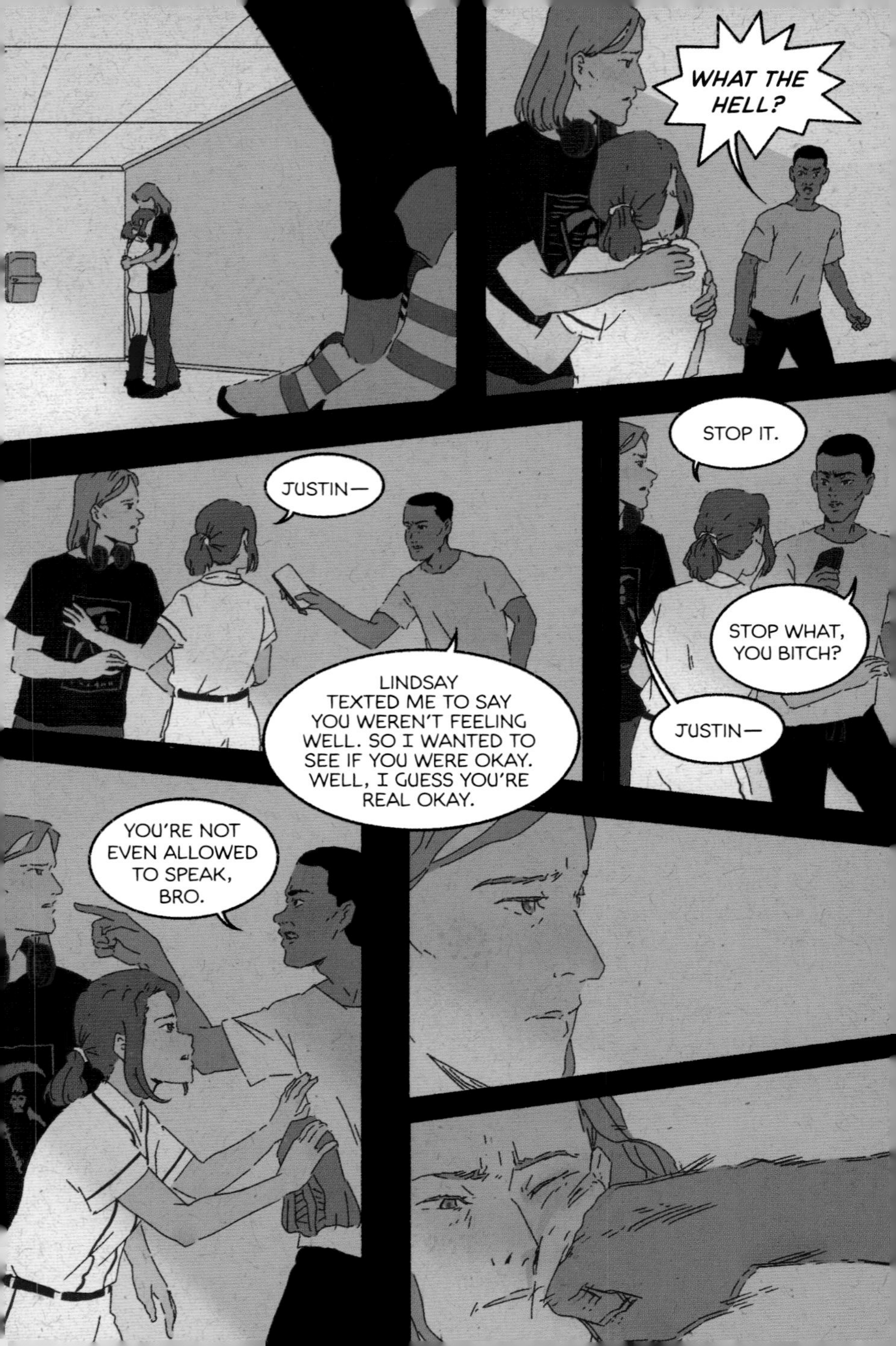
WHAT THE HELL?
JUSTIN—
STOP IT.
STOP WHAT, YOU BITCH?
JUSTIN—
LINDSAY TEXTED ME TO SAY YOU WEREN'T FEELING WELL. SO I WANTED TO SEE IF YOU WERE OKAY. WELL, I GUESS YOU'RE REAL OKAY.
YOU'RE NOT EVEN ALLOWED TO SPEAK, BRO.

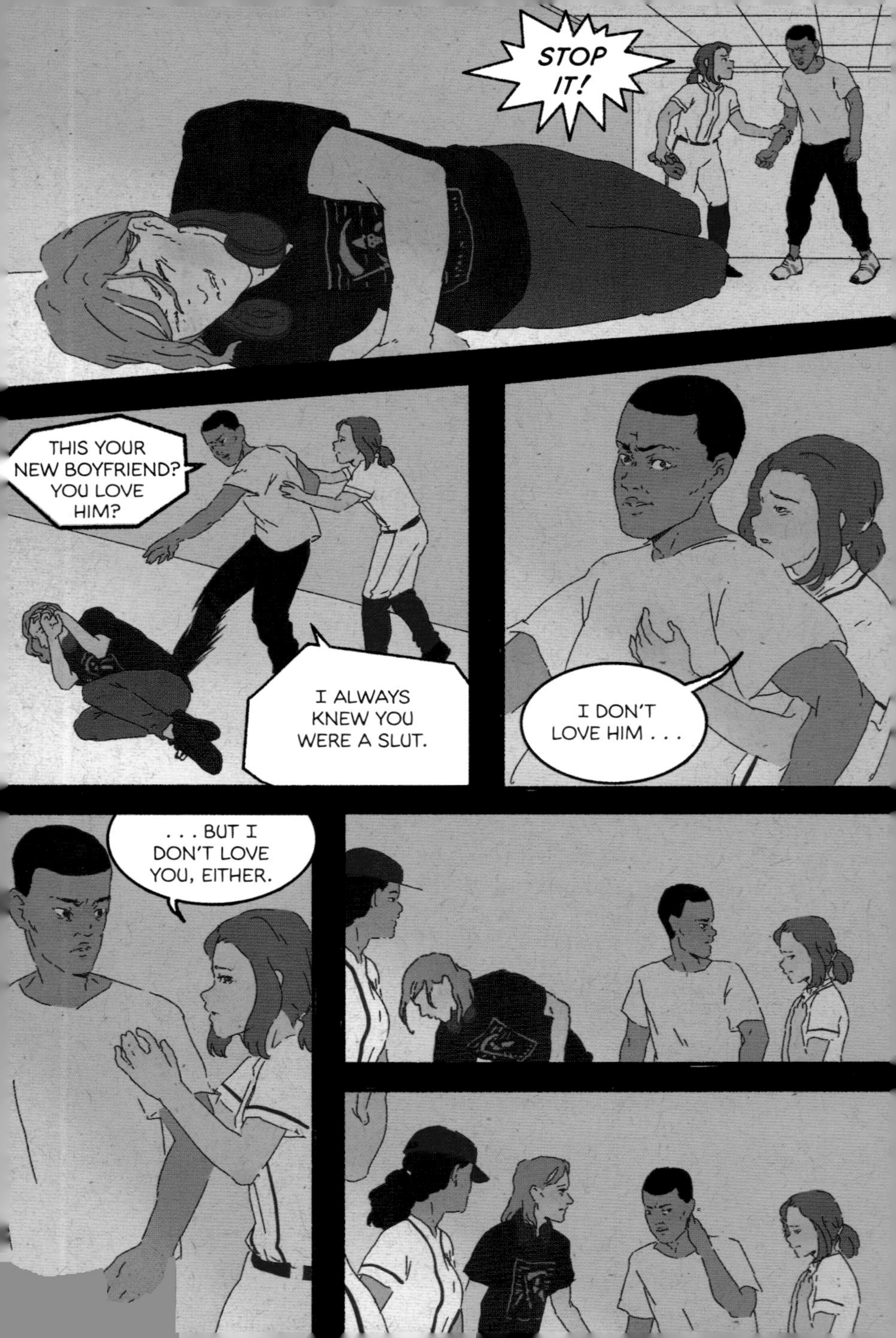
STOP IT!
THIS YOUR NEW BOYFRIEND? YOU LOVE HIM?
I ALWAYS KNEW YOU WERE A SLUT.
I DON'T LOVE HIM . . .
. . . BUT I DON'T LOVE YOU, EITHER.

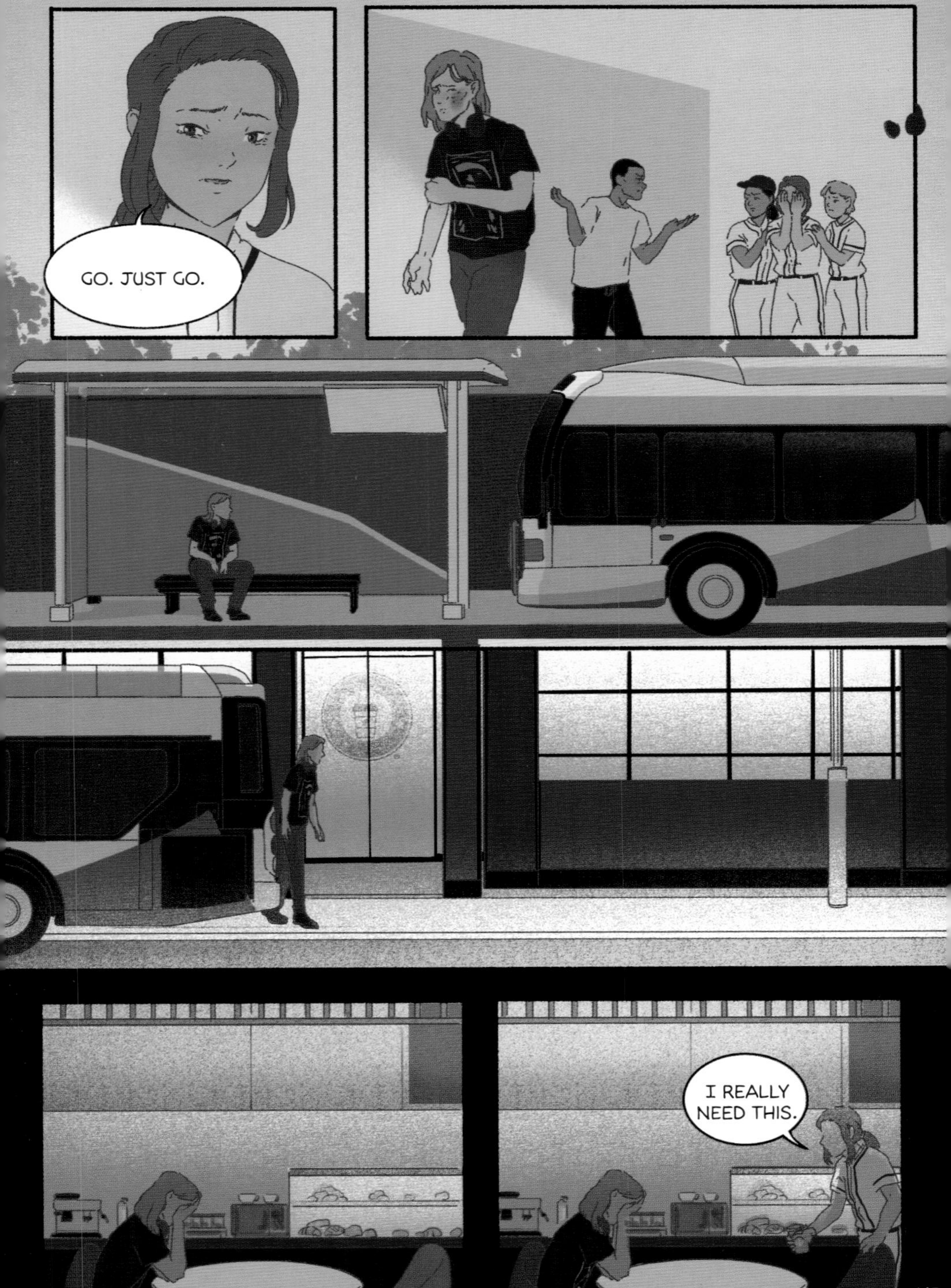
GO. JUST GO.
I REALLY NEED THIS.

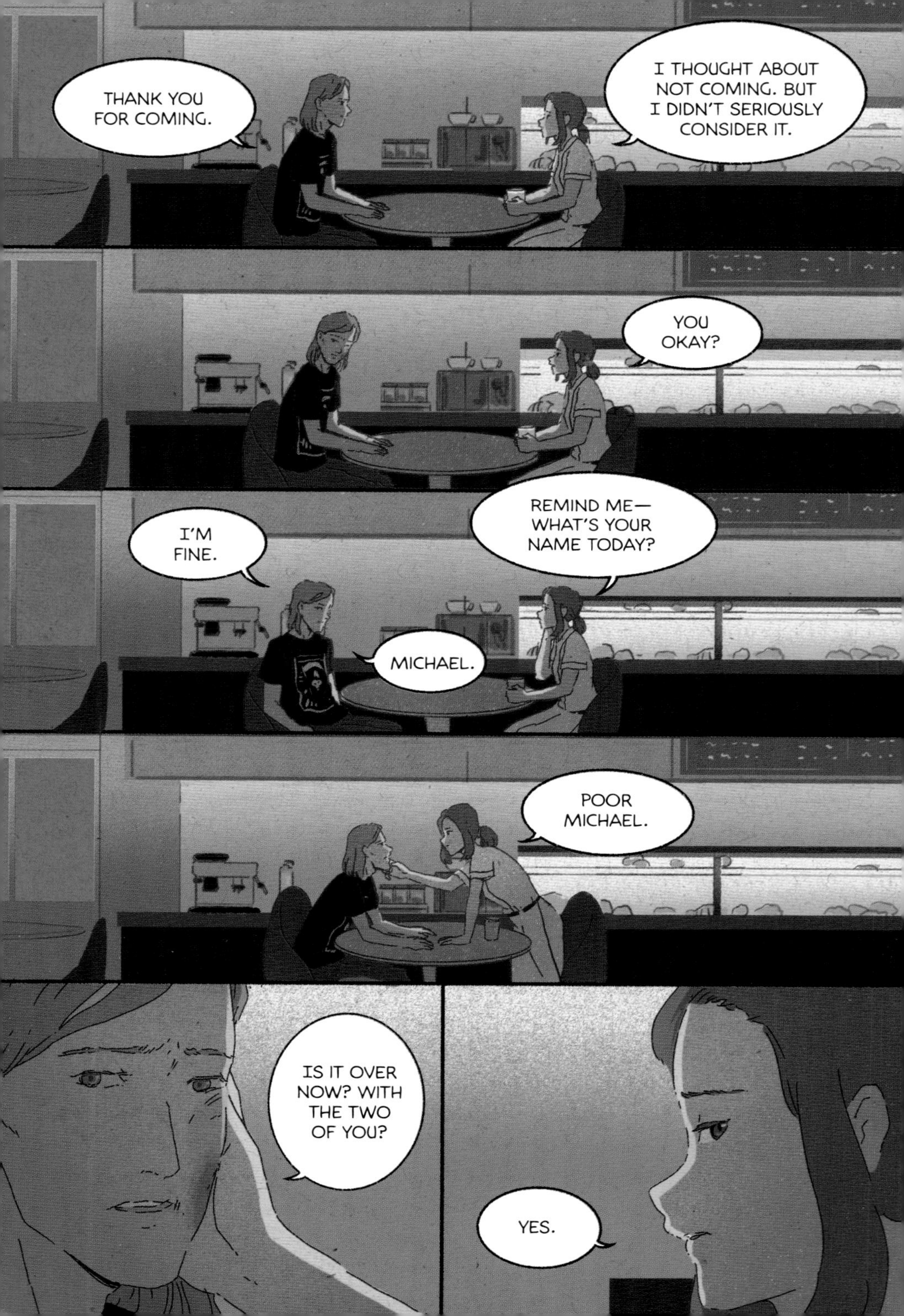
THANK YOU FOR COMING.
I THOUGHT ABOUT NOT COMING. BUT I DIDN'T SERIOUSLY CONSIDER IT.
YOU OKAY?
I'M FINE.
REMIND ME— WHAT'S YOUR NAME TODAY?
MICHAEL.
POOR MICHAEL.
IS IT OVER NOW? WITH THE TWO OF YOU?
YES.

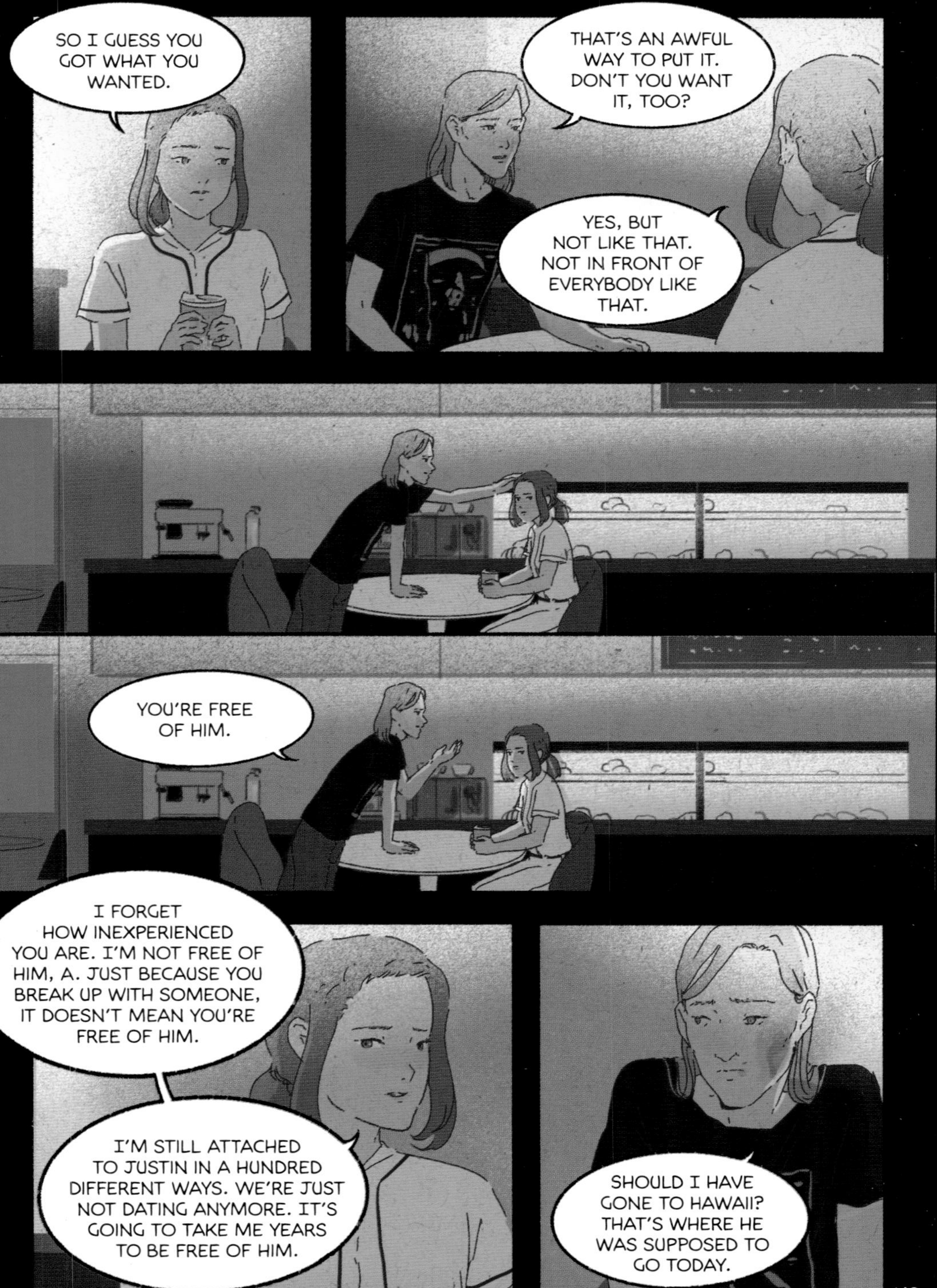
SO I GUESS YOU GOT WHAT YOU WANTED.
THAT'S AN AWFUL WAY TO PUT IT. DON'T YOU WANT IT, TOO?
YES, BUT NOT LIKE THAT. NOT IN FRONT OF EVERYBODY LIKE THAT.
YOU'RE FREE OF HIM.
I FORGET HOW INEXPERIENCED YOU ARE. I'M NOT FREE OF HIM, A. JUST BECAUSE YOU BREAK UP WITH SOMEONE, IT DOESN'T MEAN YOU'RE FREE OF HIM.
I'M STILL ATTACHED TO JUSTIN IN A HUNDRED DIFFERENT WAYS. WE'RE JUST NOT DATING ANYMORE. IT'S GOING TO TAKE ME YEARS TO BE FREE OF HIM.
SHOULD I HAVE GONE TO HAWAII? THAT'S WHERE HE WAS SUPPOSED TO GO TODAY.

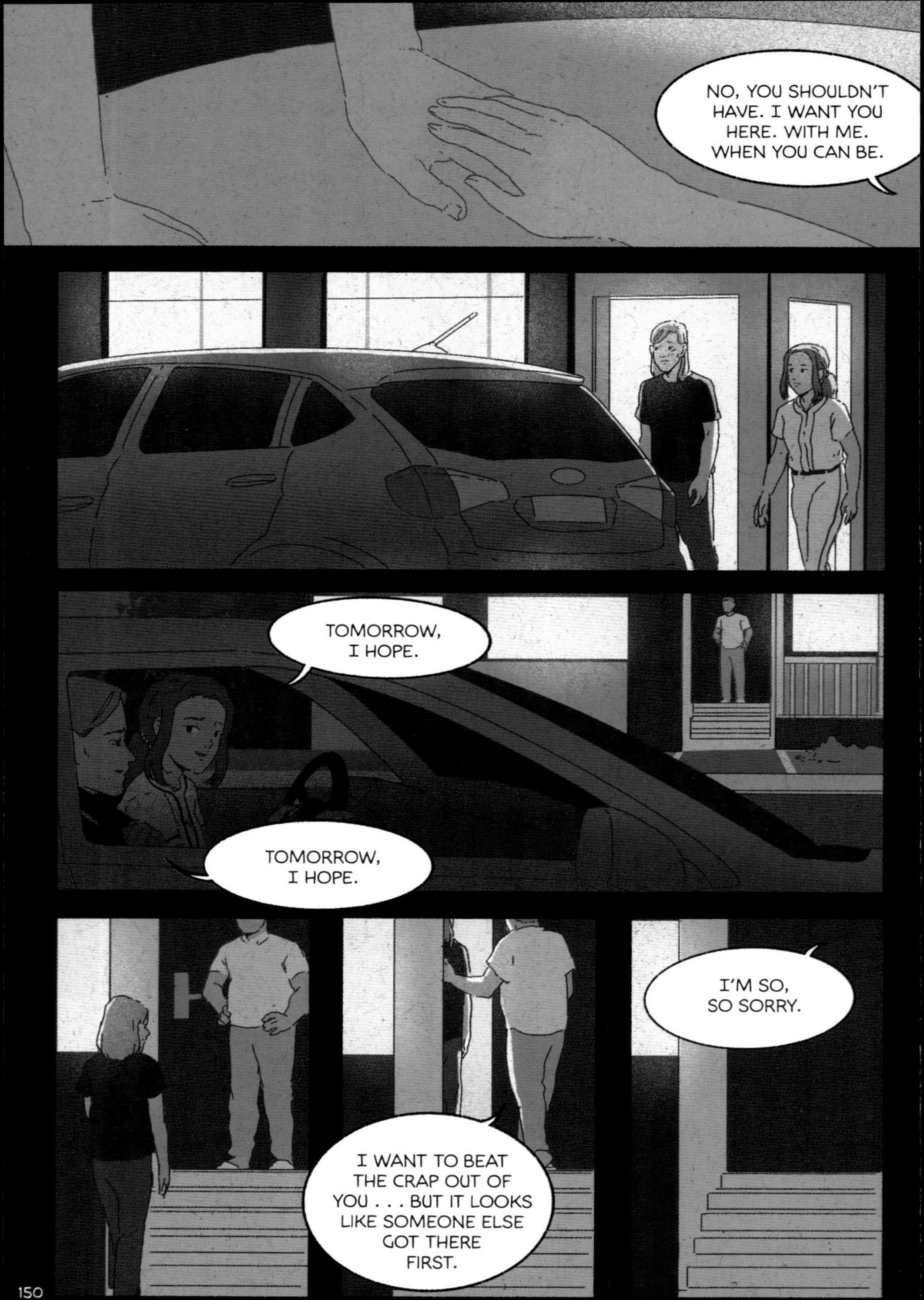
NO, YOU SHOULDN'T HAVE. I WANT YOU HERE. WITH ME. WHEN YOU CAN BE.
TOMORROW, I HOPE.
TOMORROW, I HOPE.
I WANT TO BEAT THE CRAP OUT OF YOU . . . BUT IT LOOKS LIKE SOMEONE ELSE GOT THERE FIRST.
I'M SO, SO SORRY.

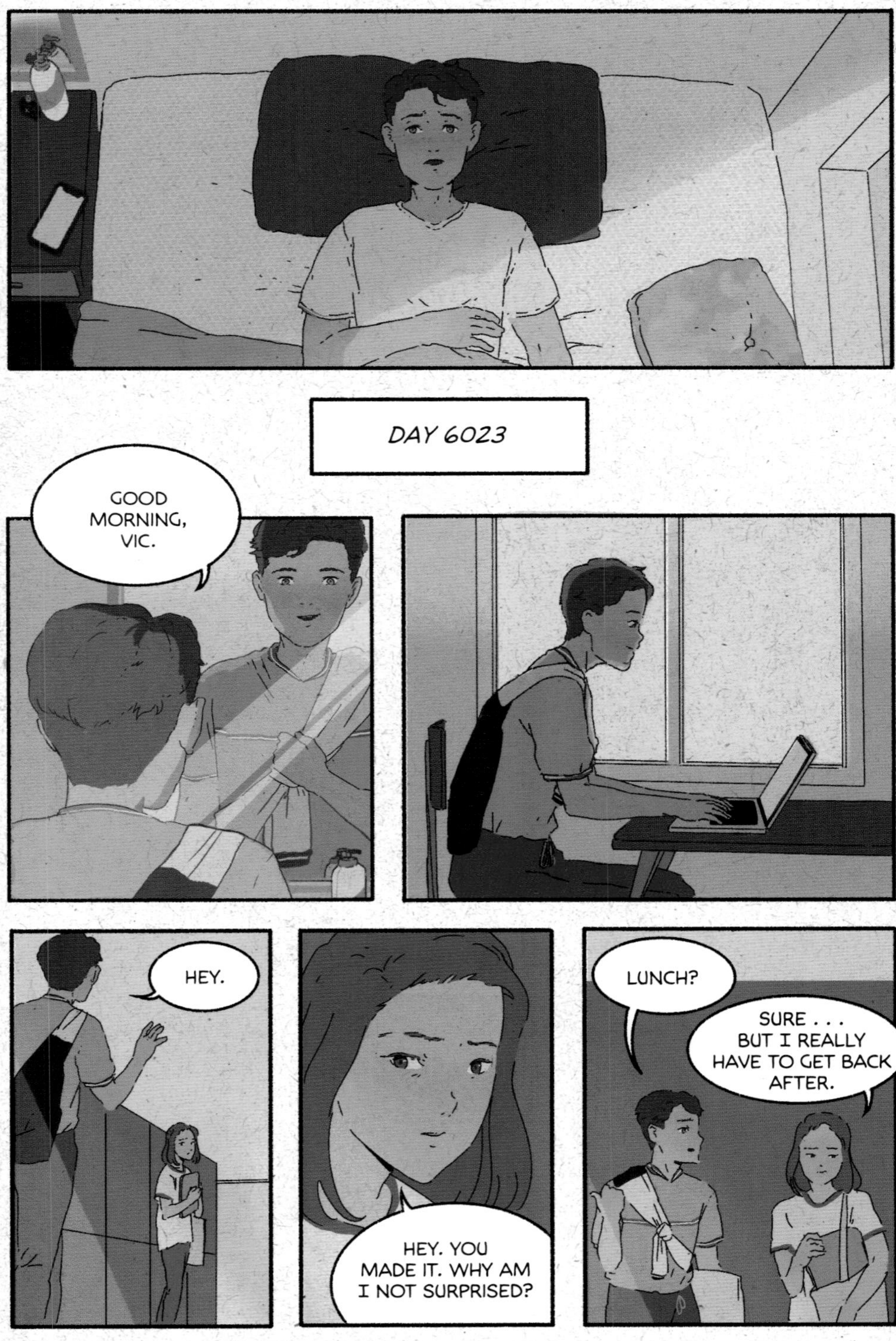
DAY 6023
GOOD MORNING, VIC.
HEY.
HEY. YOU MADE IT. WHY AM I NOT SURPRISED?
LUNCH?
SURE . . . BUT I REALLY HAVE TO GET BACK AFTER.

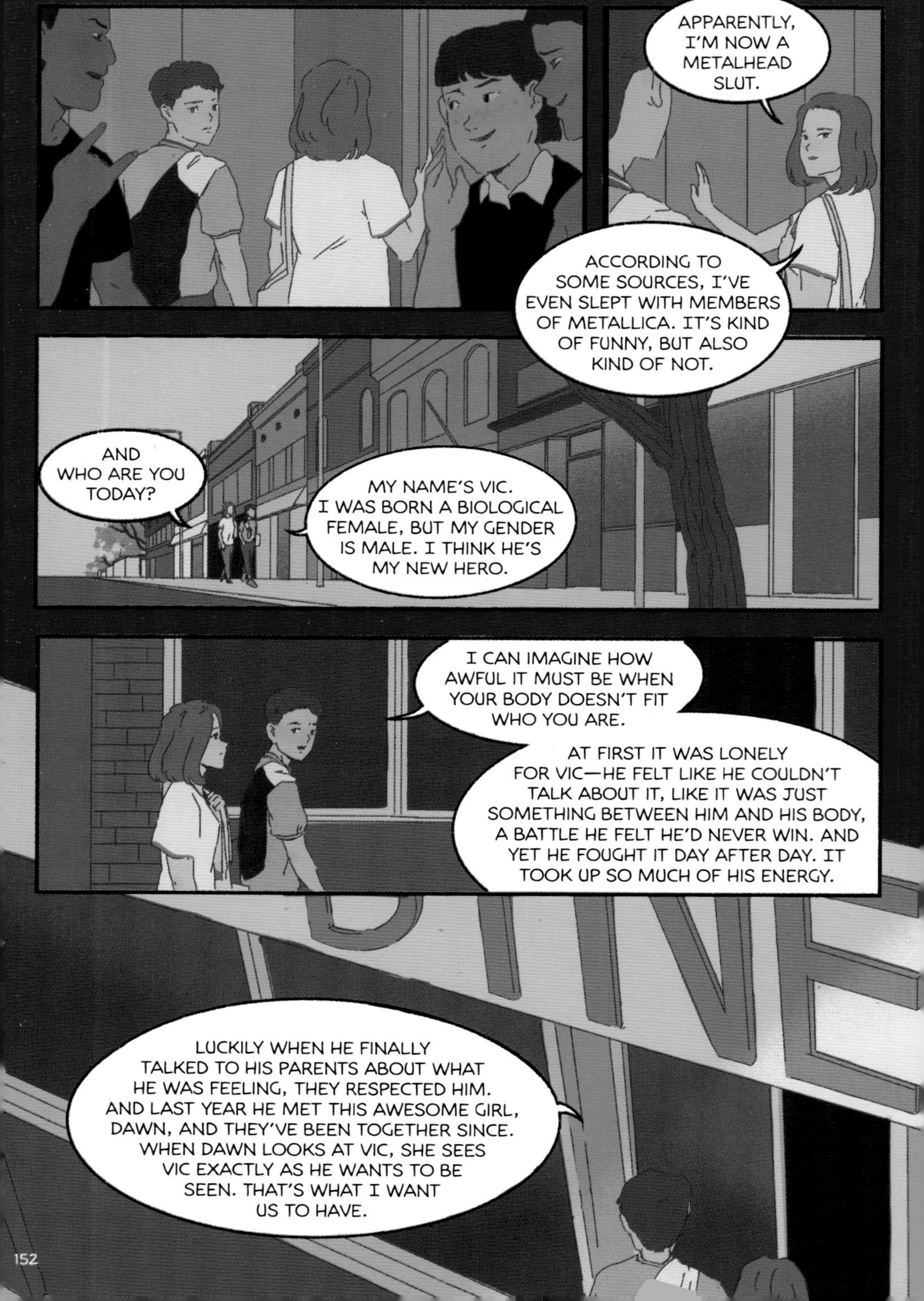
APPARENTLY, I'M NOW A METALHEAD SLUT.
ACCORDING TO SOME SOURCES, I'VE EVEN SLEPT WITH MEMBERS OF METALLICA. IT'S KIND OF FUNNY, BUT ALSO KIND OF NOT.
AND WHO ARE YOU TODAY?
MY NAME'S VIC. I WAS BORN A BIOLOGICAL FEMALE, BUT MY GENDER IS MALE. I THINK HE'S MY NEW HERO.
I CAN IMAGINE HOW AWFUL IT MUST BE WHEN YOUR BODY DOESN'T FIT WHO YOU ARE.
AT FIRST IT WAS LONELY FOR VIC—HE FELT LIKE HE COULDN'T TALK ABOUT IT, LIKE IT WAS JUST SOMETHING BETWEEN HIM AND HIS BODY, A BATTLE HE FELT HE'D NEVER WIN. AND YET HE FOUGHT IT DAY AFTER DAY. IT TOOK UP SO MUCH OF HIS ENERGY.
LUCKILY WHEN HE FINALLY TALKED TO HIS PARENTS ABOUT WHAT HE WAS FEELING, THEY RESPECTED HIM. AND LAST YEAR HE MET THIS AWESOME GIRL, DAWN, AND THEY'VE BEEN TOGETHER SINCE. WHEN DAWN LOOKS AT VIC, SHE SEES VIC EXACTLY AS HE WANTS TO BE SEEN. THAT'S WHAT I WANT US TO HAVE.

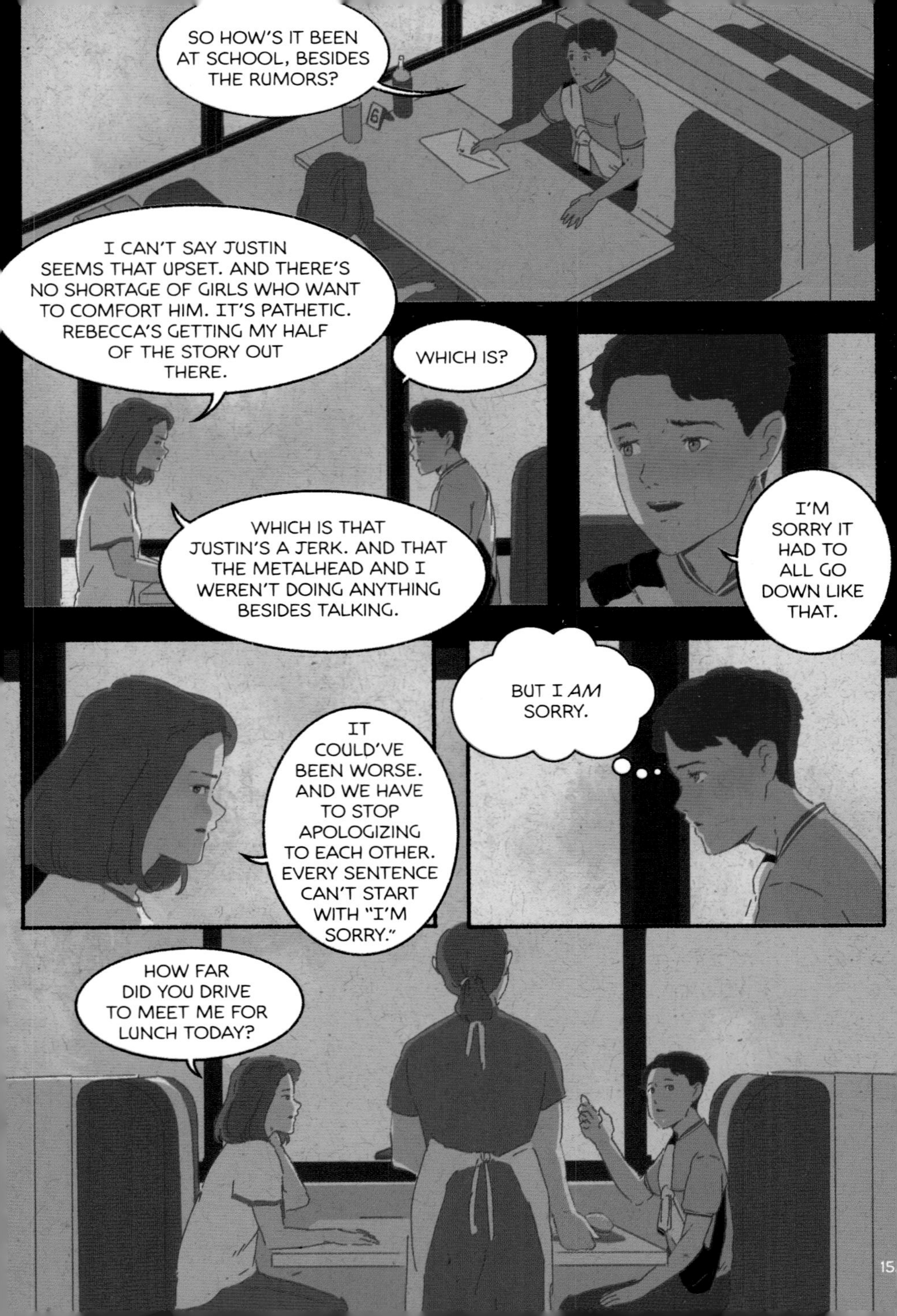
SO HOW'S IT BEEN AT SCHOOL, BESIDES THE RUMORS?
I CAN'T SAY JUSTIN SEEMS THAT UPSET. AND THERE'S NO SHORTAGE OF GIRLS WHO WANT TO COMFORT HIM. IT'S PATHETIC. REBECCA'S GETTING MY HALF OF THE STORY OUT THERE.
WHICH IS?
WHICH IS THAT JUSTIN'S A JERK. AND THAT THE METALHEAD AND I WEREN'T DOING ANYTHING BESIDES TALKING.
I'M SORRY IT HAD TO ALL GO DOWN LIKE THAT.
IT COULD'VE BEEN WORSE. AND WE HAVE TO STOP APOLOGIZING TO EACH OTHER. EVERY SENTENCE CAN'T START WITH "I'M SORRY."
BUT I *AM* SORRY.
HOW FAR DID YOU DRIVE TO MEET ME FOR LUNCH TODAY?

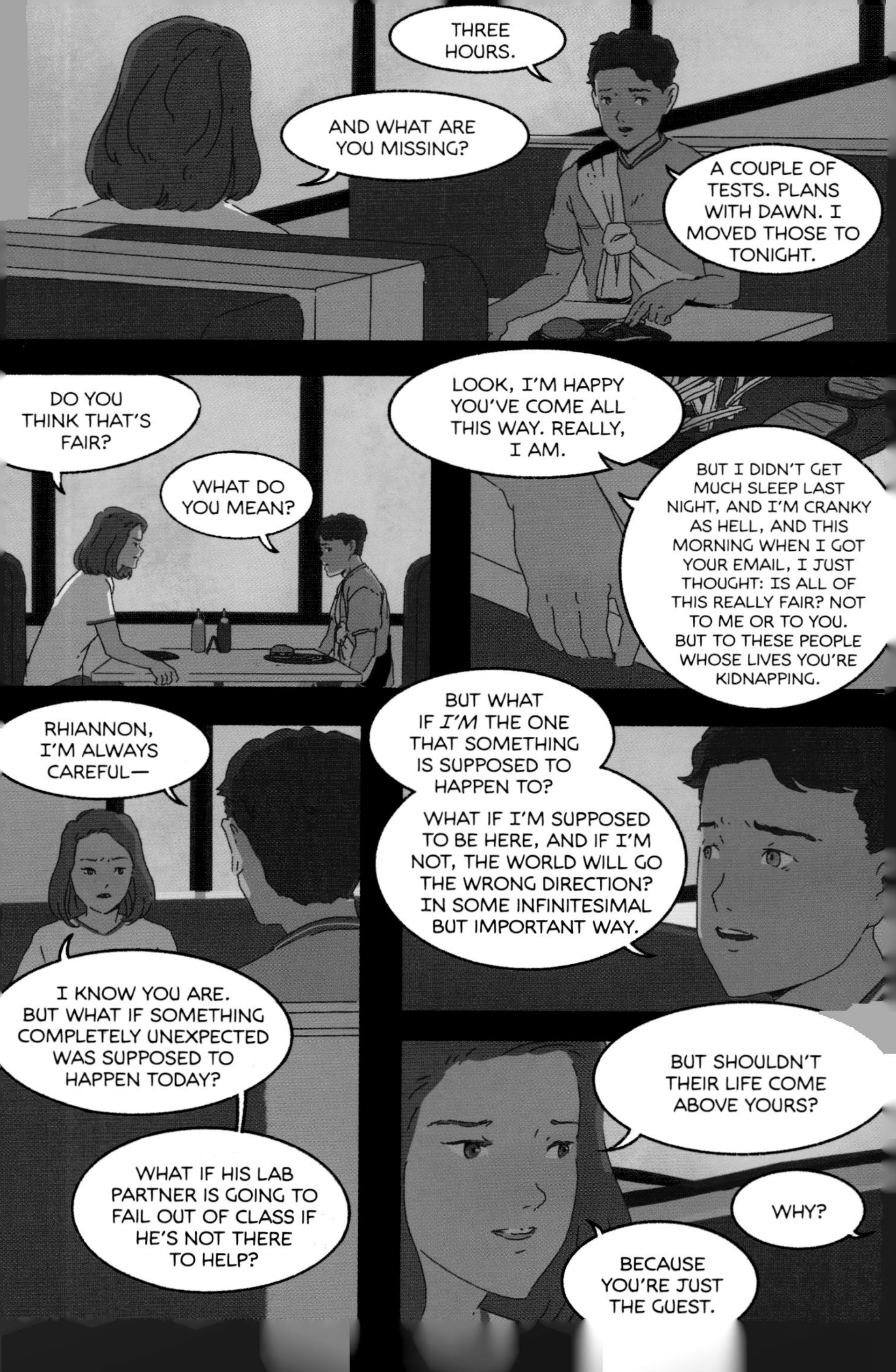
THREE HOURS.
AND WHAT ARE YOU MISSING?
A COUPLE OF TESTS. PLANS WITH DAWN. I MOVED THOSE TO TONIGHT.
DO YOU THINK THAT'S FAIR?
WHAT DO YOU MEAN?
LOOK, I'M HAPPY YOU'VE COME ALL THIS WAY. REALLY, I AM.
BUT I DIDN'T GET MUCH SLEEP LAST NIGHT, AND I'M CRANKY AS HELL, AND THIS MORNING WHEN I GOT YOUR EMAIL, I JUST THOUGHT: IS ALL OF THIS REALLY FAIR? NOT TO ME OR TO YOU. BUT TO THESE PEOPLE WHOSE LIVES YOU'RE KIDNAPPING.
RHIANNON, I'M ALWAYS CAREFUL—
I KNOW YOU ARE. BUT WHAT IF SOMETHING COMPLETELY UNEXPECTED WAS SUPPOSED TO HAPPEN TODAY?
WHAT IF HIS LAB PARTNER IS GOING TO FAIL OUT OF CLASS IF HE'S NOT THERE TO HELP?
BUT WHAT IF *I'M* THE ONE THAT SOMETHING IS SUPPOSED TO HAPPEN TO?
WHAT IF I'M SUPPOSED TO BE HERE, AND IF I'M NOT, THE WORLD WILL GO THE WRONG DIRECTION? IN SOME INFINITESIMAL BUT IMPORTANT WAY.
BUT SHOULDN'T THEIR LIFE COME ABOVE YOURS?
WHY?
BECAUSE YOU'RE JUST THE GUEST.

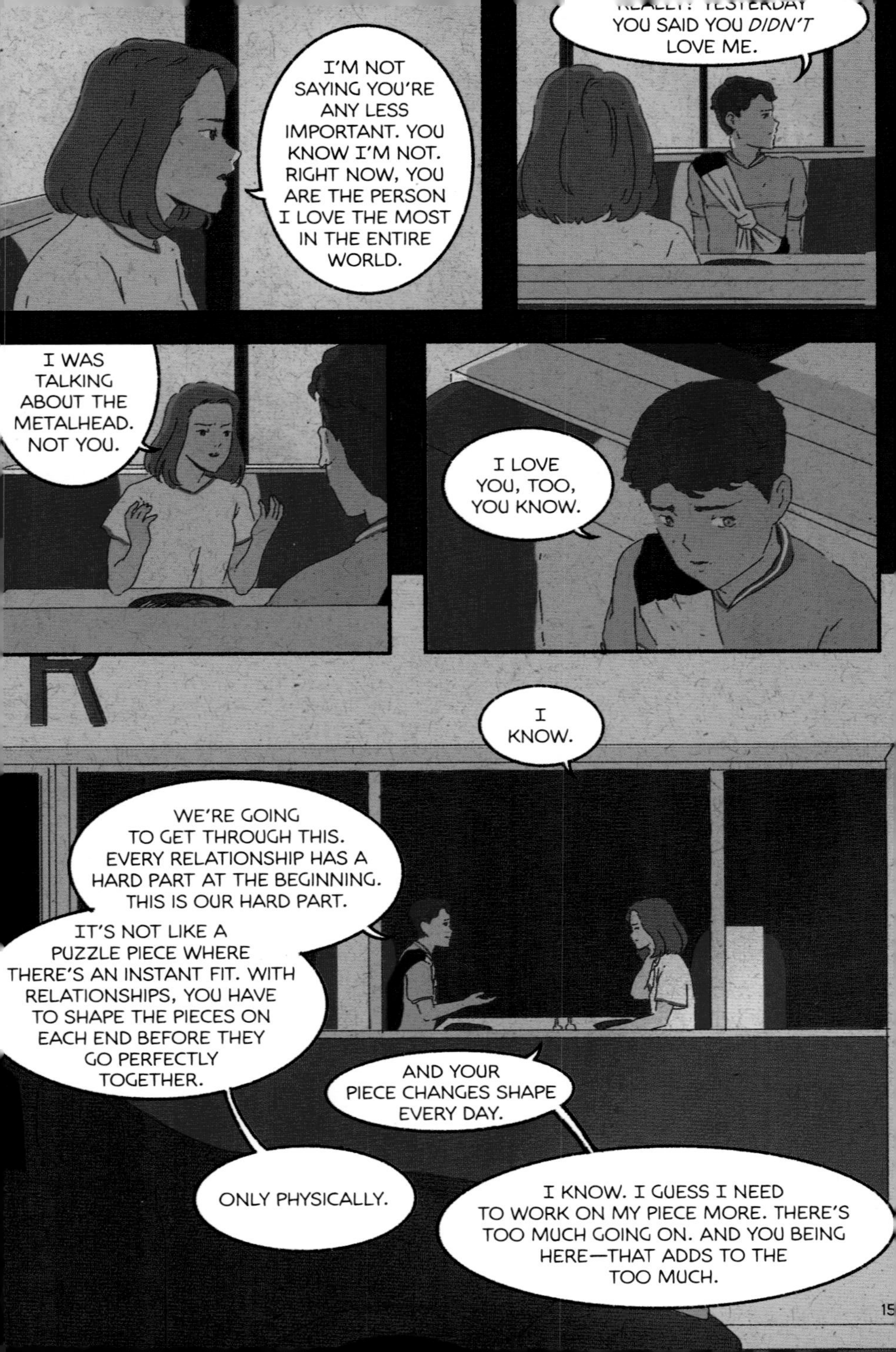

I'M NOT SAYING YOU'RE ANY LESS IMPORTANT. YOU KNOW I'M NOT. RIGHT NOW, YOU ARE THE PERSON I LOVE THE MOST IN THE ENTIRE WORLD.
YOU SAID YOU *DIDN'T* LOVE ME.
I WAS TALKING ABOUT THE METALHEAD. NOT YOU.
I LOVE YOU, TOO, YOU KNOW.
I KNOW.
WE'RE GOING TO GET THROUGH THIS. EVERY RELATIONSHIP HAS A HARD PART AT THE BEGINNING. THIS IS OUR HARD PART.
IT'S NOT LIKE A PUZZLE PIECE WHERE THERE'S AN INSTANT FIT. WITH RELATIONSHIPS, YOU HAVE TO SHAPE THE PIECES ON EACH END BEFORE THEY GO PERFECTLY TOGETHER.
AND YOUR PIECE CHANGES SHAPE EVERY DAY.
ONLY PHYSICALLY.
I KNOW. I GUESS I NEED TO WORK ON MY PIECE MORE. THERE'S TOO MUCH GOING ON. AND YOU BEING HERE—THAT ADDS TO THE TOO MUCH.

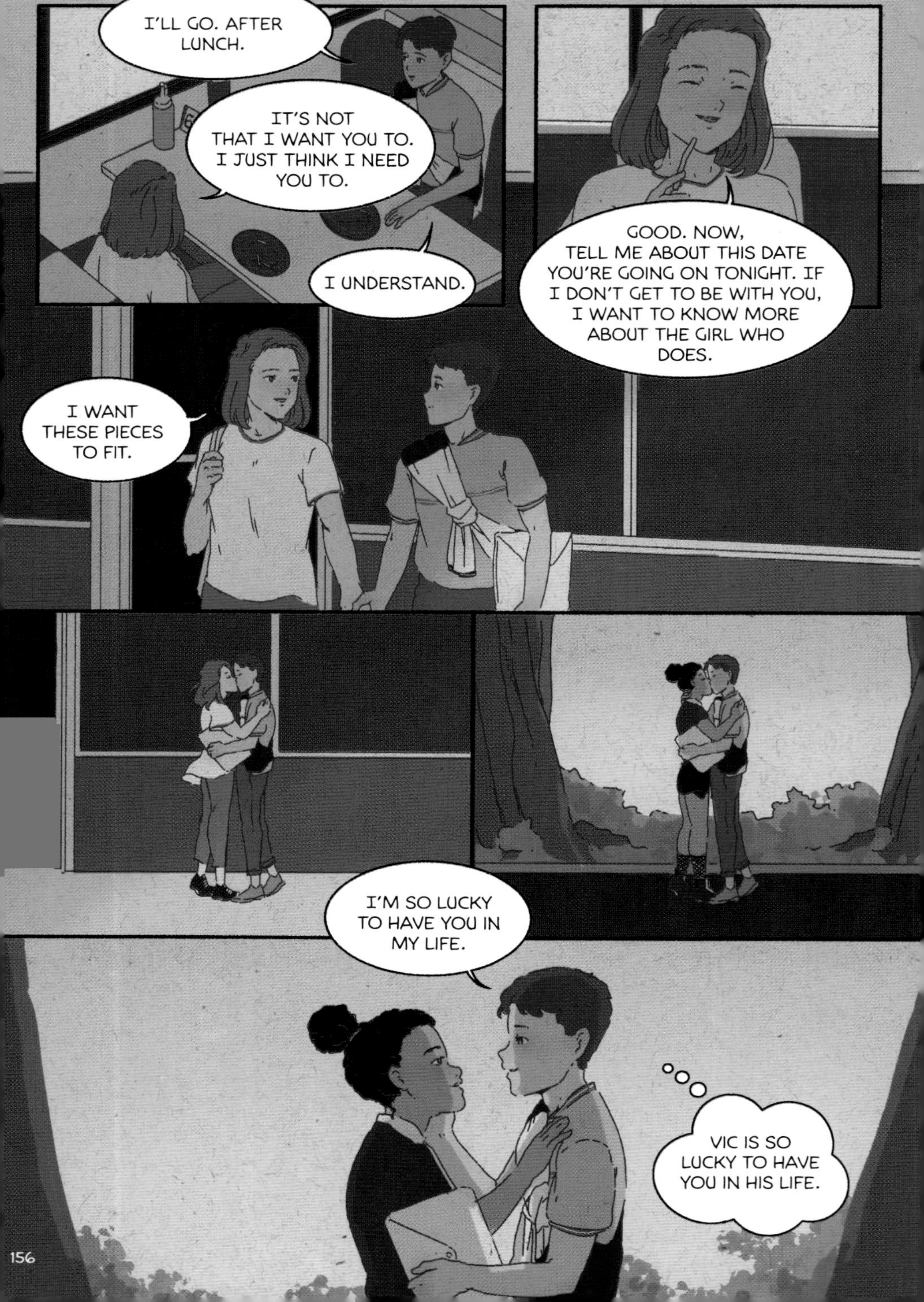
I'LL GO. AFTER LUNCH.
IT'S NOT THAT I WANT YOU TO. I JUST THINK I NEED YOU TO.
I UNDERSTAND.
GOOD. NOW, TELL ME ABOUT THIS DATE YOU'RE GOING ON TONIGHT. IF I DON'T GET TO BE WITH YOU, I WANT TO KNOW MORE ABOUT THE GIRL WHO DOES.
I WANT THESE PIECES TO FIT.
I'M SO LUCKY TO HAVE YOU IN MY LIFE.
VIC IS SO LUCKY TO HAVE YOU IN HIS LIFE.

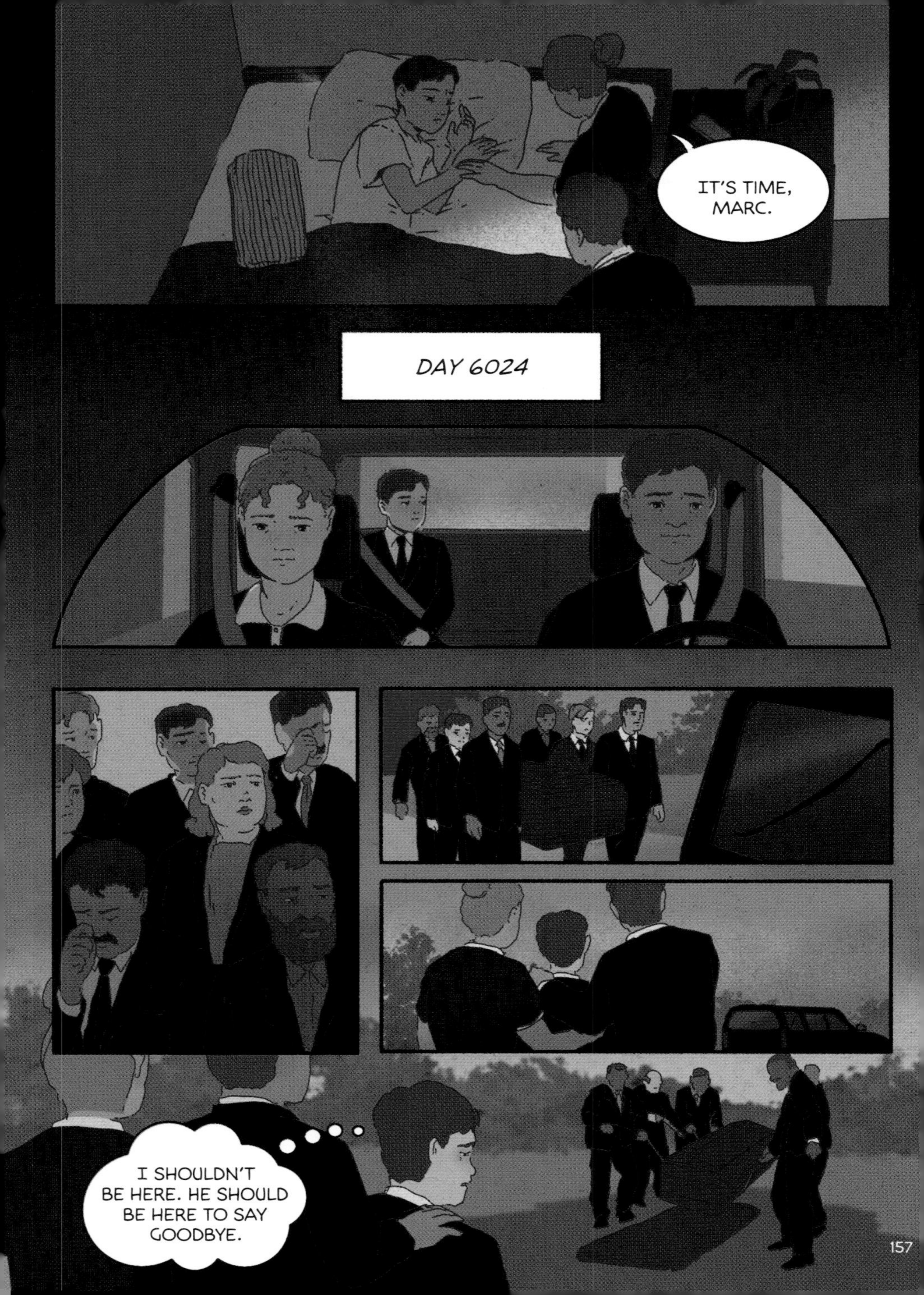
IT'S TIME, MARC.
DAY 6024
I SHOULDN'T BE HERE. HE SHOULD BE HERE TO SAY GOODBYE.

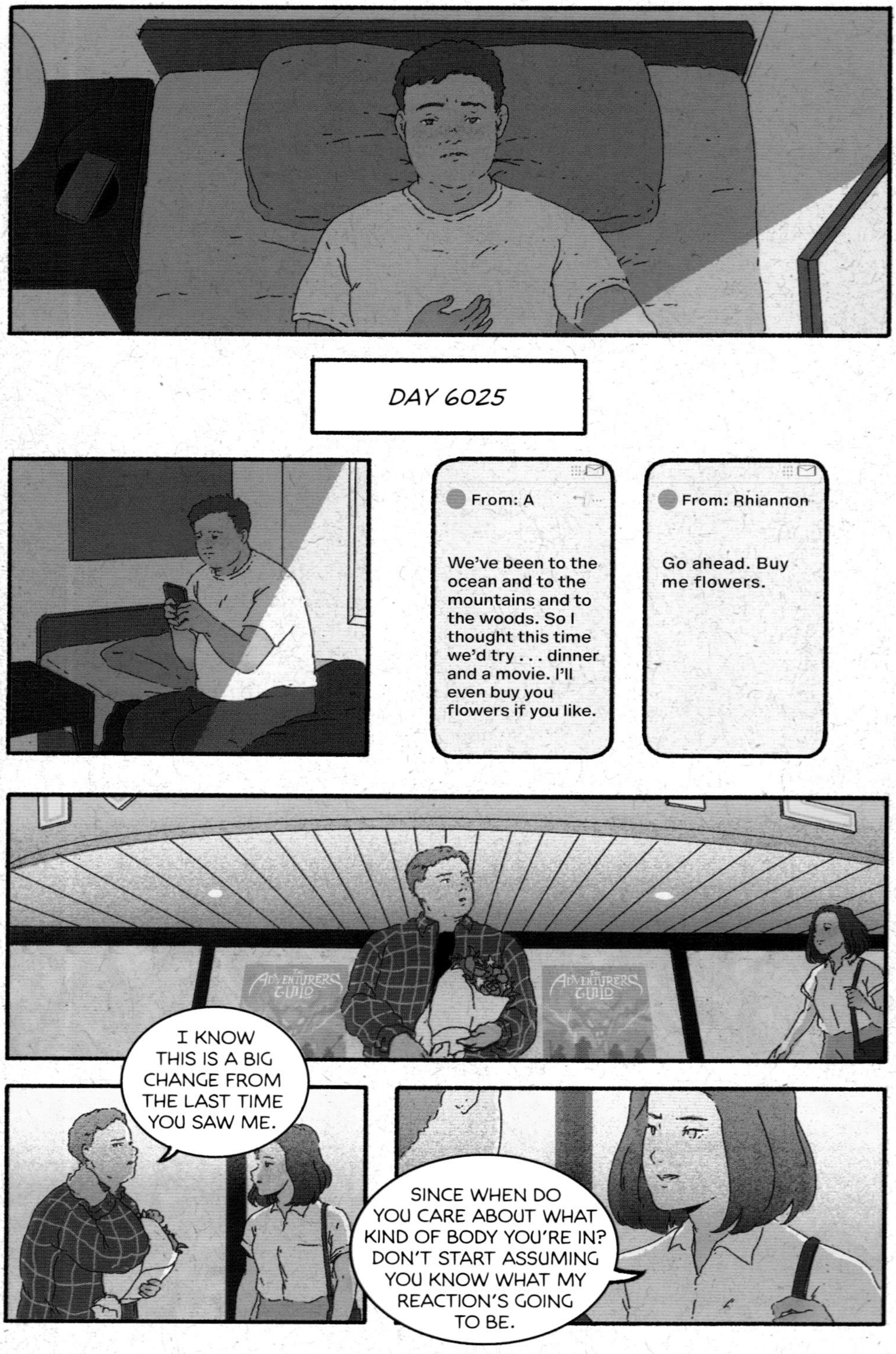
DAY 6025
From: A
We've been to the ocean and to the mountains and to the woods. So I thought this time we'd try . . . dinner and a movie. I'll even buy you flowers if you like.
From: Rhiannon
Go ahead. Buy me flowers.
THE ADVENTURERS GUILD
THE ADVENTURERS GUILD
I KNOW THIS IS A BIG CHANGE FROM THE LAST TIME YOU SAW ME.
SINCE WHEN DO YOU CARE ABOUT WHAT KIND OF BODY YOU'RE IN? DON'T START ASSUMING YOU KNOW WHAT MY REACTION'S GOING TO BE.

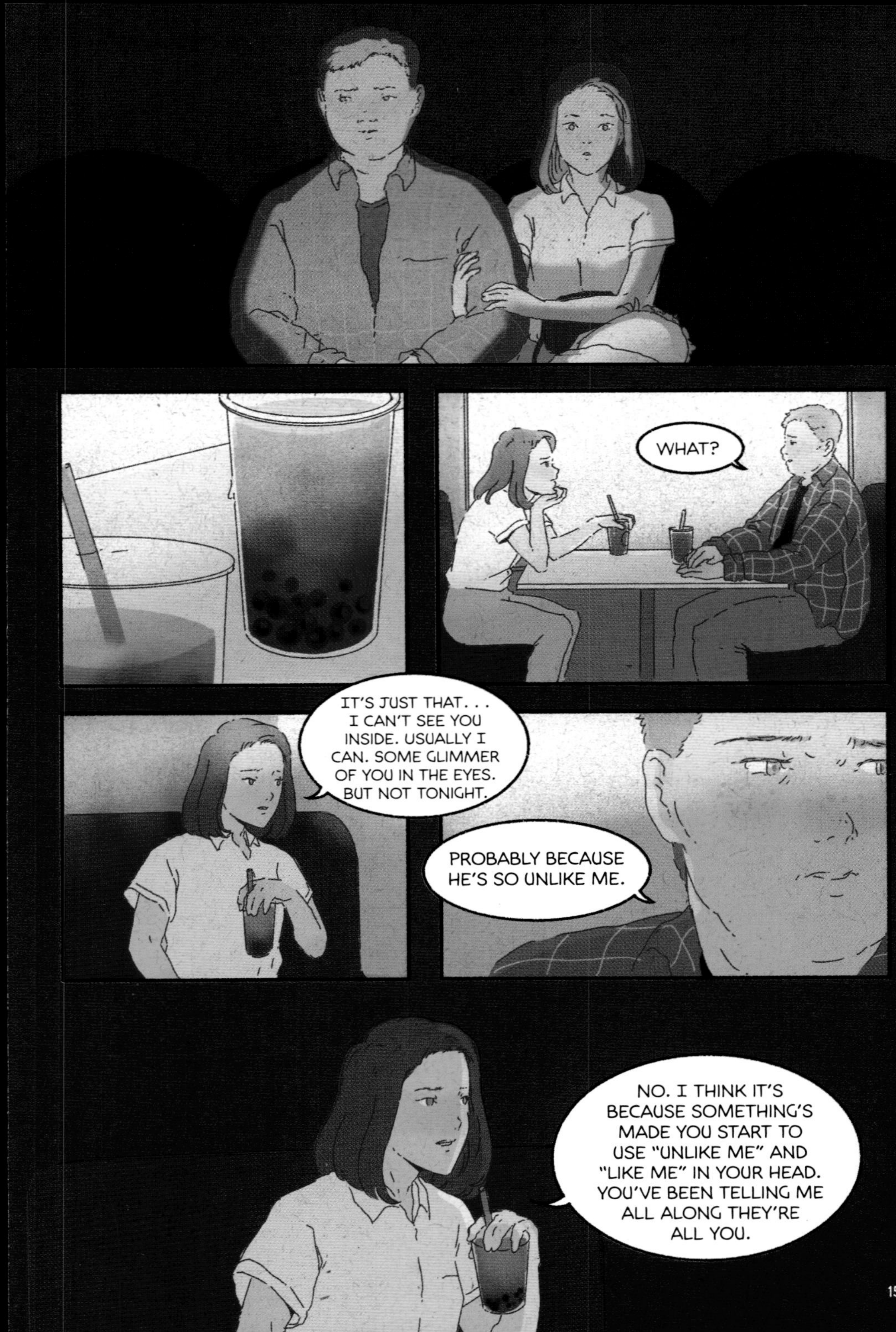
WHAT?
IT'S JUST THAT. . . I CAN'T SEE YOU INSIDE. USUALLY I CAN. SOME GLIMMER OF YOU IN THE EYES. BUT NOT TONIGHT.
PROBABLY BECAUSE HE'S SO UNLIKE ME.
NO. I THINK IT'S BECAUSE SOMETHING'S MADE YOU START TO USE "UNLIKE ME" AND "LIKE ME" IN YOUR HEAD. YOU'VE BEEN TELLING ME ALL ALONG THEY'RE ALL YOU.

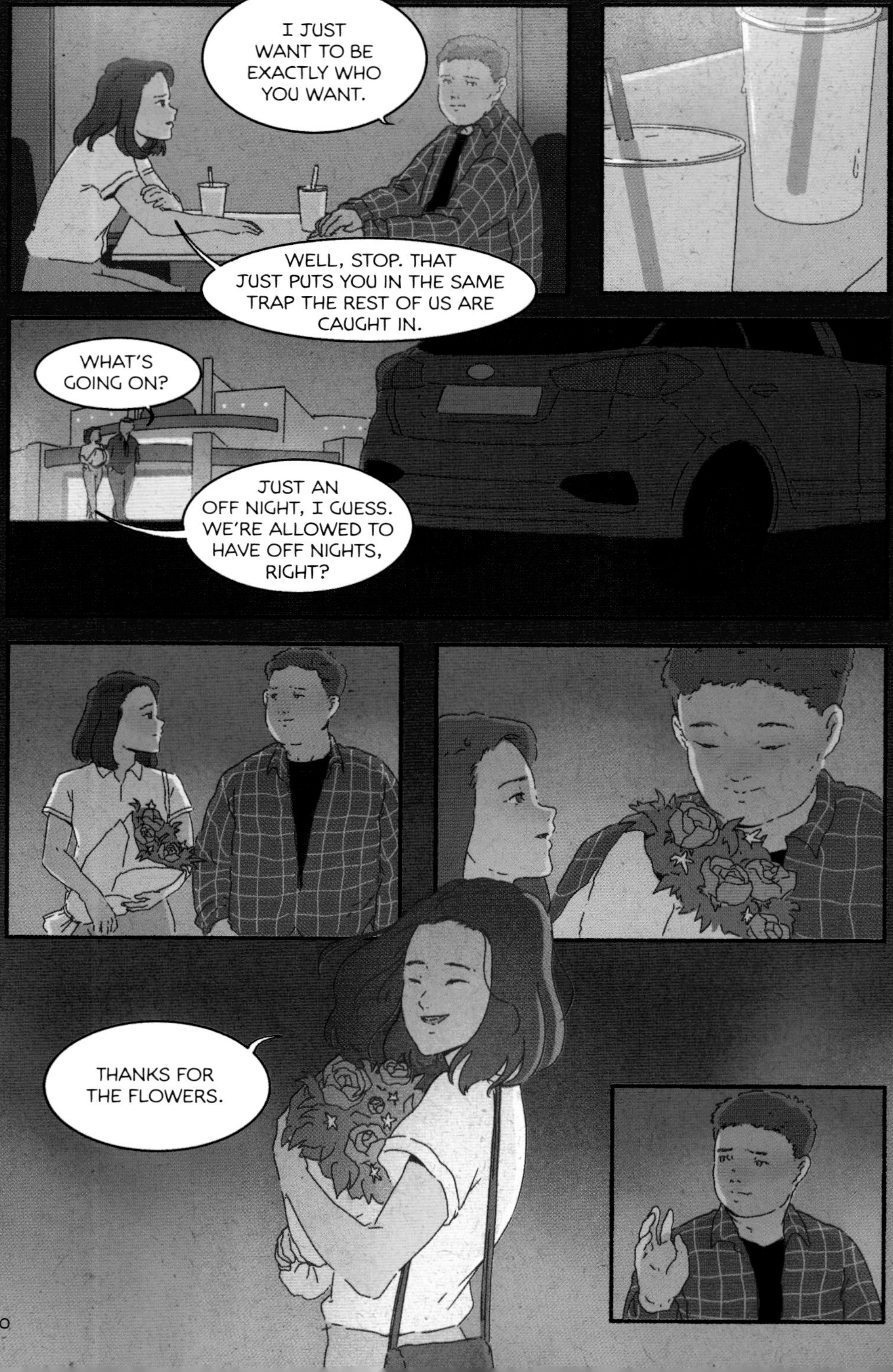
I JUST WANT TO BE EXACTLY WHO YOU WANT.
WELL, STOP. THAT JUST PUTS YOU IN THE SAME TRAP THE REST OF US ARE CAUGHT IN.
WHAT'S GOING ON?
JUST AN OFF NIGHT, I GUESS. WE'RE ALLOWED TO HAVE OFF NIGHTS, RIGHT?
THANKS FOR THE FLOWERS.

DAY 6026

From: Rhiannon

I really want to see
you today.

From: Rhiannon

We need to talk.

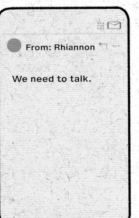

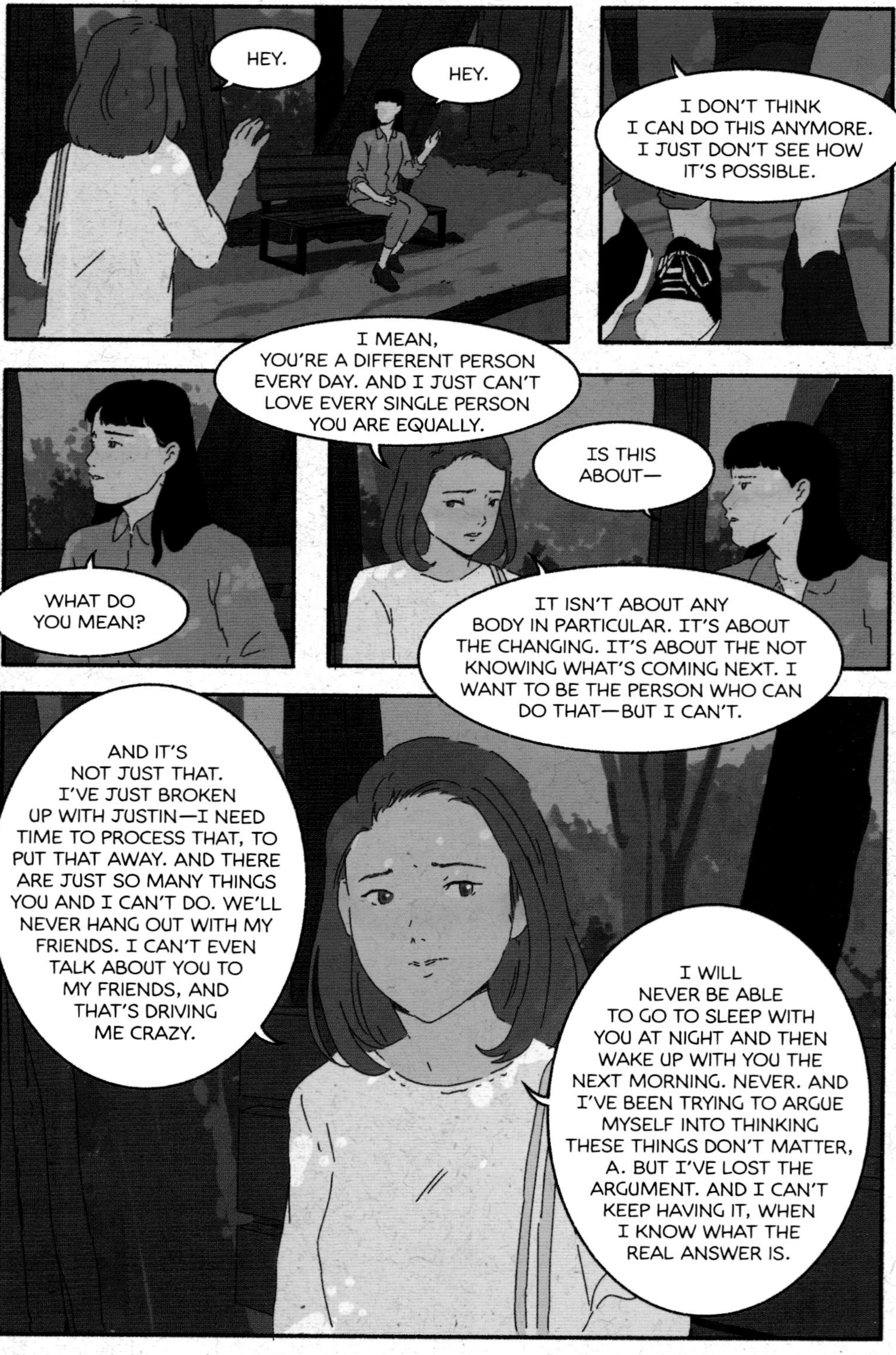
HEY.
HEY.
I DON'T THINK I CAN DO THIS ANYMORE. I JUST DON'T SEE HOW IT'S POSSIBLE.
I MEAN, YOU'RE A DIFFERENT PERSON EVERY DAY. AND I JUST CAN'T LOVE EVERY SINGLE PERSON YOU ARE EQUALLY.
WHAT DO YOU MEAN?
IS THIS ABOUT—
IT ISN'T ABOUT ANY BODY IN PARTICULAR. IT'S ABOUT THE CHANGING. IT'S ABOUT THE NOT KNOWING WHAT'S COMING NEXT. I WANT TO BE THE PERSON WHO CAN DO THAT—BUT I CAN'T.
AND IT'S NOT JUST THAT. I'VE JUST BROKEN UP WITH JUSTIN—I NEED TIME TO PROCESS THAT, TO PUT THAT AWAY. AND THERE ARE JUST SO MANY THINGS YOU AND I CAN'T DO. WE'LL NEVER HANG OUT WITH MY FRIENDS. I CAN'T EVEN TALK ABOUT YOU TO MY FRIENDS, AND THAT'S DRIVING ME CRAZY.
I WILL NEVER BE ABLE TO GO TO SLEEP WITH YOU AT NIGHT AND THEN WAKE UP WITH YOU THE NEXT MORNING. NEVER. AND I'VE BEEN TRYING TO ARGUE MYSELF INTO THINKING THESE THINGS DON'T MATTER, A. BUT I'VE LOST THE ARGUMENT. AND I CAN'T KEEP HAVING IT, WHEN I KNOW WHAT THE REAL ANSWER IS.

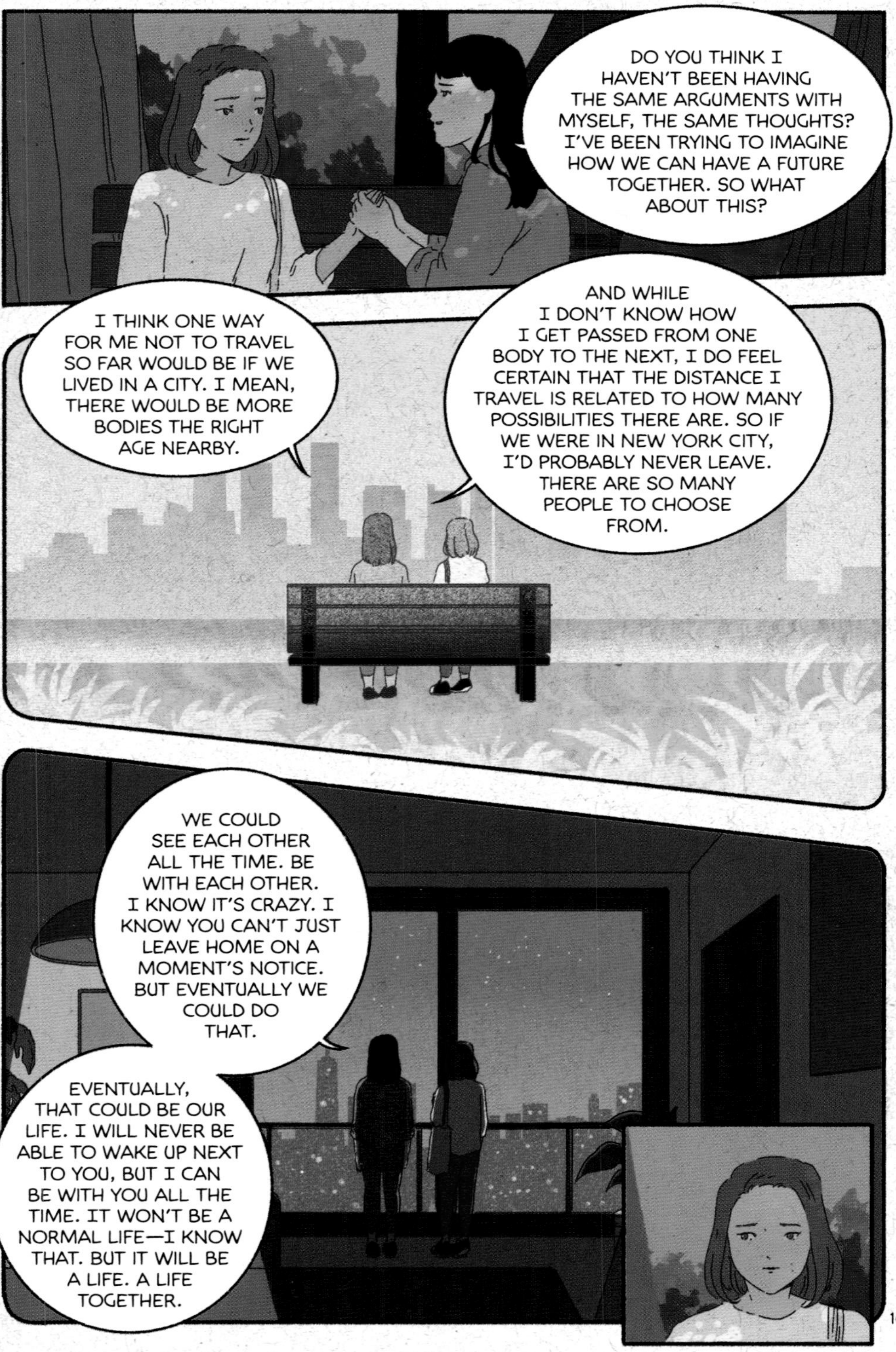
DO YOU THINK I HAVEN'T BEEN HAVING THE SAME ARGUMENTS WITH MYSELF, THE SAME THOUGHTS? I'VE BEEN TRYING TO IMAGINE HOW WE CAN HAVE A FUTURE TOGETHER. SO WHAT ABOUT THIS?
I THINK ONE WAY FOR ME NOT TO TRAVEL SO FAR WOULD BE IF WE LIVED IN A CITY. I MEAN, THERE WOULD BE MORE BODIES THE RIGHT AGE NEARBY.
AND WHILE I DON'T KNOW HOW I GET PASSED FROM ONE BODY TO THE NEXT, I DO FEEL CERTAIN THAT THE DISTANCE I TRAVEL IS RELATED TO HOW MANY POSSIBILITIES THERE ARE. SO IF WE WERE IN NEW YORK CITY, I'D PROBABLY NEVER LEAVE. THERE ARE SO MANY PEOPLE TO CHOOSE FROM.
WE COULD SEE EACH OTHER ALL THE TIME. BE WITH EACH OTHER. I KNOW IT'S CRAZY. I KNOW YOU CAN'T JUST LEAVE HOME ON A MOMENT'S NOTICE. BUT EVENTUALLY WE COULD DO THAT.
EVENTUALLY, THAT COULD BE OUR LIFE. I WILL NEVER BE ABLE TO WAKE UP NEXT TO YOU, BUT I CAN BE WITH YOU ALL THE TIME. IT WON'T BE A NORMAL LIFE—I KNOW THAT. BUT IT WILL BE A LIFE. A LIFE TOGETHER.

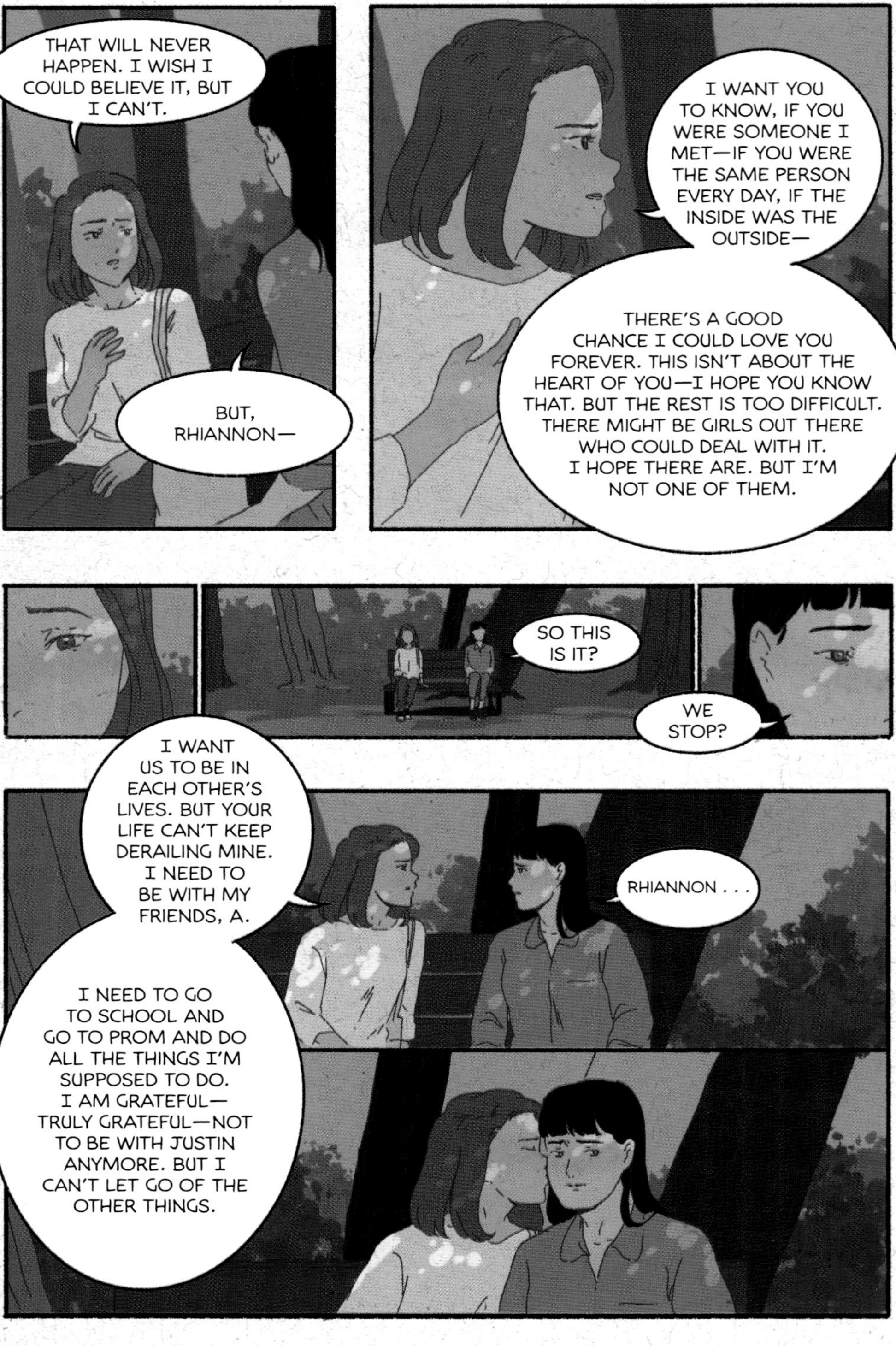
THAT WILL NEVER HAPPEN. I WISH I COULD BELIEVE IT, BUT I CAN'T.
BUT, RHIANNON—
I WANT YOU TO KNOW, IF YOU WERE SOMEONE I MET—IF YOU WERE THE SAME PERSON EVERY DAY, IF THE INSIDE WAS THE OUTSIDE—
THERE'S A GOOD CHANCE I COULD LOVE YOU FOREVER. THIS ISN'T ABOUT THE HEART OF YOU—I HOPE YOU KNOW THAT. BUT THE REST IS TOO DIFFICULT. THERE MIGHT BE GIRLS OUT THERE WHO COULD DEAL WITH IT. I HOPE THERE ARE. BUT I'M NOT ONE OF THEM.
SO THIS IS IT?
WE STOP?
I WANT US TO BE IN EACH OTHER'S LIVES. BUT YOUR LIFE CAN'T KEEP DERAILING MINE. I NEED TO BE WITH MY FRIENDS, A.
RHIANNON . . .
I NEED TO GO TO SCHOOL AND GO TO PROM AND DO ALL THE THINGS I'M SUPPOSED TO DO. I AM GRATEFUL—TRULY GRATEFUL—NOT TO BE WITH JUSTIN ANYMORE. BUT I CAN'T LET GO OF THE OTHER THINGS.

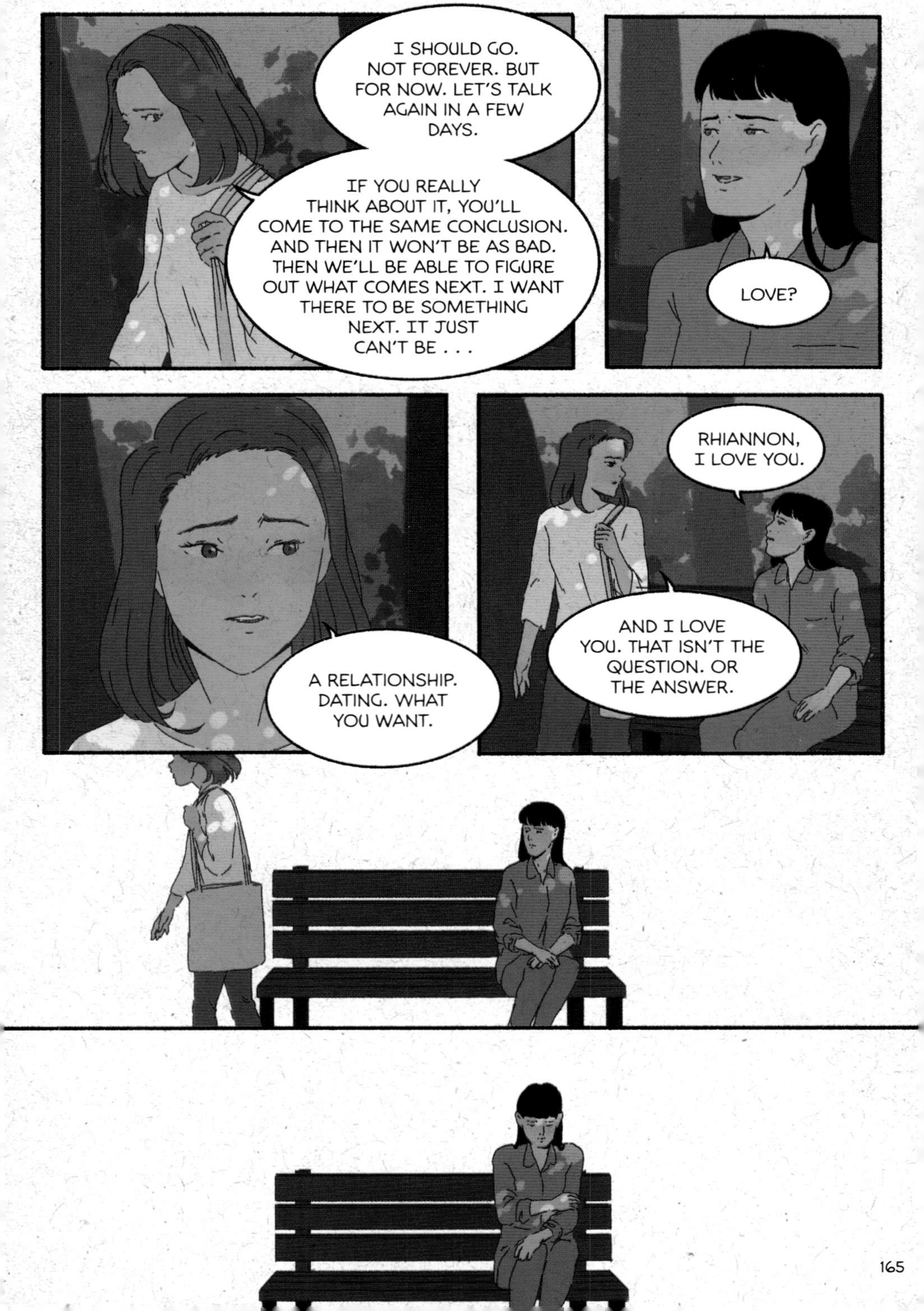
I SHOULD GO. NOT FOREVER. BUT FOR NOW. LET'S TALK AGAIN IN A FEW DAYS.
IF YOU REALLY THINK ABOUT IT, YOU'LL COME TO THE SAME CONCLUSION. AND THEN IT WON'T BE AS BAD. THEN WE'LL BE ABLE TO FIGURE OUT WHAT COMES NEXT. I WANT THERE TO BE SOMETHING NEXT. IT JUST CAN'T BE . . .
LOVE?
A RELATIONSHIP. DATING. WHAT YOU WANT.
RHIANNON, I LOVE YOU.
AND I LOVE YOU. THAT ISN'T THE QUESTION. OR THE ANSWER.

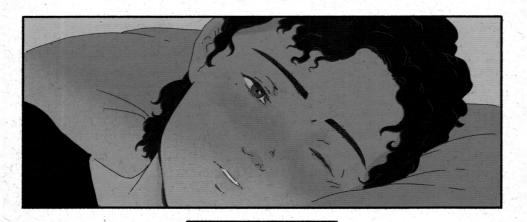

DAY 6027
From: Nathan Daldry
All I ask is for an explanation. I will leave you alone after that. I just need to know.
From: Nathan Daldry
From: Nathan Daldry
From: Nathan Daldry
From: Nathan Daldry

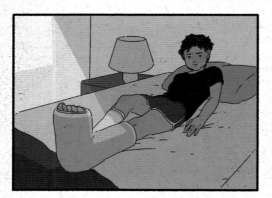

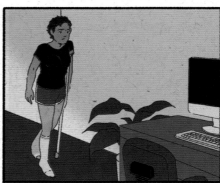

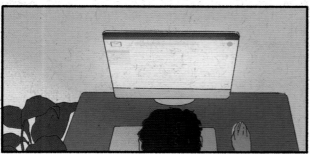

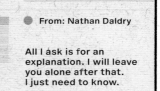

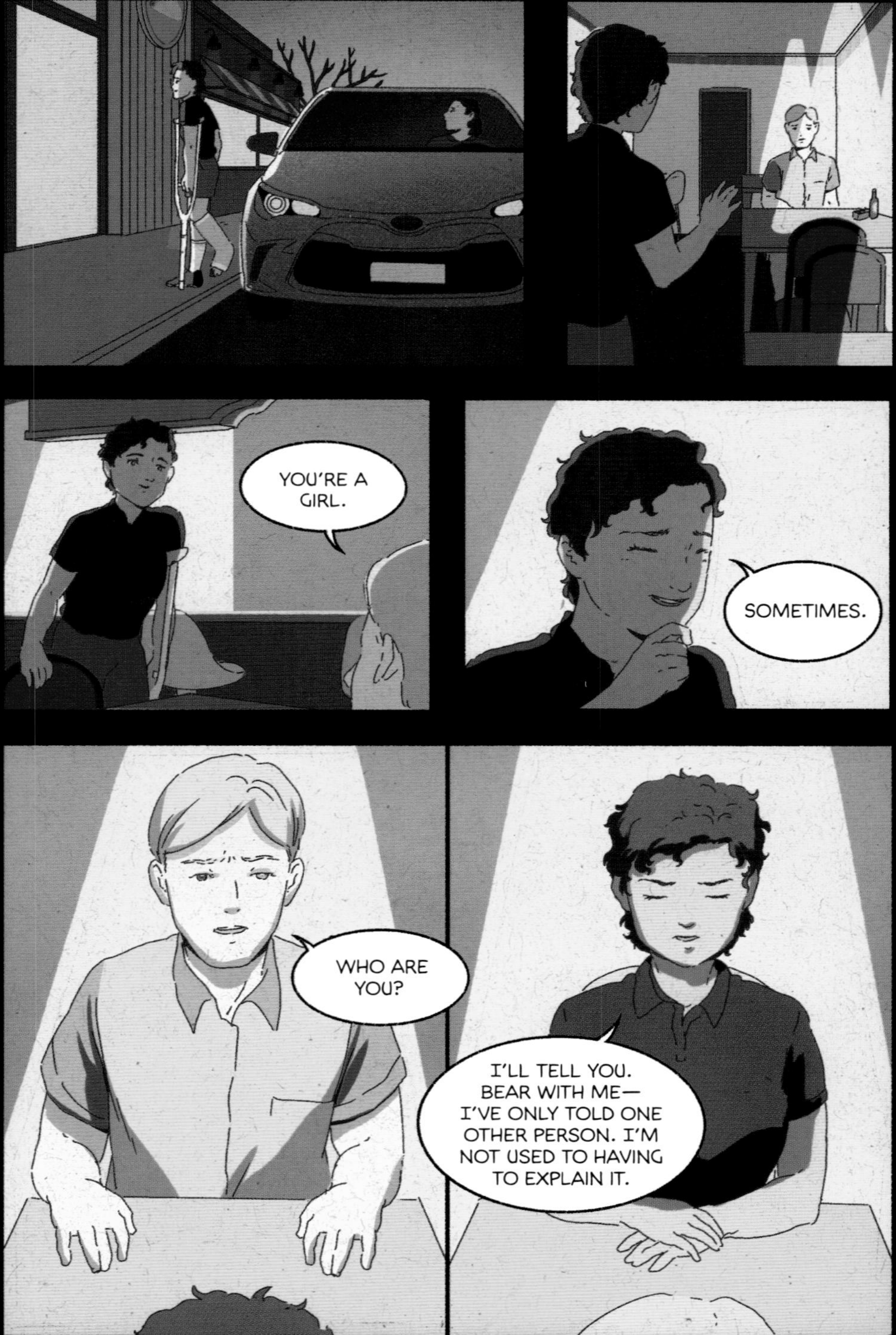
YOU'RE A GIRL.
SOMETIMES.
WHO ARE YOU?
I'LL TELL YOU. BEAR WITH ME— I'VE ONLY TOLD ONE OTHER PERSON. I'M NOT USED TO HAVING TO EXPLAIN IT.

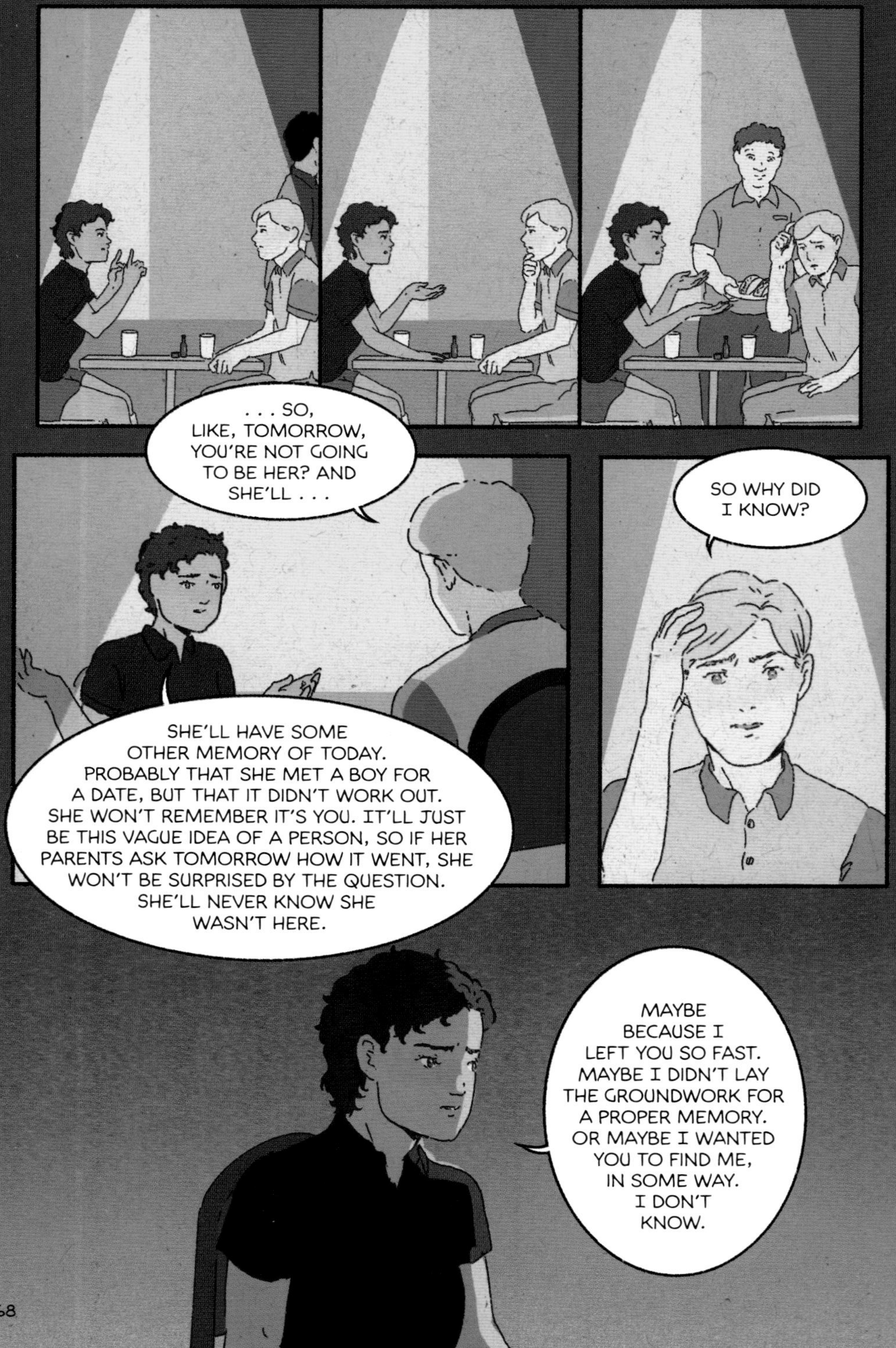
. . . SO, LIKE, TOMORROW, YOU'RE NOT GOING TO BE HER? AND SHE'LL . . .
SO WHY DID I KNOW?
SHE'LL HAVE SOME OTHER MEMORY OF TODAY. PROBABLY THAT SHE MET A BOY FOR A DATE, BUT THAT IT DIDN'T WORK OUT. SHE WON'T REMEMBER IT'S YOU. IT'LL JUST BE THIS VAGUE IDEA OF A PERSON, SO IF HER PARENTS ASK TOMORROW HOW IT WENT, SHE WON'T BE SURPRISED BY THE QUESTION. SHE'LL NEVER KNOW SHE WASN'T HERE.
MAYBE BECAUSE I LEFT YOU SO FAST. MAYBE I DIDN'T LAY THE GROUNDWORK FOR A PROPER MEMORY. OR MAYBE I WANTED YOU TO FIND ME, IN SOME WAY. I DON'T KNOW.

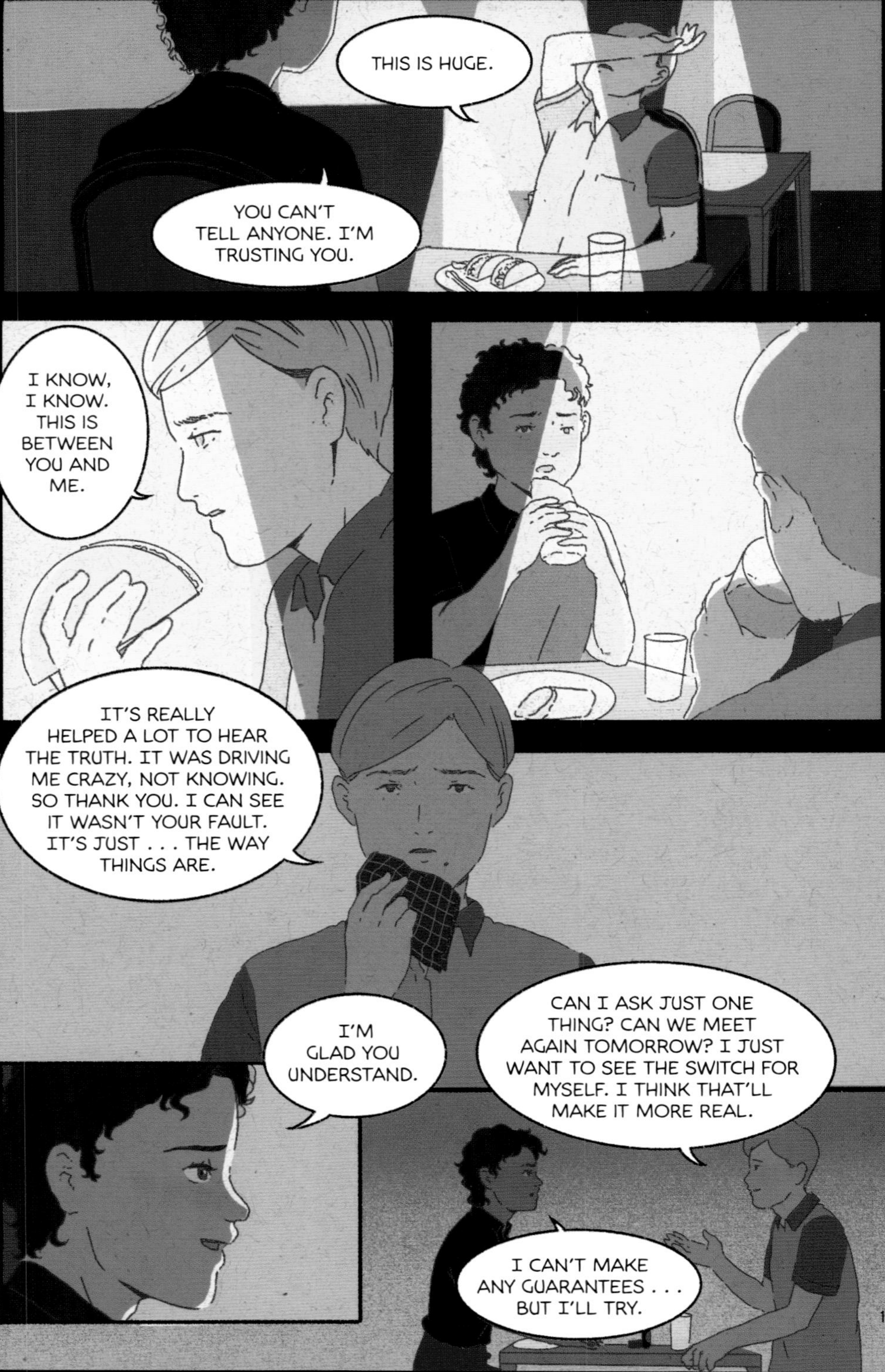
THIS IS HUGE.
YOU CAN'T TELL ANYONE. I'M TRUSTING YOU.
I KNOW, I KNOW. THIS IS BETWEEN YOU AND ME.
IT'S REALLY HELPED A LOT TO HEAR THE TRUTH. IT WAS DRIVING ME CRAZY, NOT KNOWING. SO THANK YOU. I CAN SEE IT WASN'T YOUR FAULT. IT'S JUST . . . THE WAY THINGS ARE.
I'M GLAD YOU UNDERSTAND.
CAN I ASK JUST ONE THING? CAN WE MEET AGAIN TOMORROW? I JUST WANT TO SEE THE SWITCH FOR MYSELF. I THINK THAT'LL MAKE IT MORE REAL.
I CAN'T MAKE ANY GUARANTEES . . . BUT I'LL TRY.

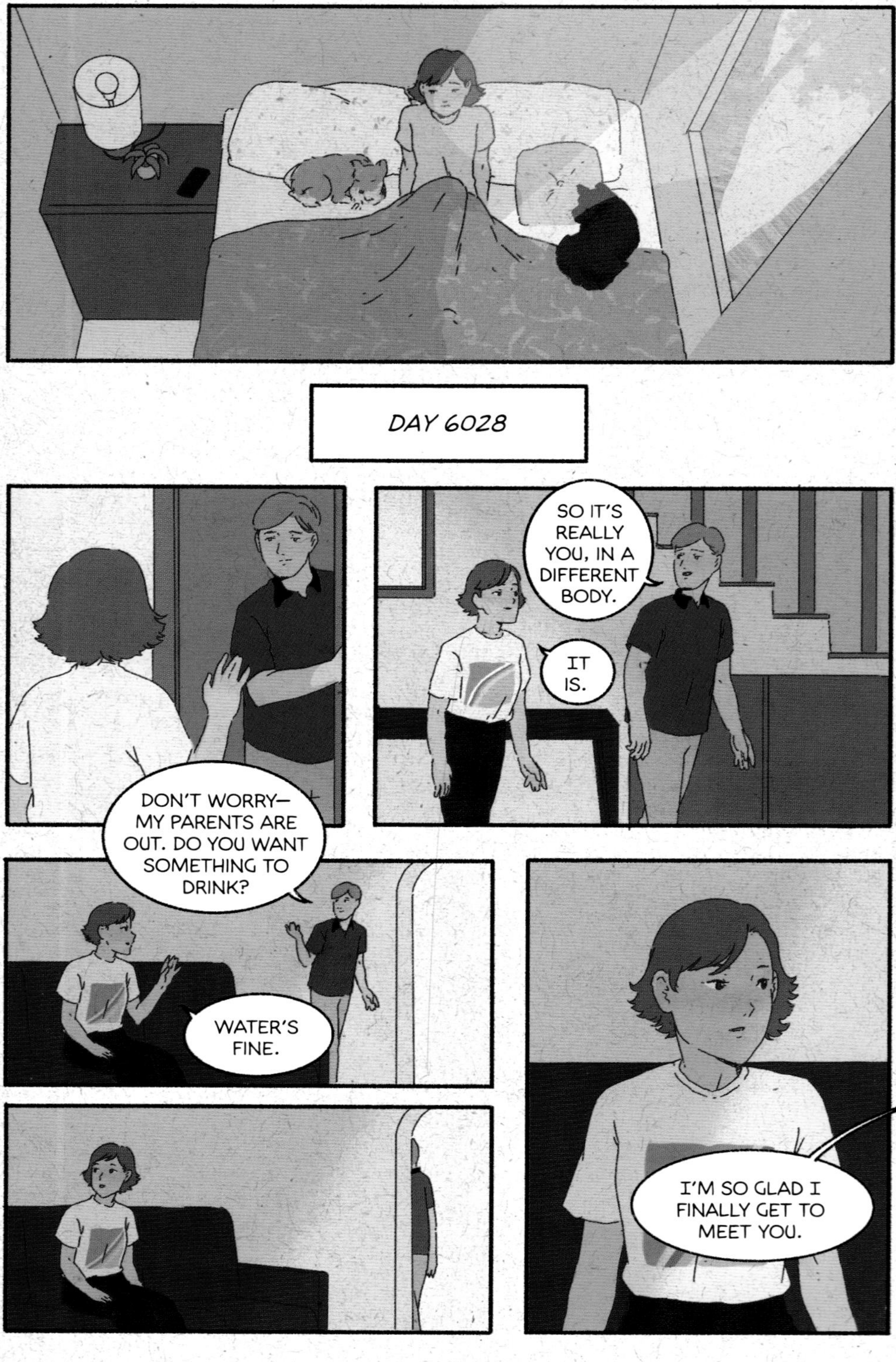
DAY 6028
SO IT'S REALLY YOU, IN A DIFFERENT BODY.
IT IS.
DON'T WORRY— MY PARENTS ARE OUT. DO YOU WANT SOMETHING TO DRINK?
WATER'S FINE.
I'M SO GLAD I FINALLY GET TO MEET YOU.

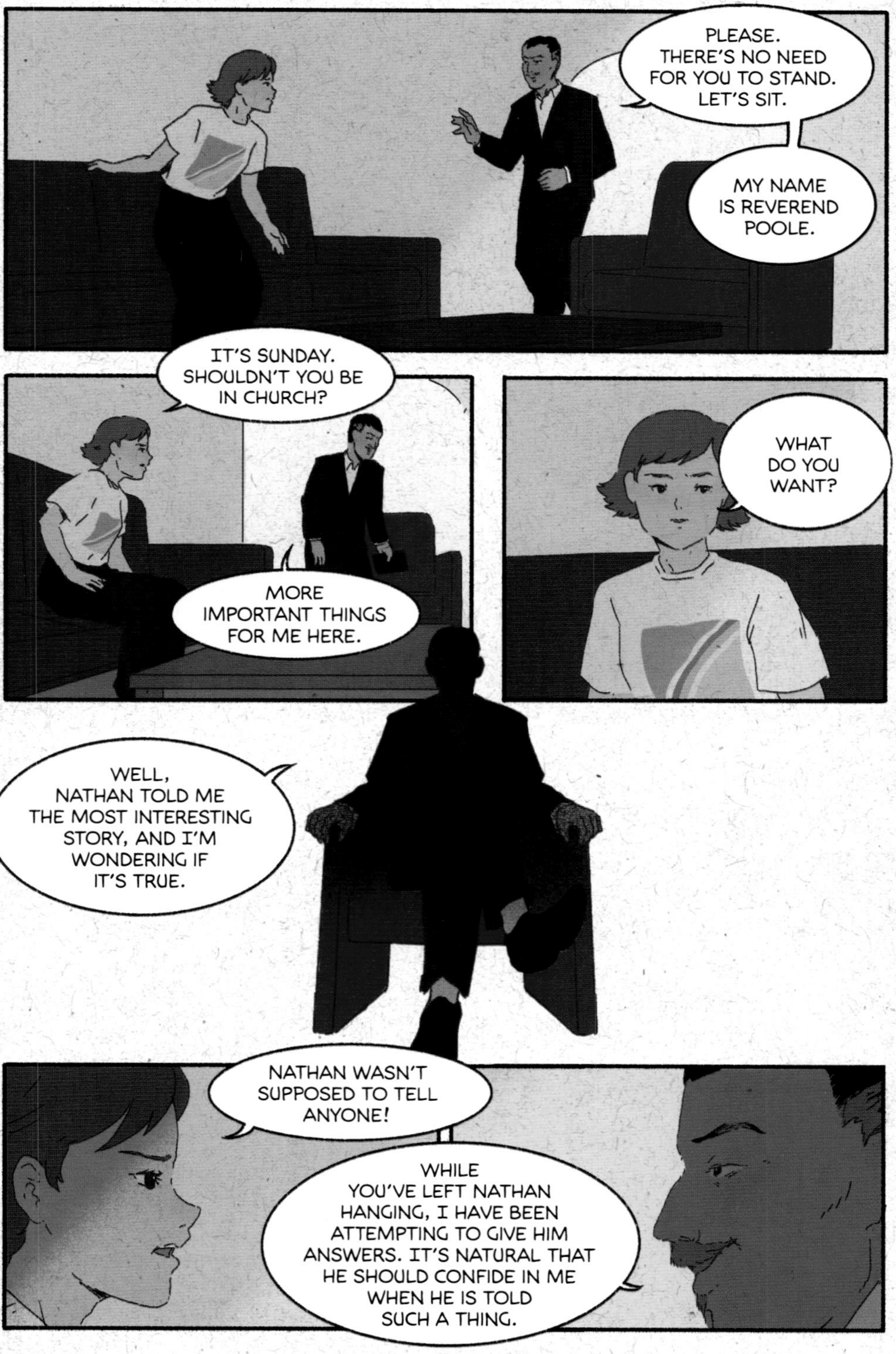
PLEASE. THERE'S NO NEED FOR YOU TO STAND. LET'S SIT.
MY NAME IS REVEREND POOLE.
IT'S SUNDAY. SHOULDN'T YOU BE IN CHURCH?
MORE IMPORTANT THINGS FOR ME HERE.
WHAT DO YOU WANT?
WELL, NATHAN TOLD ME THE MOST INTERESTING STORY, AND I'M WONDERING IF IT'S TRUE.
NATHAN WASN'T SUPPOSED TO TELL ANYONE!
WHILE YOU'VE LEFT NATHAN HANGING, I HAVE BEEN ATTEMPTING TO GIVE HIM ANSWERS. IT'S NATURAL THAT HE SHOULD CONFIDE IN ME WHEN HE IS TOLD SUCH A THING.

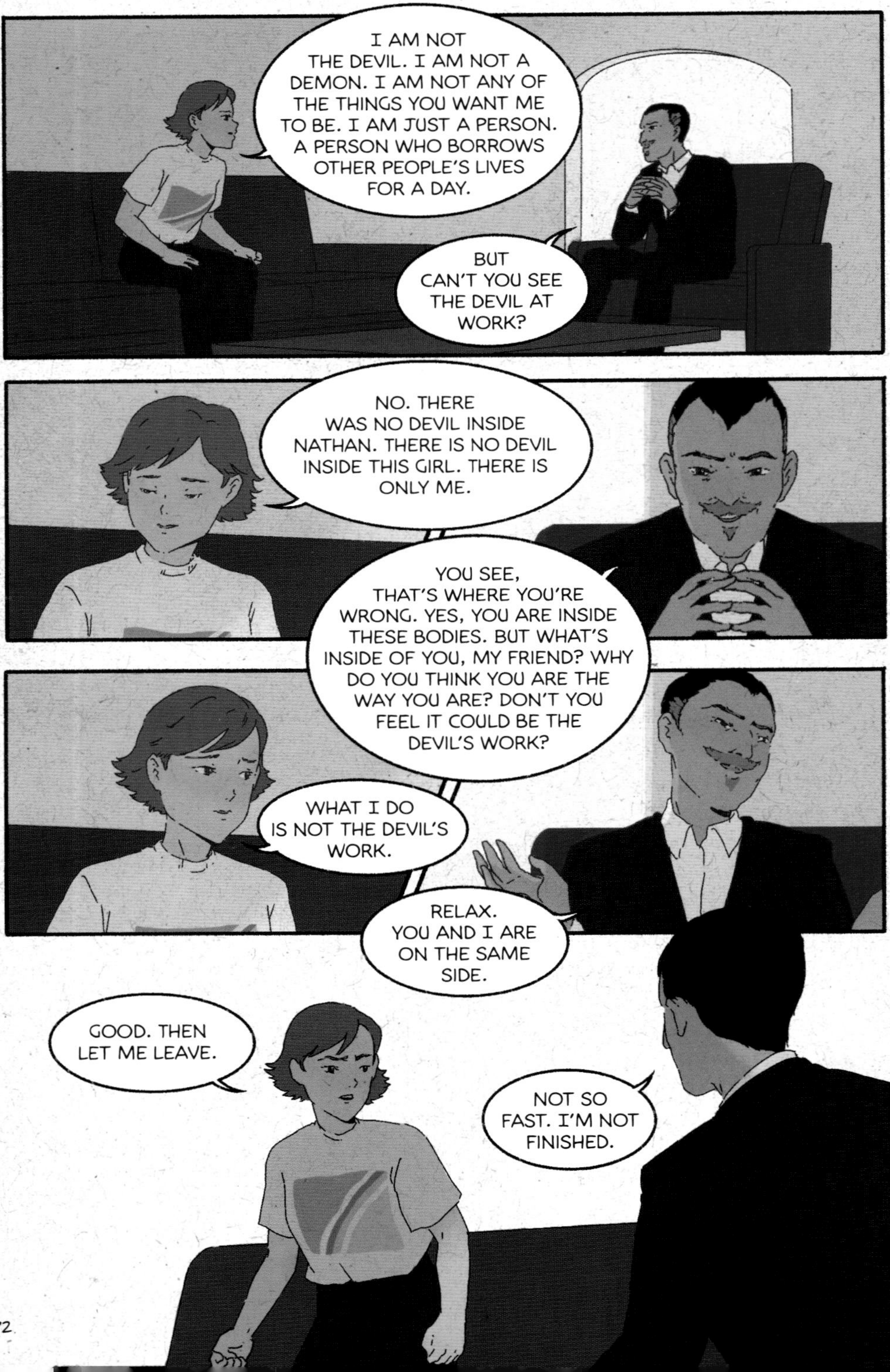
I AM NOT THE DEVIL. I AM NOT A DEMON. I AM NOT ANY OF THE THINGS YOU WANT ME TO BE. I AM JUST A PERSON. A PERSON WHO BORROWS OTHER PEOPLE'S LIVES FOR A DAY.
BUT CAN'T YOU SEE THE DEVIL AT WORK?
NO. THERE WAS NO DEVIL INSIDE NATHAN. THERE IS NO DEVIL INSIDE THIS GIRL. THERE IS ONLY ME.
YOU SEE, THAT'S WHERE YOU'RE WRONG. YES, YOU ARE INSIDE THESE BODIES. BUT WHAT'S INSIDE OF YOU, MY FRIEND? WHY DO YOU THINK YOU ARE THE WAY YOU ARE? DON'T YOU FEEL IT COULD BE THE DEVIL'S WORK?
WHAT I DO IS NOT THE DEVIL'S WORK.
RELAX. YOU AND I ARE ON THE SAME SIDE.
GOOD. THEN LET ME LEAVE.
NOT SO FAST. I'M NOT FINISHED.

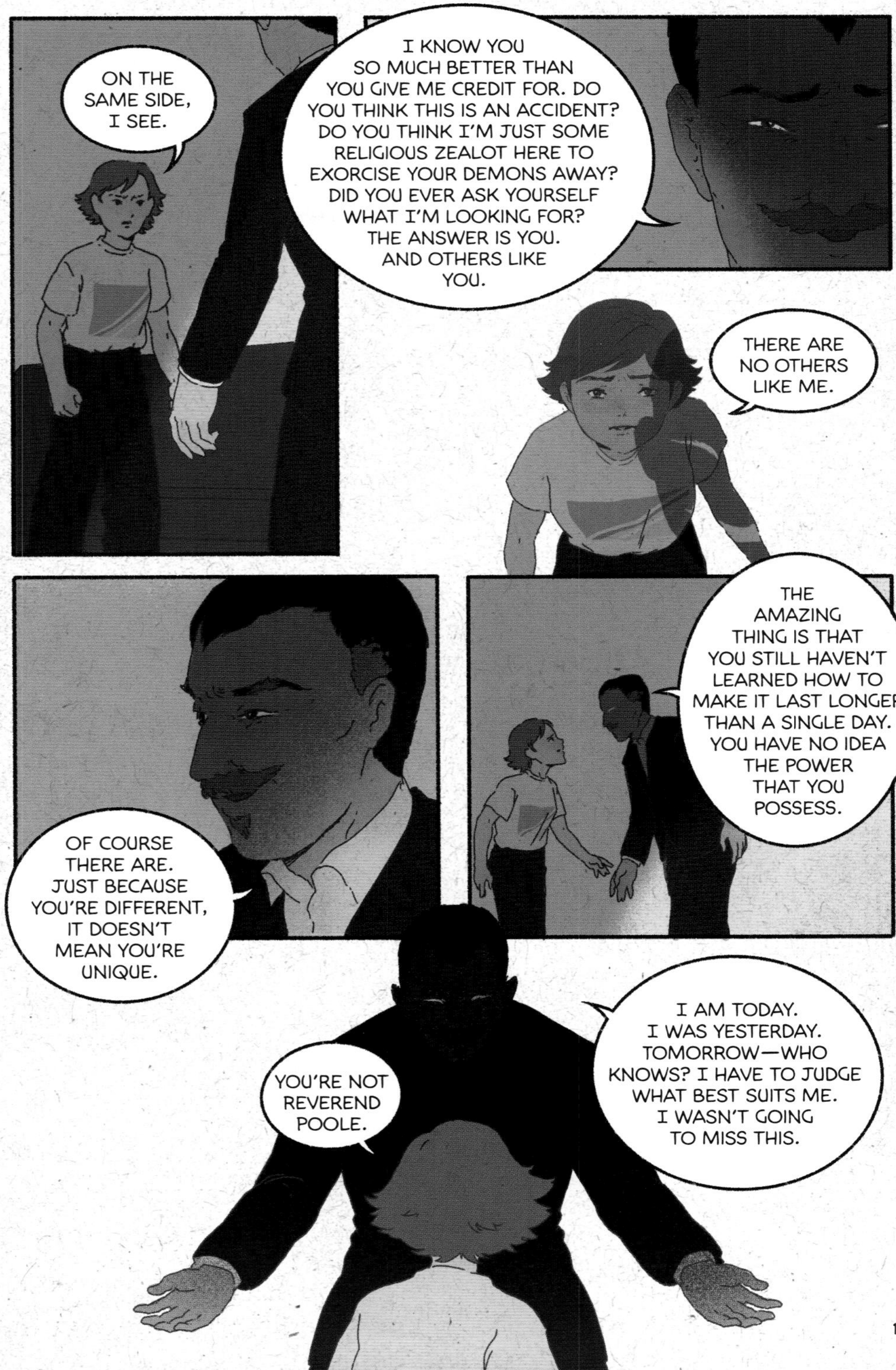
ON THE SAME SIDE, I SEE.
I KNOW YOU SO MUCH BETTER THAN YOU GIVE ME CREDIT FOR. DO YOU THINK THIS IS AN ACCIDENT? DO YOU THINK I'M JUST SOME RELIGIOUS ZEALOT HERE TO EXORCISE YOUR DEMONS AWAY? DID YOU EVER ASK YOURSELF WHAT I'M LOOKING FOR? THE ANSWER IS YOU. AND OTHERS LIKE YOU.
THERE ARE NO OTHERS LIKE ME.
OF COURSE THERE ARE. JUST BECAUSE YOU'RE DIFFERENT, IT DOESN'T MEAN YOU'RE UNIQUE.
THE AMAZING THING IS THAT YOU STILL HAVEN'T LEARNED HOW TO MAKE IT LAST LONGER THAN A SINGLE DAY. YOU HAVE NO IDEA THE POWER THAT YOU POSSESS.
YOU'RE NOT REVEREND POOLE.
I AM TODAY. I WAS YESTERDAY. TOMORROW—WHO KNOWS? I HAVE TO JUDGE WHAT BEST SUITS ME. I WASN'T GOING TO MISS THIS.

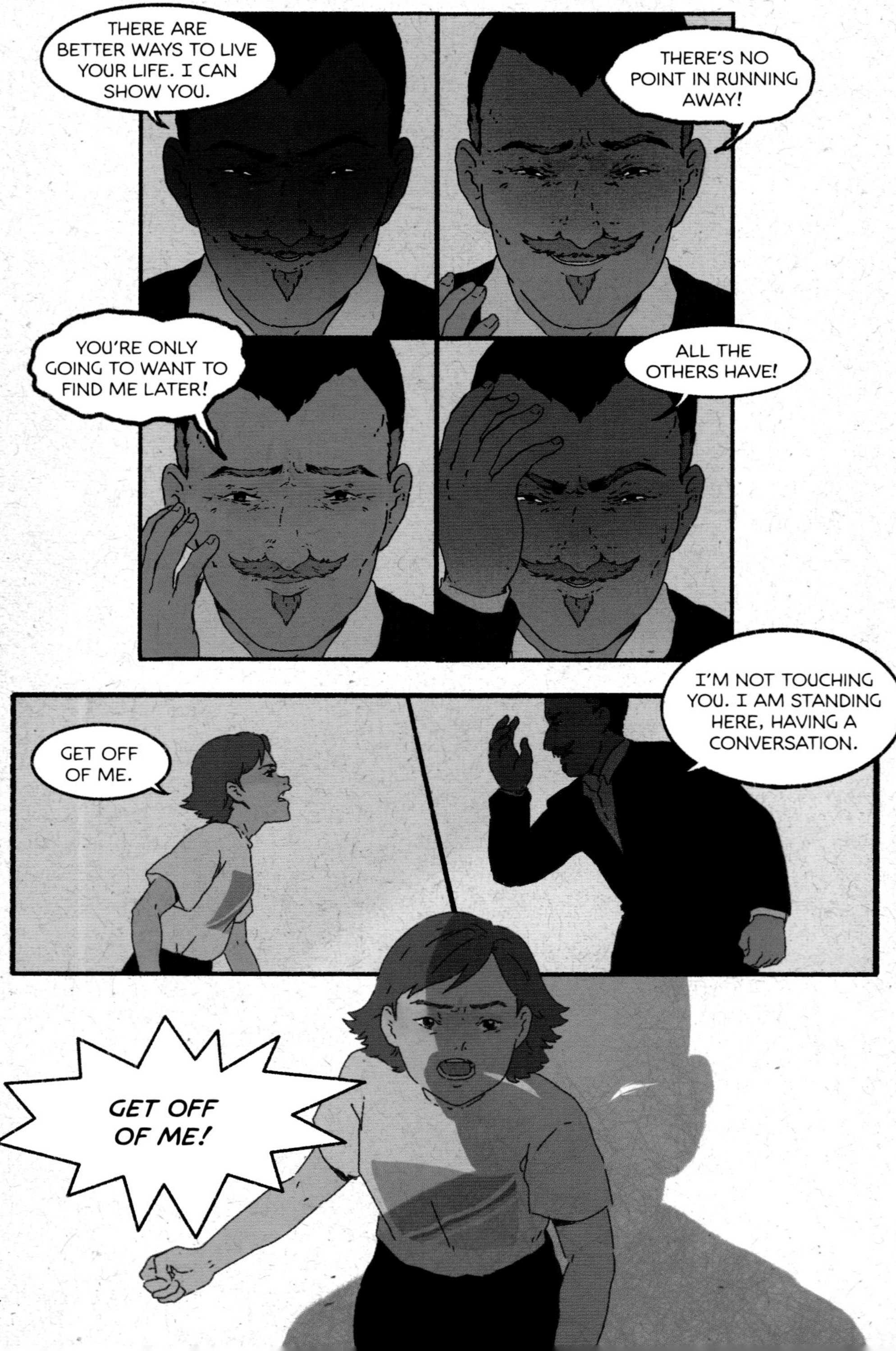
THERE ARE BETTER WAYS TO LIVE YOUR LIFE. I CAN SHOW YOU.
THERE'S NO POINT IN RUNNING AWAY!
YOU'RE ONLY GOING TO WANT TO FIND ME LATER!
ALL THE OTHERS HAVE!
GET OFF OF ME.
I'M NOT TOUCHING YOU. I AM STANDING HERE, HAVING A CONVERSATION.
GET OFF OF ME!

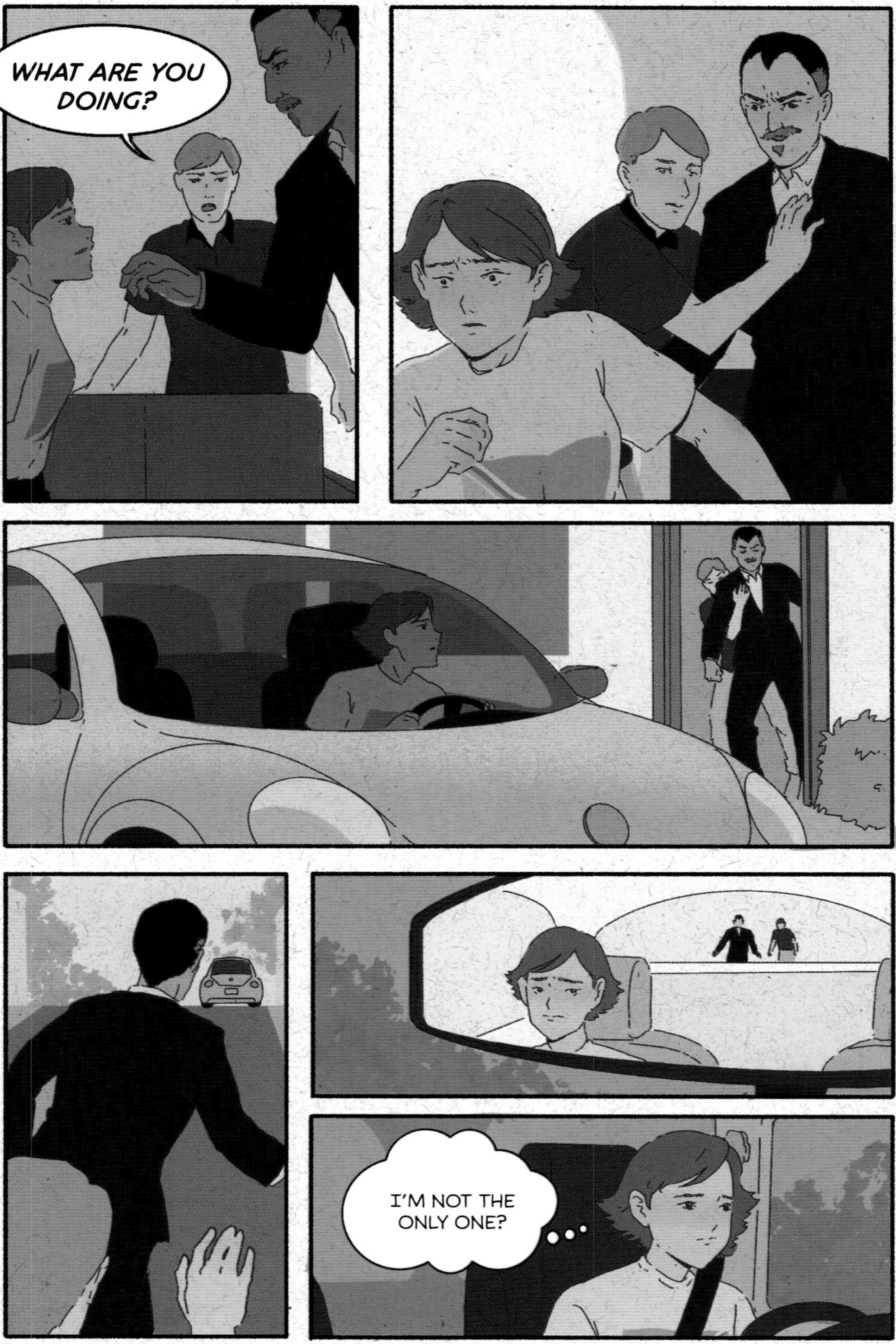
WHAT ARE YOU DOING?
I'M NOT THE ONLY ONE?

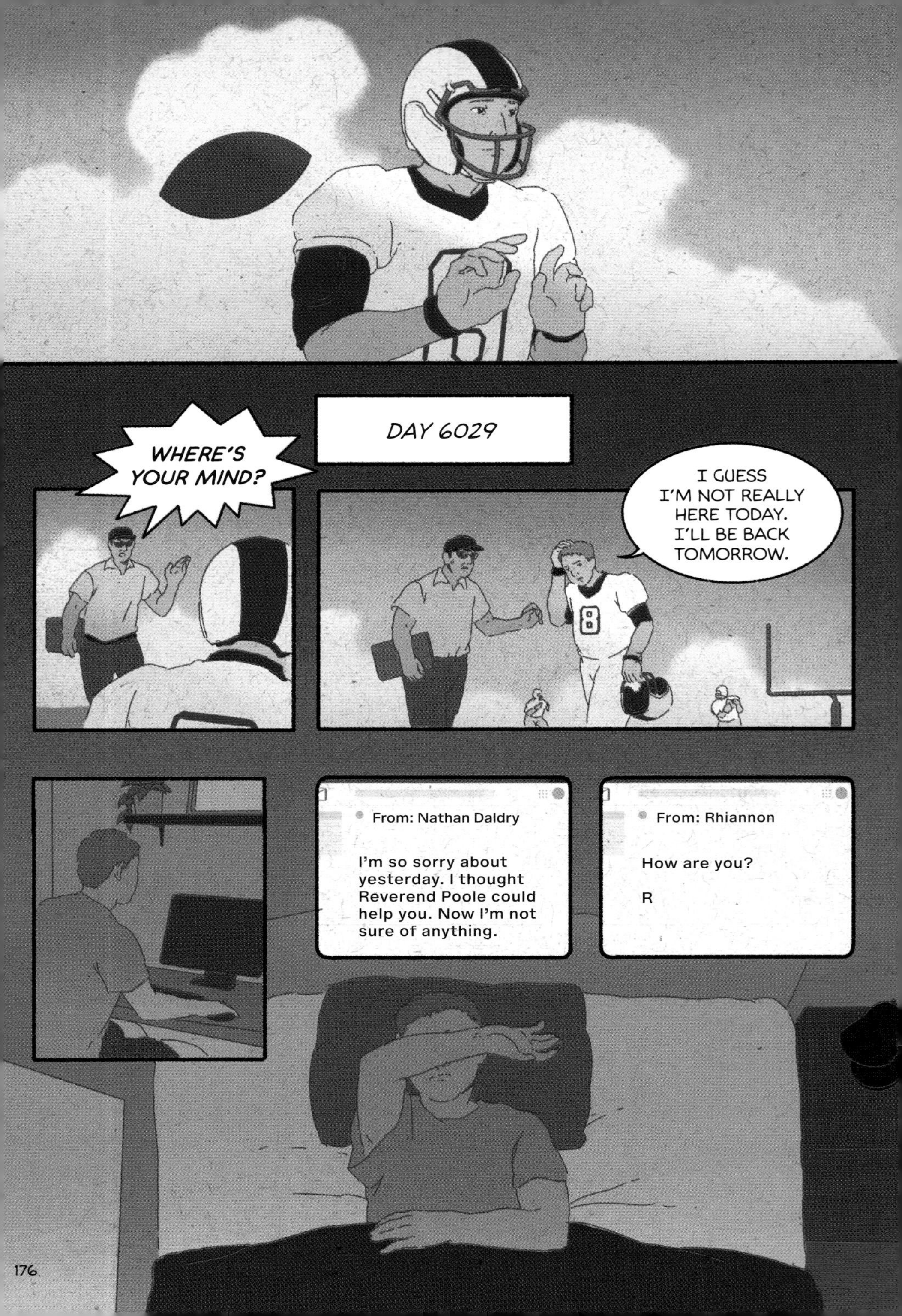
DAY 6029
WHERE'S YOUR MIND?
I GUESS I'M NOT REALLY HERE TODAY. I'LL BE BACK TOMORROW.
From: Nathan Daldry
I'm so sorry about yesterday. I thought Reverend Poole could help you. Now I'm not sure of anything.
From: Rhiannon
How are you?
R

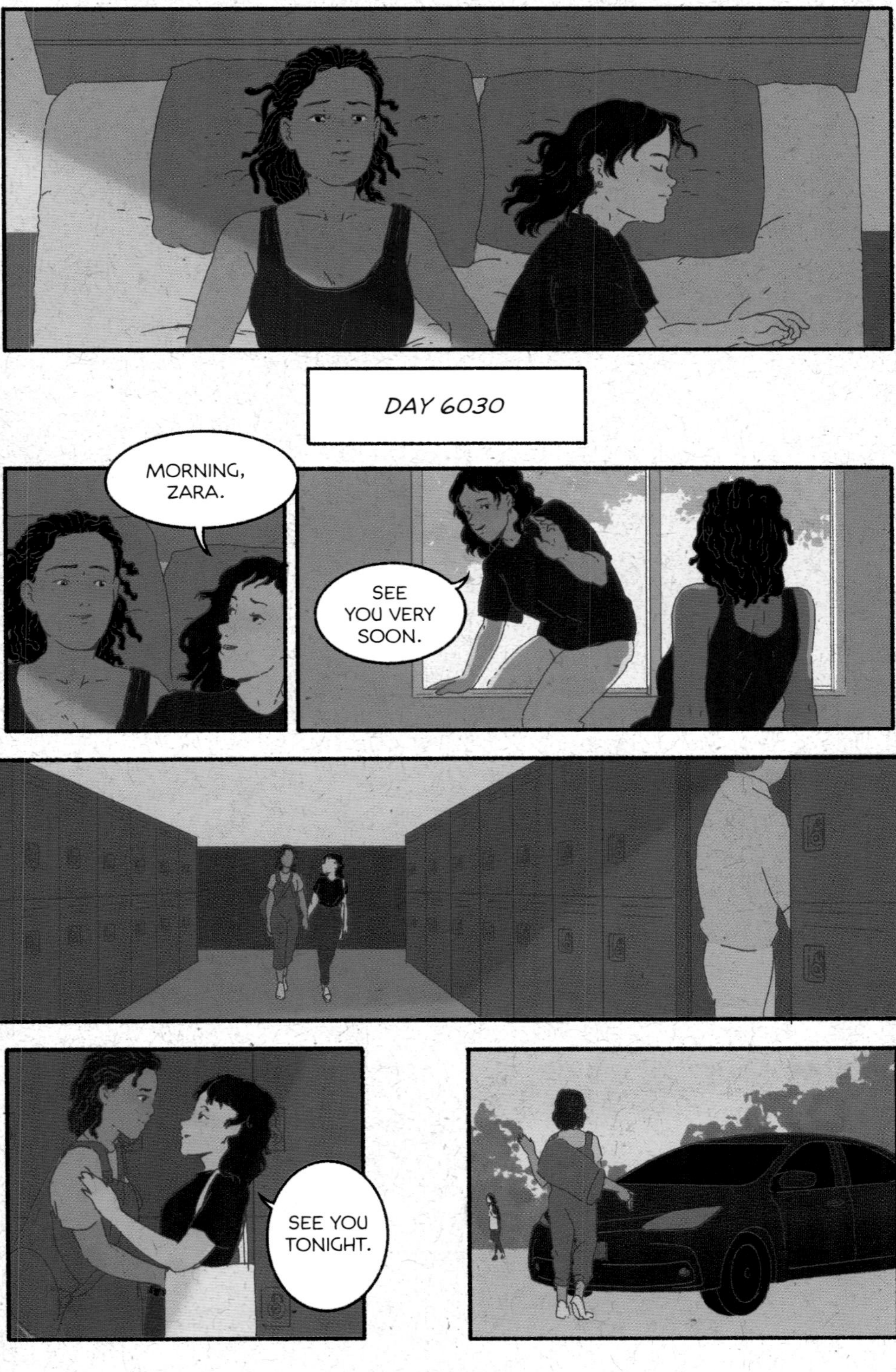
DAY 6030
MORNING, ZARA.
SEE YOU VERY SOON.
SEE YOU TONIGHT.

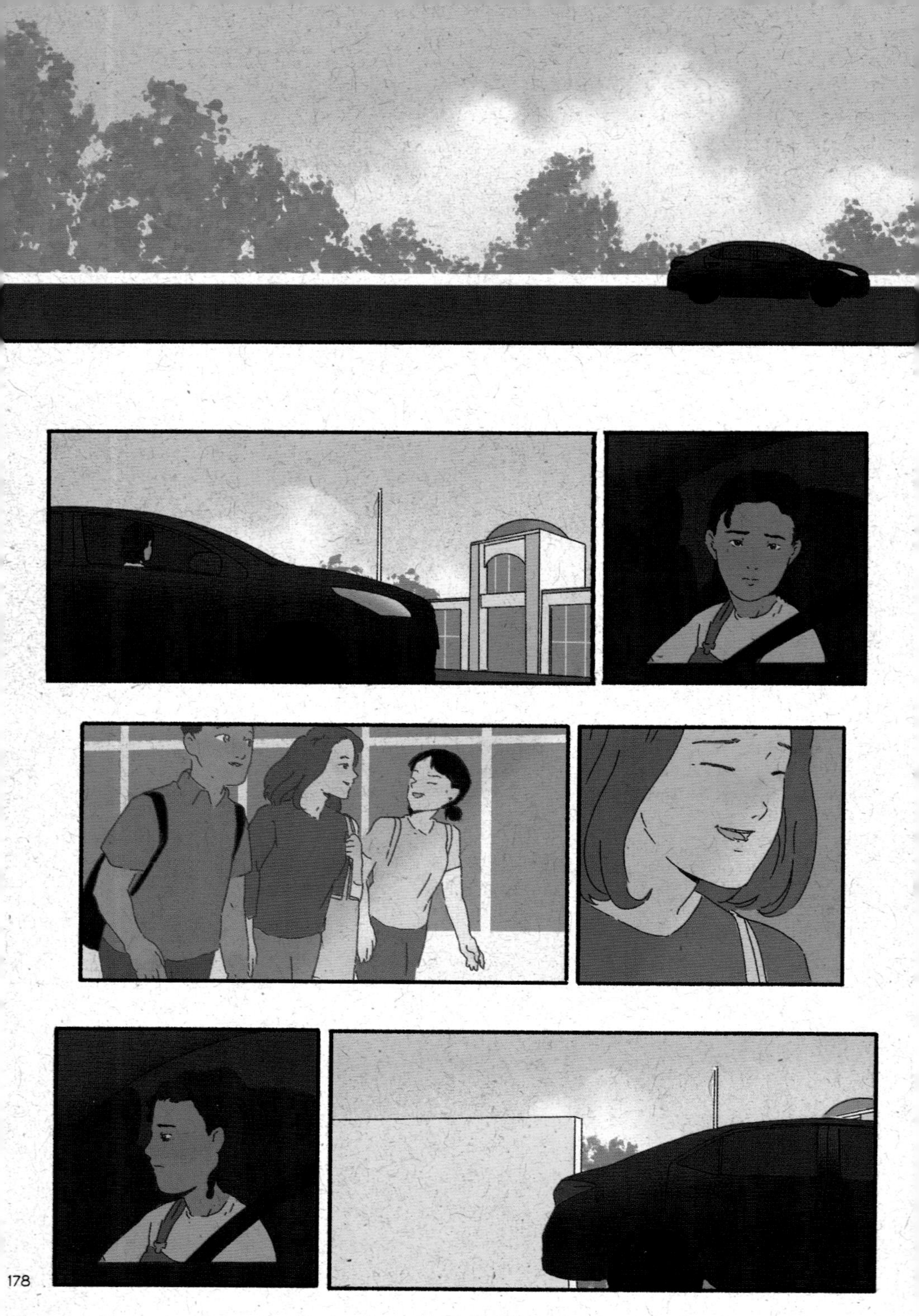

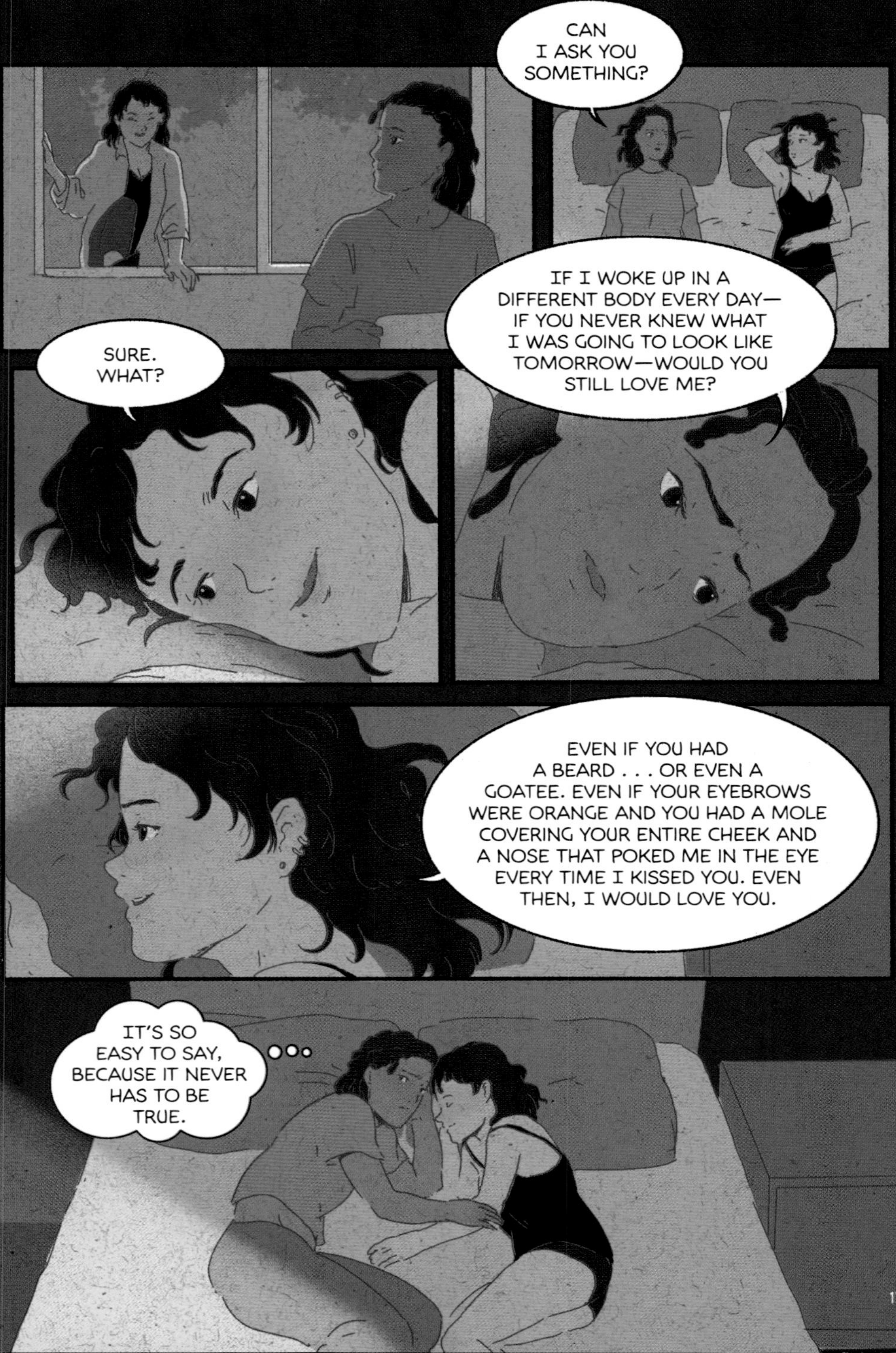
CAN I ASK YOU SOMETHING?
SURE. WHAT?
IF I WOKE UP IN A DIFFERENT BODY EVERY DAY—IF YOU NEVER KNEW WHAT I WAS GOING TO LOOK LIKE TOMORROW—WOULD YOU STILL LOVE ME?
EVEN IF YOU HAD A BEARD . . . OR EVEN A GOATEE. EVEN IF YOUR EYEBROWS WERE ORANGE AND YOU HAD A MOLE COVERING YOUR ENTIRE CHEEK AND A NOSE THAT POKED ME IN THE EYE EVERY TIME I KISSED YOU. EVEN THEN, I WOULD LOVE YOU.
IT'S SO EASY TO SAY, BECAUSE IT NEVER HAS TO BE TRUE.

DAY 6031

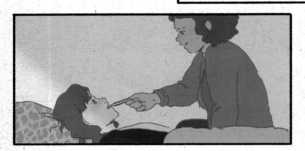

DAY 6032

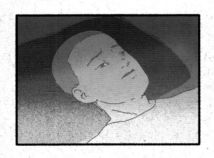

From: Rhiannon

I want to see you, but I'm not sure if we should do that. I want to hear about what's going on, but I'm afraid that will only start everything

again. I love you—I do—but I am afraid of making that love too important. Because you're always going to leave me, A.

R

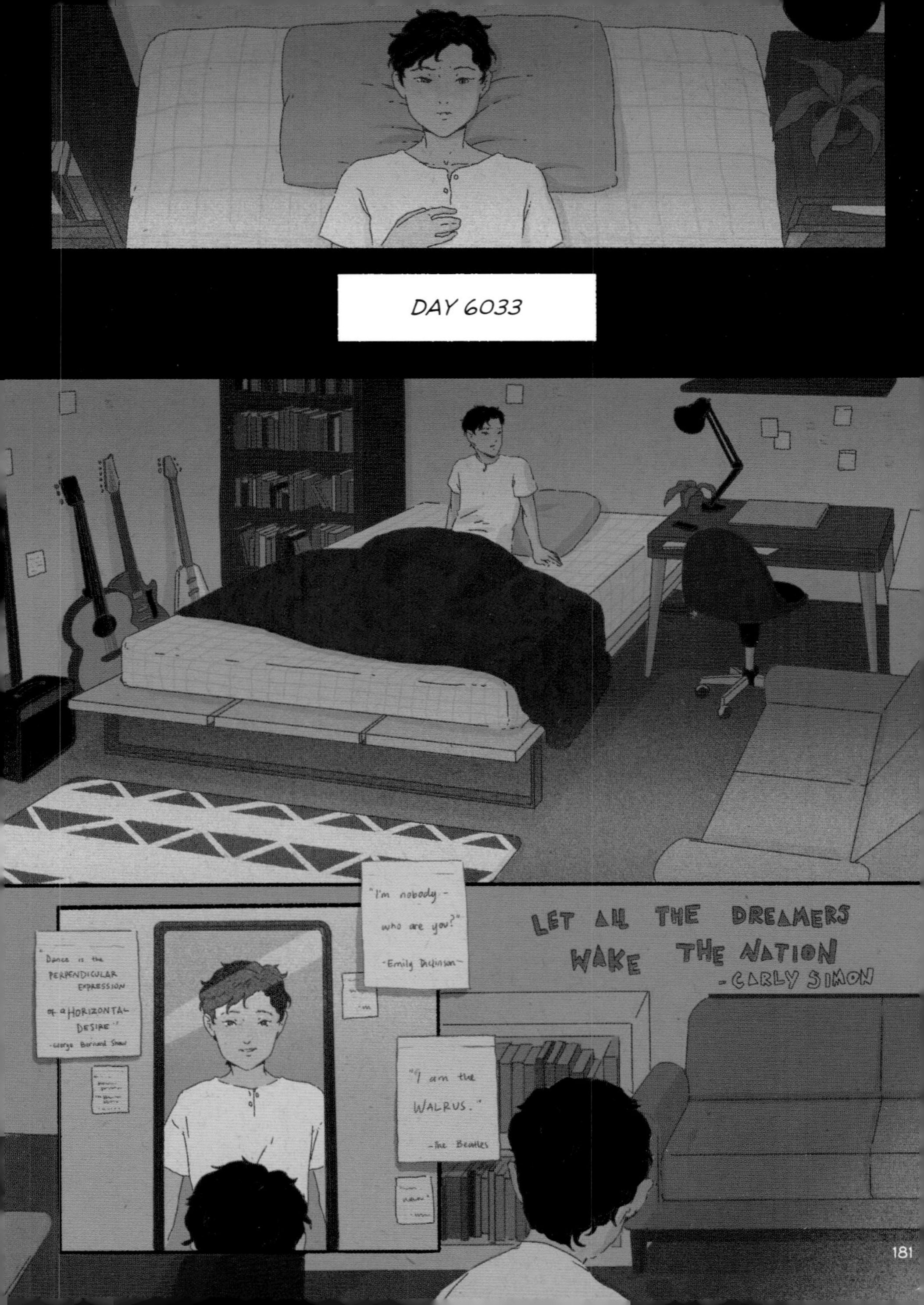
DAY 6033
"Dance is the PERPENDICULAR EXPRESSION of a HORIZONTAL DESIRE."
-George Bernard Shaw
"I'm nobody - who are you?"
-Emily Dickinson-
LET ALL THE DREAMERS WAKE THE NATION
-CARLY SIMON
"I am the WALRUS."
-The Beatles

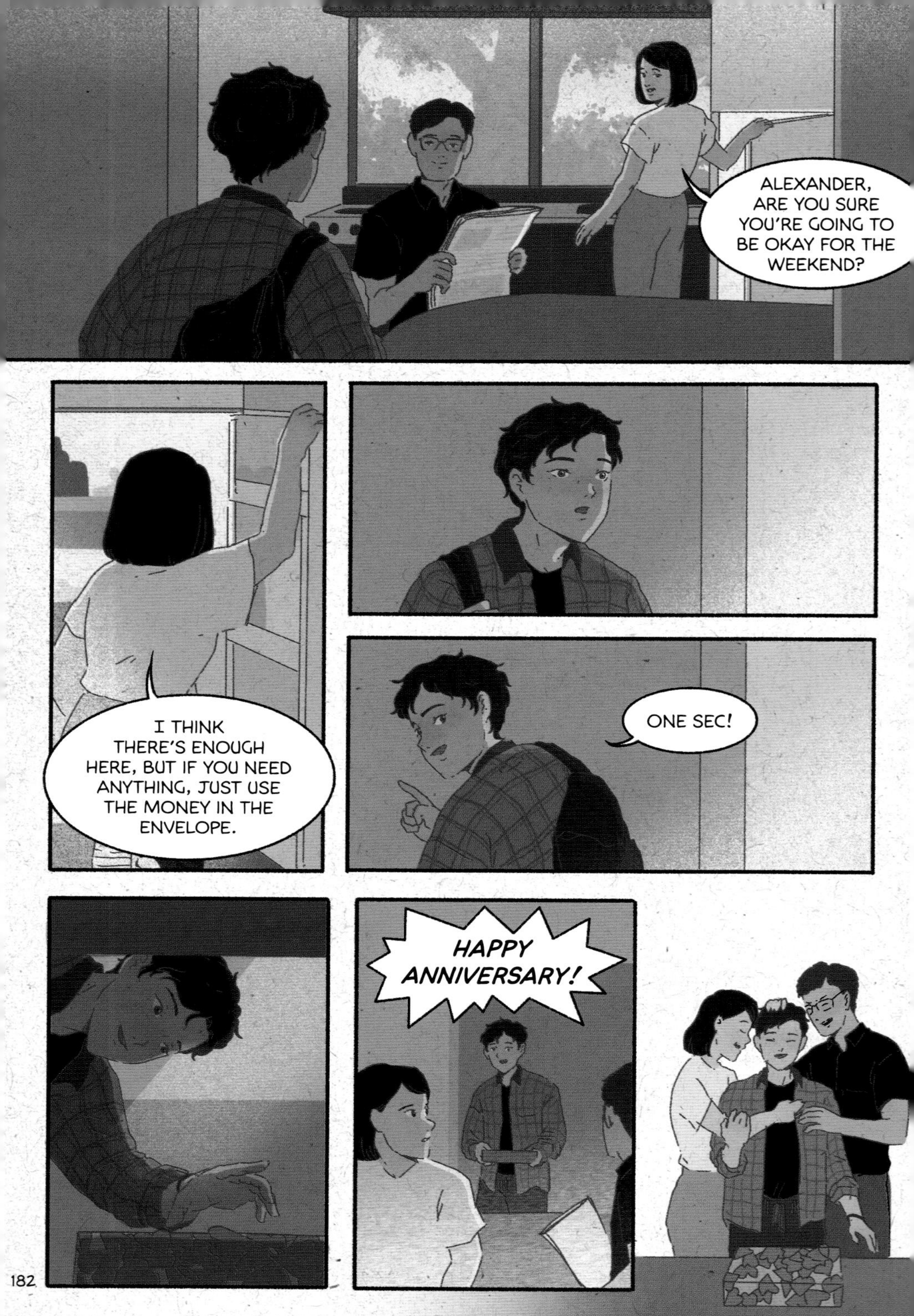
ALEXANDER, ARE YOU SURE YOU'RE GOING TO BE OKAY FOR THE WEEKEND?
I THINK THERE'S ENOUGH HERE, BUT IF YOU NEED ANYTHING, JUST USE THE MONEY IN THE ENVELOPE.
ONE SEC!
HAPPY ANNIVERSARY!

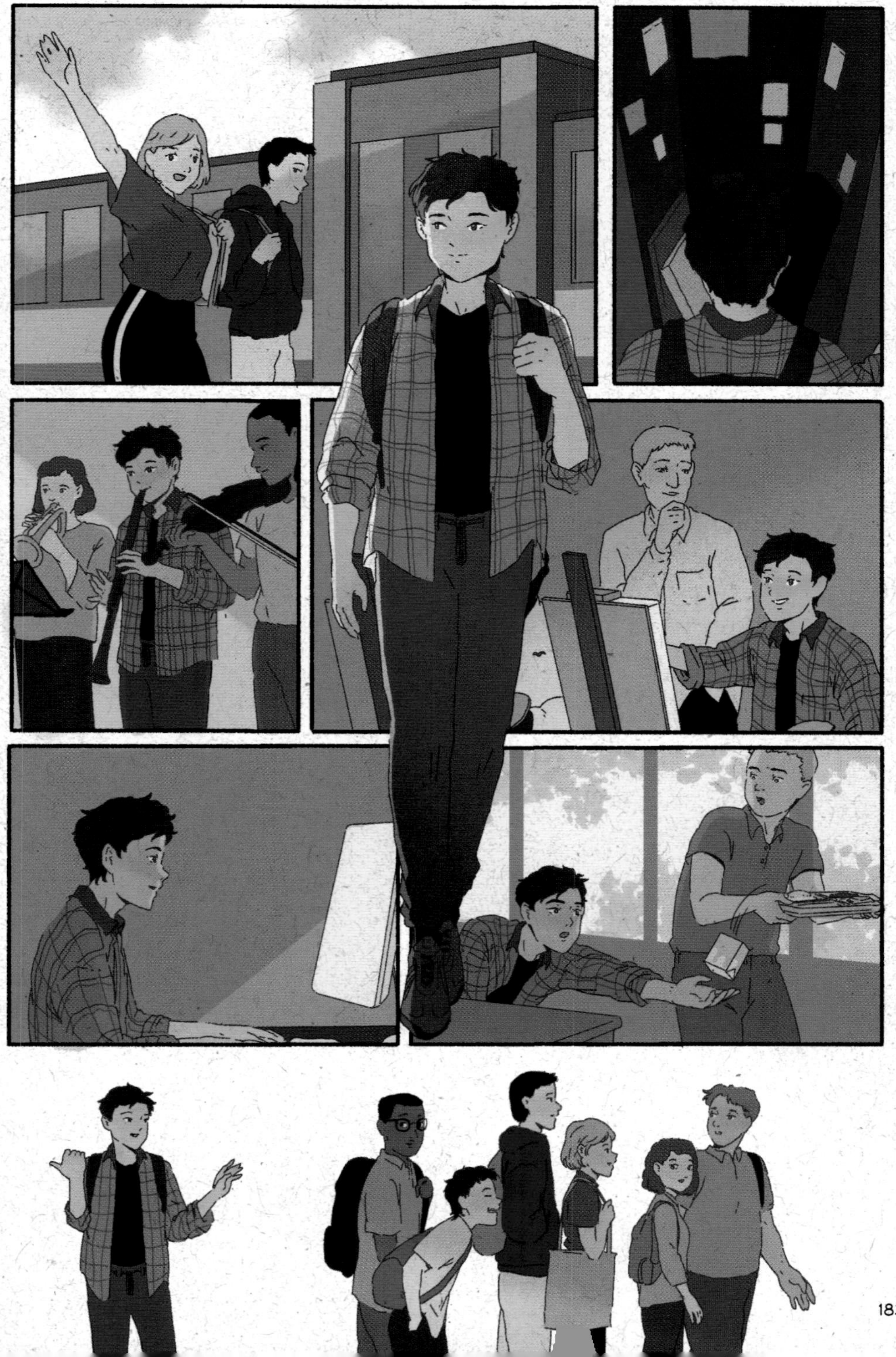

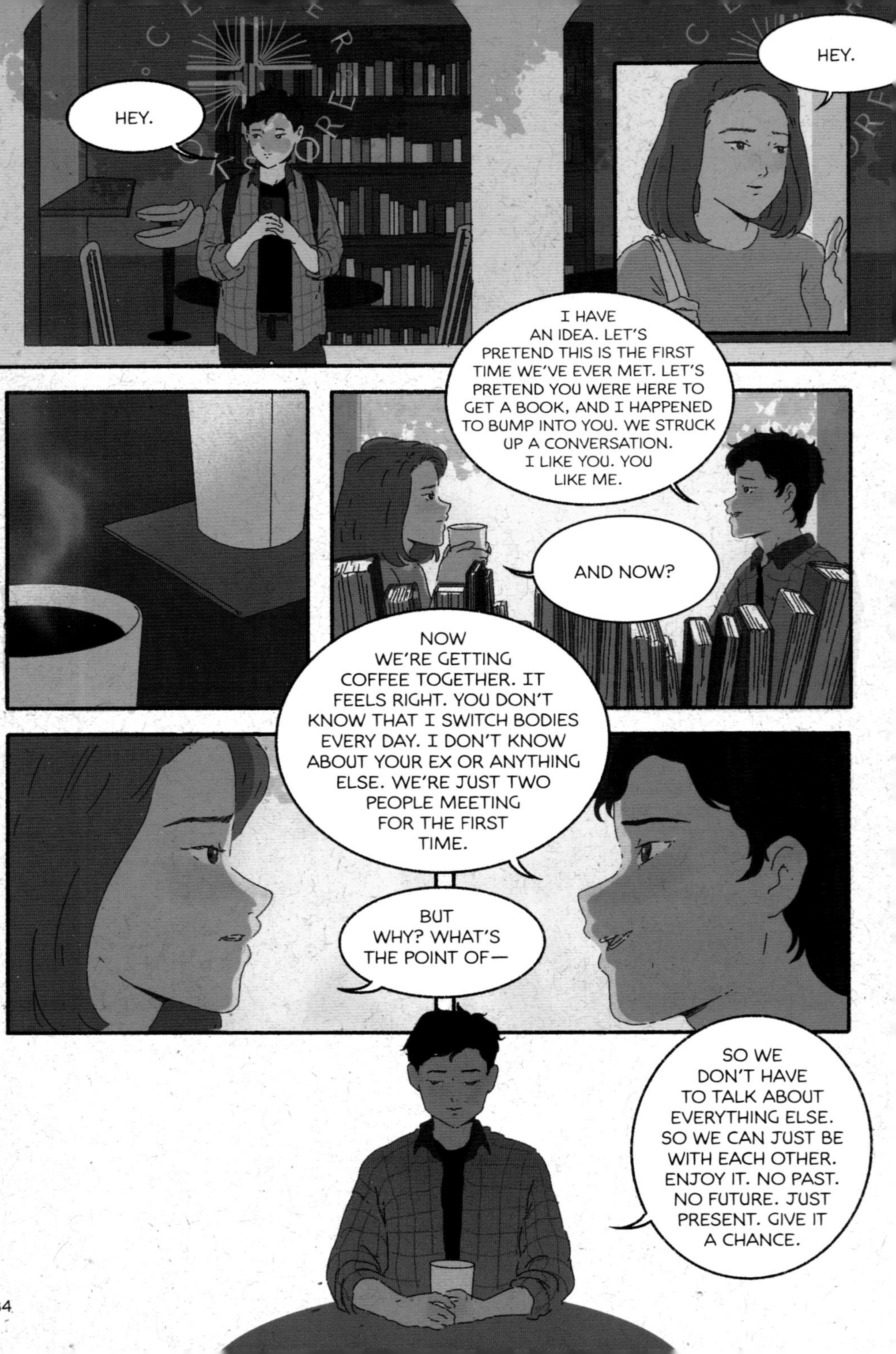
HEY.
HEY.
I HAVE AN IDEA. LET'S PRETEND THIS IS THE FIRST TIME WE'VE EVER MET. LET'S PRETEND YOU WERE HERE TO GET A BOOK, AND I HAPPENED TO BUMP INTO YOU. WE STRUCK UP A CONVERSATION. I LIKE YOU. YOU LIKE ME.
AND NOW?
NOW WE'RE GETTING COFFEE TOGETHER. IT FEELS RIGHT. YOU DON'T KNOW THAT I SWITCH BODIES EVERY DAY. I DON'T KNOW ABOUT YOUR EX OR ANYTHING ELSE. WE'RE JUST TWO PEOPLE MEETING FOR THE FIRST TIME.
BUT WHY? WHAT'S THE POINT OF—
SO WE DON'T HAVE TO TALK ABOUT EVERYTHING ELSE. SO WE CAN JUST BE WITH EACH OTHER. ENJOY IT. NO PAST. NO FUTURE. JUST PRESENT. GIVE IT A CHANCE.

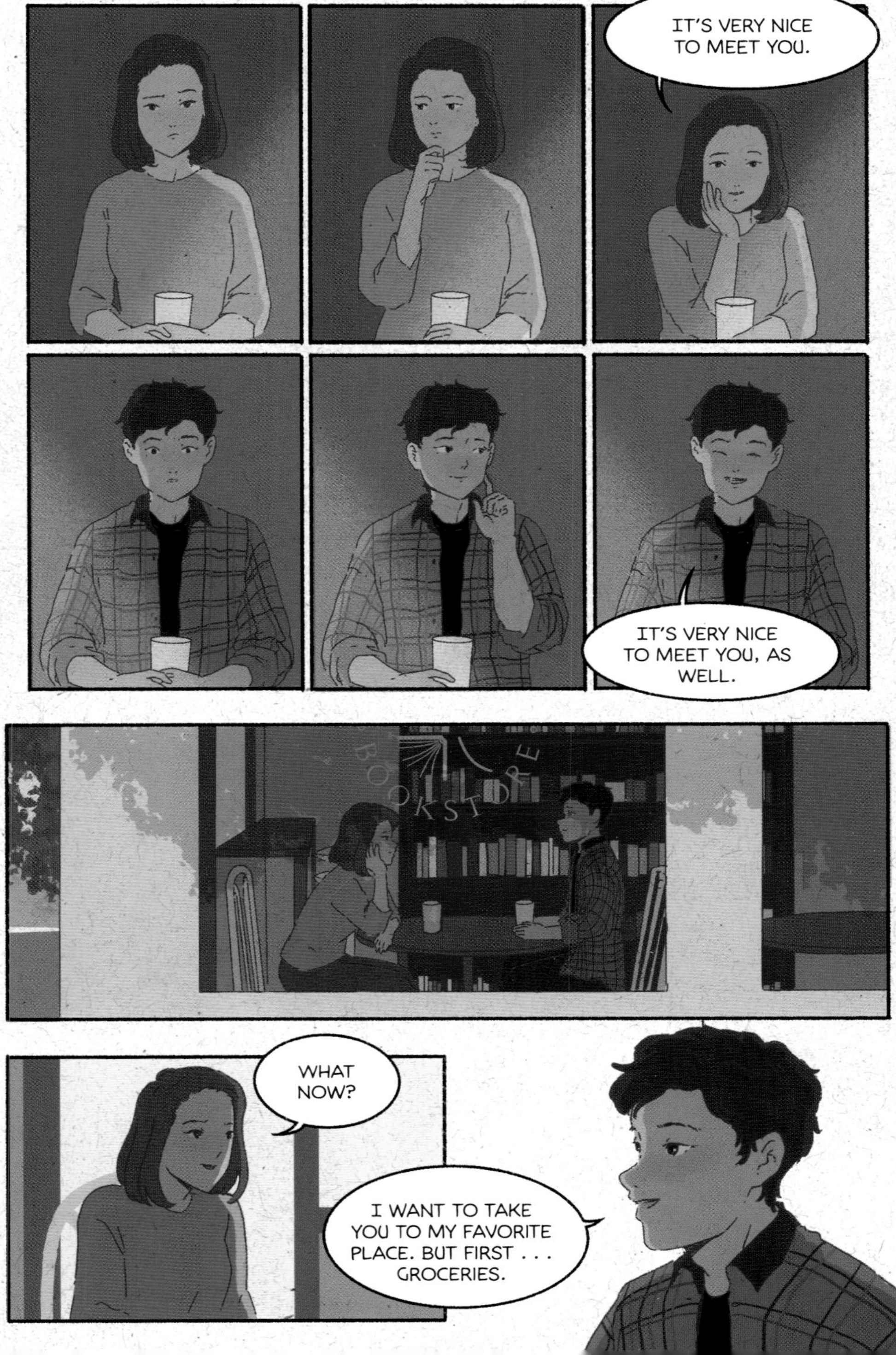
IT'S VERY NICE
TO MEET YOU.
IT'S VERY NICE
TO MEET YOU, AS
WELL.
BOOKSTORE
WHAT
NOW?
I WANT TO TAKE
YOU TO MY FAVORITE
PLACE. BUT FIRST . . .
GROCERIES.

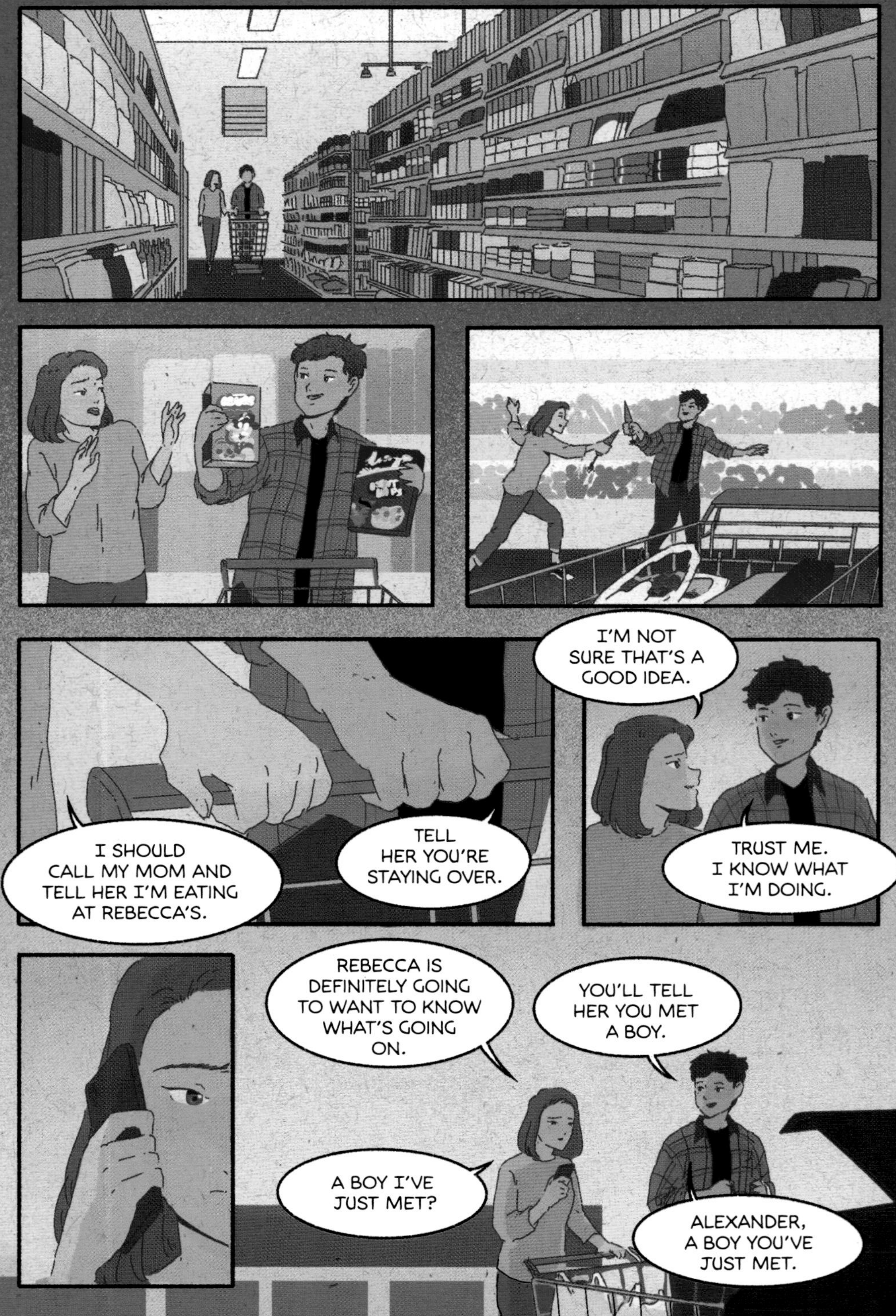
I SHOULD CALL MY MOM AND TELL HER I'M EATING AT REBECCA'S.
TELL HER YOU'RE STAYING OVER.
I'M NOT SURE THAT'S A GOOD IDEA.
TRUST ME. I KNOW WHAT I'M DOING.
REBECCA IS DEFINITELY GOING TO WANT TO KNOW WHAT'S GOING ON.
YOU'LL TELL HER YOU MET A BOY.
A BOY I'VE JUST MET?
ALEXANDER, A BOY YOU'VE JUST MET.

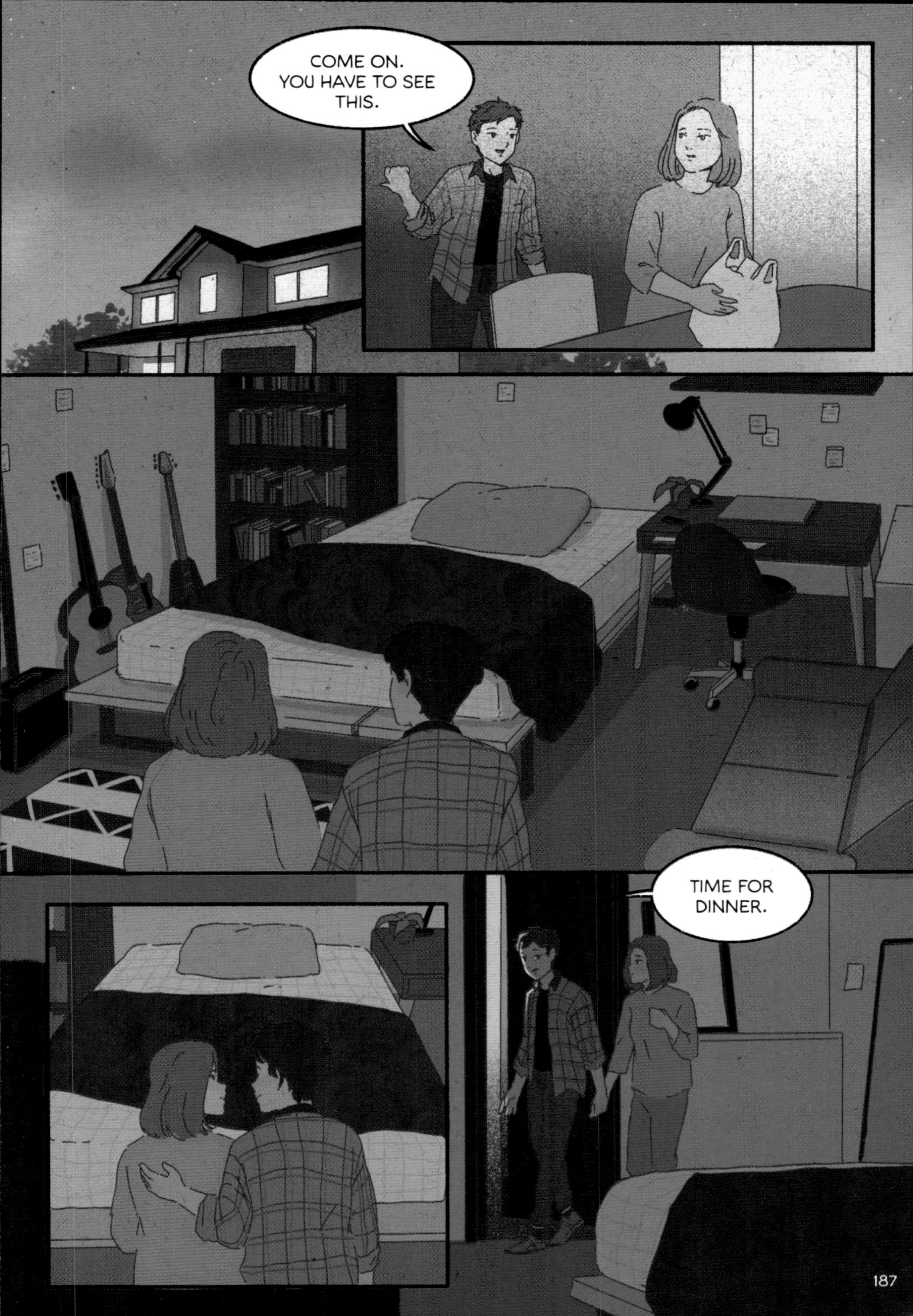
COME ON. YOU HAVE TO SEE THIS.
TIME FOR DINNER.

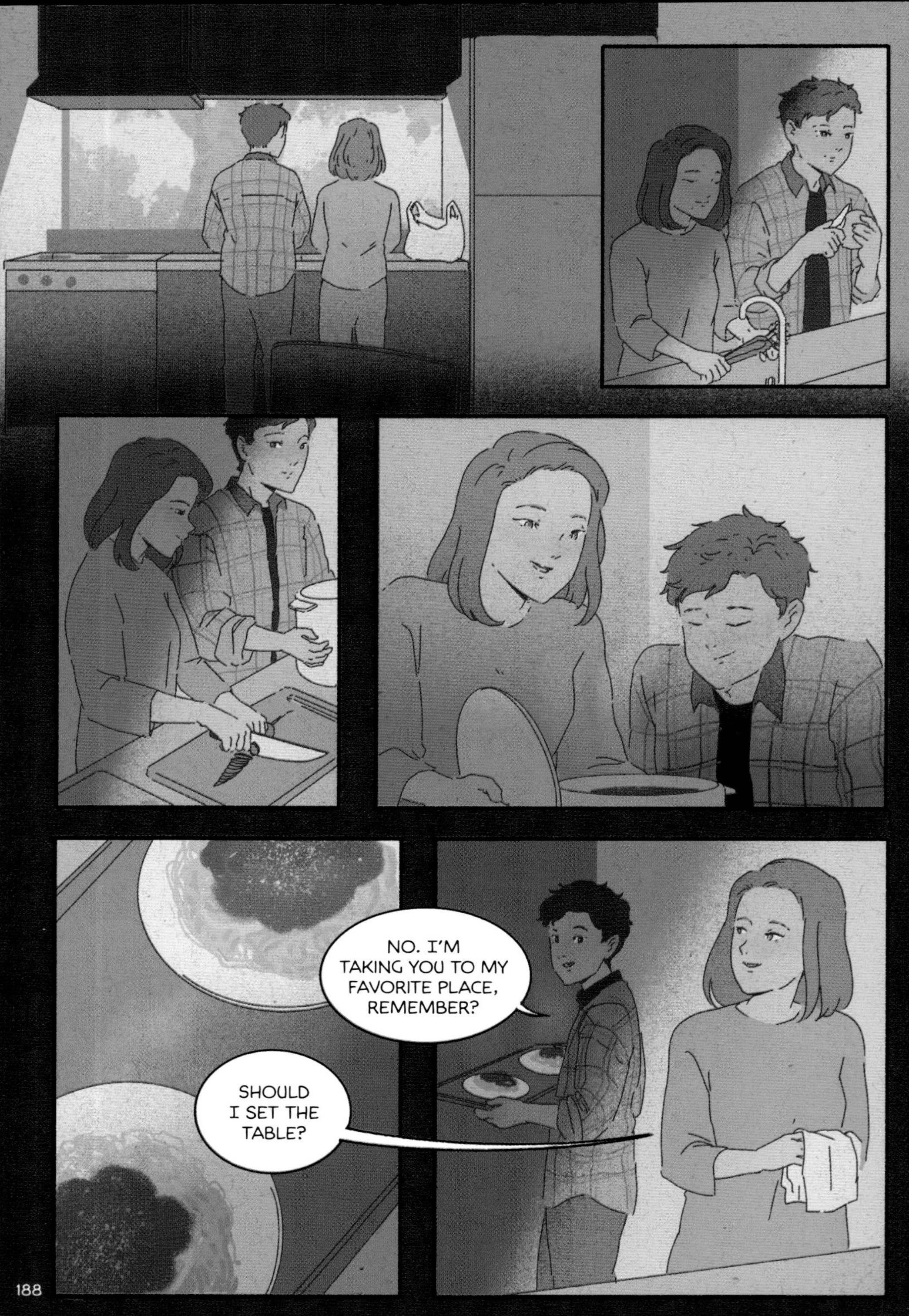
SHOULD I SET THE TABLE?
NO. I'M TAKING YOU TO MY FAVORITE PLACE, REMEMBER?

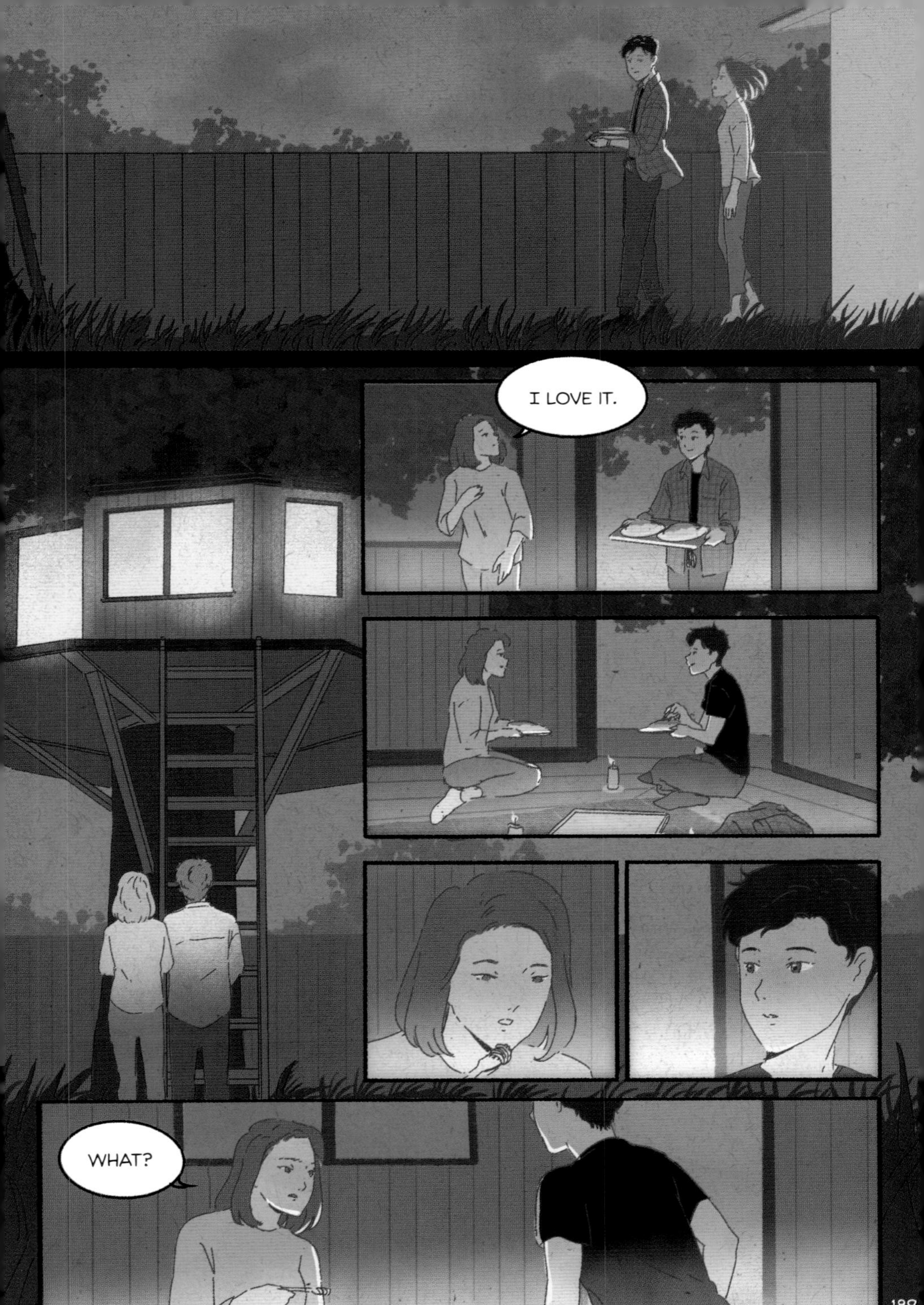
I LOVE IT.
WHAT?

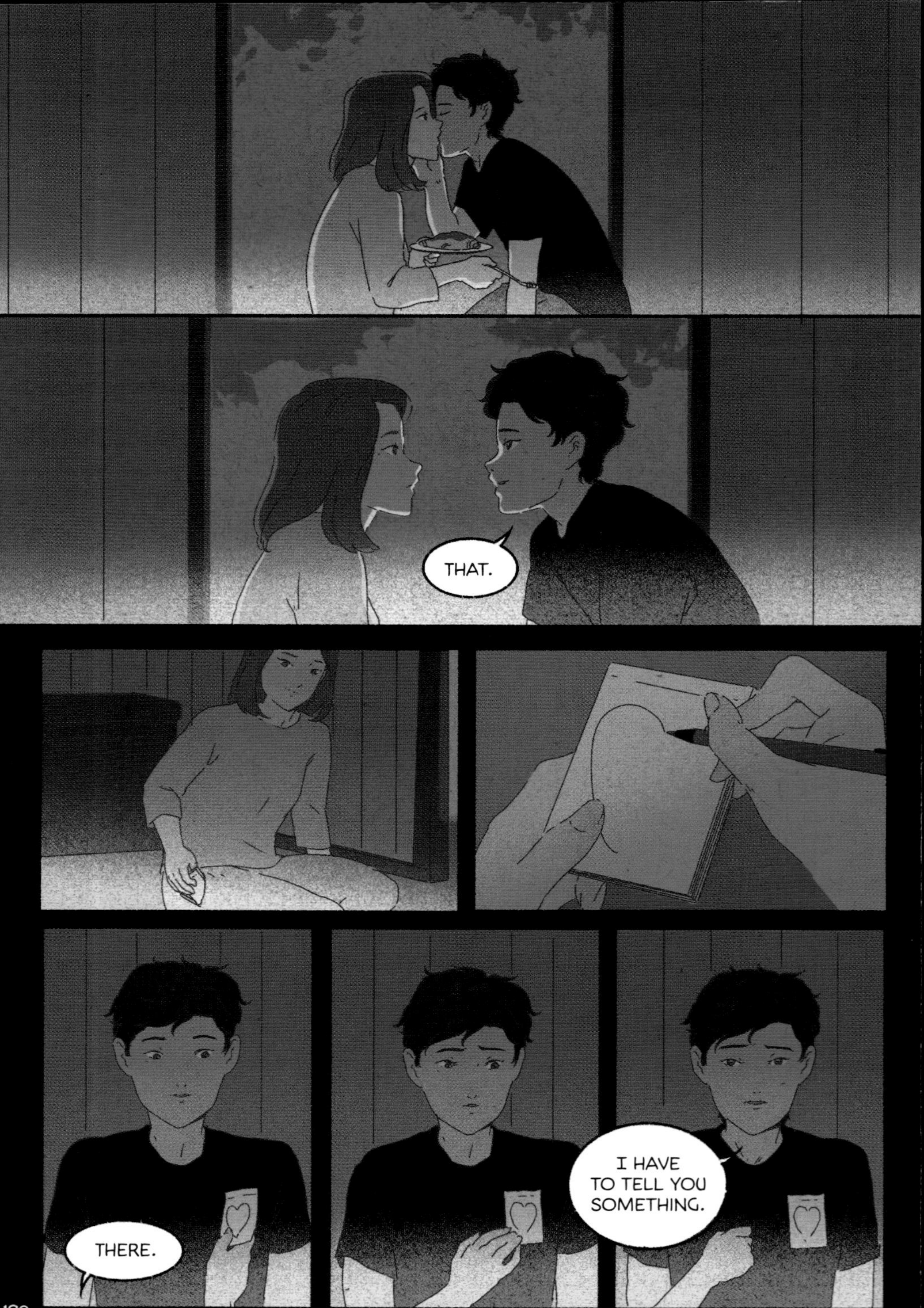
THAT.
THERE.
I HAVE TO TELL YOU SOMETHING.

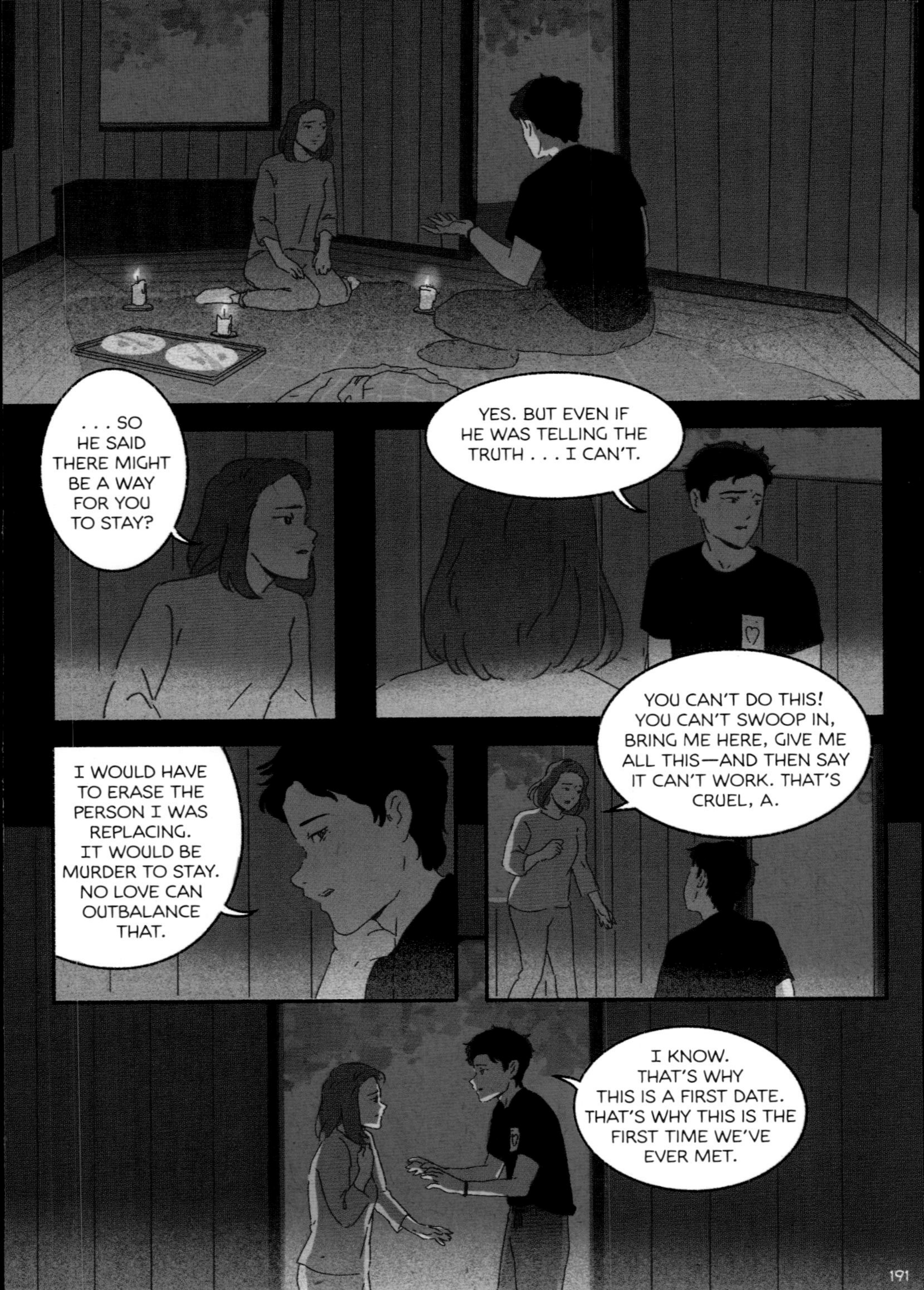
. . . SO HE SAID THERE MIGHT BE A WAY FOR YOU TO STAY?
YES. BUT EVEN IF HE WAS TELLING THE TRUTH . . . I CAN'T.
I WOULD HAVE TO ERASE THE PERSON I WAS REPLACING. IT WOULD BE MURDER TO STAY. NO LOVE CAN OUTBALANCE THAT.
YOU CAN'T DO THIS! YOU CAN'T SWOOP IN, BRING ME HERE, GIVE ME ALL THIS—AND THEN SAY IT CAN'T WORK. THAT'S CRUEL, A.
I KNOW. THAT'S WHY THIS IS A FIRST DATE. THAT'S WHY THIS IS THE FIRST TIME WE'VE EVER MET.

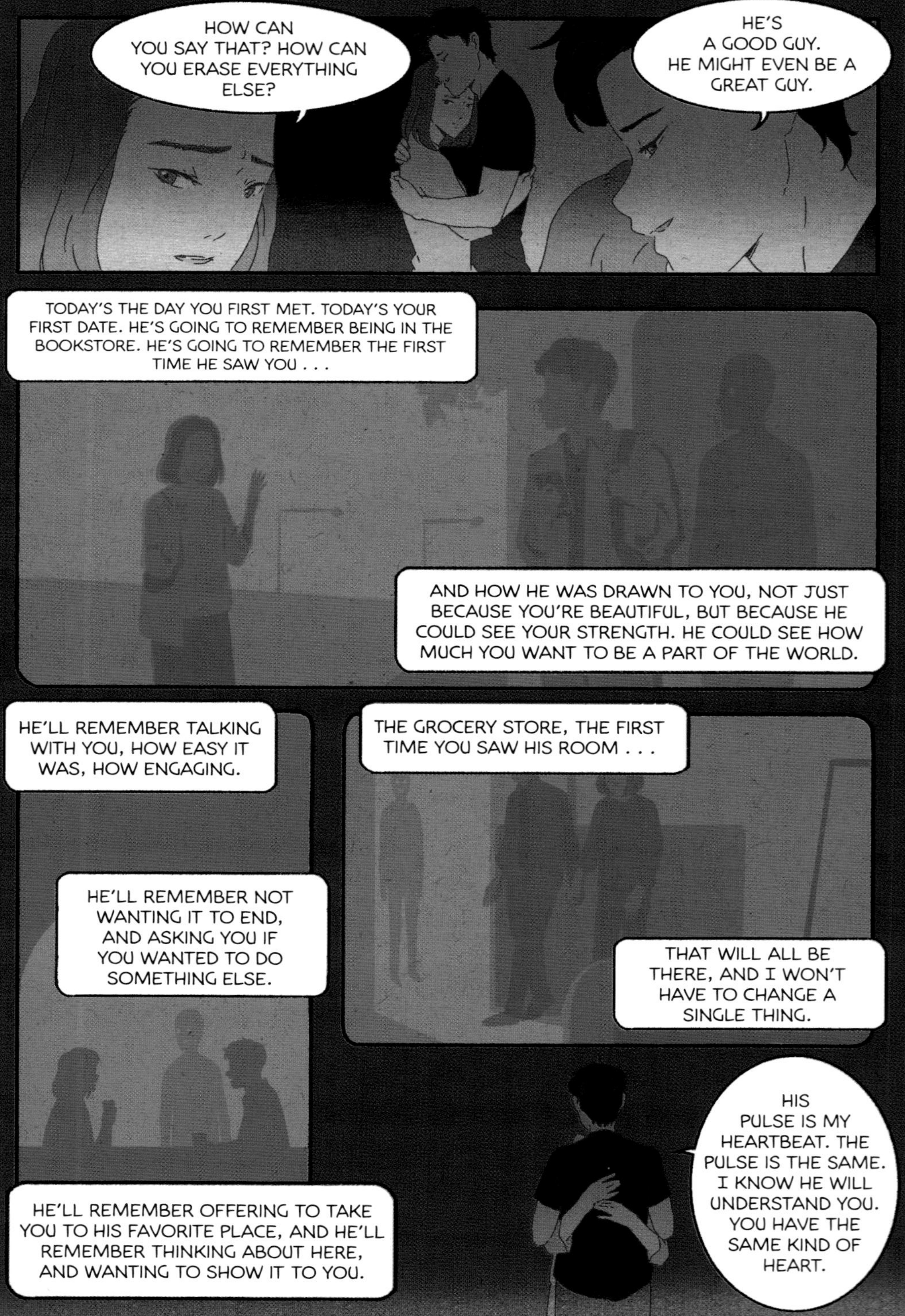
HOW CAN YOU SAY THAT? HOW CAN YOU ERASE EVERYTHING ELSE?
HE'S A GOOD GUY. HE MIGHT EVEN BE A GREAT GUY.
TODAY'S THE DAY YOU FIRST MET. TODAY'S YOUR FIRST DATE. HE'S GOING TO REMEMBER BEING IN THE BOOKSTORE. HE'S GOING TO REMEMBER THE FIRST TIME HE SAW YOU . . .
AND HOW HE WAS DRAWN TO YOU, NOT JUST BECAUSE YOU'RE BEAUTIFUL, BUT BECAUSE HE COULD SEE YOUR STRENGTH. HE COULD SEE HOW MUCH YOU WANT TO BE A PART OF THE WORLD.
HE'LL REMEMBER TALKING WITH YOU, HOW EASY IT WAS, HOW ENGAGING.
HE'LL REMEMBER NOT WANTING IT TO END, AND ASKING YOU IF YOU WANTED TO DO SOMETHING ELSE.
THE GROCERY STORE, THE FIRST TIME YOU SAW HIS ROOM . . .
THAT WILL ALL BE THERE, AND I WON'T HAVE TO CHANGE A SINGLE THING.
HE'LL REMEMBER OFFERING TO TAKE YOU TO HIS FAVORITE PLACE, AND HE'LL REMEMBER THINKING ABOUT HERE, AND WANTING TO SHOW IT TO YOU.
HIS PULSE IS MY HEARTBEAT. THE PULSE IS THE SAME. I KNOW HE WILL UNDERSTAND YOU. YOU HAVE THE SAME KIND OF HEART.

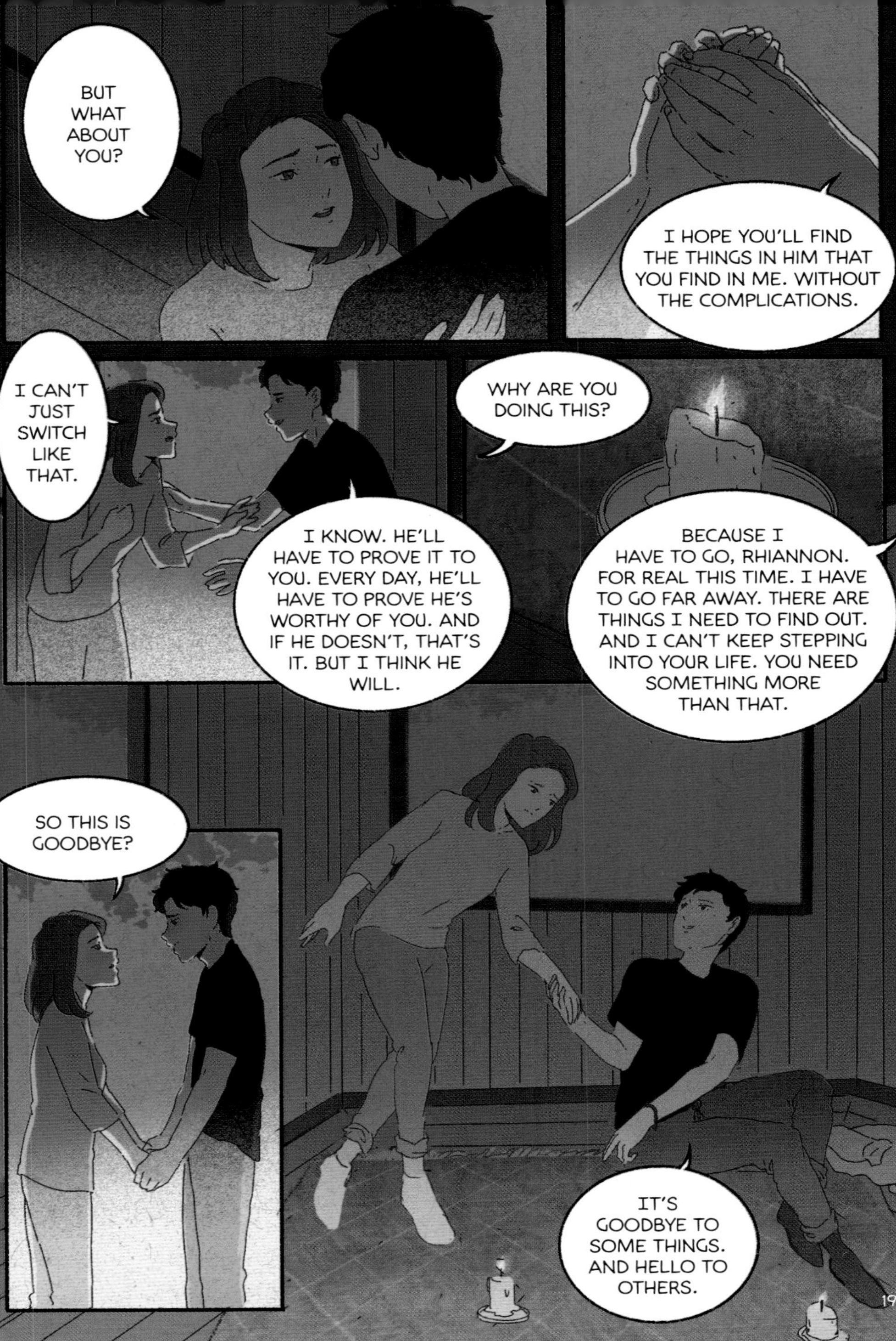
BUT WHAT ABOUT YOU?
I HOPE YOU'LL FIND THE THINGS IN HIM THAT YOU FIND IN ME. WITHOUT THE COMPLICATIONS.
I CAN'T JUST SWITCH LIKE THAT.
I KNOW. HE'LL HAVE TO PROVE IT TO YOU. EVERY DAY, HE'LL HAVE TO PROVE HE'S WORTHY OF YOU. AND IF HE DOESN'T, THAT'S IT. BUT I THINK HE WILL.
WHY ARE YOU DOING THIS?
BECAUSE I HAVE TO GO, RHIANNON. FOR REAL THIS TIME. I HAVE TO GO FAR AWAY. THERE ARE THINGS I NEED TO FIND OUT. AND I CAN'T KEEP STEPPING INTO YOUR LIFE. YOU NEED SOMETHING MORE THAN THAT.
SO THIS IS GOODBYE?
IT'S GOODBYE TO SOME THINGS. AND HELLO TO OTHERS.

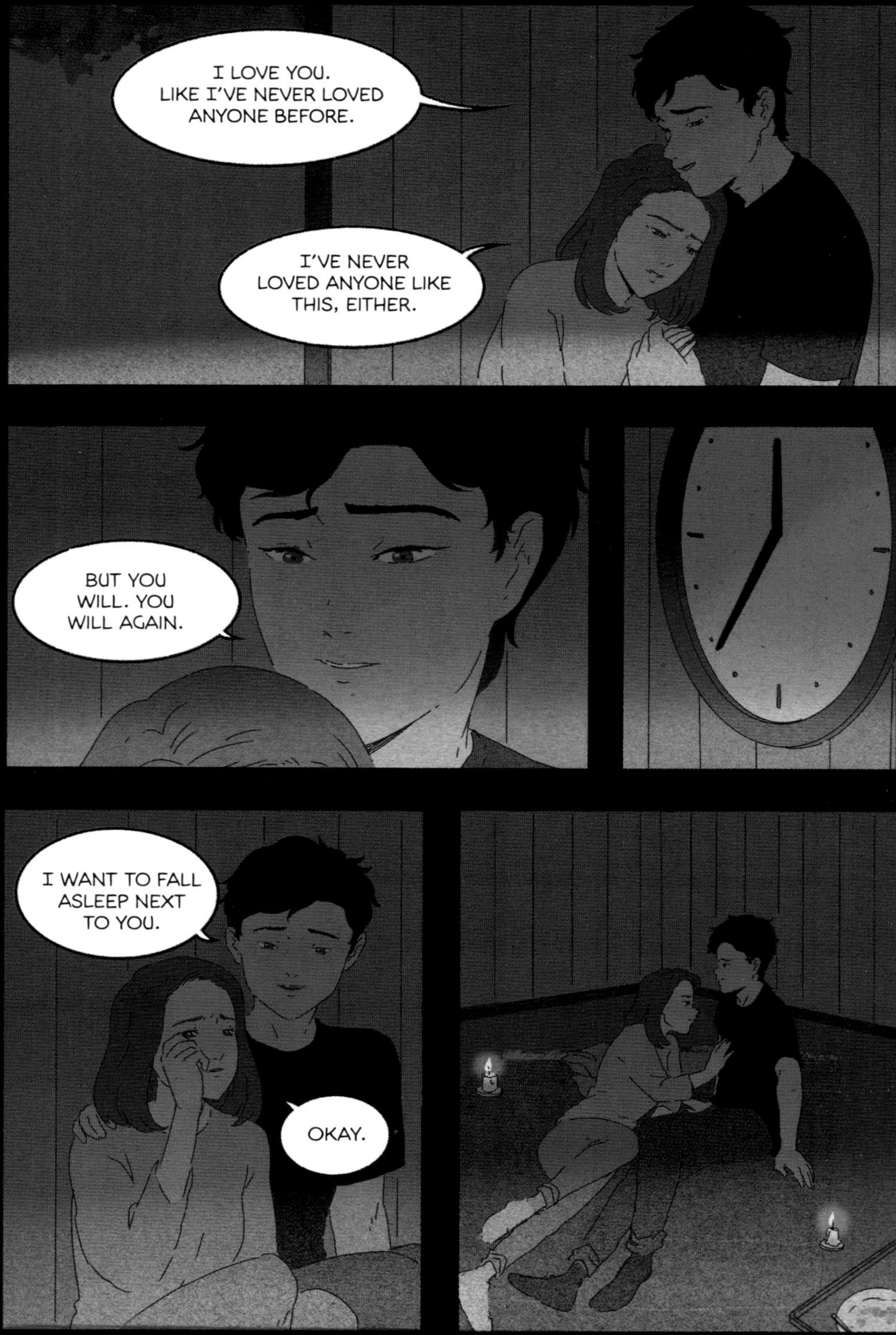
I LOVE YOU. LIKE I'VE NEVER LOVED ANYONE BEFORE.
I'VE NEVER LOVED ANYONE LIKE THIS, EITHER.
BUT YOU WILL. YOU WILL AGAIN.
I WANT TO FALL ASLEEP NEXT TO YOU.
OKAY.

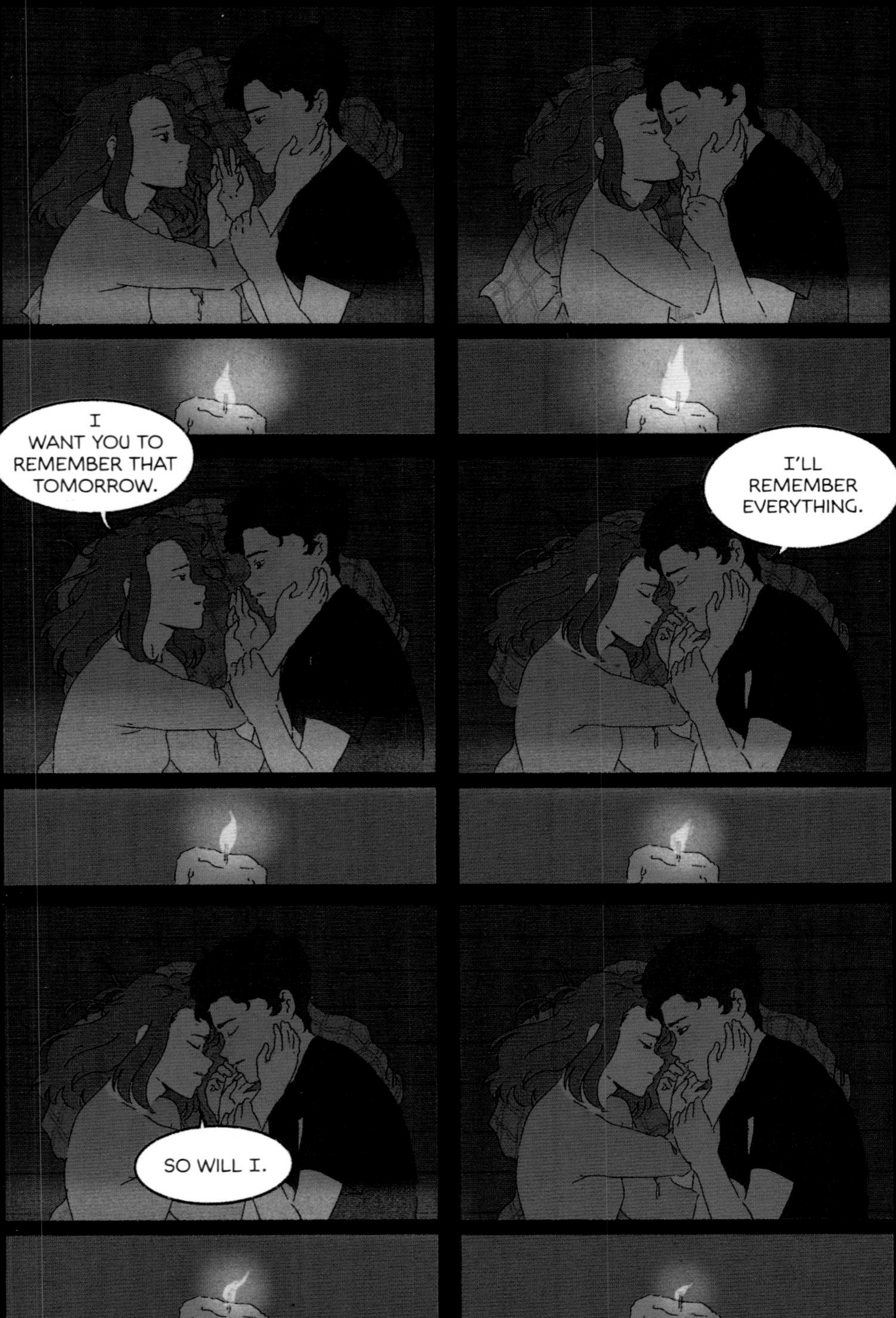
I WANT YOU TO REMEMBER THAT TOMORROW.
I'LL REMEMBER EVERYTHING.
SO WILL I.

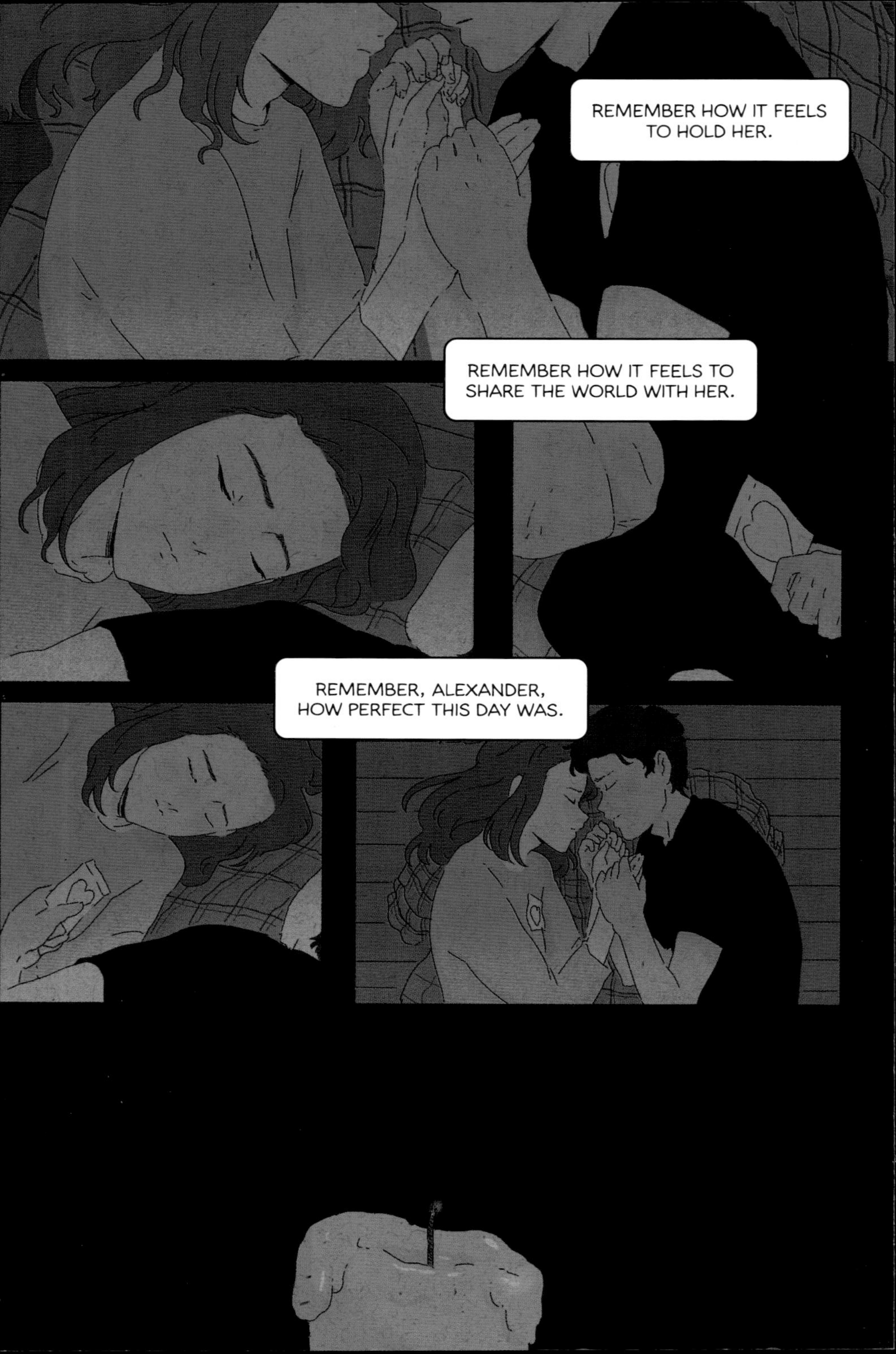
REMEMBER HOW IT FEELS TO HOLD HER.
REMEMBER HOW IT FEELS TO SHARE THE WORLD WITH HER.
REMEMBER, ALEXANDER, HOW PERFECT THIS DAY WAS.

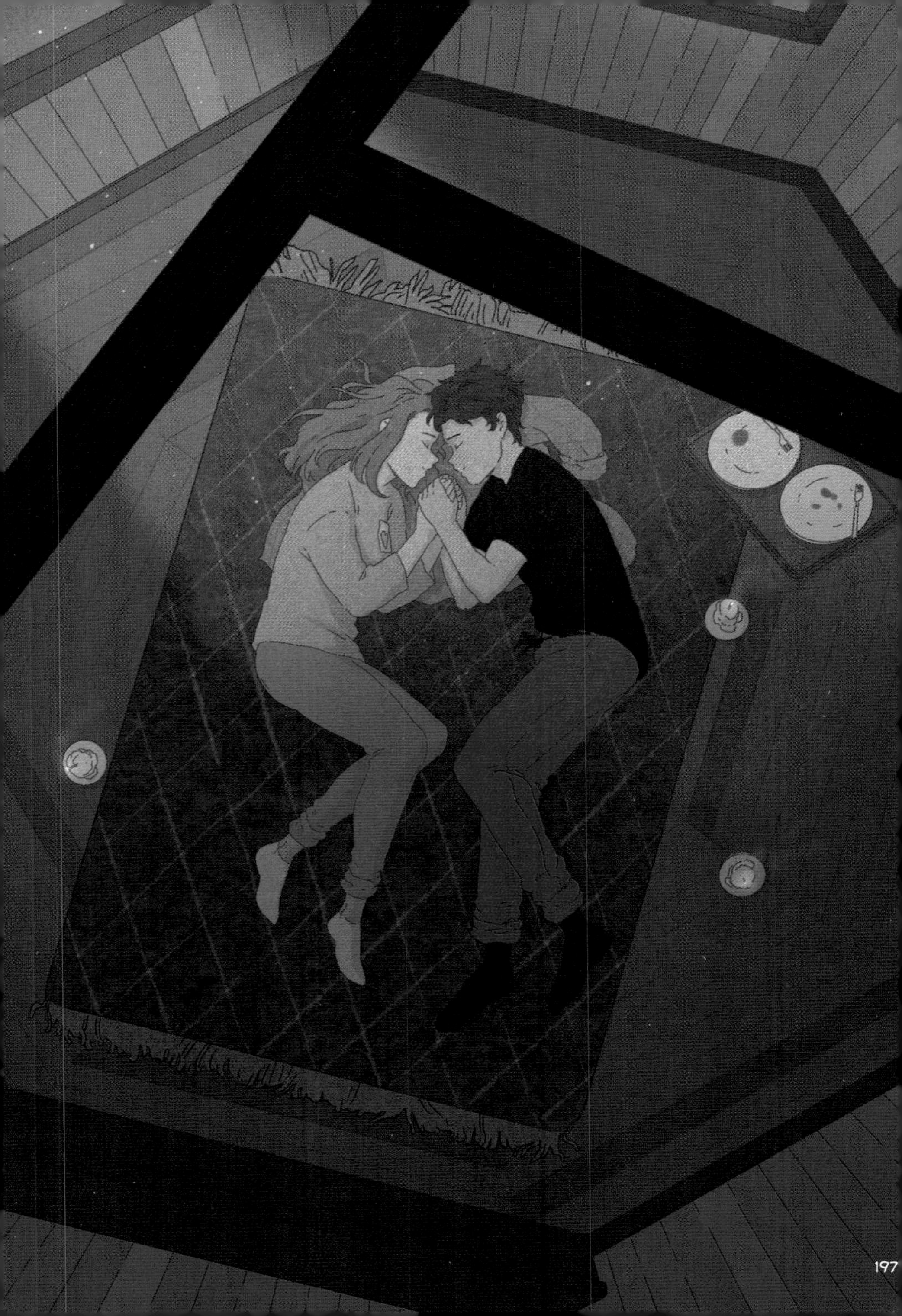

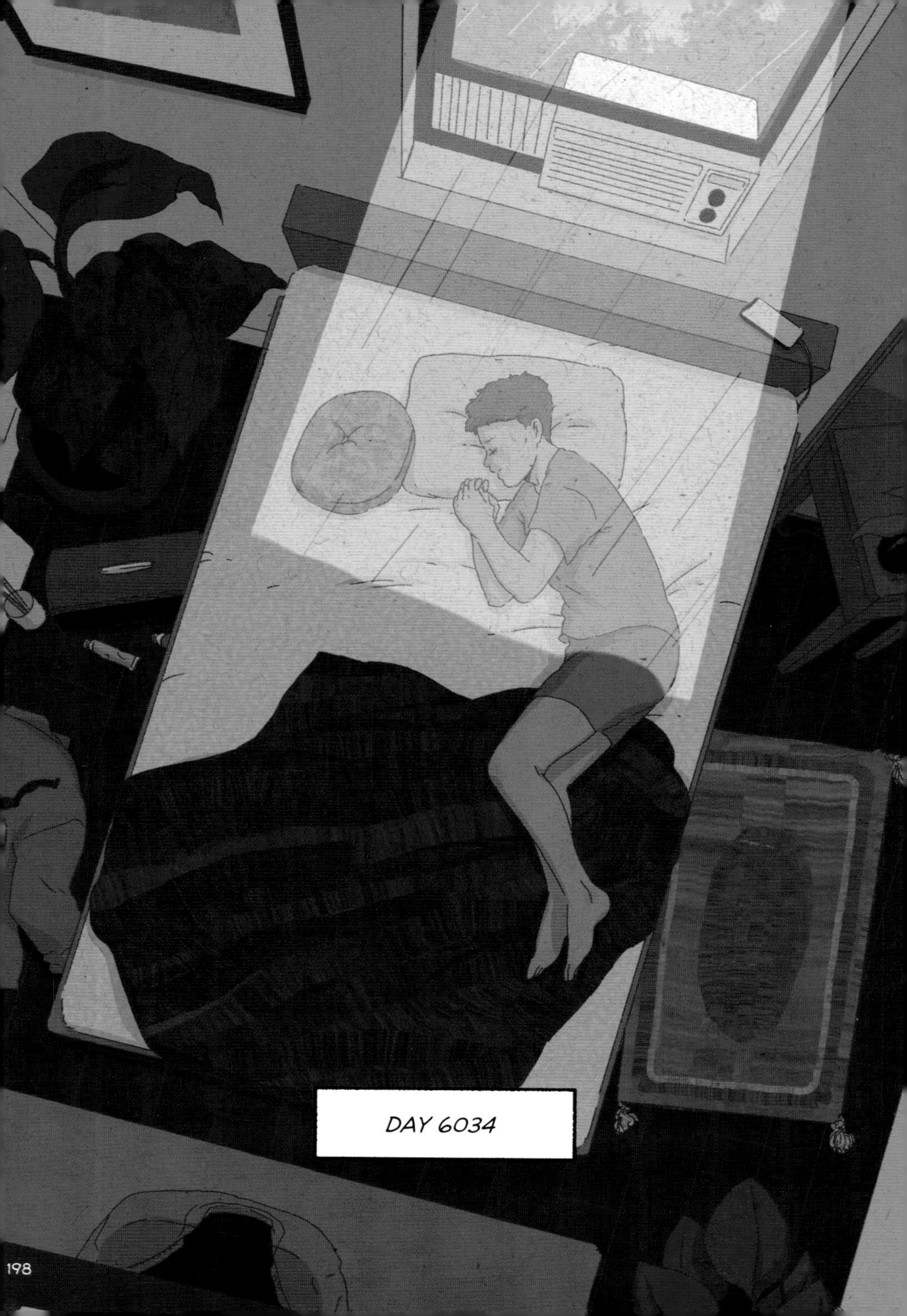
DAY 6034

Acknowledgments

From David Levithan:

Thank you to all of the readers and friends who've talked to me about the novel that this graphic novel is based on—those conversations have certainly informed how I see the book now, and how it's been adapted. Thank you to the book's original editor, Nancy Hinkel, and to this version's editor, Marisa DiNovis, as well as everyone else at Random House Children's Books, who have already given A's story such a wonderful life. Finally, thanks and appreciation to Dion MBD for making this part of the story's life so vibrant. I am grateful that a quote from the book was paired with your art, and that I saw it on Twitter, where I so rarely go.

From Dion MBD:

My eternal gratitude to: my partner, Fanny, for sharing our quality time with this project and constantly reminding me to keep hydrated; Mamah and Ayah for giving me space to concentrate when I stayed at your place; and my assistants, Shania, Nat, and Nao, for helping me complete this project without having to go to physical therapy.

From *New York Times* bestselling author

DAVID LEVITHAN

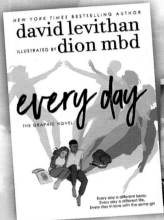

Read David's other love stories!

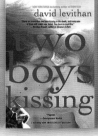

GetUnderlined.com